Cat Behind
The Window

Short stories by Francesco M. Marincola

with contributions by:

Catterina Coha
Jamie Marincola
Anna Loza

Copyright

Cover Art

Front Cover: *"Cat Behind the Window"* – Pastel and pencil portrait of Lucy by F. Marincola, August 29th 2015, Doha, Qatar

Back Cover: *"Aging Gardenia"* Pastel – Sketch by F. Marincola, May 2016, Doha, Qatar

Table of Contents

Authors' Biographies...5

Foreword...7

Preface...9

Introduction...11

Cat behind the window..13

Lovebirds...15

The Experiment...23

Wife (or a very short story)..29

Scrooge 2011..33

The Visit...45

A Rebellious Story...59

The Leopard..67

The Rider..79

The Eve..87

The Encounter...97

The Impostor Syndrome..103

The Speech..113

The Homeowner...115

Tiger...131

The Soldier..165

The Art of Gardening..181

Hotel Room...183

The Box...201

Untranslatable Communication..205

A Walk in the Park...211

The Old Boys Academy..223

Sabrina...285

Metamorphosis..301

"Mush"...305

Authors' Biographies

Catterina Coha is a physician and scientist living and working in New York City.

Anna Loza is the pen name of **Anna Panchenko,** who is a biophysicist by background, and currently works at the National Institutes of Health. Anna moved to the USA from Russia in 1993 to pursue her dream of becoming a scientist. In her spare time, she writes fictional stories which are focused on feelings and emotions, rather than the scientific facts she is used to dealing with. Ultimately, however, all her scientific and fictional writings are about getting a glimpse of the laws of nature.

Francesco M Marincola is Distinguished Research Fellow at AbbVie Corporation, Redwood City California. He was previously Chief Medical Officer at Sidra Medical and Research Centre in Doha, Qatar and before then, tenured Senior Investigator at the U.S. National Institutes of Health. He is the past president of the Society for the Immunotherapy of Cancer and Editor–in–Chief of the Journal of Translational Medicine and the sister journal Translational Medicine Communications. He received his MD summa cum laude at the University of Milan and Surgery training at Stanford University. His scientific work deepened the understanding of the mechanisms leading to rejection of tumors, transplanted organs graft–versus–host disease and by autoimmunity. He published his first novel in 2013: The Wise Men of Pizzo that was awarded the "Corrado Alvaro Award for Literature" in 2016. His site can be visited at https://authorfrancomarincola.wordpress.com

Jamie Marincola is an engineer at the U.S. Environmental Protection Agency in San Francisco. He graduated from Stanford University and lives with his wife and dog in Redwood City, California. Although this is his second print publication, he authors the ongoing web comic: *The Duller Image* http://www.thedullerimage.com.

Foreword

By Giuseppe Masucci

I am convinced that it is not so easy to put together a collection of short stories whose content stands on its own. The author opened his soul portraying situations and characters conceived not only from his imagination but extracted from the often-harsh reality of life and tailored according to his fantasy. For sure, the introspection inspired by the individuals who populate the story give life to a miniature version of Honore' de Balzac's "La Comedie Humaine". The author considers, describes and presents the anguish, the solitude and sometimes the desperation of human beings as they carry the burden of life. There is a great deal of self–analysis. The challenge for the reader is to extract himself from the *"canovaccio"* upon which different scenes are animated by the improvisations of the actors in the open drama of life.

Francesco is able to describe and investigate, through the protagonists, the deepest corners of one's conscience and soul. Take *"The Leopard"* and *"The Visit"* for instance. It seems that they portrait two opposite attitudes of human character: the laws of nature and its illogical unfolding in those who persecute and hunt the leopard in Africa or the criminal sentenced to death in far-away America. This contrasts with the analysis of the noble feelings that enliven an old father and his son's relationship. In reality, both stories talk about the expression of the intimate drama that each one of us experiences throughout life, i.e., to find or refuse an explanation to our existence. The circumstances may be distinct but the struggle for a meaning remains constant.

Is the author just an observer and an extremely talented artist? I believe that the apparent shield, behind which the author shelters himself with the pretense of creating an imaginary world, is uncovered by his engagement and precision used to describe characters and situations; a precision that can only come from first hand or at least very close experiences. Each vignette in the short stories claim a clear introspection of the author's own feelings that are exposed indirectly as best exemplified by *"A Rebellious Story"*.

The reader finds her/himself involved and entrapped in situations and the emotions released by the stories glue to the soul long after reading – for perhaps for a lifetime.

Francesco gives us, also, the opportunity to dwell in the twilight between "love and solitude", two universal emotions seemingly different but, in reality, very much connected to each other. In *"The Lovebirds"*, without a doubt, hope and solitude (not loneliness) are the source of energy that gives birth to a "solid" dream. The reader does not feel anguish in these lines but a flash of happiness spiced by a speck of sadness. We carry our life alone no matter what, with or without birds, cats or fairy princesses. Dave (could be me or anybody else) justifies his solitude through the dream of the real love in resignation and acceptance that at least, for him, there is no other way out. The lovebirds along the river and a sketch of a dreamed woman are his only companionship. The reader might expect a different end to this story but the conclusion does not matter: the events within the story are built to inspire the reader to find a different end to her/his own story.

I would like to end this foreword by citing the author himself, who elegantly reflects upon the question above:

"Thus, writing is not about publishing but it is about living an additional life and searching for a cathartic harmony with our own deeper self. What comes afterwards is just gravy".

Giuseppe V. Masucci. December 2014

***

Giuseppe V. Masucci was born in Italy where he spent his adolescence. After obtaining his MD, he moved to Stockholm, Sweden where he has been living since 1977 working at the Karolinska Institute. Devotion to poetry is a part of his life since adolescence but he published only recently. He writes his poems in Italian, Venetian, Swedish and English. His first début is "Iris Color Arancio/ Orange Colored Iris" (Ed. TGBOOK) in 2011, presented in Turin (Library 451) and Treviso (Library Lovat). His second collection is "La Rabbia del Lupo/The Anger of the Wolf" (Ed. TGBOOK). He also recently published his very first English collection of poetry entitled Dry Petals in 2017. Readers can visit his website at: https://gvmasucci.wordpress.com

Preface

Some of these stories precede the writing of my first novel: "*The Wise Men of Pizzo*". I am quite attached to them as to a firstborn. Short stories correspond in writing to photos while a novel compares to a movie. They intend to be a high-resolution sketch that captures ephemeral yet meaningful moments; occurrences deserving distinction from customary life for the weight they will bear in our memory. Some are based on true events narrated by friends or complete strangers, who entrusted them to me.

I entitled the collection: "*The cat behind the window*"; an image inspired by Lucy, a friend's cat who spends most of her life looking out behind the window. And she has become so used to it that she dwells there even when she could go out. I feel that this image very well describes my inner self and it is the genuine source of the stories.

I compiled all short stories (including those already published in "*The Leopard and Other Stories*") into this selection and I added those contributed by my son Jamie and two good friends: Catterina Coha and Anna Loza. Our stories are meant to share impressions that may reverberate in the reader's deepest emotions, or at least we hope so. Most end where others' would start. This is to empower one's own creation. As a writer, I never know where a story will end up. No matter how precise the outline at the conception is, the narrative gets out of hand as the characters gradually take control. And I am happy to let them go unbridled, just as much I wish I could do the same rather than watching my own life pass by from behind the window. Perhaps, by training in the fictional world, we may learn one day to create a better reality for ourselves and for others by waking from the torpor of conformism.

I had the privilege to share the experiences of a precious woman. I learned by listening to her that diamonds can be human with a soul, heart and mind and that the external perfection hides internal turmoil. I recalled the ambivalence of youth, the anguish of decision, the angst of aligning the uncertainty of the future with the lessons from the past, the excitement of the unknown with the admonition of the known, the unease of trading hopes for the shelter of security, the freshness of passion against the staleness of compromise. She told me that my stories helped. So, thank you again for dedicating a little bit of time to my stories, perhaps some will become a meaningful part of someone else's far away life.

I want to thank the readers who gave feedback and helped me improve the pre-published edition at: https://authorfrancomarincola.wordpress.com. I learned good lessons from the comments! Not only about writing, but above all about the intricacies that obfuscate the distinction between fiction and reality. Thank you!

Introduction

By Laura Caria and Giuseppe Masucci

This collection of short stories that Franco has put together, again, with his usual determination and passion for writing, is characterized by several "leitmotivs", which are recognizable in his friends' contributions too, one way or another, consciously or not.

The Crisis of Identity is one. This moment in the life of some of the characters has no identity and it reveals itself anytime the cloudy sky of the soul is able to give the sun of introspection an opportunity to show up.

Not easy, certainly, for Luca.

Wherever in this collection Luca is the protagonist, we can perceive his attempts to reach out to this "Introspection" in order to desperately find an explanation if not a solution to his crisis.

Can Luca really have the open mind necessary to understand the truth that lies within every human being? From the moment we are born, until the day we die, we spend our life in permanent solitude. Our soul and body never separate until death comes.

The transformation and the understanding of Love is a second one.

Many of the short stories in this book deal with Love, in its many different forms: brotherly love, love for the family, passionate love and so on.

To love for the sake of love, as in the story of Sabrina. It is not easy to grasp the reason why the two women are sacrificing to that extent for the beloved.

And finally, there is what it can maybe be considered the dominant leitmotiv, linking all the stories to one another and which intrigues the reader, urging him/her to carry on until the last page.

We are not One, we are several characters in one body, depending on where we find ourselves and who we interact with. We keep wearing different masks, more or less consciously, depending on which of the life situations we deal with and which ones of our feelings are predominant in that moment in time.

With this in mind, we can see how well our soul and mind are able to perform their own act, always different, always challenging.

It is in this key concept that lies the real drama of life, in which we are all performing as the main characters.

Shadows of silence

(Unpublished original text by GV Masucci 2017)

Drop the
Curtains on the
Scene of
Existence

A violet
Drape
Separates
Actors from
Audience

Who's
Whispering
Almost
Soundlessly
Behind the
Wings and
Doesn't
Reveal
His
Mind to
Others

It's a
Perennial
Talk
Between
Masks and
Reality

In the end,

Silence
Lays
Like a
Shadow as
Limelight
Fades away

Cat behind the window

I see things out there,

Interesting things,

Exciting things,

Inviting things...

I wish I could touch them, play with them, be part of them,

As if they were material

And I wonder, are they really there?

But, whether they belong to my present, to the past or to the future

Whether they are memories, realities or hopes

Whether they are just the fruit of my imagination

...It does not truly matter

The glass will keep them away from me.

I reckoned that a long time ago

Yet, I keep staring at them.

Lovebirds

As a day, it had been even worse than usual; the kind of day that only those among us who carry a meaningless life can recognize. When a sense of painful loss supersedes the customary monotony, a panicky sensation of vanishing opportunities, and the premonition that day after day, but more acutely today, we are relinquishing any chance to overcome the idleness of our lives.

It had first started with a series of annoyances, trifles like not finding the car keys, spilling the coffee and staining the shirt, finding holes in your socks, etc. etc. Later on, his supervisor had summoned him in the office to reiterate the need to be more thoughtful in his writings and to avoid negligent inaccuracies such as not addressing doctors with the proper appellation, missing essential elements of somebody's affiliation, misspelling surnames and other minor details important to those who have the energy to inspect such pedantic corners of life.

But it was Kate who had certainly ruffled the day and, indeed, completely spoiled it.

"I do not want to hurt you, Dave..." she said, staring at him in the eyes with a serious look, protruding thoughtfully her chin and pursing her lips as if she was about to suck with a straw his soul out of the brain.

"I am sorry if I misled you, but I really do not care for you in this way. I have been nice and affectionate because I was sorry for you... always so shy and withdrawn, ...never saying anything... could not even finish a joke. But I am not interested in you as a man. You know what I mean? You are a nice person but..."

He had heard that before, like when his wife left him:

"I am sorry Dave, it has been a mistake. When I married you, I was young and naïve. I thought you were ambitious and intelligent. But you are not! You are a nice person, but not an alpha male, not a man women would be attracted to and love". That's what she said as she packed her stuff to move in with her alpha male.

The settlement had been straightforward. They both worked and had no children. As a result, he was left with an empty apartment that with the resonating silence of its bare walls had suddenly grown to be disproportionate to the minuteness of his negligible life. No matter how inquisitively he scrutinized those familiar walls to revive memories that could alleviate his solitude, they would just remind him of the lonesomeness... the complete seclusion that embodied his existence currently and for the time to be. Not even the cat was left. She had taken it with her and he missed the little creature more than the wife since only in it had he been able to reclaim any endorsement of his presence and even, occasionally, a hint of affection.

As Dave was walking along the riverbank, his brain persisted on reflecting over Kate. Surely, he could not blame her; it had been entirely his unsubstantiated presumption to suppose that she would be interested in a loner.

In fact, passed the turmoil instigated by the embarrassment of the rejection, he had felt relief even... all the anxiety of the last few days! That arguing with himself to find the resolve to accost her, ...all those rehearsals in front of the mirror, ...all those affectations to create a creature of better appeal that did not exist...and all those pretenses to align his façade to an image that he could not even conceive. All this euphoria did not need to exist anymore. If he could just accept the fact that he would never be loved, he could carry on a peaceful existence following his comfortable routine without having to go through all that anguish again.

"Yet, even birds can be loved" he thought, looking at a couple of mallards floating in harmony along the riverbank.

"They say that these mallards are monogamous for a lifetime". He told himself.

"Look how content if not happy they are. And why would such a beautiful bird like him love a homely partner like her; so identical to all the other mallards in the neighborhood and perhaps in the world. And why would she love him? True, he is handsome but not any better looking than the other male mallards... and is he smart and ambitious? Is he funny? Not at all, he is just a simple mallard. Yet she has been with him since God knows when and she will forever be. What does she see in him that none can see in me?"

And he fancied to kidnap the male mallard for a whole day to find out how she would react:

"Would she panic? Would she look around searching for him? Would she wait for his return? Would she fly away and find another mallard? Would any of her behaviors unveil the true meaning of love?"

By observing the mallards, and pondering on the essence of their instincts, he soon realized that his premise had no answer. He reckoned that no experiment could ever explain their love, or whatever one might call the natural companionship that he was just witnessing first hand, fresh like the loveliest rose of May.

He concluded that there is no need to find a reason for love, or at least no need to articulate one. Those mallards, with their unsophisticated mind, did not know how or why, but they loved each other in the simplest possible way. They wished to be together now and in the days to come without a foreseeable end. They felt no need to explain anything; there were no expectations or paradigms. There was the simple desire to be together today, ...and every day would just be another today.

***

The air was tepid and the afternoon sun still high. The sunrays warmed a solitary bench along the riverbank where Dave settled his body as if to settle his thoughts. It would have been depressing to go home directly to engage in the tedious monotony of his evening sequence: a little cooking followed by dish washing, a little reading, sitting in front of the television with a few mouthfuls of grappa in a crystal cup that was a remnant of the obsolete dowry, waiting for the drowsiness that dampens the pain as the fog shelters the eyes from the burning light.

The surroundings were glorious, disproportionately contrasting with his feelings. And in fact, a gradual osmosis of emotions brought a tinge of happiness onto his deserted soul.

He looked at the mallards that were amicably floating toward him in the anticipation for a few crumbs of bread. The gentle birds waited patiently for a short while and then left with dignity because they understood that not all people carry crumbs to the riverbank for their pleasurable consumption.

And they went shopping for crumbs somewhere else, in their vast and unending world. And Dave thought that, although not for him, there were still nuggets of love and companionship on Earth, and that thought comforted him.

***

Then, he was talking to a stranger over a subject that was probably interesting enough to justify a conversation. But, as he talked, he followed with the corner of the eye the lovebirds still shopping for food together up or down the placid river instinctively following the magic path of their life, when...

She appeared. She came literally out of nowhere. She was the most beautiful woman he had ever seen and it seemed to Dave that his chest was lighter in her presence and the flow of the air down the windpipe was much fresher. She was beautiful because she had sweet and reassuring eyes that looked straight into his own, and she had a smile and a face like the one that a common man like himself could only dream of. It was the portrait of a fairy, or a princess that could have been drawn for children's fantasies mixing the soothing emotions of a mother's love with the hopes of eternal companionship.

***

"I entice you! Do not miss the party tonight" she said giggling and touching his shoulder. 'Will you come?"

And he seemed to remember something about a party, somewhere sometime; one of those affairs he never considered to be meant for his own inclusion. But instead he said:

"Yes, of course I will be there" while his heart was throbbing and his eyes were beaming like they had not done in a very long time.

What a strange illusion is love, an unknown face looking at you, a smile, two empathetic eyes, the hope that somebody really cares... and you are in love!

***

When he entered the room, she was already there, in the middle of the real people, those who are not afraid of life, not afraid of being judged, who talk without listening to themselves and behave as if there were no one thousand mirrors judging them, those who can laugh at a joke spontaneously rather than pretending to.

She looked toward him but she did not see him. He realized that he did not know anybody there and started looking around with affected composure. The room appeared to him full and empty at the same time. There were people and furniture, and there were burning candles and wine bottles, glasses, carpets and photographs on the walls, but none of that was familiar to him, nothing he could connect or pretend to connect to.

He felt an urge to leave when a cat, bigger than any cat he had ever seen, pounced on the drawer close to him. The feline licked his paw, then arched his back, stretched his tail straight up and looked at him expecting affection. Dave went to caress it because he loved cats and missed his own, but most preeminently, because that occupation gave him something to do, something to quench his shame and irritation for coming to a party where he did not belong, coming to chase a prize that he did not deserve.

The cat kept purring in a friendly way and Dave began to calm down when his arm was squeezed gently, and at the smell of a woman he heard:

"I am glad you came ... I am so... so happy you came! Let's go somewhere else where we can be alone" and she took him by the hand and they went away, in another room, where things were familiar, almost like his own apartment.

They sat and waited for something to happen, then they were in bed, she was hugging him and she was moving gently rocking her hips, as if she was ready to be loved. And he made love to her, ...or he thought he did. Most importantly they hugged and her hugs where tender and needy. She was so happy to be with him... so it felt.

Then she raised herself up and he did the same. Touching his hair and looking into his eyes, she whispered:

"I love you".

And the light shone while he was trying to reciprocate.

But, the brightness became overwhelming and there was a bustling of dust particles crawling up the sunrays as the sun was preparing to set. The mallards were still there but she was gone together with the dream that had brought her to him.

At first, he was disappointed but then he thought:

"How could this be just a dream? I never met her and yet she was so authentic. Why would I suddenly make up something so different from what I know? Yes, yes, it may not be true but then what about those religious people? Don't they believe in a God whom they have never seen, not even in their dreams? Yet, they do, and they trust that their love is reciprocated! Why can't I be loved too? Yes, she was true and she loves me, she just came to me through a dream but she truly exists."

And thinking along these lines and rehashing over and over his dream he stood up, turned around to look at the love birds one more time and went home.

***

As soon as he arrived home, he drew a sketch of her on a notepad. He was a decent draftsman, not a professional artist, not even an amateur, but he mused himself by sketching trees, boats, landscapes and even people sometimes. He reconstructed her on the paper, as well as he could remember. He had no precise recollection on one side, and on the other, a vivid impression. In the end, the sketch did fit the anticipation of his senses. Perhaps, its fidelity was not as accurate, but it was good enough to reenact the feelings she had stirred in him.

He looked at her and he whispered to the drawing:

"I love you too".

And then the apartment was fuller and livelier... and suddenly all objects around appeared meaningful. The frames on the wall definitely needed to be straightened, the spills on the counter cleaned and what a mess the room was! Thank God she was not there to see it! His energy was restored and soon, the kitchen was spick—and—span. It was just as good as when his wife lived there before she went with the alpha male. When he still trusted that they loved each other, when they still shared a dream and when he believed that they were building together a nest for the progeny to come. It felt just exactly like those lost times on that enchanted evening.

And at nighttime he just could not sleep. He opened a book and read through a few pages, but the remembrance of her kept hauling his thoughts afar and he had to restart the chapter over and over. Meanwhile, as his eyes were running over the printed words, he kept blaming himself. He wished he had the promptness to tell her that he loved her with the same tenderness she had demonstrated toward him before disappearing. How volatile and impalpable can a dream be?

Then the room became dimmer, the furniture moved to the side, the cat came back and, this time, it was black and the size of a panther. The feline did not jump or pounce but stretched on the sofa regally. Dave tried to get close to pet it but the cat stared in the distance without recognizing him.

So many other things happened that night till, at the verge of dawn, a pallid light created a new day. He was attracted to the window. There he saw her. She was coming home! She looked up and smiled at him and waved her hand. He ran to open the door and, by doing so, he woke up, ...once again too early.

He wished that he could have had better control of his dream to keep it alive just a little longer, just enough to allow the time for her to come home and to have a chance to hug and kiss her and to tell her:

"I love you too".

But the light of the day had extinguished the dream and it was time to go to work.

***

That day at work, things were different. The supervisor had gone over the letters that Dave had presented to him the day before.

He smiled and said to Dave:

"Good!" putting them to the side before resuming to sip his coffee and to read the paper.

During the break, the normal people no longer seem so extraneous to him. He felt he shared a story in common with them. A story of love! Like the ones they were bragging about all the time, but this one was not vulgar because of her beauty and kindness. He also calculated that he would never relate yesterday's events to anybody because he reckoned that they would consider him odd. It was going to be his lifelong secret!

Even Kate was not as threatening. She appeared just as a regular human being, a pathetically lonely woman with that veiled expression of solitude that is so revealing and archetypal of those who had never experienced love. He almost felt contempt for her but he controlled himself; he did not want to be arrogant and insensitive like others had been to him in the past.

Yet, for the first time, he felt superior to his coworkers and he wondered if any of those people had ever experienced true love, if any of them ever had a lovebird to share their life with.

Most of all, he was eager to go home, to the place where his dream lived.

***

On the way home, he saluted cheerfully the lovebirds at the river and it seemed to him that the male mallard winked at him.

He bought some good food and made a good dinner, nothing special but definitely elegant, not for her, because he knew she would not come till later, but in respect for him. Being loved makes someone feel worthy.

He looked with pride at the cleaned-up space, at the kitchen and the tiny studio. He thought she would have liked it and, with a glass of wine in his hand, he stretched on the couch waiting for the trance that would bring her back.

And soon, he was in the middle of a square, and there were pigeons; a neatly dressed businessman walked by and smiled at him, ...and then there were fireworks, and the day was not even over although it was already night.

And many other things happened but she did not come back that night, not ever after.

***

Several years have passed. Dave continues to carry his negligible life with dignity. But the kitchen counters are stained and the frames on the walls are crooked. He does not look at the sketch of her anymore when he goes to bed.

Yet, lying down, more often than not, while waiting for sleep to come, he recollects the day when he was loved, and in those moments, he wonders where she could be and he wishes over and over that he could have had a chance to tell her at least once:

"I love you too".

Along the riverbank, the lovebirds continue their content if not happy life, and they follow their magic path together without knowing why till death they will part.

The Experiment

It is seven o' clock in the morning on Sunday and Luke is up already. He is eager to execute a long–planned experiment. Luke describes himself as a behavioral scientist, albeit amateurish, following the steps of the great Konrad Lorenz. Today, he is going to the riverbank to separate the male mallard from the female and observe her reaction. For some time, he has obsessed about the essence of the relationship between those birds that are supposed to remain monogamous throughout their life. By understanding their behavior, he hopes to uncover the primordial roots of love. After all, what is love but an incoercible desire to be together, an instinctual craving for companionship? Do we really need to understand to love and be loved; don't we just feel love when it is there and, even more, long for it when it is not? How can those simple birds take for granted what we cannot comprehend?

***

Having heard him rise from bed and take a shower, Luke's wife is busying herself preparing coffee to accompany a cheerful breakfast. To please his wife, he sits and distractedly eats, drinks the coffee, kisses her on the forehead and goes out.

'When will you be back?"

"Don't know."

"Will you be back for dinner?"

"Probably, I will call if I won't" he replies with a tad impatient tone.

***

The day is shiny. The recent rain left moisture around and in the cleanest air, the fragrances of spring are inviting. Luke leaves the car and runs gaily down the riverbank, where the humid soil crumbles under his weight, and rolling little pebbles cheerfully follow him like ducklings after their mother.

There is nobody around. The perfect time to concentrate without disturbances on the experiment!

Luke walks to the river, and soon, he is recognized by a couple of mallards. He is welcomed by their purposeful approaching. He throws bread crumbs at first in the water, closer and closer, and then up in the riverbank to entice the birds to climb the gentle incline, where the frost melting under the rays of the sun shine in ordered little pearls on the tip of the immature grass.

The mallards respond to the invitation happily. Without suspicion, they soon graze around his feet waiting for the next crumb, wagging their tail with satisfaction and quacking approvingly.

After giving one more look around to be sure that nobody is watching, Luke bends down and, holding a crumb in his hand, waits for the gloriously colored mallard to come even closer. And when the mallard is picking at his hand, he catches it gently and lifts the beautiful bird up in his arms.

***

At first, the mallard is not concerned. He rather seems surprised, not being quite sure about what is happening, and Luke, as if comforting a baby who just woke up, gently caresses his plumes and teases his neck.

The female companion also does not seem too concerned and looks at Luke and at her mallard as if they were just one thing, a big monument to the beauty of nature, the glory of spring and the friendship among beings on Earth.

Encouraged by this preliminary success, Luke slowly turns around and starts walking toward the car. There, he had left a birdcage to hold the mallard while he could return to the riverbank to observe undisturbed the behavior of his companion.

But, looking back after taking a few steps, with the mallard resting in his arms, he observes that the mate appears concerned, or, to better describe it, she acts surprised. Why is her lifetime companion leaving her? Why is he going away with that strange animal? What is happening so unexpectedly? And, as she bends her neck toward one or the other side to better look up, it seems to Luke that she is thinking:

"Why is he leaving me? Wasn't I a good companion? Did I do something to displease him? Didn't I smooth his feathers when he wanted me to? Didn't I always let him have the first crumb of bread from strangers? Wasn't I always by his side, day after day, with the rain and the sunshine? Why is he leaving me now?"

And that scrutinizing gaze reminds Luke of something that he cannot determine.

As Luke walks further away, the male mallard loses sight of his companion on the ground, loses composure and starts calling for her. His sharp quacking cuts the silence in the cool air breaking the stillness of the morning. At his call, the mallard understands that her companion is not leaving her but he is in distress and needs help; thus, she quacks:

"I am coming! Wait for me"

And with the courage of a lion, she wobbles towards Luke with her wings half stretched out unsure whether she should fly or run.

At this point, Luke calls off the experiment. There is nothing to learn by stressing further the poor animals. They are obviously wedded against any circumstances.

He stops and turns around. The mallard stops calling, his companion stops running and peace is restored along the riverbank.

She looks up again, bending her neck and staring not at Luke but at her mallard. Then Luke bends down and, after a last caress, releases the beautiful bird.

With a dignified wobbling step, the liberated mallard first mumbles something that may be translated as:

"I knew all along that it was just a mistake, I was not worried at all".

Then, he shakes his feathers underneath his wings, smoothing them with his beak.

Determined, his companion walks toward him and attentively uses her beak to complete the job carefully, restoring her companion's elegant attire.

Then they both wobble gracefully toward the river, but Luke, remembering that he had some leftover crumbs, whispered to them:

"Not yet, there is more breakfast for the lovers," and he spreads more crumbs around his feet.

And the mallards, content and peaceful, come back and graze again around him, wagging their tail and quacking approvingly as if nothing had happened. And their behavior restores Luke's feelings as he admires one more time the happy couple.

Suddenly, out of nowhere, a retriever appears barking loudly and chases the mallards. The lovebirds elegantly take off flying over the polished water toward the warmth of the shiny sun.

Luke and the dog stand there looking at the birds. The latter wags its tail straight up proud of completing its ancestral duty of chasing the intruders away and the former wanders about the future of the friendly couple.

Patting the insolent dog, Luke gradually rises from the stupor in which he had fallen and, turning around, puts his hands in his pockets and walks back to the car as the dog, following an invisible trail that only its nose can map, soon disappears in the crescent grass with only its tail sticking out.

As he walks, Luke thinks again of the mallard's puzzled gaze and, once again, he cannot point to what he is reminded of.

***

It was too early to go home for Luke, who detested Sundays at home. Particularly on that day, the prospect of spending the rest of the day with his wife was unmanageably depressing. He reflected upon the reason but could not identify any specific one.

He married her three years before. She was formally educated, was pretty and loyal; in so many ways, she was complementary to him. He was outgoing and ambitious and she was modest and withdrawn. She made him feel needed and he had liked that feeling then.

He married her almost on a charitable impulse but that generosity had rapidly vanished and what he saw now in his wife was a plain, uninteresting woman worried about the routine of life, of being a good housewife, dreaming of a future with children, what they would do, she talked about how to prepare a comfortable nest, and she worried about carpets and linens, about walls and colors, most importantly, she worried about making him happy by satisfying necessities that were more of distractions than true values along the tracks of his own perception of life.

Of course, there was nothing wrong about it; he had to admit it. But still, Luke's expectations were broader. There were still vast horizons in need of being explored according to his young vision of life; undefined potentials that would surely emerge in the next future, those unpredictable but forestalled turns of luck that only a young and inexperienced mind can dream of; those hopes that drive the inexperienced, while any seasoned traveler knows that, except for misfortunes, life is despairingly predictable.

In other words, life to Luke was as bright and open ended as that crisp Sunday morning and the future was consistent with this feeling, while going home was in sharp contrast, a desecration of all.

***

Luke had a lover.

Unlike his wife, she was sophisticated and a regarded professional. She was older than he was and divorced with two children of whom she had joint custody.

"This weekend, her kids are staying with their father" he thought, and that thought erased the image of the ducks and the boring afternoon.

***

After opening the door with the keys left for him in the usual place, Luke found her sitting on the sofa with a cold bottle of Prosecco waiting for him with the excitement of thousands of bubbles surging to the top to welcome him.

According to the usual procedure and following the standard protocol, he sat close to her and asked how she was doing, and then he listened and talked when she paused, and sincerely pretended to care. Then, he kissed her neck and touched her breasts and legs till they went to bed.

She was passionate, and it took very little for Luke to forget everything else for a few moments of excitement.

Then, as the ardor became extinguished, not much was left to do. They both lay down looking at the ceiling with their belly up, and Luke heard the ticking of the clock. It appeared to him that it was particularly loud that day, as if wishing to remind him that had he been a good Christian he would have gone to Mass; or had he been a responsible scientist he would have read and studied.

He also thought that the same ticking was measuring his wife's day in his other world and he shook off an uncomfortable sensation of guilt by searching for something else to think about.

He then recalled a conversation he recently exchanged with a friend:

"You know," the friend said "there is no such thing as time in the universe. Time is a human invention created to explain causality and it is based on observable repetitions. It is the metric that measures the lapse between cause and effect. But the Earth that goes around the sun, the sun that travels around the galaxy and the galaxies altogether do not measure time. This is why eternity is not relevant; because there is no such thing as time to measure its boundaries."

Yet, that ticking, whatever it represented, and in as much as it separated him from his bright future to come, by far represented in the current state of affairs the most exciting preoccupation in what appeared to be an otherwise tedious existence.

***

When he woke up, he reached for her with his hand but she was no longer in bed. The clock was still ticking, and because it had been keeping track of terrestrial time during his sleep, it was telling him that it was getting late.

To please the clock, he went to the bathroom and energetically brushed his teeth, cusp by cusp, in and out, tongue and palate as if the harder he worked, the more effectively he could compensate for the time wasted during that self–indulgent lazy afternoon.

Then, he went downstairs and found her sketching something on a piece of paper as she used to do to contain her crossness: it was a woman looking out of a window.

He repositioned behind her ear a curl of hair that had fallen down her cheek and then kissed her on the forehead. Then, feeling guilty for falling asleep, he navigated his hand toward her breast with purpose but she caught his hand and, turning around and smiling at him, she said:

"No more for today. You did your job. You can go back to your wife now."

At the beginning, he felt relieved and was pleased for the validation of a job well accomplished. But then, the word "wife" echoed deeply in some remote emptiness of his soul. And he thought of the incessant ticking of the clock and wondered how often that day his wife measured that time that did not exist.

He poured another glass of Prosecco. But this time, the bubbles did not run up with the anticipation of before. Rather, they seemed to orderly follow their destiny for the sake of some dull physical principle mechanically ascending one after the other.

He drank the warm wine, kissed her one more time and left.

***

As he was driving home, he saw at each intersection opportunities spreading in so many incalculable directions. He thought of the different paths waiting to be explored. Each crossroad reminded him of the different places he could go if he did not have to go back to his wife. Perhaps in one of them would he find happiness and, with that, peace in his tormented soul.

27

And so it was that: between a stoplight and a truck arriving from the left, Luke resolved to leave his wife.

As he pressed on the accelerator, he pondered about the future. He recognized that it was not right to continue on the current path. It had been a wise decision to refuse to have children saying that he was not ready.

It would have been easy to ask for a divorce and move on. She would not have liked it of course at the beginning, but in the end, she would be happy. He convinced himself that he was doing this for her and not only for his own benefit.

"She deserves to be loved!" he thought and he saw himself one day in the future meeting her occasionally and saw her happily embracing him as an old good friend. She would tell about the children that she had had with the right man, their successes, and how good they were and she would thank him for making this hard but sensible decision for the both of them before it was too late.

And he smiled and wondered what he would be by then, and he could not place himself except for being free and alone.

"To achieve something, I must be free!" he thought.

***

Entering the house, the emptiness overwhelmed him. He heard the silence while the darkness of the evening completed the stillness of the day.

As he was about to take off his jacket, his wife came to the door to greet him. She looked at him without saying a word, and in her inquisitive stare, he recognized the eye of the mallard – and it seemed to him that she was thinking:

"Wasn't I a good companion? Did I do something to displease him? Didn't I take care of him when he needed me? Didn't I always let him have the first choice of everything we share? Wasn't I always by his side, day after day, with the rain and the sunshine? "

And he went close to her and kissed her on the forehead, and she smoothed his hair, which was ruffled, and she straightened his shirt.

Then she asked:

"Are you hungry? I made the soup you like".

In silence they ate, and he ate voraciously after a day of fast, activity and sex; and he drank wine and looked at the clock in the kitchen but could not hear its ticking.

All of a sudden, he remembered that he wanted to say something to her about divorcing, or maybe just separation, or maybe, just simply mention their differences.

But, as he touched her hand, it seemed to him that indeed there was no time, no space, no universe out there but just that little kitchen with a dim light and a pleasant fragrance, where he was bound by destiny to his lovebird whom he would never leave.

Wife

(Or a very short story)

It is time to get up, to extinguish the buzz of the alarm clock, to rub one's own eyes, to engage the slippers, to follow the cat to the bathroom, to sit on the toilet, looking at the same photos in an old magazine, to scrutinize oneself in the mirror, to look down at the tooth brush, to enter and then to exit the shower, to dress, to look for the watch and the wallet and to go downstairs.

Downstairs, coffee is ready. John's wife has been up in the meanwhile. She prepared cereals and put the newspaper on the table.

John says: "Good morning" and sits.

He likes to keep the routine short in the morning. In fact, he could definitely do without breakfast; any minute wasted and the congested traffic could become unmanageable. He is eager to go to work and he could get coffee there.

Yet, it feels nice to smell the coffee in the morning, to sit briefly, to be pampered for a while. Like an inpatient cat, he lets his wife kiss him and hug him. If he had a tail, he would wag it right and left to compensate for the uncontrollable purring of his throat – demonstrating in this way the ancestral conflict between receiving love and owning freedom.

Then, he grabs his backpack and out he goes.

"Call when you can," says his wife at the doorsteps.

When is about to enter the car:

"Would you like Chili for dinner?"

Forbearing a surging tsunami of irritation, he replies:

"Yes!" and he drives away.

***

The day passes.

***

When John opens the door and shakes his boots from the snow, he is welcomed by the satiating smell of rosemary. The wife, who did not come to greet him, is busy in the kitchen taking out a huge standing roast with roasted potatoes.

"Sorry, I found this beef on sale and thought you would like it even better than chili."

He puts down his backpack and goes to kiss her in the forehead.

"How was your day?"

"Fine."

He cannot remember whether anything had happened that day. It seems all so far removed already... and in any case, the last thing he wants to do, coming home, is to worry about what happened during the day, particularly when nothing of relevance had happened anyways and the evening is meant to reprogram his life, clearing it of its daily annoyances.

The wife pours a glass of chilled white wine for him just as he likes it and a few drops for herself because she knows he likes to drink in company.

They cheer and drink and, after a little while, things appear sweeter to him. The permafrost over his meaningless life thaws. He regains cheerfulness and even remembers a joke that he heard at work. It was some kind of version of the reason why the chicken crossed the road. He did not think it was that funny then, but now he recounts it expecting a laugh. The wife smiles while he stalks her around in the kitchen till he grabs her breast and kisses her gently in the neck.

***

They eat.

***

Then, he feels tired and yawns. He had one too many glasses of the no–longer–so–chilled wine.

The wife gets up and clears the table and he pretends to help. But she stops him with an authoritative expression, the only time when she is bossy to him.

He freezes with pleasure, sipping the last drops of wine and then goes to the sink where she is busing herself with the dishes. He kisses her in the neck again and says:

"See you upstairs".

Lying down in bed, he becomes inpatient.

"What is she doing downstairs? How long does it take to clean up after two people?" He questions.

 "Mary!" he shouts, "Are you coming soon?"

"Yes, honey" and the noise of the running water suddenly vanishes. Few metal sounds announce the rearranging of a few pans and here she appears, still beautiful after all these years.

Then, there is the bathroom routine:

"Why does she have to take so long? She is just as pretty the way she is."

Finally, in a silky nightgown, she comes under the blankets and hugs him with her cold feet and hands. He loves that chilling feeling in contrast to the warmth of the rest of her body and there, he makes love to her.

***

Later, staring at the ceiling adorned by the moving shadows of the streetcars, he reflects:

"What a good wife I have. She has been always on my side. Even when we disagreed, she made me feel loved. She has raised these beautiful children while I was mostly away, and now that they are away, she keeps the family together with her motherly trepidation. And she is still so pretty and affectionate. I have been really lucky. Many people do not have a wife like her."

And he thinks of something that had indeed happened recently at work which he had forgotten until then. Somebody in the office, who had gone bankrupt because of his wife's recklessness, ended up committing suicide.

"Maybe I should tell her more often that I love her," and he cannot remember when he last said so.

He argues with himself that maybe it is not necessary to tell her because she already knows ...of course!

"But still, I should tell her!" and turning toward her, he touches her shoulder and says:

"I love you."

But she is already peacefully asleep.

Resting his head on the pillow, he then thinks:

"Maybe I should write a poem for her birthday," and although he has not taken up a pen in a long time, he fancies himself sitting at a desk with a candle light in front of a papyri and other scraps of paper or notebooks that poets must use, with the cat sleeping on a nearby sofa, holding with his left hand a cup of tea which a woman from another century that looks just like his wife had brought him with a smile.

He navigates the uncharted seas of creativity; and as he dozes off, he murmurs a not–so– original but quite an accurate verse:

"To my wife, the Angel of my life..."

***

Fortunately, for the sake of decent literature, the poem was never written – although it would have been much appreciated in any form by the intended recipient.

Instead, the next morning was at least as gloomy as the previous one. The slippers were lost under the bed, the cat yawned but did not get up to accompany him to the bathroom and the poem had been forgotten as the cycle of life resumed its tenuous balance atop the unsteady rope of ephemeral emotions.

Scrooge 2011

The alarm went off at 6:30 and mechanically, as if pre–programmed, Julius stood up, scratched the back of his neck, and turned off the alarm. Then, still following his long–established routine, with a firm gait (he was still young and strong,) he approached the window and looked down at the deserted, still lit, street. Soon, a few cars will start their engine and the early risers will be walking swiftly to the metro to get to their jobs. Observing from the height of his apartment that momentary peace and silence, he felt empowered as if it all belonged to him.

He then turned back and looked at her still sleeping, at her beautiful shoulders and the straight black Asian hair flowing down her side.

He could have thought about what a perfect companion she had been for the last three years; how she had always been there for him when he wanted her and left him alone and free when he needed space. And how she remembered everything that mattered to him and never complained that he never remembered anything that mattered to her, from her birthday, to the anniversary of the day they met, to her little preferences such as whether she liked sugar in her coffee or not.

Alternatively, he could have thought about how lucky he was to own this beautiful woman who despite having the perfect body, the most charming smile, the most passionate affection – is still loyal and unassuming: a perfect toy for an important and handsome man like he was, who could have had all he wanted but preferred a relatively simple and programmable life; with all the conveniences that a man needs around the only thing he truly cares about: his work.

But, most likely, he did not think about anything close to those thoughts as he quickly recovered from the spell and remembered that a meeting was soon going to happen at work, where a decision needed to be made about something he had not made up his mind yet. What would have happened, he did not know – and this idea excited him and made him long to be already in the office with a cup of coffee at his side and his people around the conference table briefing him and trying hard to impress him with their alacrity.

Therefore, he hurriedly went to the bathroom, turned on the light – that shone in the bedroom, straight on her face – while he took his shower.

Then, after recovering his clothes scattered around the floor from the previous night, he dressed and, before leaving, he sat at the bedside and, admiring his toy, he touched her hair and bent to kiss her forehead, perhaps to absolve a duty, perhaps giving into a burst of spontaneity.

In response, she lifted her arm and wrapped it around his waist. Then, she said:

"Merry Christmas... if I do not see you again before".

"Merry Christmas to you Sabrina, what are you going to do for Christmas?"

"I am going to Jersey to stay with my parents. Of course, you are invited. You are very welcome to come if you would like".

"No thanks, I will stay in New York... bye." and checking the time once again, he left.

In the elevator, he thought that it was nice of her to invite him – but why should he go? Having Christmas with an old Chinese couple and their only daughter, without knowing what to say ...just smiling and nodding?

Besides, he hated Christmas and holidays in general.

Nobody would be at the office to plan and discuss new concepts, even stores would be closed and, in any case, it would not have mattered since he did not care about shopping. Just as well, shows, movies, bars, restaurants, meals with the family, and walks in the park were not the kind of activities he could relate to. Even watching TV, whether sports or family shows, was not of any interest to him.

Tomorrow, he would spend Christmas as always: sleeping an extra half hour, adding a little extra cream to the coffee, reading the newspaper, and maybe finding some book to read about finance. He condescended most of that finance and economy literature written by people who had gone to fancy schools but had made no money starting from scratch as he had done. All that theoretical gibberish that did not take into account the most important aspects of success: hard work, dedication, perseveration, focus, shrewdness, and intuition. All those naïve attempts to create formulas that would fit it all. Still, it was amusing for him to read those treatises as they would be for an anthropologist informing himself about how the Neanderthals prepared a meal.

By the time he reached the ground floor, he had forgotten about Sabrina, her parents in Jersey, and most importantly, about Christmas. Today, for others, was Christmas Eve, but for him, it was a day like any other and he was going to fully enjoy it by working hard and forgetting the upcoming misery of the following day.

***

When he stepped into the conference room, everybody was already waiting for him except for his CFO.

Things were not exactly "business as usual". People wore childish red and green stuff on their business attire and silly jokes sprouted from side to side while everybody was waiting for the meeting to start. It was just the kind of environment perfectly tailored to rouse Julius' irritation.

It took a few cold glances to restore the behavior of the insubordinates and get everybody focused even in the foreplay of the meeting on what they were there to do.

At exactly 8 o'clock, the CFO entered the room being, together with Julius, the only one dressed properly without any unnecessary fringes.

Though he knew that the CFO would be there, Julius was relieved to see him.

His CFO was the most reliable person Julius had ever dealt with, the only one who could even closely match his own character and, for this reason, he respected him and his judgment.

Let's put it this way: he represented his second opinion, whether it was matters of finances, marketing, product design or whatever else. Whether it was directly relevant to the CFO's job or not, it was equally important for Julius to solicit his opinion, and pretty much a "...not sure about this..." from the CFO was enough to kill anybody else's enthusiasm.

At 8:03, the meeting started.

It revolved around some important decision about future investments.

In truth, it could have been postponed to another day as there was nothing urgent about it but, at the same time, why postpone something that can be done on a regular business day?

As the various opinions where dealt around the table, Julius observed, through the glass walls of the conference room, that the snow was heavily coming down and for some reason, that snow, chaotically twirling around without control, that impertinent snow that was not obeying the rule of gravity, stuck in his mind as he was trying to refocus on the meeting.

Yet, disobediently, his thoughts kept returning to the twirling snow and to some memories attached to that vision, and soon, he saw his Mom busying herself in the kitchen while he was watching her from the table. And then he saw his Dad come in, neatly dressed for the Holidays and holding his hand to take him for a walk up the little town while waiting for supper.

And then, he saw his Dad bending toward the ground to collect a leaf from the fresh snow mantle that still sported a wisp of life in the form of a few green veins along the yellow stem. And his Dad was holding the leaf between his thumb and index finger and blew into them to spawn a trumpet's sound.

Then, he remembered trying to imitate his Dad without being able to reproduce the sound, and his Dad would smile, patting him on his bushy hair and telling him that one day he will be able to: he just needed more practice.

And then, he saw himself with a friend on the snowy riverbank, fishing in the silence of Christmas Eve when nobody, not even a fish, was around.

And he recollected the river's flow, slow and majestic in a pledge for eternity and the landscape that rested indifferent and harmonious, boasting a supernatural peace that did not belong to him and that he could only envy.

***

"So what do you think?"

Everybody was looking at him suddenly as he woke up from dreaming about the ghost of Christmas past:

"I do not know, I will have to think about it," he said, buying time.

Then, turning to the CFO, he asked:

"Jack, what do you think?"

"It sounds reasonable to me."

"OK, let's go ahead then" and in this way, he made the first impetuous decision of his life and as he realized that, he did not seem to care too much, after all, this was not that big of a deal and there was not much to lose.

As the meeting was adjourning, he saw people looking at him with expectation, some standing, and some still sitting, as if they were waiting for him to say something.

He knew that they were trying to remind him with their stare that it was Christmas Eve, but he pretended not to notice and, with a forcedly gay tone, he said:

"OK, let's go back to work!"

***

Back in his office, he suddenly felt conscious that he had let a decision slip away without really having thought it through and he felt uncomfortable.

He walked to the CFO's office to seek reassurance and there he saw Jack with his concentrated look as usual, frowning in front of the computer.

As he walked closer, he saw that he was looking at clothes and other amenities online.

Disregarding this vision as an illusion, he went on and asked:

"So, what do you think, Jack, was it really a good decision? I am not quite sure about it, what do you really think?".

But Jack was distracted and, turning toward him, he said:

"I am sorry, I was distracted, I was looking online for something last minute for my wife and kids, or at least just to get something ordered online; there is no way I can get out of here in time to buy anything before driving out of town and I totally forgot to get them anything the last days, we have been so busy. At least I could show them the pictures of what is to come ...Sorry, what were you asking?"

Julius, biting his lower lip gently, another way to buy time, then said:

"Nothing, I just came here to say that you are doing a great job; remind me to talk about a raise next week, and... Merry Christmas to you and your family."

***

Back in his office again, Julius could not find a thing to do next, but rather, he walked to the glass wall that was sheltering him from the rest of the world.

And he looked down toward the street. It was 73 floor removed, but the people busying themselves, engaging each other in the streets, sorting their path in the crowd, no longer look like ants to him, but now it seemed that each one of them was as big as he was, but, differently from him, had a family to go to, sounds and cheers to look forward to, children running at the door to merrily yell: "daddy is home!"

In other words, it appeared to him, for the first time, in a long time, that life was there to be lived.

And he imagined the traffic sounds and, for the first time, in a long time, he thought of it not as an irksome noise but a cheerful Christmas Carol.

Back at his desk, he thought that he also had sort of a family, or if not family, he had at least Sabrina. She was a close friend after all. Probably, he should have bought a present for her. But then, she did not get one for him, and that thought made him at par with a menacing sense of guilt.

But, as he was moving on to more constructive thoughts, he remembered spotting that morning a nicely wrapped box on his bedside table. Obviously, it was a present for him as she had managed to trick him the previous years.

He honestly thought that he should buy her something this year, but what? A ring? No way, he would not want to give her false expectations, and in any case, he did not even know what she would like.

She was so simple and easy to please! She had been wearing for two years that silly necklace from Tiffany he bought her impulsively one day walking down 5th avenue. He just purchased it because it looked like a good deal: a real sale! It was a little platinum heart hanging from an invisible platinum chain.

"I guess it is time to upgrade that necklace" he thought, and he knew that he had enough billions to buy for her the whole New York City, but he really could not see the point of wasting it on something as indulgent as a diamond necklace.

Even though they say that jewelry keeps its value and you can always sell it, you really never get the true worth when you do, so it's nothing like a real good investment.

Giving her a valuable jewel would probably not be as wise of an investment as giving her some money that she could use for something more tangible any time, even after he would leave her.

"Maybe I will write her a check" he thought; "or maybe I will try to remember next year".

And relieved by having solved this nuisance, he went back to work.

Or he thought he would, when another annoying consideration crept up his mind:

...This time, it was his Dad. Mom died almost a year ago, just after Christmas, and his Dad found himself alone for the first time. True that he had called him last Sunday and his Dad told him that all was fine, to not worry about Christmas, that in fact, he liked being alone, shuffling around the home without worrying about anything, just reading or watching TV. He did miss his wife a little, but being alone gave him a chance to think about her and paradoxically feel closer to her. After all, his Dad had always been a positive and jaunty person, a pathologic optimist, and he would have really been just fine.

Still, the idea of leaving Dad alone bothered Julius:

"I am still his son, and I think he would not mind seeing me".

Impetuously, Julius got up from his desk and walked out of the office:

"Sarah, call early dismissal… everybody home! Also call Toni and tell him to pick me up with the limo in 15 minutes, I am going upstate to see my Dad. Tell him to be prepared to spend the night there too."

And, to Sarah's incredulous face, he added with a cheerful and natural smile:

"And, Merry Christmas to you!"

The drive to upstate New York, where he was born and where he lived till he moved for college, had been routine for him. He had done it at least once a month till last year when Mom died. It had become less regular after then – not because he was not as close to his Dad, but his Dad was less vigilant about visitation. He had lower expectations and devotion to routines. So, like for everybody else around him, he had taken his Dad for granted simply because his Dad did not have the courage or the willingness to ask.

But this time, the white hills, the impertinent snow, the humming of the driver, had changed the trip from a dutiful chore to a lively adventure.

He started imaging how his Dad would deal with the surprise. He would probably act as if nothing was happening, give him a hug and while shuffling around the house, invite him to start a fire, or ask whether he wanted coffee, or may be show him the fixing he had done around the house.

He then would have asked about his work, listening with the biased ears of a provincial Dad, who, far from caring to understand subtleties, was prone to catch a few words that best suited his fancy and that he could boisterously repeat to his friends in the days to come… and, indeed, that is exactly what happened when he arrived.

***

But Julius was not someone who could stay still for long, and as much as he loved his Dad and enjoyed the thought of being with him, pretty soon became bored and, with the excuse of taking a walk and going to buy something "special" for dinner, he left the house.

And, step after step, with the day still being young, he found himself following an old path that brought him to the home of an old girl friend of his.

If anybody would have asked him whether he had ever loved anybody, he would have pointed at her. They had been classmates since kindergarten. They had played together with snowballs in the winter or climbed trees in the summer. They had been a couple of lovebirds that was looked upon with a smile by the whole town.

But as he grew up, he had become more sensitive to the complexities that govern the rules of engagement between genders and, while she flourished into a wonderful young woman ready to be loved, he never had the initiative, intention or perhaps even the thought of telling her that he loved her. As for most of his relations, he had grown accustomed to taking love from others for granted without considering the need to demonstrate reciprocity.

So, as time passed, the pretty girl, Susan was her name, got courted by handsome suitors and, on one hand observing Julius' indifference to her attempts to stir his jealousy, and on the other hand, accepting the possibility that another man could be as good, after refusing proposals a few times, she eventually yielded to Paul, the handsome son of the town's Mayor.

At her wedding, Julius felt a pang in his chest; a strange impetus to cry. He had suddenly realized that he had lost something that should have belonged to him. He decided to leave town. This resulted in a very productive move. Whatever ensued was done with zeal and commitment. Whatever he did was successful: studying, mastering his business, and becoming a legend for the little people in the little town who now greeted him with awe.

And people smiled and said they envied him whenever he entered the grocery store, or the barber shop and he was forced to report about the life in the big city about which, in reality, he knew and cared very little beyond the walls of his office.

***

Still living in what used to be her parents' house, Susan was busying herself with domestic chores, with the kids still playing outside and the husband working in the shed immersed in loud Christmas music.

It was the most joyful welcome that Susan reserved for Julius when she opened the door, almost as if she had been expecting the surprise.

She jumped on him as if she was still a little girl and she hugged him with the enthusiasm of when they saw each other again after summer camp.

And, for a few seconds, he reminisced the same happiness.

But then, gently, he pushed her away as he remembered that time had passed, that she was married and had children and that he had sworn eternal devotion only from a distance, fancying that he could pursue an old dream without interfering with her current life.

"Perhaps," he had almost subconsciously thought a long time ago: "she chose Paul because he is more handsome than I am, but I will show her that I am a clever man and one day, when I will be powerful, she will regret her choice and she will long for me".

And this naïve thought had surprisingly sculpted the life of this otherwise smart man.

But she was difficult to keep away. She held his arm and ruffled him up left and right, as if they were still two little kids, totally irreverent of his important status.

Susan still treated him as if he was still the scrawny, introverted little boy of thirty years ago.

Then she yelled:

"Paul, come here, see who is here. Mister Scrooge came to spend Christmas in the silly old town!"

And because Paul did not hear her, she dragged Julius to the shed, inadvertently forcing him to admire the realization of his dreams inside another body.

Finally, Paul's attention was conquered and, recognizing an old friend, he dropped the saw and, with a big manly hug, he lifted Julius up and down a few times.

"Let's go inside and have a beer," said Paul with a warm smile. "How are things? What brings you here? Is your Dad OK? I drop by to see him almost every day and to bring him some treats and he looks just fine, better than all of us. Do not worry. I will take good care of the old man for you. How long are you going to stay?"

But while he was being dragged by Paul into the kitchen, dreading to spend a precious part of the afternoon with the least of the persons he wanted to be with, Susan came down bundled up in a furry coat and, with the most coquettish smile, took him by the arm and said:

"Paul, you take care of the kids and I will go for a walk with Prince Charming!"

Paul smiled and, slapping him on the shoulder, said:

"Take good care of the old lady; I guess she needs a little excitement from the city mouse".

Susan had changed very little. She still could not walk slowly, and she jumped two–tree steps ahead and then waited. She looked forward while saying something and then turned back to look at him at the end of each sentence to examine the effect of her words:

"So, do you have a girl friend?"

They were at the riverbank, where the smooth flow of the water transforms suddenly into a rapid current and the reserved silence of the upper river translates into the refreshing murmur of an awakening.

"No" he said, but then he remembered Sabrina:

"Actually, I am seeing somebody"

"How is she?"

"She is a petite Chinese woman, very pretty actually, I have been seeing her for three years and she seems to be nice, low maintenance."

"I meant, how is she as a person?"

"She is a doctor, an internist, they say she is a good one with a successful practice in New York. She even won an award last year..."

"Julius, this is not what I am asking about, are you ever going to grow up? What I meant was, does she love you and do you love her. Do you know that you are starting to get some white hair and it is time for you to..."

"I think she cares for me, but she has never told me that she loves me. Also, I am not Chinese and maybe her parents are strict about this, you know how the Asian culture is; but maybe she loves me"

"Did you ever ask her? Did you ever tell her that you love her? Or are you going to do what you did to me? Are you still waiting for a miracle to make things happen? Listen Julius, I loved you and you know that, and I still love you and I will forever. I am the sister you never had, but now it is time for you to move on, it is time for you to be happy as you deserve. Just go tell her that you love her and marry her, for Christ sake!"

"I can't"

"And why?"

"Because the day you got married, I swore to myself that I would devote the rest of my life to you in spite of all, and I would be loyal to you forever just as we used to say when we were kids: that we will stand by each other forever ...like that time under the oak tree. As you know, I might be excessively compulsive, but I am what I am; I have to keep my promises.

Life has been good to me. I live well in my own crate without emotions. I know my business better than most, only few can compete with me and even they respect me. I do not have friends but I also do not have enemies. I fairly treat those who deserve it. I do not ask for anything from anybody except that they do their job, and I live contently because one really does not need to be happy to survive.

And this is the way my life will be. And one day, maybe, when you will be tired of Paul, the kids will have grown, or maybe Paul will not be there anymore, then maybe, you will come to me that day."

If you have ever been on a snowy Christmas Eve at the side of a rushing river, listening to your own words, and then returning your attention to the moving waters, you might picture how Julius heard his own; it seemed to him that his words, or what provoked them and, more specifically, his entire life up to then was being washed away by the river.

Susan was thoughtfully looking at a whirlpool and at a log stuck in it when she said:

"Julius, that will never happen, or even if it will, the chances are so low that you do not even want to think about it. Life is here to be lived and the truth is that you care for Sabrina. I could see how proud you were talking about her. But wake up! How can you even imagine a woman staying with somebody for three years, particularly an egocentric jerk like you, if she does not love him?"

"Julius, I am serious now," and she looked straight into his eyes like the little girl that used to scold him when he was being too silly on summer evenings at the fair.

"You have to learn to listen to the silence of people. She never told you that she loves you because she understands you, she knows that you may not want to hear that. But believe me, I can tell you as a woman, knowing how a woman thinks, that she loves you and I want you to marry her. You are relieved of your silly promise to me and to yourself... Go and be free as a bird out of a cage, that is the best Christmas present I can bestow upon you and that you could bestow upon me."

***

Back at home, the two kids greeted Susan and "uncle" Julius. Paul once again offered the beer and started talking with a smile about how miserable life was with such a bossy wife and two terrorists for children; and his complains felt as joyful and insincere as the sorrow of the man who had too much wine and food.

Then, Paul said:

"Come on, get your Dad here and you can have dinner with us. It will not be as fancy as the dinner you are used to in the Big Apple, but I promise it will be good. The old lady here knows some good tricks to keep a man's belly happy!"

But Julius answered:

"Thanks Paul, maybe next time. I think I will go to Jersey to a friend's home for dinner".

And a few tears trickled down Susan's eyes.

"Do not forget to tell her that you love her!" she screamed as the swirling snow and the descending night swallowed Julius' image.

***

"Sabrina, it is me, what do you think if I come for dinner to your place in Jersey?"

"Where are you?"

"I am upstate at my Dad's place"

"Yes, of course and what about your Dad? Bring him with you!"

***

"Hi Toni, check out of the hotel and pick me up in 15 minutes, we are driving to Jersey for dinner. I want to be there soon."

***

When he entered his Dad's house, Julius said to him:

"Dad, we are going to Jersey for dinner, to a friend's home".

And the Dad replied:

"Is it a woman?"

"Yes, she is Chinese and her parents are Chinese too, and they speak only Chinese and eat Chinese food. I hope it is OK! Come on, let's go!"

"I guess somebody had to come all the way from China to put some sense onto you!" mumbled his Dad while walking obediently to his bedroom.

"And Dad, do not forget to wear a tie!"

"Of course, I always put a tie on when I go out of state".

"And bring the pecan pie we are having for tonight".

As they were walking toward the limo, the Dad suddenly stopped and, taking a few steps in the snow, went under a tree and pinched a leaf that still bore a little green trait of life off the old bush. He squeezed it in between his hands and blew the trumpet's sound.

"Come on Dad, let's go, it is late!"

In the car, the Dad asked:

"How do you say *hi* in Chinese?"

"Ni hao, which means: you good".

"niaoww, niaoww... niaowww..." muttered his Dad thoughtfully.

***

When they arrived, the whole family came to greet them at the door.

Sabrina took Julius' Dad from Toni's care and brought him in, and the old Chinese lady smiled and nodded her head while the Chinese Dad looked sternly at the son and his Dad.

The latter said "niaowww, niaowww" a few times, but even a cat could not have related to that sound.

Then, as Julius' Dad was brought in the house by the old woman to enjoy the ghost of Christmas present, Sabrina's Dad said to his wife something in Chinese that meant:

"Should we ask him to take off his shoes?"

But the old lady pretended not to hear.

Then, Julius held Sabrina in the atrium and asked:

"Do you have 200 dollars? I have no cash".

She opened her wallet and gave him the money.

He went out and, while she was waiting at the door, he held Toni by his shoulder and said:

43

"Go home, I can go back to New York with my friend tomorrow after dropping off my dad at his place... and take this, good night and Merry Christmas."

Then, he went back to his shivering woman, who was waiting for him at the doorstep, and he held her in his arms and said:

"I love you," and he kissed her.

And this kiss felt different from those before. There was the tenderness that one feels only for a wife, a sense of eternity that is deeper than infinite itself.

And when he let her go, she had tears in her eyes and she said:

"I love you too".

I will let the readers imagine the obvious end to this story and the ghosts of Christmas future that followed with full of cheerful sounds from children. To those of you who are more interested in details and may wonder how Julius' Dad enjoyed a whole Chinese meal, I will happily report that it went just fine. In fact, he even refused to use Western utensils. And as for the Chinese Dad, who used to be a teacher, he patiently taught him how to use chopsticks so that far from mastering the technique, the American Dad managed to bring the food to his mouth and, in the end, this is all that really counts.

The Visit

"Quid Concupiscam Queris Ergo? ...Dormire"
(What I desire most of all now, you ask me? ...To sleep)
Epigram X.74 – Marco Valerio Marziale – 1ˢᵗ Century A.D.

As with many stories before, it started with a beautiful morning. The sun had been patiently climbing the sky on the left, dispensing just the right amount of warmth to the skin of Christian's arms. Seemingly above the sun, scattered clouds were rushing from right to left to an unknown place, distant in space and spirit, unaware of terrestrial things and posing no threat.

The air was crisp and a cool breeze, also coming from the right, tempered the warmth of the sun and all together contributed to that misleading feeling of hopeful expectation that such mornings impose on the human soul: that for no apparent reason, today will be better than yesterday and many days before.

***

Even Christian, who had watched many mornings in his long life, gave into that feeling. Sitting on the veranda, he held in his left hand a newspaper folded so tidily to give the impression that it had never been opened. The right hand had been periodically ferrying a cup of coffee to his lips, while a cell phone rested on the coffee table. The hands and the objects lent an awareness of purpose to the scene while, in veracity, there was none.

Lately, Christian had taken to perceive the future as a mere extension of his own past rather than a legitimate reality, and this was principally because he had grown bored of life in whatever direction one might look at it. It also appeared that the feeling was reciprocal, as life around seemed to have grown just as tired of him.

He donned trousers of good quality linen but shabbily worn that ended at one extremity too early above his ankles and too far on the other with the belt above the navel. The white shirt was open at the neck and a tinge of yellow could be discerned along the collar, while the vest was sprinkled with flakes of dandruff that had probably been there for days and for which there was nobody to blame but life itself with its negligent disposition.

The ring tone of the cell phone was programmed to play Für Elise, which he liked very much because it brought back bittersweet memories with its enigmatic notes that are happy and sad at the same time. But the ring tone had almost completely ceased to perform and the phone, reflecting the sky and the migration of the clouds, sat silent at his side as a reminder of the slowing pace of life.

That he had not completely given up on life, stood witness the fact that he still carried the phone with him during the day and, at night, he laid it gently on the

45

bedside table and hooked it to the charger, perhaps with the unconscious wish that the charge would not only kindle the battery but his soul.

***

Indifference was what he recalled. When his mother died and he was sitting at her side crying and asking what was he to expect next, he saw indifference in her face, absorbed in her own journey toward eternity. Such a caring woman, who shivered at every familiar call, had completely abandoned and forgotten everything.

And indifferent had been his Dad, lying in his coffin with a strange smile as if he had been relieved of all the anxieties that had crowded his latest life: indifferent to things that mattered so much before.

And indifferent was his wife the morning he found her dead at his side. Not sure about what to do, he rose from bed and mechanically went to the kitchen. Like every single morning for so many years before, he prepared two cups of coffee and brought them to the bedside. He put one on her bedside table and he set at her feet drinking his. He touched her feet, and then her belly and breast, and stood up to kiss her lips and caress her hair. But she, who had loved him so much and would quiver at his touch, remained indifferent, just as his Mom and Dad had done before, as if they all had suddenly realized from the other world that life itself was just a deception not worthy of attention.

He saw indifference around himself, in the sky and in the birds, in the clouds and in the sun, he saw indifference in the inmates of the retirement home whose smiles, how do you dos, take care of yourself etc. hanged like abstract figures out of a crooked canvas.

And he was returning the indifference with indifference of his own. He barely read the newspaper and he regarded the news as mere curiosities, as if the world out there did not really exist or it had no bearing on him. He played cards with the inmates but he did not care whether he won or lost. He expressed opinions to be social but he did not bother defending them. He read novels but he did not remember them and, when he occasionally watched TV, he was distracted by thoughts that brought him back to some specific moment of his past that had long gone and had no reason to be exhumed.

His thinking was still sharp, but the emotions, just the emotions had failed him. Perhaps, more than indifference, it was detachment that ruled his life. Possibly, he protected himself by not caring, and this was an ancestral skill developed over time, starting who knows when in the remote shadows of his past.

***

One after the other, more and more clouds had gone by, and Christian's eyes had started to feel heavy, the right hand had long quit carrying the cup to his lips and the newspaper deposited at the side of the cell phone with its corners flapping at the rhythm of the breeze had remained folded.

It was then that a man of around fifty appeared in front of him. He had a spacious forehead that bordered into boldness and a thin moustache that partly covered a row of shiny white teeth. He sported an ironic but pleasant smile, and he looked straight up at the sun with impunity. His eyes were golden when he looked into the sun and returned green when he looked at him.

As to answer an obvious question, he introduced himself as:

"I am the Angel of Death. It was decided that you need counseling and this is why I am here for you".

And he continued after a pause. "...You see, most people keep bustling about till the day they die. They keep themselves busy till the end with trifles; and, when they die, they rest in their coffin relaxed and smiling; happy to leave those stupid worries to the world ...And then, of course, there are the religious ones. Most do not even believe in God but religion serves them as a diversion. Every time that the Big Question comes, they cross their chest. And they have their churches, where they chant and pray and cheer each other up. Their leaders speak conventional wisdom, and their words deflect the reality of death. By the time one of my colleagues comes to take them away, they do not argue and, for the sake of consistency, they take the blessing from their minister and jump in the coffin having no clue of what happened to them as they pass to the next generation, their God, the prayers, the flowers, the incense, the chanting, the litanies and all their religious armamentarium that protected them while alive on Mother Earth".

The Angel then focused his stare right into Christian's eyes and continued.

"But you are different. You are one of those who look at life and death as if they were the same thing and, forgetting to live, spend most of their time preparing to die... of course, quite unsuccessfully."

Here, the Angel stopped talking and looked again into the sun as if he was reading some notes engraved in the flames. When he fixed his gaze again into Christian's eyes, the sun rays were still burning inside his pupils and Christian, who could not bear the glare, bent his face.

Then, the Angel sipped from a cup and looking up toward something in the sky that only he could see, smiled again.

"You see, people like yourself feel that the process of life must be controlled, although they realize that they cannot do it themselves. Yet, they do not know where to turn for help. Religious people turn to God, atheists believe there is nothing to be explained that cannot be supported by their own minds but agnostics like you are condemned to continual anguish ...You would like to know where your mother, your father, your wife are ...if they are. You believe that they are gone forever, yet you are not sure. You would like to know the purpose of all that has passed, but yet, there may be no purpose..."

After another pause the Angel asked:

"Why don't you just believe in God and be happy, keep yourself busy with prayers and good actions, do not question what cannot be questioned. It will not make any difference in the end but in the meantime, you will have a better life...and we would not have to worry about you. Believe me, Angels are not lazy, I am not trying to save work for myself but it pains us to see people like you suffer so much while they are alive when in the end it will make no difference. All of you people of the Heart will end up the same. Why don't you just go with the flow? Tell me...tell me please...why don't you just believe in God?"

It seemed to Christian that an explanation came out of his mouth according to the following words:

***

"When my son was a little boy just about three years old, I was recounting a bedtime story in the darkness laying at his side and hoping that he would soon fall asleep. It was just before Christmas, and like all children, he was impatiently anticipating the magic of Christmas Eve, the milk and the cookies waiting for Santa on the coffee table in front of the fire place, the thank you note that Santa would leave with familiar hand writing, and of course, the bewilderment over the colorful landscape of presents that materialize in the silence of that magic night just as the snow does outside.

...My son cherished Christmas more than anything else and his anticipation for it kept building like a tsunami day after day as the time approached... those were wonderful times! But I am losing my train of thought.

...Anyways, I was telling him the story... I do not recollect exactly which one, and at the same time, I was paying attention to his moves because I was tired after a long day at work and I was longing for the embrace of my own bed. And in fact, I savored the silence and the stillness; no more questions about why this happened, who did this, was he a good or a bad fellah, was he really that mean, was she really that beautiful?

...As I held my words and even my breath, silence seemed to have taken control of that peaceful night in which my son was sleeping and dreaming of the good things to come.

Slowly, gently, carefully, I put one foot on the floor. But the foot had barely touched the carpet when his trusting and harmonious voice questioned the silence:

"Dad?"

"Yes Joseph, aren't you sleeping yet?"

And Joseph answered:

"If you do not believe in Santa, does he still bring presents?"

"Of course not!" I replied with an appalled tone!

(You see, I am agnostic but I always "believed" in Santa, in the magic of Christmas and I wanted my son to experience the same for as long as he could).

Silence followed and once again, I put my foot down; but once again, as the foot touched the floor, the voice that I loved so much asked...

"What if you do believe in Santa... but.... you are not really, really sure... would he still not bring the presents?"

And understanding the depth of his conflict, I reassured him:

"Do not worry, as long as you believe, even a tiny little bit, he will bring the presents, you do not have to be sure."

You see? This is exactly the essence of being agnostic. My son really wanted to believe, but he could not force himself to do it. You cannot manipulate your mind, you cannot coerce it to follow your wishes no matter how badly you would like to. You cannot just lie to yourself ...and this is the curse of the agnostics".

And the Angel then asked:

"But, if you do not believe in God, how do you explain your own existence? You really think there is nothing out there? Do you really think that your life was just a temporary illusion?"

Now Christian interrupted the Angel:

"Why do you ask me? You should know better than I do and ...you should tell me! You have lived longer than I did and have seen things far away that humans cannot reach."

But the Angel, turning his smile into a thoughtful expression said:

"The truth is that I have never seen God. May be as an Angel, I am closer to God than humans like you are, but still I have never seen Him or heard Him. I do not know what eternity or infinity is. You see, even if I lived forever, I would not know a beginning because there is no beginning to eternity, and even if I traveled the universe forever and ever in a straight line, I would never see its origin because the ocean of infinity has no horizons.

But, just because I do not remember a beginning or an end, it does not mean that there isn't one. In some ways, the situation for us Angels is similar to that of humans, except in a vaster dimension in space and time.

I will share with you a conundrum around which I have been pondering for a long time. I am curious to know what you would answer ...listen carefully before answering:

Do you think that it is easier to imagine an infinite universe or one that ends? On the same token, is it easier to imagine eternity or a beginning and an end?"

And here, the Angel pointed his index finger toward Christian's mouth:

"Do not answer right away! Think it through carefully and keep in mind.... I did not ask you what you think the truth is, but rather ...what is easier to imagine and conceptualize."

But Christian felt he had an easy answer and reacted impulsively:

"Probably a beginning and an end! It is impossible to imagine something that never ends; and it is the same for time, how can something be forever?"

The Angel nodded his head as if he was expecting that answer. Then, squinting his eyes, he appeared to look very far in the distance, through galaxies and universes... exploding and imploding ones, the darkness and the light, the infinite and the timelessness.

Then he said:

"Yes, this is what most people answer, but I personally do not agree.

Think about it, imagine that you could travel the distance of space at your leisure; let say that you could reach the end of it all; can you imagine or conceptualize what it would look like? Would it be a wall? ...Or would it look more like a fence?

And then, what would you see beyond that wall or that fence? Would it be empty space? And would empty space represent something or nothing? In other words, how does the End look like?

What if there was no empty space, what would be the substance of that nothingness that fills a space that is not there? I am just talking about the physics of it. Forget the spiritual stuff.

...I do not know. For me, it is easier to imagine and conceptualize infinity and eternity although it is difficult to comprehend it because these concepts do not require the creation of a something that is different from what we are familiar with and experience in the known universe, except for accepting unending and timeless boundaries. In some ways, it is like trying to rationalize a logical end to the infinite repetitiveness of periodical numbers. Isn't it easier to let them go forever?"

And the dry smile reappeared on the Angel's face:

"Perhaps I am as agnostic as you are, but with a positive spin! I just accept that something that we cannot comprehend can still be out there and this thought gives me comfort.

To you now, life looks like a collection of scattered events to which we try to attach a meaning.

What was the meaning of holding your Mom's hand while taking a photo on your first day of school? And proudly walking with your Dad in the park, dressed in a Harlequin suit for Carnival? And watch your team win a game? Listening to your son's first words? Bragging with your wife about your son's achievements? What do they have to do with each other, what is their sequential logic, buried as they are in the blanket of the past and kept together by the puzzle of memory?

You feel that life threw all these events at you and you were passively washed downstream by their uncontrollable flow.

It would be best if you desist, and like us Angels, accept that the meaning is beyond our comprehension. Does this comfort you?"

***

Whether this conversation really happened, I am not sure, but by the end of it, the Angel had gone and Christian's chest moved up and down following the rhythm of a mellow snore.

"Dad...Dad!"

As he woke up, Christian saw the image of his handsome son standing in front of him.

It should be clarified that the only reason that kept Christian from completely giving up on life and swaying him to recharge the cell phone at night was his son and the grandchildren toward whom he carried very conflicting emotions.

He loved his son of course; as for Christian, Joseph was still the same little curly–haired boy around whom his life had spun from the day of his birth. But there was a dissonance between this love for his son and his own philosophy of life.

As the Angel had said:

"What is life but just a collection of scattered events glued together by our own memory?"

How come he still cared so much about something that, like the past things, if it will soon be over? Christian could not reconcile those emotions with the rest of his existence, but still, when the joyful thought of his son emerged from his deserted soul, he surfed on it with pleasure and he did not question further.

Besides, he admired Joseph, like all Dads do. He thought he was extraordinarily handsome, he looked much like his mom, and he had the same gentle smile though mitigated by a natural virility, an aura of self–confidence that made him look like a giant.

After spending a few seconds admiring his son, Christian interrupted the silence by saying:

"Hi Joseph, what a nice surprise, what brought you here?"

"Hi Dad, how are you? Long time–no see; you look good".

And Christian, holding his son's arm, began to rise from the chair.

Dad and son were both doctors. They had gone to the same school, trained in the same place and both entered a similar field aimed at the treatment of cancer.

Although the Dad had been an established academician, as for everything else, his son had taken the lead and he would gently patronize the dad about anything that could be thought or said. This was not out of arrogance, but simply because, since he was a little boy, he wanted to be like his dad and part of this was to act like a dad himself. Finding no resistance from the dad, he had gradually reversed the roles and he now acted as a big man leading the dad around as if the old chap was a little boy just about to start kindergarten.

"Dad, you should take better care of yourself," he added, patting the dandruff off his vest and gauging the belt to a more dignified and manly position.

A twinge in Christian's chest, whose significance a doctor could very easily appreciate, distracted him for a moment, and with the pretense of adjusting his shoe, he hesitated for a few seconds before rising completely.

Then, he turned to the side table and with an unhurried elder's pace, Christian methodically collected the unfolded newspaper, then the phone and lastly, the cup.

Finally, holding his son's arm, he stood up. Turning their back to the sun that by now was above the clouds, and to the migrating clouds and to a flock of geese that was passing by going in the direction opposite to the clouds, son and dad, following their own shadows, walked toward another veranda where they could find some coffee and a few other amenities to celebrate their encounter.

During that short walk, Joseph had been repeating one too many times how happy he was to see his dad and how beautiful the weather was, for Christian not to become increasingly suspicious that something serious, even painful, was in his son's mind.

Besides, it seemed that Joseph kept starting to say something but every time, rubbing with his index and middle finger his forehead and wincing his nose, he postponed the thought while something light and predictable came out of his mouth instead – like the cleanliness of the place, the color of the roses, the shape of the trees or other things that are raised to the level of conversation only when we need to buy time.

Christian had known that behavior very well.

It reminded him of his school days, when an insufficient grade was needed to be reported. It took a very long time, through a very contorted path, before the news found their way out of Joseph's mouth.

Suddenly, a little kitten walked out of a bush and, meowing loudly and insistently, said to them in its feline language:

"You big people, don't you see, I am just a little kitty who needs attention."

Christian had known that kitten for a while since the little creature had taken for more than a few times the liberty to select his belly for a concordant nap during the sunny hours of those lazy afternoons when nobody seemed to be around. Although it would be an exaggeration to state that the kitty was Christian's best friend at the nursing home, it was close enough to draw a smile from a face that had become resistant to joyful emotions.

Joseph, who loved animals, squatted on his knees like when he was a child and rubbed the kitten on the top of its head, and let him trace its whiskers against his fingers while it, purring as loudly as a steam engine and keeping its tail straight like a lightning pole, released a few meows that meant:

"See, I told you that you could make me very happy with just a little gesture"

Christian, who barely bent and stretched his arm to pet the kitten, observed that the anguish had gone from his son's eyes and his beautiful smile had returned to rival the glory of that glorious day.

But then, a butterfly also came out of nowhere and became the kitten's duty to stalk the impudent insect, and squatting and waving its butt to get ready to pounce, the animal forgot the humans and their kindness.

Straightening up, Christian felt the twinge in his chest again and he held his son's arm a little tighter waiting for the pain to go away. But Joseph did not notice it and, little by little, step-by-step, they arrived to the veranda where Bernie was preparing the chair for the old man while greeting Joseph at the same time.

Bernie was a middle aged Filipino man, who had been working at the retirement home for as long as Christian had been there. He was very kind to everybody and was caring. He was fond of "his" old people and of their visitors.

"May I bring you the usual?" he asked, and receiving consent, Bernie left:

"You are lucky to have him! He seems to really care and he takes good care of you" observed Joseph.

Bernie was particularly fond of Joseph not only on the account of the generous tips he gave but also earnestly because of the respect and gratitude that Joseph made sure to express to him each time for the care he gave to his Dad.

Not that the tips were irrelevant – Bernie maintained a restrained existence, saving every penny to send to his family in Manila, and visiting his children for a month every two years –but this is all there was to say about Bernie as he lived a very simple life and talking about Bernie was the last of the distractions.

Silence followed, and Christian, having become impatient to know the cause of his son's torment, did not do anything to break it.

Looking at the ground, with his middle finger gently stroking the side of his mouth, Joseph said:

"Mary's cancer has recurred".

"Where?" asked the dad, who had been expecting the news, for Mary's breast cancer had all the characteristics of an aggressive type.

"She just had a PET scan and the liver and bones lit up".

Although Christian had spent his whole life dealing with cancer patients and their family, he still had not found an optimal solution about what to say and, like he had always done around those situations, he started by lying. It was not a flat lie of course, but it was that form of a lie that we would rather define as "positive thinking":

"You know, nowadays, there are all these new experimental treatments ...I have a few friends I could call in New York or Texas. You will see: she will be fine!"

...And seeing that Joseph had no intention to speak but continued to look at the floor this time, rubbing his eye with his index finger, he continued:

"You have no idea how many people with advanced cancer I saw healing with experimental treatments during my lifetime. Not all respond to therapy, but you never know. Those who do are cured! Better than a miracle! Do you want me to call Kevin? He was a post–doc with me and is now chair of oncology at M..."

"Dad, I am an oncologist myself, I know who to call... thanks though... but you know as much as I do that she is dying, let's not fool ourselves."

"Does she know?"

"Of course, Dad, we are in America, people have the right to know".

Christian nodded. Of course, he knew that they were in America and that people had the right to know. Yet, he thought of the Angel, and he thought of the religious people who believe what best suit their own needs. But Mary was agnostic as he and Joseph were, and she did not believe in God but just in her own cancer that was going to kill her soon.

"How is she dealing with it?"

"She is very pragmatic about it. She has been telling me what to do with the house, and the children, how I should take care of them, even the dumbest details about how to cook, clean, iron etc. I guess this is her coping strategy.

...But then she sits at the side of the bed, close to me and she says:

'I can't believe this is happening to me.'

And I lie to her and say:

'Do not worry Mary, there are all these experimental treatments, I have a lot of friends whom I could call, you will see, it is just a setback.'

And she smiles. She squeezes my arm and, standing up, she says:

'OK doctor, now I am becoming an interesting case!'

...And then she says:

'Let's go, let's worry about the important things!'

...And she goes in the kitchen, or the pantry.

And I do not know how to deal with it myself. I try to make love to her, and I lay over her, and as I make love, I wonder what she is thinking, and when we are done, we lay down side by side in silence, then she gets up and goes to the kitchen, and I smell the coffee, and she starts cleaning and cooking and doing other things, and another precious day goes by without anything I can do to stop or at least slow the progress of time..."

"And what about you? How are you coping with it?" asked Christian.

"You know dad, sometimes I feel in control, I feel I know what to do all the way to the end ...and even after, but sometimes I am scared, I am just so scared."

And Christian looked intensely into his son's eyes and he saw how painfully his used–to–be–little boy tasted the true flavor of life.

"You know Dad, what scares me the most?"

"Yes, you are afraid of being alone," and as he said this, Christian realized that he had impulsively revealed with a short sentence the essence of the last thirty years of his own life.

"How did you know?"

Now, I ask my readers, how can you deliver such an obvious answer? Isn't being alone what we are all afraid of? Why do men become dictators or politicians, and why do boys want to impress girls, why do we want to impress our parents or our neighbors? Is it not just to attract attention to ourselves and to savor the momentary illusions that we are not alone?

But Christian answered:

***

"You were always afraid of being alone... remember that time (you must have been about four years old) when we went bear–hunting in the woods in the back of our home? I just gave you a toy riffle with a cork at its end. And we were carefully listening for any noise, and we walked silently side by side... and then, a noise arose from a bush a few feet away and I told you:

– There is the bear! Did you see it...lets surround it, you go left and I will go right. I will move slowly toward him and when I come close enough, I will yell and scare him and it will run toward you and you shoot him! –

And you looked at me, with your big eyes wide open and did not say anything.

– OK then, let's go – I said,

...And you walked two or three steps your way as I went mine, but then you said:

"Dad, I would rather come with you."

And so we walked silently by each other's side all the way to the bush to discover that, of course, there was no bear.

 And I said:

"Sorry Joseph, we must have scared him away with our noise."

And you took a deep breath and did not seem disappointed at all.

And as we walked home, your steps were swift and you held my hand tightly, and once in a while you looked back till we arrived home.

I remember your curly–haired head being just at the level of my hips, the smell of rosemary and roasting turkey when we opened the door, and you running to the kitchen to find your mom ...and this is all I remember about that day."

"I know," reflected Joseph "you told me this story so many times that I am starting to believe that I remember it too".

"You know dad, I came here not because I needed your professional help, I can deal with all that needs to be done myself; I came here because I needed somebody to talk to, it is just too painful to be at home pretending, pretending, pretending…"

At this point, Joseph lost his thread of thought and he looked tired – very, very tired.

"You know dad, in the end, you are all I have, I tell you. I loved the way you were with me, your gentle way. It was amusing to observe how positive you always pretended to be, as if I could not read your thoughts. When you liked something, you would be so excited and positive. But when you did not agree, you would ask me whether I was really sure I wanted to do this or that, it was so cute how you could not simply say that you disagreed.

…And yet, I cared so much about your opinion, I knew all the time exactly what your thoughts were. And I remember when mom died, how you tried hard to make me feel "OK", and you told me about Angels in the sky, and how they hide behind the clouds, and how mom was one of them and she would look down and check on me …and she would cry if I was sad and it would be a rainy day. That was why I should be happy …and most of the time, she would smile at us from up there and the days would be as shiny as today

…And even then, I knew that you did not believe a word of it. But I pretended to believe you since there was no point not to."

"You know Dad, sometimes I think you are my only friend".

And Christian looked up at the sky and the clouds, and like the Angel in the dream, he squinted his eyes to see even farther, searching for something from up there, something like a sign, a reassurance that there was a meaning to all of this, to his and his son's life, to all that had been and had to come.

***

The morning turned into a peaceful afternoon, rich with memories and stories till the time came for Joseph to leave.

When they walked toward the car, the sun was still shining and the clouds were still migrating to an unknown place. It seemed to Christian that they were going faster than before as if they were hurrying somewhere. And it looked as if they were retiring from a big event that was now over, rushing to their home in another universe.

His son held his hand tightly and Christian remembered when he, many years before, had walked his son on the first day of school, hand in hand with his wife on the other side.

"Are you going to take the family to see the July 4th fireworks tomorrow?"

And the son answered:

"Yes, of course…good bye Dad"

And as Joseph walked back to his own life with steps not as purposeful and steady as they used to be and his shoulders no longer as straight, it occurred to Christian that he himself should soon be gone, and that his son would be as alone, and his life as empty has his own now. And no matter how big the bears hiding behind the bush are, he would have to deal with them by himself because nobody would be there to hold his hand. And a feeling of uncontrollable helplessness descended upon him, presenting itself like a weight in the chest that could not be lifted.

And he felt sorry for his son, and he imagined Joseph sitting with his head in his hands, beside the indifferent corpse of his dad, asking him why he abandoned him. He imagined that his son would have nobody, neither his Mom nor his Dad, to ask what happened to the hopes and dreams that had decorated his earlier life. Profound sadness and a sensation of disempowerment fell upon him, and he remembered what his own Dad had once told him:

'Life is a very strange thing... in truth, you live alone to die alone".

***

That night, memories kept pouring on Christian like raindrops in a summer storm, warm like tears and heavy like steps in the mud. They would not come in order, but he remembered holding his mom's hand on the first day of school, and holding his dad's hand in the park dressed like Harlequin, and meeting his wife and her beautiful smile, and the day his son was born, and his graduation from high school, and then from college, and his wedding with Mary and the grandchildren, and, although these memories came like a series of separate events, he imagined that on the other side of infinity, there was a logic, a meaning just as the Angel had said.

Then, he felt tired and, looking at the clock, he saw that it was one in the morning. One more time, he checked to assure himself that the cell phone was charging and that his slippers were waiting for him right where he would want them to be in the morning and, turning to his side, he closed his eyes.

The twinge came back in the middle of his chest and it seemed to him that the past, the present and the future had all come together. He saw his mom, his dad, Joseph and Mary and the grand children, all together smiling at him as in a big family picture, and he smiled too.

***

"...And now, for the weather forecast, we are looking at a wonderful July 4th Independence day, shiny day with highs in the mid–eighties and lows in the sixties, dry air with very low chance of rain and a 10–mile per hour breeze from the west....etc., etc., etc. and ...etcetera, etcetera, etcetera".

But Christian heard nothing of all these, as he had died during the night.

A Rebellious Story

Whether Otto was a good, or at least a decent writer, we will leave it to his readers to pronounce. Here, I will describe the technique that he used to develop a plot and how once it went awry.

Otto enjoyed letting his imagination wander. On the plane, waiting in line, driving to work and, most of all, lying down during sleepless nights, he would propose a theme and would then let the characters build the story by giving them outmost freedom.

In fact, Otto carried with his characters a symbiotic existence or, more precisely, his characters followed him wherever he would go and, though others would perceive him as a loner and a withdrawn character, he was circled by a wealth of relationships that kept him busy like a bush surrounded by bees in hot summer days.

Besides, it was easy for him to settle and relax while watching the story evolve along uncharted territories rather than obsessing on minute details to please the demanding hypothetical reader. This way, stories took on their own life while he rested aside, enjoying the evolving comedy as a spectator on a velvet armchair at the theater.

But once, things did not exactly go the way they were supposed to. The theme itself was quite straightforward. The characters needed to reach a catharsis during a holiday after a dysfunctional period in their relationship – a way, through heartfelt conversations, to open their hearts to each other.

He had tested something similar in a previous story where he asked his main character to verify the existence and define the significance of evil.

What is evil? Is it just a social convention? Does evil really exist, or is it a way by which humans set rules to avoid self–destruction? In the end, the character which, like Otto, was agnostic and even materialistic, concluded that evil exists as a material thing that can be uncovered in the faces of those who suffer, in their pain – both physical or emotional. The character also concluded as a corollarium that those who cannot see and empathize with others' pain are, according to all human standards, evil or, in medical terms, sociopaths.

Granted that this theory cannot compete in depth with the perspicacity of Ivan Karamazov's views in Dostoyevsky's story, it was still good enough to keep a reader busy on a rainy afternoon.

***

This time, however, the characters refused to follow the plot. The patriarch went to the family room after lunch to watch TV and kept dozing off. When he was awake, he went on telling old and foolish anecdotes that everyone had heard thousands of times.

The matron busied herself in the kitchen or in the laundry room, and when she would appear, she would either scold the husband because he was not sitting correctly, the son for the mess in which his hair was, or the daughter for not helping, leaving her to deal with everything by herself.

The daughter, on the other hand, was incessantly on the phone – talking to her friends or texting, and the son, pretending to read something, was hypnotizing himself with computer games.

In vain, Otto kept trying to discipline each character one at a time. As one was languidly trying to listen and follow the orders, the others wondered around in different rooms, or took a walk outside or got on the phone again and again so that it never happened that all of them were in the same room at the same time and could even initiate any meaningful conversation whether constructive or destructive.

Eventually, in a desperate final attempt, Otto was able to arouse from his torpor the son, who as a character was the most related to his own personality.

Making himself invisible to the other characters, he sat at the coffee table in front of Michael, firmly removed the computer game from his hands and, looking straight into his eyes, told him:

"Listen, this may be your last chance to become a real character in a published story and, more importantly, to come to a closure with your own family. Your parents are getting old; who knows how many chances you will have to chat with them, to let them know that you love them after all, to let them tell you that they are proud of you for what you are.

With a little effort, you can go far in solving the anger that lingers in you when you think about your family and we can both gain. You will be happier and I will have a decent story to relate to my readers. Come on, you can do this! I will let you be now," and as magically as he appeared, he quickly disappeared wrapped in guilt for, contrary to his principles, interjecting his will into the story.

After Otto's disappearance, Michael did not grab the computer game but, rather stunned by the thought that his parents were getting old, began meditating.

✳✳✳

Michael was an angry person. He was angry with his mother because she never listened to him but was just worried about the color of his socks or the length of his hair. He was angry with his sister because she was dumb. He was angry with his employer because he exploited him, and with acquaintances because they had demands that he did not want to satisfy. And he was angry at the world because it was too big and indifferent, and with those who were happy because he was not.

He was also angry with himself for being paralyzed in such a funk and doing nothing about it, but most of all, he was angry with his Dad. He felt that he never had a deep relationship with him and that this impasse was not his fault. He agreed with Otto that he should take this opportunity and make an effort to finally straighten things up with his Dad.

To be truthful, his Dad was not a bad person. He had taken care of and provided for his family throughout. He had been a devoted husband, he never spent a penny for anything unnecessary and had lived a humble and boring life, swinging from work to home as regularly and precisely as a pendulum.

Yet, he never made any effort to communicate with his children. He did take Mike to school every day when he was a little boy and picked him up in the afternoons, and he would hold his hands too, but he would barely say a word to him.

When Michael would ask him a question, he would shrug his shoulders and say:

"I do not know, you should ask your uncle who went to college" or...

"This is not something I would know anything about," and he would let his hand loose, pat Michael's shoulder opposite to him and then hold his hand again while saying:

"One day, if you will do well in school, you will have the answers to all these questions".

And to compensate for his dismissiveness, in the cold weather, he would stop at the store and buy him a hot chocolate, and when it was warm, an ice cream.

As he grew a little older, while they were walking down Main Street on a Sunday, Michael had asked his Dad whether he believed in God.

"I do not know," he replied, "You should ask your Mom who goes to church and listens to the sermons".

Often, like in this occasion, he would attach a barely relevant story or joke to these miser conversations.

"What I know is that I am not God; like that father who asked his daughter's Ascetic Jew boyfriend what he was planning to do if they would get married and, after he repeated several times that God would provide while he would spend his time in prayer and meditation, the Dad concluded that the boyfriend meant that he expected for him to be the God!".

This sort of conversations was as deep as his relationship with his Dad could go. Yet, his father was, otherwise, fond of him and was even too fond – often in an embarrassing way.

In front of his Dad, he felt like an exotic pet or an imaginary hero like a modern Don Quixote, ready to confront windmills of any size and shape as the Dad would boast with his friends about truthful achievements that grew disproportionately with each word, forcing the son to correct and disclaim with embarrassment the queries of the admiring crowds.

What really irritated Michael most of all was that his father was not dumb. In fact, he had managed all his personal and business life quite successfully and was as wise of a man as any person who had received a formal education.

Michael felt that his dad just did not want to express his thoughts and feelings. He sported this dismissive attitude for which he had no clear explanation: was he afraid to be caught in an unpleasant confrontation? Was he simply lazy? Was he embarrassed for not having received formal education? Was he too busy to waste his time to talk to his own son?

Michael just could not find a reasonable explanation and, by so meditating, he once again thought that Otto was correct, that it was time for closure and, therefore, he said:

"Dad,"

To which the Dad, staring at the TV, replied:

"What?"

"I thought we could talk a little."

To which the Dad, still staring at the TV and holding the remote, replied:

"About what?"

Encouraged by the established contact, Michael thought of ways to switch the channel of his father's thoughts from the football game to a more substantive subject.

"Maybe we could talk about our lives, about the way you think we came out as your children. Are you disappointed? Are we the way you hoped for us to be?"

"You were a fine boy and your sister was quite a fine little lady indeed," said the Dad, trying to look thoughtful.

...Silence...

"That is all, I cannot complain, everything went just fine," he added, but all of a sudden, he was distracted by the fireplace and realized that right at that moment, more wood was needed.

He got up, went to the fireplace, rearranged the burning wood, and stepped out to get more.

"Dad, do you ever read anything or do anything other than vegetate in front of the TV? Why did you even bother having a family, why did you bring us to this world – just to eat, sleep, barely communicate with each other, and wait to die? What was the point?" Michael said after the Dad had settled himself again on the armchair.

The Dad did not answer but kept watching the TV.

Then, he pursed his lips as if he was going to blow on a trumpet, and then he rubbed his neck, keeping Michael hanging while he was waiting for his Dad to blow out some words assembled under such herculean efforts.

But little followed this pantomime and, releasing a big sigh, the Dad said:

"I don't have much to say, I am not like you kids who went to college and know how to debate about everything. I could teach you how to make a cabinet, that is all I know, but you would not care, would you?".

"Dad, I am trying to tell you that I do care. Stop pretending that you are not a clever man. You lived a savvy life, you took care of the family, of our education, we are fine now around you and not many children can say that".

And again, the Patriarch pursed his lips and held his breath and, when he was about to expire, released a bigger sigh and said:

"Yes, I had my share, you should ask the old lady in the kitchen, she has seen quite a few things," and Michael heard the rattling of dishes and wondered about what could the old lady have seen besides dirty socks and lost buttons.

"What was it Dad, what did the old lady see?"

"Never mind, the past is the past; you have to always look ahead," replied the Dad.

"But then, why did you bring it up? Stop playing games, talk to us like grownups for once."

"You know, this reminds me of the joke about that guy who wants to buy a parrot, and the first one he sees is beautiful but too expensive, then he sees one that was a little older and less opulent and he asks for the price; when he learns that it is even more expensive, he wonders why and the seller explains that it is because he is a Doctor: "it cannot only say "Hello...how are you," but if you ask him: "I have a headache, what should I do?" you will see that the parrot will help. In fact, the parrot prescribed: "Take an aspirin!". The guy dropped his jaw, but still, that parrot was too expensive for his pocket. Finally, the same guy sees a very old parrot, with few feathers hanging around its neck and he asks: how much for this? And the store owner replies: "Oh, this is even more expensive, he is the Chairman of the Department!""

...And the Dad waited for a laugh. But Michael was distracted as he was trying to reaffirm in his mind what they had been talking about before the joke and to understand why that story was relevant at all to the previous discussion.

"I guess, once again you managed to avoid talking to us," Michael finally concluded.

"I just do not understand why you always try to express yourself through apocryphal conversations. Can you just think out loud for yourself and say what you think through your own words? We are not judging you for your literacy!"

"A−po−crfl" pronounced the Dad, probably trying to memorize one more piece of evidence that could be repeated to his friends in the morrow as a testament of his son's sophistication.

And then, after the "neologism" was safely stored in his memory, the Dad said:

"Mike, I am trying my best to tell you what I know. Do you remember the story of the priest who always prayed to God? And one day, a flood came and the church was flooded, and everybody fled... but he stayed and prayed and, as the waters swelled, he went to the roof to continue to pray. A boat came to rescue him but he refused to go – rather, he continued to pray to his Lord for help. Then the water reached the base of the steeple. Another boat came and, again, he refused to go, saying: "God will take care of His sheep," and the water went up to the top of the steeple. Finally, one more boat came, but he was praying so intently that he shushed the boatmen off with a wave of his hand: "God will take care of His sheep". Eventually, he drowned and his soul reached Paradise where he was warmly welcomed. But when he was in front of God, he respectfully asked: "How come, My Omnipotent Sir, you did not help Your faithful sheep?" and God replied: "What do you mean? I sent three boats to get you out of there!"

"I guess you are telling us that we do not understand and appreciate you as you are. I just have no idea what you are talking about Dad, can you just be normal?"

But the Dad got up and slowly walked to the powder room, leaving Michael shaking his head.

"Why did you have to harass Dad like that? What is in your mind? Who are you to drive him crazy with this nonsense?" asked his sister.

"I do not know, I wish I could have an adult conversation with him for once, without jokes, just with some logic attached to it, some ways for me to feel respected as a person and not just patronized."

"He is not patronizing you. This is the only way he knows how to communicate: by images. He has never learnt to express his feelings 'congruently'" she said with an effort before she went back to texting her boyfriend.

Michael felt uneasy and, to put behind his unnecessary belligerence toward his Dad, he attacked his sister and her possessed texting:

"You should stop worrying about that idiot, or if you are really worried that he is going to leave you, just worry about your weight. Men do not like fat, trust me, and just try to look better".

And he observed his sister get up and go to what used to be her room when they still lived there.

Alone, in the living room, Michael, not willing to accept his faults for ruining a perfectly fine day, started commiserating with himself: how stupid everything was and how miserable it was to be stuck on that couch.

Mother came and wondered where everybody went. But, as Michael was about to explain, she interrupted him upon noticing some spots on Michael's shirt:

"You spilled the sauce on your shirt, give it to me, I can put some talc on it to absorb the fat".

Then the Dad came out of the powder room looking a little frail and pale, but most remarkably with the fly open.

"George, look at you, what is going on here? Button up that thing!"

And as she was saying this, a catastrophic metallic sound arose from the kitchen:

"Someday, I will kill that cat," she said, rushing to the scene of the crime.

Then, Michael and his Dad were left alone, and Michael was about to apologize when the Dad said:

"I have some sort of indigestion. Don't feel too well," and he lied down in the armchair one more time and, after a deep breath, he turned his head toward the other side.

"OK Dad, I got it, you got out of it one more time," and putting his jacket on, he went to the kitchen, kissed his mother on her temple and went back to the living room. There, he said:

"I am sorry Dad; I love you," but the Dad did not reply and, with his head reclined, kept his eyes closed.

***

Driving back, Michael was remorseful for his behavior and thought angrily about Otto.

"What was the point of stirring all of this? Was he trying to put sense into life? Why ask ourselves questions that cannot be answered? A philosopher may not know the answer to the simplest questions and we bother each other with existentialism? Let Kierkegaard, Dostoyevsky, Nietzsche, and Sartre argue about this stuff in their spare time! Why us on a lazy Sunday? What is life aside from being a blind jump into a journey that begins by chance and leads to nowhere? Maybe Dad is the true philosopher, maybe Dad is correct in turning everything into a joke... isn't life itself just a joke?"

And, keeping his mind absorbed in such and similar thoughts, he unexpectedly found himself home.

After parking, while walking to the apartment, he turned on his cellphone and noticed a voice mail waiting, but he did not check it. Rather, he walked to the apartment like a hermit crab, instinctually feeling more comfortable in recovering in his own shell, from which he could stare suspiciously at the world outside.

In the apartment, after depositing the mail, and taking off his jacket and scarf, he dialed with his thumb his phone's passcode and opened the voice mail:

"Michael, Dad is dead! I have been calling you forever! When I came back from my room, he was lying unconscious on the armchair. I tried to wake him up but he had no pulse. We called the meds, they did CPR and gave him a shock; they took him to the emergency room and there, they pronounced him dead. Come as soon as you get this".

***

But Michael did not go right away. Instead, he walked to the bathroom, put his head under the trickling water and let the flow of cold water run over his head –

perhaps to wash away the news, perhaps, in an attempt to wake up from a nightmare.

Then he looked up – around the bathroom and around the apartment. Everything seemed unfamiliar. The living room reminded him of pictures of the Gobi Desert he had recently seen: the same indifference and desolation, the same emptiness buried under infinity, the absurdness of any hope for interaction.

He tried to remember what happened. He recalled the phone call, recalled his Dad's head quietly reclined to the side, and recalled the joke of the old parrot and, looking at the mirror, he saw himself smiling.

***

After finally jotting the story down, turning off the computer, Otto reflected on the unexpected events and, while partly proud of his clairvoyance for predicting the demise of the Dad, he felt guilty at the same time for not creating a more perspicacious character in the son.

"Perhaps, if the son was less self–absorbed, he would have noticed that the Dad was laying down gray on the arm chair and he could have checked on him – perhaps even saving his life".

But, most importantly, if he had created a more sensitive character, he would not have gone through an insensible rampage of anger with his family on the last day of his father's life. He would have controlled himself and a more constructive end to this story would have been written".

Of course, Otto was well aware that, being the writer, he could easily modify the story, but this was against his philosophy as he treated his stories the way he treated his own life, of which he felt he retained very little control.

***

That night, Otto called his Dad:

"Hi Dad,"

"Otto my boy, what's up?"

"Nothing, just felt like telling you that I love you".

Silence and then...

"Gotcha! You remind me of the Budweiser commercial. Remember one of the sons and his dad fishing together and the son telling his Dad how much he loves him etc. etc. and the Dad:

"Still you are not getting my Bud!".

And then both laughed and, for the first time in a long time, Otto appreciated the humor in his Dad's stories.

The Leopard

It was the dry season of the Serengeti. The immense pastures of the savannah had morphed from the rolling green of the long rains to a parched and lifeless tawny hue. The wildebeest, the zebras, the gazelles and most other game had vanished and only predators endured. It was as if God had, in a burst of anger, capriciously turned Eden into Hell. Evil creatures were wandering the wretchedness inflicting anguish to each other in the overbearing silence disrupted only by sounds of agony. A premonition of tragedy pervaded the atmosphere: a guarantee that no mercy would spare even the mightiest among the creatures of the great prairie.

***

At the breaking of dawn, the mother was wide–awake. The crawling of creatures during the night had interrupted fleeting fragments of sleep. None encouraged a hunt. None justified the abandonment of her remaining cub for a meager catch.

The monotonous chirp of the crickets had languished and had finally subsided, and the enigmatic silence of the early morning was interrupted only by calls from distant birds. There was an undertone of anticipation in the air for something either benevolent or horrifying, but above all, mysterious. It seemed that the savannah, perplexed about the days past and weary about those to come, was making an effort to listen to itself in search for clues to reprogram its course.

As the sun rose, her mouth stretched into a famished yawn. There was hunger in her veins and she sensed the hunger in her cub's tremor. The cub also woke up with the first sunrays and became active. Without his sister, he attacked his Mother in playful mood. From the lower branch, he reached for her swooping tail with a fervor heightened by hunger. In excitement, he pounced to the upper branch to catch her elusive tail and in frustration, he attacked his mother's ear with the baleful growl of an apprentice hunter.

The discomfort provoked a much more menacing growl from the mother that shuddered the cub, who nimbly found protection under her belly. There, he stood waiting for the storm to pass, perhaps judging that what had appeared to come from his mother was in reality a special kind of thunder. When peace was restored, he peeked from his shelter and, noticing his mother's mood restored and her gaze distracted, resumed his play by attacking her tail and ears in turn, but this time with gentler nibbles.

Meanwhile, with her whiskers retracted, the mother was searching the horizon. While her nostrils were sifting the breeze for the scent of prey, her mood was vexed by a recurrent memory from the previous evening. It was the remembrance of her other cub being killed by hyenas. They were returning from a fruitless hunt when they were circled by a cackle. The two cubs had run in different directions and while she was protecting one, the other was snatched. The prudence of the savannah forced her to escort one to the first tree at the cost of losing the other.

It was the right choice dictated by Mother Nature to which she submitted to cope with the inexorability of the wilderness. But that memory recurred and troubled her. Alas, this had been her first litter and her first encounter with the finality of parting from loved ones in the great savannah.

***

Suddenly, her rhythmic panting stopped and her gaze froze. Her tail recoiled and her nares widened. Her neck stretched and her head cringed. She had spotted in the grounds a worthy pray. The cub, perceiving the tension, interrupted his play.

In keeping with the commandments of nature, it was not an ordinary pray for a leopard. It was rather a last resort for the desperate mother. It was a calf that had strayed from the herd. Cattle are not wild game. They are strange animals that do not mind the vexing dogs and that coexist with the Maasai people, who walk holding spears in their hands. Cattle do not interest predators till the dry season, when hunger is disproportionate, their litter is starving and the unthinkable is considered.

The leopard's muscles tightened. Abandoning her cub, she swiftly reached the ground from the far side of the tree. Stealing for a few steps and finally pouncing, she executed the calf that, upon dying, released a high–pitched moo.

The Maasais, the herd and the dogs were alerted. The mother cow rushed in rescue of its calf, just in time to witness the extinction of its progeny. It stopped at the sight of the leopard that, without turning, emanated a menacing growl. Mooing in return toward the calf, she instinctively thrust her horns toward the leopard as a tentative intimidation, but it was too late. It was just a visceral gesture without concrete purpose for the powerless mother. The leopard did not pay attention while she was taking the best hold of her pray to carry it up the tree to her hungry cub. And even this ignorant beast would soon realize that it was of no avail to challenge a hungry leopard.

Meanwhile, the moos had attracted a hyena that suddenly appeared behind the leopard, laden with the game. Adult leopards do not fear solitary hyenas and the mother would have gone to the tree unimpressed by that escort, had not the hyena made the fatal mistake of looming too close. That sensation, that closeness to the hideous smell that reminded the mother of the day before, triggered the unpredictable. The pang that had been smoldering in her chest since the night before burst into explosive anger. Suddenly, the mother dropped her catch and, while the encouraged hyena approached even closer to snatch it from her, she bounced in the air and, dropping on top of the enemy, hit it with a prodigious jab that made the animal roll on its back. Before the hyena could react, the leopard was onto its jugular, cracking her neck with her portentous jaws. Dissatisfied with the swiftness of the success, the mother jabbed the dying animal a few more times till, recovering survival instinct, she remembered the pray and its purpose and resumed the journey to the tree where the cub was waiting.

Other hyenas, alerted by the commotion, teemed around the dying one – but they did not finish it. They were repulsed from devouring one of their own. It's the honor code of the jungle. So, the carcass became the feast of the vultures that enlivened the desolate place and cleaned the skeleton to the last living cell.

A pride of lions appeared, directed from an unknown place to the next one. A young lioness noticed the leopard and, carried by an impulse of curiosity, clambered upon the tree. She raptly sniffed the bits of bark doused by blood and leaked some, then she glanced at the unreachable leopard and left to catch up with the rest of the migrating pride.

***

Alerted by the turmoil, a Maasai boy had also ran to the scene to witness from suitable distance the massacre of the calf he was supposed to protect. Likewise, the dogs growled from the distance, then contently followed their master to the village.

At dusk, the leopard and her cub were still lazily working on their meal when an assembly of Maasais appeared from the direction of the village. They were holding spears and were speaking loudly as to impart courage to each other. Leading them was the owner of the herd and of the piece of land where it was grazing. Nowadays, Maasai people possess their land and it belongs to them and it is not to be shared with other creatures of the savannah.

To no avail, the Chief of the tribe tried to negotiate the sparing of the leopard. He had studied in America. He was a wise leader and a gentleman. Most importantly, he loved his country with a special appreciation for those who have parted for a significant amount of time.

He offered pecuniary compensation for the loss of the calf with funds made available for such unusual occurrences by animal protectionists and other similar organizations. But the victimized Maasai had no intention of forgiving the leopard that had transgressed the rules of the Maasais' sovereignty. The animal ought to be castigated by him and by his own people. He believed that any lack of firmness would encourage further ravages by other predators, as if animals could talk and teach each other respect for human property. It ought to be a lesson for the entire savannah.

The Maasais gathered around the tree, on top of which the leopard was holding in between her paw and the branch the dismembered remains of her pray. They yelled and cursed. They spat at the leopard. They questioned it. Why did it rob them? What made it think that it could get away with it?

But the leopard looked at them without repentance. It was not in her nature to understand and empathize. She had killed because she was hungry and because her cub was hungry. She could not understand what that commotion was all about.

Gradually, the shouting became louder and the gestures more menacing. Finally, the leopard, reckoning that all that uproar was directed against her and her cub, became unnerved. As a result, she climbed higher up the tree followed by the cub.

The Maasais began to fling spears and stones at it, but the leopard was unreachable. A Maasai attempted to climb the tree but others discouraged him. Ultimately, an elder advised to start a fire under the tree to displace the beast. They collected sticks and dry leaves and ignited the fire with each one carrying more combustible to enhance its power.

The Maasais then threw burning sticks onto the tree. The same Maasai, who gave up before, reattempted the ascent. This time, he carried a scorching stick, but the smoke from the ground was too dense and the heat too unforgiving for him to endure.

Finally, the leopard panicked, she realized that she needed an escape. Swiftly, holding her cub by the nape, she pounced from one branch to the other to reach the ground and spring away from the Maasais. But as she was about to flee, a spear entered her lower abdomen, penetrating the joint of the hind limb, immobilizing her. By instinct, she released the panic–stricken cub that ran away behind another tree. As she was attempting to rise, she looked at the angry faces of the Maasais, trying to understand what they had against her, but as she was opening her mouth in a deterring grimace, another spear entered her throat and impaled her neck. She thought of her cub and tried to turn around to see whether he was safe, but the spear had immobilized her neck. She looked one more time at the angry assailers without understanding... until all vanished.

***

Ten thousand miles away, in the United States of America, Jeremy Scarpa had just awakened. As usual, he struggled to recall where he was. He was not a quick thinker and his thoughts, like the early morning fog that needs the warmth of the sun's rays to dissolve, had to be recalled one at a time from the murkiness of the night by the lethargic brain.

Nonetheless, a perfunctory glance at the bare walls of the cell reaffirmed his monotonous routine, quickly dissipating any possible confusion bequeathed by nocturnal dreams. No matter how vast life could be in the outside, those four walls had somberly encrypted his existence for almost two decades.

Yet, today was going to be special! He reckoned it was Super Bowl time! Inmates in death row are not allocated televisions in their cells. But, as his last wish, he had negotiated to watch the game on the big screen. This was going to happen just before the execution performed on the same day... on God's day, to allow the victims' families coming from far away to attain their long–awaited closure.

As a youngster, Jeremy had not been particularly bright. Instead, he was rather simple–minded. He took things literally. Once, a boy grabbed from his hand a toy soldier and ran away. As soon as Jeremy arrived home from school, he eagerly reported the robbery to his dad expecting advice. The dad, in response, slapped him in the face.

"Next time", the dad said, "you should take care of things yourself. You can't let people step on your toes".

Therefore, the next day, he prowled the kid who stole the soldier and, when he finally cornered him, hit him over and over, scratched him, bit him and pulled his hair till somebody noticed and parted them. He was reported to the school principal and was punished.

At home, he recounted the episode to his dad just as it happened. The dad slapped him in the face and told him that he was stupid for being caught.

"One takes care of business quietly, you blockhead! Not in front of everybody! Just take care of things on your own, never trust anybody but yourself!"

Thinking that his son was too innocent, the worried dad thought it best to provide him with valuable advice. With a rope, he tied Jeremy's hands behind the back. Then, he hauled him up to stand over the kitchen table and ordered him to jump. When Jeremy hesitated, the dad told him not to worry because he would be there to catch him. As Jeremy still hesitated, the dad looked straight into his eyes and said:

"Don't you even trust your father?"

Thus, Jeremy jumped. The dad kept his arms crossed and Jeremy hit his face against the floor and his nose bled.

The dad smirked at him with contempt.

"I hope you will remember this lesson." he said, "Remember: never trust anybody".

Consequently, from that day on, Jeremy followed his dad's instructions and vouched not to trust anybody, unsure whether he could even trust himself. Gradually, defensiveness against others turned into diffidence, then mistrust and finally into a paranoiac persuasion that people, like a pack of hyenas, were after him – not for any specific reason beyond the fact that he happened to carry beef on his bones and they were hungry.

He compensated for the loss of confidence in relationships by building his body, obsessing with martial arts, as if insecurities could be deterred by punches and kicks. By crude force, he eventually succeeded in extracting respect from his peers with whom friendship was not an option.

In high school, he made the football team. During his first season, when the coach directed him to "go get them", he cracked a few of the opponents' bones till, after a few warnings, he was expelled from the team. That really confused him. The more he sought to accommodate people's wishes, the angrier they turned against him. Finally, he renounced belonging to the human species with which he shared no empathy.

When, members of a competing team, in revenge for the fractured bones of a teammate, cornered him in a dark alley and beat the berserk out of him, but he was not resentful. According to his simple mind, those guys had acted just as he would have in similar circumstances. That made sense to him; in fact, he was to blame for being caught unprepared.

***

Eventually, he joined a gang, bonding to chaps who did not fool with his mind. When they asked him to take care of business, he would. When the job was done, he received praises and cash. It was linear. It finally made sense. Within a few years, he gained quite a reputation as a hitman and Don Carmine, a local Mafia boss, offered him a job with good pay, stable and reasonable hours, just at par with his cushy expectations.

He took his job seriously and everything was accomplished professionally. Following the path of crime with extreme discipline, he never used violence without a good reason. Indeed, aside from his profession, he remained quite a reserved character, a decent fellow, who would not even hurt a fly. This held true but for a single transgression.

There was an Irish fella nicknamed Iceberg, who kept toying with his nerves. He bragged unrestrainedly and talked too much with a loud voice, wrapped within a foul breath. With his corpulence, that churl suffocated the atmosphere. He talked through the interlocutor as if the latter was a microphone while the message was meant for the rest of the audience. His contumely consisted of reiterated quotes, recycled jokes and remarks and rehashed mockeries that would make nobody laugh – save for a few desperate junkies, who linger in pubs grasping for affirmation.

Such countenance would have barely afflicted Jeremy, who much favored minding his own business. But a waitress, who detained a special affection for him and one–sidedly chose him for a confidant, sat one night in front of him during a break. She crossed her legs, wiped her sweaty forehead, composed her posture and revealed that she was raped by Iceberg. She hated the guy but did not know what to do about it.

Jeremy had little to say. He did not know what to do either and, most pertinently, he could not find a reason for him to intervene since empathy was not part of his portfolio.

After all, it was none of his business.

He, therefore, looked at her with his transparent green eyes and with the frozen gaze of the one who looks but does not see. It seemed that his gaze, blazing through the transparent woman, was searching for hidden thoughts or memories buried into an invisible casket.

In the end, he said nothing.

Yet, those melancholic eyes, the waitress' armless resignation, her inexplicable reliance on him, all of this internal turmoil resurrected buried sentiments – reminiscent of a pang he suffered a long time ago when a toy soldier was snatched from his hands.

Thus, each time he encountered Iceberg at the pub, he turned his eyes away to shun from the temptation of an unnecessary quarrel. After all, as he kept repeating to himself:

"It is none of my business".

But Iceberg was truculent and vexing like a hyena. He sported the same empty gaze; defiantly staring in expectation, and unquestionably Jeremy did not like to be gawked. Gradually, Iceberg became cockier. He took unopposed control of the pub that in his eyes was his miniature smoky kingdom. As a malevolent and angry drunkard, he took satisfaction in harassing the patrons. Misinterpreting Jeremy's detachment as a sign of vulnerability, he began bullying him as well.

In turn, Jeremy, who was determined to avoid haphazard conflicts, did his best to dodge a brawl and, on account of the drunkard's short attention span, he easily swerved the provocations by deflecting the hostility onto other costumers. But the harassment of others soon bothered him just as much, and he continued to repeat to himself:

"It is none of my business".

But he could no longer shake the annoyance which kept building like a summer storm. Ultimately, one night, when Iceberg was especially drunk and particularly vexing, Jeremy, who had also hoarded a good portion of alcohol, left the premises discreetly. As soon as he was out, the fresh air somewhat restored his thoughts and he thought about cutting the night short and going home.

Instead of going home, however, he put on his leather gloves and quietly waited for Iceberg in a dark alley. When Iceberg exited the premises, he was so drunk that he walked past Jeremy without even noticing him. Jeremy, sensing the odor of alcohol mixed with the man's perspiration, acted on the irritation that had been smoldering in his chest and had turned into anger. Jeremy swiftly crashed Iceberg to the ground and, as Iceberg tried to reach for a gun, he swindled it from his opponent's hands.

Iceberg was on his knees, staring at his own gun pointed toward him and said:

"What are you fucking doing? Are you fucking going to kill..."

But he did not finish. Blood came out of his mouth and from between his blank hyena's eyes. Dissatisfied with the swiftness of the success, Jeremy shot him one more time in the head and then dropped the gun at Iceberg's side. He then took off the gloves and composedly walked home.

In the morning, after the fumes of alcohol had dissipated, he recollected the events of the night. When his sluggish brain confirmed that they really occurred, he argued with himself. Why such an impulsive blunder? Why did he kill for no good reason? It was against his well–established professional principles. Yet, for the first time, he felt satisfaction and purpose in his actions and he thought of the waitress. He wondered how she would react to the upcoming tidings of the execution.

***

Besides this unusual circumstance, Jerry carried, as we said, a constrained and well–disciplined criminal career. His life would have proceeded with ease had, on a lovely autumn morning, as he was completing a job in the suburbs, a little blond girl appearing from nowhere and shouting: "leave my Dad alone!" not get in the line of fire. It was too late, and the bullet had already started its journey that ended in the little girl's head.

The little girl immediately collapsed, her shiny blond hair rested on her shoulder, her arms stretched on the ground and a pool of blood heaped up in between them. Few eternal seconds followed, as if the glacial age had returned in the tiny shop of the little town to freeze everything.

Nobody moved – neither Jeremy nor the intended victim, who looked at him with expressionless eyes. Jeremy did not like to be looked in the eyes and, recollecting the purpose of the visit, he shot the witness in the chest first and then in between his eyes.

The mother came out from the back of the shop where the accident occurred, drawn by the shout of her girl and the shots that had killed little Mary and her husband. Jeremy, without moving his cringed head, raised his eyes to encounter the gaze of the powerless mother. Her stare was sad and inquisitive, as if she was asking to be removed from this world together with her beloved by a merciful bullet. Her expression was impotent, not because she feared him, but because the poor mother had instantly recognized that it was of no avail to challenge the finality of parting from loved ones in the great savannah of life.

Jeremy raised the gun and pointed it at her, but after one long second, he dropped it and left.

Exiting the shop, he hesitated. He reckoned that he was making an unforgivable mistake by not killing the witness. He nearly turned back to complete the job but he knew that he would never be able to do it.

Composedly, he walked for a block, turned a corner, boarded a car that was waiting for him and left. In the car, he did not say a word, but as he was staring at the passing trees, he conceded that this had been his last job.

Things became complicated after that episode. The little town was upset. The detectives could no longer turn their eyes away. That same night, the SWAT team broke into his apartment. They squashed him to the floor, handcuffed him behind his back and took him out where a mob was waiting.

They yelled and cursed him. They spat at him and questioned him. But Jeremy looked at them without repentance. It was not in his nature to understand and empathize. He could not comprehend what the commotion was all about, why they all turned against him. He had done nothing against those strangers.

***

Detectives were deployed. Evidence of crimes committed by Jeremy piled up. When indisputable evidence was provided by new technologies, Don Carmine washed his hands. Any of his tie with the Mafia was severed. Jeremy also did not spill information. He was a man of honor and he knew that he had to pay for his mistakes; once again, he was the fool who had been caught.

The prosecutor proved beyond any possible doubt that, besides gangsters, a few good law–abiding citizens, who had refused to submit to Mafia's protection, had been subject of retaliation. All crimes brought to trial had been pre–meditated save for the murder of the little girl – all were the result of a professional job. Mary's mother served as an unattackable witness and Jeremy refused to confute her testimony against his court–appointed lawyer's recommendation. Iceberg's case never came up as that crime had been forgotten together with its victim.

The court–appointed lawyer tried to negotiate a guilty plea in exchange for his client's life. But Jeremy declined. He had no patience for lawyers and their elaborate lingo. He did not understand the reasoning behind admitting guilt. Moreover, why should he trust anybody: a lawyer, a jury of peers? He had no familiarity with that concept. Weren't they all human creatures that he was not supposed to trust?

He also did not feel remorse for the pain he inflicted; it truly was not in his nature to empathize. He was not repentant or sorry for the little girl. He had not meant to kill her. It was not his fault that she stood in the way. Parents do not watch over their kids nowadays as they should. The only regret and shame he felt was for being caught. That truly embarrassed him. He thought of Don Carmine who, like his father before, would smirk and disparage him.

In the end, he was sentenced to death. He seemed neither surprised by the verdict nor interested in the judge's homily, as if all of it was a predictable farce. How could those who had shared nothing with his life condemn it? How would they understand the instincts that drove his actions – entrenched as they were in the orthodoxy of civilization?

Sure, it would have been nice to live a little longer and watch a few more football games but, in the end, let's be frank: he had been caught and he was receiving the slap he deserved for his foolishness.

He refused to appeal. He had no family behind to fight for him. His parents had long broken ties with him. He had no friends and all acquaintances had vanished. He did not want an appeal also because he was weary of all that legal gibberish, the rubbish of depositions, the unending questioning, the interrogations and counter interrogations that bewildered him; and that hunt for inconsistencies just for the pleasure of cornering him. He did not want to be exposed to that unrelenting embarrassment any longer.

Under inquisition, he tried to cooperate to expedite the end of the torment. But his cooperation was sloppy and dishonest. Stories were hurriedly created in the hope of dismissing the investigator. Unfortunately, the officers kept accurate record of all his statements as if they had nothing better to do. When the stories were assembled, they made no sense, giving ground to further inquisition and further embarrassment. He would rather end it all and not sit through further pestering. He simply had enough of that nonsense and all he wanted was to be left alone since his life was determined by instincts rather than logic. He would unreservedly trade the rest of it for a few moments of peace.

***

Jeremy interacted only with me as his social worker. Like a leopard in a cage that accepts its guardian, he became accustomed to my presence, mostly because I did not vex him with overbearing questioning but just brought treats and let him act freely.

We played chess or checkers. He had learnt to play in jail and he played by himself most of the time, and with me when I visited. He was not a good player, and neither was I, but the game allowed the passing of time and enabled the interjection of few, amicable questions.

He was polite and responsive, though shallow and, at times, condescending. He pretended to pay attention to my attempts to communicate, but he was obviously distracted either by the game or by an uncontrolled stream of thoughts and visions. He would stare far away, to a distant point hidden beyond the walls of the cell, as if he was searching for something past the horizon. There was no expectation in those gazes, no anxiety. He looked like a captain of a liner who scrutinizes the vastness of the ocean without anticipation, knowing that besides a few adjustments to the course of the vessel, nothing will ever appear in the distance that would bring any notable change to the course of his own life.

He rarely turned his eyes toward me and he almost never made eye contact.

Once, I asked him:

"What do you feel when you kill somebody?"

He thought it over for a few seconds and then replied:

"Nothing...I feel nothing. Do hunters feel anything when they shoot a deer? It is like killing something belonging to another species".

"Would you kill me?"

Extraordinarily, he stared at me and muttered:

"Why would I do something like that?" and he continued: "...You are a friend".

I felt that I belonged to his "species".

***

The day of the execution by lethal injection had finally arrived.

He showered in the morning and asked for the big screen. He was then brought chained to a bare room, where the big screen had been set up just for him. He had been a good prisoner, not a troublemaker, and the guards were lenient toward the unassuming inmate.

The game started. They brought him chips with salsa and one and then another bottle of beer. It was a good Super Bowl: lots of TDs and, even better, lots of roughness. It reminded him of the good old times when he still belonged to the human species: when he had teammates, if not friends, to stand by.

In the middle of the fourth period, a catholic priest came. Jeremy had no faith in humans and had no good reason to trust that unknown entity called God. It was not his intent to speculate about God's existence because in the end, it was none of his business. He could also not appreciate his worth. How could Jeremy understand mercy when he had never experienced it? It was too ethereal of a concept for his simple and practical mind. In summary, he had no sense of belonging: not to mankind and, even less, to a transcendental entity.

I convinced him to take confession before the execution. He agreed. What was there to lose? And most decisively, wasn't it the speediest way to get rid of that cockroach?

The priest endeavored a conversation in the attempt of practicing his duty and of inducing repentance. But, since Jeremy, distracted by the game, paid no attention, the frustrated priest lost patience and suddenly exclaimed:

"Jeremy! Jeremy! You killed at least eight innocent people! You destroyed families! You killed a little girl! Don't you feel sorry? Can't you ask for forgiveness from the Omnipotent? He could save your soul for eternity".

Jeremy was startled by the loud voice. He turned his green and glacial eyes toward the priest for one second and, returning his eyes toward the game, he mumbled:

"I am sorry!"

That seemed to satisfy the priest. He whispered some undecipherable sounds in a low voice to avoid further irritating Jeremy and nimbly left the premise. Jeremy was already absorbed by the rest of the game and did not notice his departure, rather munching the remaining chips.

At end of the game, it was three hours left before the execution. They brought him back to his cell. He seemed upset; his favorite team had lost in the last few seconds:

"Those bastards!" he murmured to himself, referring not sure to whom: perhaps the police, or the jurors, perhaps humankind, perhaps the referees of the game, the coaches and the players who had let him down on the last game he was going to watch.

In the cell, sitting on his bed, he waited for his escort. I touched his shoulder and shook his hand before leaving. He shook it without looking at me. I said:

"Good bye... see you in a few minutes. I will be there for you if you need me."

He did not reply.

They brought him shackled and dressed in orange scrubs. Through the glass, he casually scanned the audience with his detached green eyes. He encountered the inquisitive gaze of the little girl's mother and he finally understood her anguish... but he had no gun to kill her.

Then he lay down and looked at the ceiling till everything vanished.

***

Three years passed.

A boy is looking at a magnificent young adult leopard caged at the National Zoo. With his forepaws crossed and hind limbs stretched, the leopard stares absorbedly from the height of a console at a spot in the undefined distance. Neither the waving of the boy nor his calls can distract the leopard.

The boy becomes frustrated and asks his father:

"Dad, what is he starting at?"

"He is staring at his memories. He is looking at things that he cannot see. He is searching for horizons beyond the horizon. In the very far distance, he recognizes the savannah from where he came; those stripes of red earth, like wounds in the yellow grass, the trees that are a whole word of birds, the sky with a million stars, and his old home where he was a cub and where he chased the swooping tail of his mother. He is vigilant for a scent; a rustle that his spirit tells will start a chase. In his eyes, you can see the reverberation of the instincts of nature."

"What are instincts, Dad?"

"They are the imperious laws of the land that supersede those of mankind, to which we all abide – humans and animals – and they can neither be understood nor judged."

The Rider

A follow up to The Leopard

Contributed by Catterina Coha

As the gray waters, parted from the gray sky by the dark green hills, were passing by, Clara, who was observing the spectacle through the large screen of the train window, felt at peace. She did not feel happy or cheerful, but simply at peace...at peace in an inexplicable way.

It was the combination of the motion and the changing landscape that appeased her and just the fact that she was moving! It did not matter from where to where: it was about the prospect of a departure from the standstill of her current life toward the excitement of exploring uncharted destinies. It was that fantasy that offered relief from the edginess that had accompanied her for so many years – years laden by a vortex of unwelcome concessions and compromises made–God–knows–why against her own will. Granted, it was only an optical illusion, a sequitur of images that distracted her for the time being as she was composedly looking out of the window.

The ever–changing landscape seemed to reassure her that there was still a living world out there, an open scenery rich in prospects and not hopelessly predetermined as her own life was, a world that still owned its own destiny. It seemed to her that in that world, opportunities waited patiently to be picked at the right time like flowers in the green grasslands. This cornucopia of vague possibilities was passing by in a display to be observed from the tranquility of her secluded corner in a fast–moving train.

It seemed to Clara that this wealth displayed in the big screen of the commuters' train ran an advertisement to be passively admired and to be treasured in one's own memory as a fashion show with the scent of a college fair. All reminded her of one of those moments of youth when hopes are plentiful, those ephemeral moments that yet leave an indelible mark, that Pandora of hopes that occasionally reemerge later on in life and that could now be magically resurrected on the other side of the glass.

That fragrant mix of images and memories seemed to her so vivid that at times, she would pose the palm of her hand on the glass in an attempt to pick them. And that feeling of reassurance was subconsciously transmitted to her mood as the train rolled on its tracks and the world moved in the opposite direction.

***

Clara preferred routes that were the least crowded. She liked to sit near the window, and disliked being close to other people. She dreaded those who talked, whether they addressed her unsolicitedly or nattered among themselves or proclaimed loudly the details of their life that were meant only for the blue tooth.

In truth, Clara was a peculiar type of rider. Unlike most other users of the train, she was not a commuter. Clara rode the trains for her own recreation, as a hobby, perhaps a sort of self–administered therapy. It was almost an addiction.

Most often, she rode during the weekend. But in the summer, when the days were longer, she loved to ride in the early evening of weekdays. She would go along with the commuters who were returning home in the hours just proceeding or following the sunset.

For example, she would take a train from Grand Central Station in the northbound direction along the Hudson River, and enjoy the sun slowly plunging behind the hills and spreading orange and pink tones over the peaceful surface of the water.

The railroad ran through parks along the river, or through the rocky banks, where one could see people fishing, couples strolling, and families enjoying picnics.

They all looked so relaxed to Clara and she felt like she could, just by watching, soak up from them that peaceful sensation that is peculiar to the lazy summer evenings and that reenacted emotions from her own childhood.

Going out in the evening was something her parents would do only during the holidays, and this practice became imprinted in Clara's mind and she associated those lighthearted evening strolls with the cheerful tones of a festive mood: the expectation of fun, novelty, and the freedom to run bare foot in the sand, or the pleasure of eating an ice cream gloriously sitting at a table of what had then seemed fancy cafes to her innocent eyes.

Moreover, the twilight of the evening reminded Clara of the mysterious intimacy associated with her first romantic escapades, the goofy flirting of the teen years that never really fulfilled the budding anticipations and desires of her heart but were nevertheless treasurable. The thrill of the prelude to those otherwise disappointing relationships with boys had remained intact. The tentative hopes associated with the excitement of walking along the river, the fragrance of flowers in the air, the fading lights and the discreet path leading to a bench removed from friends, the elating prospect of knowing that somebody liked her. These simple flashes could still entertain her thoughts while her mind was wondering along the labyrinths of the past.

***

On a sunny Saturday morning in early spring, Clara was riding the train rather early, intending to take a boat that from Beacon was directed toward a little island on the Hudson.

Four young girls around fourteen years of age boarded the train at Tarrytown. They wore skinny jeans and colorful hoodies. Two of them had manicured nails decorated in a complex pattern. One was wearing eye–catching large earrings different from one another. Their long hair looked soft and shiny and was gathered in a ponytail gradually ranging from dark blonde to even darker and warmer tones. One girl sporting stripes of bright purple colors set her hair loose over her shoulders to better show it to her friends and said in an excited and cheerful tone:

"Look, isn't it weird?"

Receiving answers like:

"Oh my God, this is so cool! Weird cool!!!" pronounced loudly in an equally excited and cheerful tone followed by collective laughter.

The girls had not stopped chatting and laughing since they boarded the train, and this chatter did not aggravate Clara at all. Instead, these happy and innocently cheerful girls reminded Clara of a flock of young colorful birds chirping excitedly in celebration of the sunrise in an early spring morning.

So that loud flock had the effect of a fresh breeze and, for some reason, triggered a memory, not of her youth, but from an even deeper past.

Her mother struggled with poverty aggravated by the anguish of having an older sick brother whose existence casted a gloomy shadow of sadness and shame over her family in a little village plagued by ignorance and post–war grievances.

The mom had told Clara that in spite of the hovering soberness that reigned at home, there were times when, as a young girl, she could not refrain from laughing freely with her friends for no specific reason, and she would sing spontaneously, all of which were forbidden in her austere and contrite household. That image of the charming and untamable power of the delicate optimism of youth had captured Clara's thoughts. She could not recollect ever being like that. Perhaps she had on rare occasions, but that spontaneity had long been erased from her memory.

Eventually, one of her mother's friends, the prettiest one, became pregnant and she was pressed to marry not the unwilling father of the child, but an older and grumpy man who accepted to trade his forgone pride for the illusion of a love that could never be. Clara's mother did not know more about the fate of her young and pretty friend: whether she accepted her destiny and remained forever in that unhappy "safety" of marriage or whether she eventually broke free. But the dissonance between those few happy moments and the harsh reality of a tainted destiny left a mark in Clara's recollection of that memory; the acceptance that life is most often hard and only memories of youthful untarnished joy can alleviate one's burden of heart.

***

There was a seasonal character to the train rides which Clara liked – it could be observed as it reverberated over everything within and outside the train, from people's clothes, to the light, the shadows and the colors of the landscape scrolling across the windows screens, to the mood pervading the riders.

The end of summer was marked by the prevalence of teenagers commuting to school, while around the Winter Holidays, one could observe an increasing number of young children going with their parents to the city to admire the huge Christmas tree at the Rockefeller center.

Looking at the children with the colorful jackets and big lollipops, Clara wondered if they were going to truly enjoy the experience or feel frightened by the crowds of adults towering over their little bodies, like her son used to be a long time ago. The realization that her son dreaded an experience that she loved so much and that she wanted to share with her little boy, made an indelible mark on Clara's perception of the huge and beautiful Christmas tree.

More importantly, it had contributed to shaking her fragile confidence. She started questioning whether she was apt at making the right choices for her own son and she wondered what other wrong decision she had made or might make. And as the train kept running toward its destination, station after station, she wondered if that indecision, which was born from the deepest love but had turned little by little into chronic hesitation and finally total unresponsiveness, had been perceived by the young boy, in need of guidance and reassurance, as indifference: a sentiment that eventually he returned by displaying coldness towards her.

*****

It had been a relatively warm, rainy, and sad winter. But toward the end of January, a snowstorm transformed the landscape overnight, like only snow can do.

Clara sensed the snow even before waking up in the early morning hours. And parting the curtains to look out of her bedroom and finding the immaculate white coat that hid the dirty streets and the unleveled sidewalks around her small apartment building, verified that inexplicable premonition. By wiping out most of the differences between rich and poor neighborhoods, snow has an equalitarian effect.

Like when she was a child, Clara could not wait to go out and play with the snow, wondering at this marvel of nature. But old ladies, as she perceived herself, do not make snowmen or toss snowballs.

Paralyzed at first by self–consciousness, she started to walk instinctively towards the train station. It was very cold and the wind blew icy flakes onto her face. Soon, Clara's hands and the tip of her toes felt painfully frozen, and oblivious of her previous thoughts, she hurried in the fresh deep snow to reach the station and find relief. Despite the numbness in her hands and feet, she enjoyed being immersed in the cold yet intimate environment of the solitude of a snow day ... white in the ground, white in the air and white in the sky.

She could not see very far and she felt protected in this small and cozy self–contained space without walls, limits, or other physical constrains. Everything was still there like the days before, but she needed to get closer to see familiar objects, and she could rediscover the beauty of each tree and each object as each appeared one at a time to receive her undivided attention.

Like a little child, Clara stuck out her tongue to taste the snowflakes. She remembered the games she used to play with her son. There was the house of the squirrels: mama squirrel and the little boy squirrel under a big tree in the park by the river. They had to hide and run and eventually fight with snowballs against the wolves trying to get them. Clara, by nature, would effortlessly be absorbed into the fantastic world of children, feeling authentic excitement in their games just as easily as the social chatter of adults would bore her.

When Clara finally reached the station, she realized that her boots were wet and a few curls that had fallen out of her hat were encased in ice. She cleaned herself from the snow in the bathroom, enduring the pain inflicted by the blood that was flowing back into her frozen hands.

The station was deserted and, for a change, nobody was rushing. Schools were closed, as were several businesses. Very few trains were running and, despite the absurdity of having walked so long to come to a station for no reason, Clara's heart felt warm like it had not felt in a very long time.

Suddenly, Clara realized that the dense fog that had been clouding her thoughts was gone. She was not sure why, but everything was sharper, more colorful, palpable, and perceptible than it had been for years. It was such a glorious feeling that brought tears to her eyes. It was like finding somebody who had been lost and for whom she had been searching for a very long time, save for the fact that that somebody was herself.

***

After that snowy day, life did not change much for Clara. Governed by her monotonous routine and self–imposed seclusion, days did not have much to offer but work and additional annoyances. Nevertheless, on clear and sunny mornings, that feeling from the snowy day occasionally re–emerged and Clara regained, albeit momentarily, optimism and energy.

But those affirmative feelings would inevitably vanish with the passing of the day and, by evening, no pleasantness was left, leaving only darkness and cold. The truth is that Clara was incapable of evading from the shelter of her self–imposed emotional prison. She had subdued her ability to feel in avoidance of the risk of facing the anguish of an undetermined but palpable loss. Some people sail through life and never look back at the wreckages they leave behind, feeling naturally entitled to pursue their very own happiness. Others delegate judgment to a superior authority like a religion or a political doctrine, and substitute natural empathy with symbols. A few people are born with a natural strength to stand up against the adversities of life inspired by pride and integrity.

But then, there are those who are condemned to a life of uncertainty at best or self–inflicted guilt in the worst – a guilt that knows no relief because it cannot be forgiven by anybody else but oneself. It is the inevitable result of carrying an existence where the knowledge of what is right is not accompanied by the resolve to act accordingly. An overbearing mismatch between soul and willpower that feeds hypocrisy, of which there is an overwhelming abundance in this world. But some people cannot accept hypocrisy and struggle with the inconsistencies of life till their will is broken. Clara belonged to this last group.

Thankfully, it is the nature of living things to evolve in a constant struggle to regain a homeostasis – not only physical but more so emotional. We grow, then we age and, though the change is imperceptible, it occurs in a continuum day after day with the steadfastness of dripping water. An imperceptible change was slowly eroding Clara's long–standing state of withdrawal. Imperceptibly at first and more explicitly in time, she started to follow unbeaten paths, wondering streets and alleys around unplanned train stops where she had abruptly decided to disembark.

***

In one of such spontaneous excursions, Clara entered a small antique shop vending used artifacts labeled as *antiques*. The meditative mood – elicited by the dim ambience created by insufficient lighting, the old dark wood shelves and floor – welcomed her. The shelves were filled with all sorts of objects: fine ceramics, teacups, decorated glass vases, and half broken toys from generations past. There were also used party dresses and hats and a collection of old keys in all shapes and sizes.

Lifting her gaze from the sobering displays of unexciting objects, Clara noticed a large drawing hanging on the wall. The sunlight entering from the window illuminated part of the drawing and part of the wall around it, creating a strange illusion of life that contrasted the dim stillness of the lifeless objects in the rest of the store.

Walking towards the drawing, Clara felt amazement, mixed with unexplainable apprehension: the leopard's head in the drawing seemed alive, and the shadows on the wall around the leopard looked like grass waving in the savannah under the wind.

She must have been standing there for quite a long time, trying to decipher the expression of the beast, its gaze, lost in memories of past experiences, when the store owner's voice suddenly brought her back to reality.

"Do you like it?"

Clara took a moment to compose her thoughts and recollect where she was and why this small old woman wearing an exotic dress and big ivory earrings was talking to her. Undeterred by Clara's startled silence, the storeowner, eager to make a sale before closing for the day, added:

"You know, I acquired it from somebody travelling from the Middle East, who needed money. It comes with a book".

Clara finally realized why the lady was talking to her. The statement about a book confused her. Maybe the lady was trying to take advantage of her by assembling together a bunch of merchandise on false pretenses. While this last thought materialized in her mind, she heard the disconnected sound of her own voice asking inquisitively:

"A book? Related to this drawing?".

So, Clara obediently followed the old lady across the room, to a drawer from which she extracted a small book.

"Oh!" Clara said in a simple tone, betraying her childish curiosity, "Is it the story of the leopard in the drawing?"

The storeowner had not been curious enough to have read it, but knew that she should capitalize on the curiosity of her potential customer:

"Yes, dear, it is a beautiful story!"

Since it was closing time, the storeowner rushed Clara to make a decision on purchasing the book and the drawing as a package, claiming dishonestly that another customer was coming to buy it the next day as customarily claimed by several in that trade. She told Clara that she was impressed by how long she had been staring at the drawing and would give it to her if she really wanted it, even if the other customer was likely to pay more for it.

A little later, Clara left the store with a large bag and almost no money in her wallet. She was slightly irritated with herself for not resisting the pressure of the lady but, at the same time, felt an urge to possess that pair of items and, in particular, the portrait, as if the decision had already been made a long time before by an overbearing and superior power; as if by welcoming those objects into her home, she would establish a companionship with the mysterious person who had been forced to part from them for shortage of money and had left them in the custody of the pawn lady, waiting for a foster home.

***

In the evening, Clara read the story with trepidation. As she was reading, she felt strongly connected to the mother leopard losing one of her cubs, as she herself had lost one of her twin babies. But after the brutal killing of the leopard, she could not continue reading.

Clara hanged the drawing in her room so that she would see its beautiful head with those determined eyes every morning. One night, she had an intense dream born by the crescent obsession triggered by the portrait. She was walking in the savannah and she started a fight against the *Maasais* to protect the leopard in some kind of awkward way, as it can only happen in dreams; some arguing, some pushing and shoving, and anger from both sides. She woke up sweating and screaming. After a few moments of confusion, she smiled at herself. It was so childish! Dreaming that she could change the fate of the leopard in the savannah through her own nightmares.

It was a Saturday in late spring, when trees turn light green and flowers bloom. She dressed, packed a few items, and went to the station. This time, she did not board the usual Metro North commuters' trains trailing along the Hudson or along the ocean towards Connecticut. She boarded a train that went to somewhere far away, from where she never came back. Suddenly, the resolve to escape from the constraints of her own life had won and she had broken free.

Perhaps she realized that the foes that linger within us could be dealt with. She thought about the mother leopard and her attempt to escape from the Maasai. She thought about the news on the radio of children taken hostages, who perished without being given a chance to escape. And the realization that her only true enemy was herself suddenly dwarfed her pain. She felt ashamed of her misery and, in a strange way, that shame gave her the resolve to change her life. Stepping out of her apartment, Clara gave one last look at the leopard and smiled saying goodbye. Certainly, out there was a world more unpredictable than the enclosed familiar space in which she had lived for several years. Clara did not know if she would have the strength to fight "hyenas" or the wisdom required to survive encounters with callous men indifferent to her feelings, but taking chances was a small price to pay for her passage to freedom.

The Eve

Contributed by Jamie Marincola

"What was that?"

"I didn't hear anything," she responded without pausing to listen.

He slowly drifted asleep.

***

The next morning started like any other. He woke up to the tune of his cell phone alarm. She opened her eyes just wide enough to notice that he hadn't gotten up yet before prodding him out of bed. The sun was already beaming through the open window; it was hard to imagine how they managed to sleep through the sunrise, yet they seemed to achieve this feat every morning.

He started the shower before brushing his teeth, then brushed his teeth before showering.

"It's still cold," he complained to no one. His wife decided to answer.

"Just give it a minute."

But he had given it a minute. In fact, he had given it two minutes. The same two minutes he gave it every morning while brushing his teeth.

This phenomenon was unusual, but not unique. He had a suspicion which was confirmed when he flicked the light switch.

"Power's off!" He announced to his wife who was now firmly out of bed.

"Are you sure?"

He was.

"Was there a storm last night? I don't remember a storm." She continued while reaching for the TV remote. "The TV's not working," she went on to reveal.

"I don't remember anything about a storm on the news last night," he reflected, "must have been some construction or something... that development by the I–6, no doubt." He then hopped in the cold shower, already one and a half minutes behind schedule.

By the time he was dressed and packed for work, she had breakfast improvised on the kitchen table.

"I had to toast the bread in the oven," she boasted. He walked straight past her to retrieve the newspaper from the doorstep.

It wasn't there.

It was rare that the newspaper didn't make it to his doorstep, but less rare than not having electricity. In all likelihood, these two coincidences were not coincidences at all, but rather, quite related. Maybe without power, the

87

newspaper could not be printed or perhaps the delivery boy's alarm didn't go off. Or, perhaps the causation was flipped and the newspaper delivery boy ran his van into a power line. Or, perhaps both things were the result of a single incident such as all of humanity being swept away in an apocalypse overnight.

"Now there's a thought," he mused.

By the time he had returned to the kitchen, he had forgotten to mention the strange lack of occurrence to his wife. She didn't miss a beat.

"No paper?"

"Nope, no paper." And then he ate his breakfast.

***

His drive to work was quiet. There was almost no traffic. In fact, there was no traffic. With the electrical grid down, the lights were flashing red, which was inconvenient, but not overly so without the traffic.

He pulled into his office parking lot. There were far fewer cars than normal. He slid into his usual spot, just outside the shade of an old willow tree, which he was always fond of. Long ago, he would have liked to park underneath that tree, but he had been parking three spots over for many years now and didn't think it prudent to change spots today simply because one was available.

He got out of his car, adjusted his tie in the reflection of his car window, and proceeded toward the office building. As he approached, the sliding doors failed to open.

The power outage was starting to elevate from a nuisance to a downright inconvenience. Not sure of how to approach the situation, he looked inside for the receptionist to see if she might offer instruction or assistance, but nobody was manning the front–desk.

"Is it Saturday?" he began to wonder. Checking his watch, it indeed read 'Friday.' Perhaps with the three–day weekend looming, it was a popular day to take off. He walked around to the side of the building and scrounged through his keychain for the proper key that would let him through the door. He thought of how fortunate he was to have gotten that key when he first started and furthermore, that it wasn't replaced with an electronic entry system that seemed to regulate all other entrances to the building.

The side door opened up straight into a metal staircase. Knowing that the elevators likely weren't working, he didn't mind hiking up the four stories to his floor. He took a break at the midway point to catch his breath, then once more before exiting the stairway into his office. Casually strolling out of the staircase, he was prepared to make necessary small talk on the way to his desk. Surprisingly, though decreasingly so, he discovered he was the first person in the office.

Standing seven stories high, his office building was tall for the surrounding area, though it was not particularly wide. This meant that there was plenty of natural luminosity and, oftentimes, he didn't even need to turn on his cubicle light. Today would need to be one of those days.

The floor he worked on had maybe only 16 cubicles, in addition to a few offices for management. On a typical Friday, he might expect only 50% attendance. On a Friday before a 3–day weekend, the number would be even lower, but it was surprising that he was the only person there. Conceivably, this was the result of the electricity being out. Maybe there was a memo that work was cancelled due to the power shortage, however he had too much work to do to consider the implications of this potential cancellation. Besides, that was a ridiculous notion. This wasn't the first time he was the only one in the office and, thinking back on the previous day, he did not remember a single colleague mention that they were planning on coming in that day.

Not even bothering with the computer, he opened his briefcase and poured the documents onto his desk. He then opened his file drawer and unloaded another pile of documents onto the table.

He was an accountant, and a good one at that. He knew all the documents to file and numbers to add up. He could subtract and multiply, too. When he was young, many of his peers moved around to different firms or up the management chain. Some even quit accounting altogether. But not him, he wasn't going anywhere. Ultimately, it was a blessing in stability and, over time, he had come to earn a very respectable salary. He had also developed a level of autonomy by establishing a firm client base and years of seniority above almost everyone else in the company outside of the founding partners. At this particular time of year, he was especially buried in his work because the new fiscal year was fast–approaching and his clients wanted him to turn all the numbers that had been piling up in their backlogs into fancy reports and projections for the coming year.

As the day passed, no one joined him in the office. This allowed him to focus on his work, but it also added a new layer of complication because, without the support staff, he had to complete the administrative tasks that he would ordinarily hand off to others.

The day wore on, but he hardly noticed. Wrapped up in his paperwork and calculations, he almost didn't notice that it was past 5:30.

"About time to head home," he pondered. He sorted out his paperwork neatly into two piles: one for filing into the drawer and one for shoving back into his briefcase. By the time he completed the cataloging process, it was comfortably 6:00.

***

Friday was meatloaf day. He was grateful for his wife because she would cook, as he would relax on the couch getting caught up on local news and the weather forecast. It's not as though he didn't contribute, however, since he was primarily in charge of picking up the groceries on his way home from work.

"Friday is meatloaf day," he reminded himself, as though the anticipation might wear off if it wasn't continually renewed.

The grocery store parking lot was packed. He was lucky to find a spot close to one of the entrances. He got out of his car, grabbed a stray shopping cart, and approached the entrance to the store. The door was propped open, as it normally was during business hours.

Inside, the store was empty. Not only were there no customers, but no cashiers, stockers, baggers, cart pushers, bakers, butchers, or pharmacists. Although there seemed to be plenty of food, the store was completely void of people. With the power still off, the store was also quite dark, though outdoor and emergency lighting did an adequate job illuminating the aisles.

The entire scene was quite eerie, enough so that his heart began to race. Something was off: the open door, the lack of people, and the cars in the parking lot, the power *still being off*. A part of him wanted to go straight home, however, he had been looking forward to his meatloaf dinner for too long to give up on it now. He scurried over to the meat section and grabbed a pound of meat before swinging by the produce for an onion, tomato, and bell pepper. Doing one last sweep of the store and finding no one, he laid out $20 on one of the cash registers and went out the way he came in.

He sat in his car before starting it. He was going over the day's events in his head to try to make sense of it. Consolidating all the occurrences into a single commonality, he surmised:

"I haven't seen a single soul." At this point, adrenaline was throbbing at his heart and pumping through his veins. He tried to think of ways to dispel this ludicrous observation.

Starting the car, he knew exactly where to go. If he wanted to see people, he simply had to go to *The Old Saloon*. Night–or–day, power–or–none, there were always people at the town's bar. Indeed, the place must be packed on such a peculiar Friday evening, with no better way to wash away the week's memory than pint after pint of fresh ale.

This twinge of hope was immediately dispelled upon arriving to the tavern. The place was dark and empty, like everything else he had encountered that day. The bar was neither clean nor dirty; it was most certainly a complete mess. Unfinished beer waiting to be cleared, the pungent musk of sweat and ale reeked from every crevasse. The depressing ambiance was one of the more soothing experiences of the day, as it was exactly what he had come to anticipate from *The Old Saloon*. He pushed on one of the taps to observe the draught pour out before shutting it off almost immediately. He placed a dollar on the bar to offset the cost of the drink he spilled and left.

***

It was late, much later than he normally came home from work on Fridays. He needed to get in touch with his wife so she wouldn't worry, but not having charged the previous night, his phone had died hours ago. He hurried back.

"I was getting worried! Would you believe that the power's still out?" she greeted him, continuing without response, "Where have you been? Did you get dinner?"

"Honey, something's wrong."

"What are you talking about? What's wrong?"

"Have you been out of the house today?"

"Well, I went to check for the mail," she reflected, "we didn't get anything; not even any junk. I think the no—mail list I signed up for is finally working. I don't remember getting more than two pieces of spam all week." Her train of thought drifted. "Hey, did you pick up some milk? What will we drink with dinner?"

It was true that he had forgotten the milk. In his panic at the grocery store, he had not bothered to pick up milk. The dairy aisle was particularly dark and uninviting and must have subconsciously deterred him from fulfilling his duty. He attempted to explain:

"The store was closed... I mean... it was empty. There was no one there. The doors were open, but it was empty."

"What are you going on about? How did you get the rest of the groceries? Did you *steal* them?"

"No, I left money, but there was no one there to check me out."

"You are positively making no sense at all," she was visibly frustrated with the conversation, but more so with the predicament this left them in. Fortunately, she was able to rapidly contemplate a solution.

"Why don't you go back to the store and fetch some milk while I get started on the meatloaf?"

At the mention of meatloaf, his nerves somewhat subsided. He contemplated his wife's proposal and reasoned that without the TV working, he really didn't have anything better to do anyway.

"Okay, as long as you start cooking right away!"

His drive back to the grocery store was as lonely as the day leading up to it. When he got to the store, it was dark outside, which meant that it was also dark inside. He had neglected to anticipate this problem and had to wander the store in the dark. In the back was the dairy section with the milk tucked away behind a transparent refrigerator door. Inside the glass cage, the temperature seemed hardly any cooler than the temperature in the aisle outside. Touching the milk, it was noticeably cooler than room temperature, but not chilled, as he was accustomed to. Not wanting to disappoint his wife, he searched through the low—fat milk for the one with the latest expiration date.

He carried the milk to the small electronics section of the store where he grabbed a flashlight and some AA batteries. He managed to carry the bundle to the register where he dropped off another $20 bill in addition to a $10 bill. After completing his purchase, he unpackaged the flashlight and batteries for use to help guide him back to his car.

He slept through the night with surprising ease. His belly was full of meatloaf and his eyes were heavy from having to stay open all week. As long as he slept, she slept. After years of attenuation, her circadian rhythm was completely synchronized to his.

Without an alarm to wake them or a need to be up, they slept in until the exact time they normally awoke every morning. He was refreshed and alert. The previous day felt like a bad dream from many nights ago. His optimism didn't last long.

"The power's still out," chimed his wife as she jammed on the TV remote.

***

The rest of the weekend was listless. Both he and she scarcely left the house. When he did, it was for groceries and supplies. When she did, it was to check the empty mailbox.

On one of his grocery trips, he told his wife that he would be out a while. Instead of coming straight home, he took the long drive around town in search of signs of civilization. He found gas pumps resting in empty cars, 'open' signs on vacant diners, and a soccer field with cones carefully laid out ready for practice without a soul there to use them. Garbage bins that had been left out on the street were toppled over by hungry raccoons scavenging in peace. He wandered until he couldn't take the solitude anymore and returned home.

"Orange juice? Since when do we drink *orange juice*?" his wife grieved.

"Sorry, the milk was warm and we have no way to cool it." He pointed to the then–ineffective refrigerator.

"This is ridiculous! I cannot remember a time when we had to go this long without power!" her temper flared. "There isn't even a storm outside! There is no excuse for this disservice! I should march straight to the power company and give them a piece of my mind!" she exclaimed.

"Honey, I think it's something much more than the power being out. I think everyone's *gone*."

"Well the gas and water still work, so I don't know why the power company thinks they can use that as an excuse!" she deflected without comprehending the magnitude of his concern.

He backed away from the conversation, retreating to the living room. After a few hours of self–reflection, he confided to his wife:

"I was thinking of staying home from work tomorrow."

"Oh, yeah?" she pried, "Have you enjoyed sitting around doing nothing all weekend so much that you can't be bothered to go back into the office? You think I enjoy taking care of the house, cooking every meal from scratch, and picking up after you every day? Of course not! But how often do *I* ask for vacation?"

In reality, her preferred hobby was following celebrity gossip and waiting for her husband to come home so she could surprise him with holiday destination suggestions from her favorite stars. As an accountant, this made him very uncomfortable since their budget was not at all congruent with those of her idols.

"I actually wouldn't mind getting back in the routine of things," he responded, "however I'm afraid you are missing my meaning. You see, I don't know how functional I will be without any colleagues or clients."

"And how functional will this family be if you decide to stop bringing home a paycheck? This is not up for debate; you are going into the office tomorrow!"

The last thing he did before going to bed was take the trash bins out to the curb.

***

Weeks went by and still their routine seemed almost impervious to change. When the gas ran out, he purchased extra propane tanks from the hardware store and rigged them to the stovetop. When they needed fuel for their car, they siphoned some from their neighbors, always leaving compensation inside of a delicately worded note. It wasn't so easy when the water ran out, however they made due by buying water jugs and manually filling toilet tanks. She would get up early on Mondays, Wednesdays, and Fridays to water the lawn using an old watering can so that it would be green and lush enough for him to cut every Saturday.

By this time, they had also invested in a back–up generator. Although the upfront cost was not within their budget, he was able to pen out a payment plan with the vendor. Like all other stores, the hardware store was vacant. Fortunately, the tenant had been a client of his and he felt comfortable that he could represent their interests when negotiating a payment scheme for him and his wife. Although he struggled with the ethics surrounding the conflict of interest, he thought, given the circumstances, that there was no other reasonable alternative. As a gesture of good will, he did all the calculations *pro bono*, much to the chagrin of his wife who was eager to increase the scope of his billable hours.

Work had admittedly been slow without any clients around. He uncovered a few older projects that had been sitting on the backburners while more pressing work continually got shoved before him. It was certainly nice to not have the pressure of deadlines being relentlessly imposed on him by others; however, it was also unfulfilling when he didn't have those deadlines to meet.

The automated payment system, which sent him his electronic biweekly paycheck, was just as functionless as everything else, so he had to pay himself manually. Fortunately, his firm kept a reasonably large cash reserve on–hand which, given his seniority, he had access to. Calculating his payment and parsing it out into health insurance, retirement, and social security payments was burdensome, but not overly so. Besides, he billed all of his payroll work to the firm, though at a reduced administrative rate.

***

The holidays were approaching and Thanksgiving was only a few weeks away. Their routine dictated that they visit her sister in the town over, joined by a festive medley of her sister's children and, most recently, grandchildren packed into a cozy two–bedroom bungalow. Although her sister lived not far away, Thanksgiving was one of only a couple annual opportunities for her to remind her sister how liberating life without children was and for him to regurgitate what his job entailed to his brother–in–law. He would often wait to talk to his brother–in–law until the latter was sufficiently drunk such that he would have no chance of remembering the conversation the next year. This practice would leave them with enough seemingly new material to discuss every Thanksgiving.

"I was thinking of going early to help her stuff the turkey this year," she offered, as she did every year. Every year, her attempt to help was interpreted by her sister as an attempt to make her feel inadequate, as it was intended. He knew that this year, her offer would again be rebuffed, but not for the same reason as every other year.

"I'm not sure if your sister is hosting Thanksgiving this year," he began to explain.

"Not without my help, certainly not!" she agreed adamantly.

"I mean, I'm not sure if your sister will be there. There doesn't seem to be many people around these days."

"Don't be preposterous! She wouldn't have left and cancelled Thanksgiving without a note! Particularly with only a few weeks' notice! That's simply not sufficient time to allow us to make alternate arrangements." Her argument seemed to get only more substantiated as she thought out all the logical missteps in his hypothesis. He had no basis to refute these points so he conceded, as was his custom.

Thanksgiving came and went. She was very upset at her sister for not warning her that they would not be in town that year. It was altogether unclear to him whether her sister knew she was upset at her, or whether her sister even still existed, but it did not prevent him from hearing about their riff for many weeks following the holiday.

Christmas came and went as well. He was unable to find a pine tree that wasn't someone else's property, so they had to make–do without one. They kept the house warm all winter, burning forest wood and free grab–and–go newspapers that were left behind all over town.

Independence Day seemed to arrive quicker than usual that year. Although this was typically another opportunity to get together with family, she was still upset at her sister for Thanksgiving and decided, as punishment, to not attend the 4th of July celebration. This ploy backfired as it only made her more upset that her sister hardly seemed to notice when they didn't show up.

***

Years went by like this and the couple continued on their stationary way. As their health deteriorated, they cared for each other and treated each other with any medicine they could find. Their routine remained intact despite the nothingness that happened.

One weekend evening, as they sat together outside in the dusk, he became overwhelmed with doubts over his existence. He confided this doubt to his wife:

"What if this is it?"

"This is what?" his wife was confused, but intrigued.

"What if this is life? What if *we* are life? What if there is nothing else and it's just us?"

"Just us? Wouldn't that be nice if it were just we? To not have to worry about going to work, or paying bills, or family who treats us so poorly?" she said with admiration at the concept.

He kept going undeterred:

"I think we might be the only two people left in this town. For all I know, we might be the only two people left on Earth! That would mean that when we go, there won't be anyone left and that the entirety of civilization depends on our actions. What if we were meant to propagate the human race? What if I am Adam and you are Eve, and we have failed?"

"Oh, sweetie," she tried to console him, but also wanted to find a segue into another topic since his overly philosophical musings did not interest her. "Maybe you should chop a little more wood before it gets too dark? Perhaps it will help clear your mind."

"My mind has never been clearer," he was adamant. Just then, a new wave of inspiration swept over him.

"Let's make love!" he announced, "Let's make love until we bear a child! I don't care if we are too old to reproduce, God will provide us with a child and he will be strong and find a way! Come with me now and I will make passionate love to you by the fire for the sake of all of humanity!"

She was taken aback by his gusto, her libido responding in kind to the zeal emanating from her husband. But she was also tired.

"Not tonight, honey." she concluded.

She retreated into the house to clean the dishes and tend the fire. He sat around a little longer before getting up to chop some more wood before it got too dark.

They did not make love that night. They bore no children.

The Encounter

She was definitely proper... in fact, a little too much so. Perhaps, she was that proper because she was from Japan.

He was not a philosopher of any sort, not even close to being one, but he mused with unforeseen questions that surged through his mind for no explainable cause and lingered there for an unspecified amount of time, keeping his imagination busy and the solitary life endurable. They were perhaps too many crowded and disorganized questions – the sort that bore no expectation for an answer, or at least one that could be realistically sorted in one's fleeting lifespan.

It was likely because of the language barrier or, even more likely, because of her appropriateness that at the beginning, the conversation stalled. To begin with, he was not at ease with the other gender. In addition, nature bestowed upon him a reserved disposition, so he lacked the spontaneity to translate into words whatever commotion was in his mind. Finally, being unreasonably afraid of ridicule, he refrained from gratuitous naturalness to avoid any risk of exposure, so he jealously guarded a majestic collection of sentiments in the box of his heart, watchfully carrying them around wherever he went, like a spinster who would hide a bag of ordinary jewels at the bottom of the suitcase.

But when she entered his life and sat at his side in the airplane, the corner of his eye could not refrain from staring at her. Undoubtedly, she was a pretty woman – no questions about it – but it was her simplicity, her modest demeanor that fascinated him. Conceivably, George's subconscious saw its reflection in the shape of a woman.

So as she was typing cravingly at the computer after takeoff, with no eye contact whatsoever, he mastered the courage, only God knows how, to inquire about her name.

She mumbled something impossible to decipher and he did not understand it, but then, she wrote it down in a little notebook filled with Japanese characters. Her name was Umeiyama, which she explained, means Cherry Blossom Mountain in Japanese.

He explained to her in return that his name was George, that in English, it meant just exactly as what the name itself would imply: "George," but it could also be translated to different languages to become Giorgio, Georgy, Γεώργιος, etc. In an awkward attempt to impress her with the savvy of the conversation, he added that the name originated from a mythological Saint who fought against dragons that, according to the Christian orthodoxy, represent devils but that, understandably, may bear a different connotation in the Asian culture.

While he was digging himself deeper and deeper into this childish conversation, he reckoned that Japanese names are definitely more interesting and poetic than the cookie–cutter Western ones. Most importantly, they are special because they are the fruit of parents' imagination turned into an auspicious prophecy to be carried zealously for the rest of one's life. Yet, she listened politely and even thoughtfully to the explanation. Perhaps, she even understood some of it. Meanwhile, she remained composed staring at her knees, which, candid and fragile, appeared at the end of her skirt after she rested the laptop to her side.

George could not control the corner of his eye that kept turning toward this lovely lady.

And it was then that a complication intervened in the shape of a golden ring that spoiled the looks of her left annular finger. Perhaps that was the reason she was acting so excessively proper.

Endowed suddenly with the audacity of a lion, he ventured a few more awkward attempts of conversation. It was a one–way exchange, questions followed by telegraphic answers. Yet, each time, a gentler smile accompanied her response as she kept looking at her knees and bowed at every question and the subsequent answer. After learning bit by bit a little more about her, George conceded that, for the first time in his life, he experienced what others may consider love.

Nobody that I know of would ever act in similar circumstances as this timid man did in a momentary impulse. Surprising himself, George heard his voice exclaim:

"You know ...you are ...lovely!"

Now, as I said before, there was some sort of language barrier and that statement was lost in translation, confusing Umeiyama who, trying to better her understanding of the English vernacular, asked:

"You say you love me?"

Who would want to be too literal in such a predicament? So, George, to keep it simple, answered with a nod:

"Yes!"

"But, I married...I not can! I not... (checking on her translation App)... available."

That, of course, settled the conversation ...at least for a while because, as I am sure most of you would agree, love is too brittle of a concept to challenge the conformities of life.

George also fully appreciated this but, at the same time, (we mentioned that he had an inquisitive mind) he kept wondering why he nonetheless endured love for that tiny woman. It happens that a mind can play strange trickeries on a man who loosened control and, in this case, this phenomenon resulted in a movement of Γεώργιος... sorry, I meant George's lips that conveyed an inarguably improper question:

"But do you love your husband?"

What do you guess Umeiyama answered?

Well, after consulting her translating gadget, she answered:

"Sincerely to be... No."

Expectedly, that answer caused severe palpitation in George's heart. One could guess that he was not primarily concerned about the poor husband's feelings or even about the circumstances that governed her unhappiness. He rather recognized, as ignoble as this may be considered, a window of opportunity for himself.

Therefore, in this definitely Kafkaesque situation, he asked:

"Would you love me?"

Now Japanese culture is not only reserved but also compulsively precise. So Umeiyama took the proposed scenario seriously and pensively started analyzing its facets. After thoughtful consideration, she spelled out from the gadget:

"Why me love you?"

"Don't know, but I wish you would." was his answer.

Then, Umeiyama asked:

"You love me?"

"I think so."

"Why you love me?"

"Don't know, but I do" was his reply.

George resorted to staring at the panel of the bulk seat to reroute his thoughts and relieve the swelling embarrassment: how stupid could somebody be? How could he have expressed so precipitously something that he had never had the courage to extract from his body in so many years...and to a married foreign lady who could barely understand him? Wouldn't she have better things to worry about than to deal with a lunatic who happened to sit close to her in a flight from any random point A to an even more random point B? But his ears were burning, his cheeks were flushing and his heart was pounding, while he disingenuously pretended to hate that feeling that answered some of, and perhaps the most salient, questions of his life.

So, he tried to focus on more productive thoughts, allegedly related to his work and it brought him close to a dozing state ...when he suddenly heard:

...*Time out! Editor's note*: *In my role as the writer, it is my duty to interject at this juncture that Umeiyama was not just beautiful. She was the faultless depiction of beauty – of which the most striking aspect was the vision of her dark black eyes that could swallow a man's emotion in a snap, like what a black hole would do with light. Her eyes were those of naiveté and wonder, those of a little girl who loves her father and so did they appeared to George when she looked straight at him and said:*

"Perhaps I could, if you really care for me to!"

Her eyes were so black that one could not sort the pupils from the iris, and they blended into dark fawn's eyelashes, which gently flapped to erase each surge of passion to clear the path for a fiercer next one.

George felt an uncontrollable urge to hold her hand, but as he was about to do it, the flight attendant came to offer drinks and his hand froze. He asked for coffee with extra cream and a pack of sweetener, she just wanted tea.

He wished for her to reinitiate the conversation, but she went back to staring at her knees and she kept her hands on her lap, holding one with the other and turning at intervals the wedding ring clockwise and counterclockwise.

Extraordinary things happen. They happen rarely of course, but occasionally they do, and some call them miracles. I really cannot explain how it happened, but at one point, George thrust his hand on hers and held it in a tight grip.

She continued to stare at her knees but did not retract the hand.

George felt a supernatural current of air passing through his lungs that freed his spirit, but it tightened his chest. He simply forgot to breathe. Everything was frozen into the grip of that precious hand. And he stayed content for a timeless hour with his eyes closed, holding the hand of the kind little woman.

When the plane landed and the jet way opened, he handed the bag to her from the luggage compartment and smiled. She took it, bowed, and thanked him without looking at him. He gave way to her and let her go. As she was about to disappear forever, she turned back for a second, looked at him once more, and smiled.

In the hallway, she walked fast and George saw her evaporate into the crowd. Then, an extraordinary power overcame him and, as Superman would, he found himself suddenly at her side. He grabbed her hand. She did not retract it and they walked together to the luggage conveyors. They waited together, but the bags came with despicable immediacy, sporting loud priority tags that laughed at him.

"Where are delays when you need them?" George thought.

Was this the end?

***

I really do not know why I am wasting my readers' time with this obsolete story that belongs to the attic …and I apologize …and also do pardon the anachronism of the cell phone and its App, adopted as stratagem to appear more contemporary. Yes, my friends, this is a true story, but it happened such a long …long time ago that it has lost its momentum in the space of time.

Umeiyama and George are now just a boring old couple. Holding hands, they sit each morning at the veranda of their home that overlooks the Pacific Ocean, from which one could navigate, in one's imagination, all the way to Japan. George drinks coffee with extra cream and a package of sweetener while she has tea. Occasionally, George gets up and caresses her graying hair; she is still just as beautiful as an aging gardenia that impregnates the soul with its magical scent. She looks at him with those everlasting eyes and smiles. It is a contained smile because she still remains that proper lady, perhaps too proper a lady from Japan.

***

An alternate and more likely ending, considering George's intrinsic shyness, could be the following:

All that was presented as factual was, in fact, a vision stored like the rest of all his trances, in the imaginary box of fantasies carried along by George, who, after admiring the beautiful woman sitting close to him, had fallen following take off into a fast sleep and lived an unforgettable dream. He never saw that lady again and he remains a solitary man, who each morning sits in the veranda of his home that overlooks the Pacific Ocean from which one could navigate, in one's imagination, all the way to Japan. There, he drinks coffee with extra cream and a package of sweetener. At his side stands an empty armchair.

***

But just because this version is more likely, it does not mean that it is the real one! As we discussed, extraordinary things ...miracles, do happen!

If you were George or Umeiyama, and you had both the power and will to craft your life's story, how would the tale have ended?

Perhaps the two characters just said good night right after the conveyor delivered their luggage and they never saw each other again. Perhaps taken by remorse for trying to corrupt a married woman, George heroically pretended not to care after all – as Rick did to Lisa in Casa Blanca... or perhaps they just slept together in a one–night stand, or perhaps she fell in love with him and she went back to Japan after, and losing faith in a reunion, she reenacted Madame Butterfly. Or maybe she abandoned him to go back to her family and he drunk himself to death? Or perhaps they remained good friends and met occasionally in Hawaii, midway between the two countries?

There is probably a version for as many as there are of us... and we should admit it: we only know where we are if we remember were we came from and we admit to ourselves how we got here. Crafting your own story, you may build your own miracle by bridging the future with your past. An infinity of endings is waiting for us in the continuum of preference between a "do it yourself" and a pre–packaged version of life. The contradictions and the ironies linger in front of us. I could not decide whether to choose linguini or gnocchi at Italian restaurants, but I would like to believe that George had the courage to hold that woman's hand and, therefore, I personally like the original ending.

The Impostor Syndrome

"I don't care to belong to a club that would have me as a member."

Groucho Marx

***

Frank had always regarded himself as a genuine impostor ...or at best a very lucky man, a human version of what statisticians would refer to as a type one error. So, he was the happiest of men when the day of retirement came and he could relax, having to lie no more.

His inadequacies dawdled in the back of his mind as a vague, gnawing sensation throughout life. Whatever he did, it felt like walking on the surface of a dormant volcano. He sensed that deep under the surface, if someone had to dig, it would soon be uncovered that all his accomplishments were founded on nothing.

He missed his father because he was the only one who could infallibly scout what was wrong with his accomplishments no matter how seductive their appearances might be. All his achievements were – in one way or another – undeserved, since a hidden truth, that nobody else could see but his well–meaning but severe Dad, tainted them. When everybody else praised him for an outstanding grade in school, a sporting achievement, good behavior, or whatever else, his perspicacious dad could find the thorn that spoiled the rose. With time, Frank welcomed the discovery of his flaws that gave him a contorted peace of mind, distracting him from fear of exposure by admitting from the beginning that he did not deserve whatever he achieved, or at best, it must have been the fruit of a good dose of luck.

But his Dad was long gone, and nobody was there to reveal his faults and only that vague sense of guilt persisted.

Professionally, he managed to deceive for decades the smartest among academicians, who were unanimously fond of him and respected his "outstanding achievements", his publication record, and his contributions to humanity. It was obvious that Abraham Lincoln's quote: *"You can fool all the people some of the time, and some of the people all the time, but you cannot fool all the people all the time"* did not apply to him, who kept escaping scrutiny against all odds.

In truth, he had never been able to build a good argument to rectify his admirers' undeserved esteem. In fact, he himself could not find any specific wrongdoing, except for that vague sense of being a cheater. In the end, he settled that there was nothing to lose by being admired and uneasily accepted his success while hoping that nobody would ever uncover the truth.

But lies take a life of their own, and as he learnt to play the role of a successful scientist, he could not revert easily into private seclusion. Instead, he had to give lectures, participate in meetings and advisory boards, educate young scientists and advocate for the field in front of the public and politicians. In other words, he was living in a war zone, where each day, a challenge forced him to advocate and present concepts and ideas that on the surface made perfect sense, but that deep inside did not belong to him but were rather passive rehashes of other people's thoughts, materializing in the form of an indemonstrable plagiarism. And when people applauded at the end of a speech, or came to shake his hand to congratulate him, to befriend him and even explicitly adore him, he responded with rushed cordiality while trying to escape to his hotel room, where he could rest and pardon himself in front of the mirror apologizing for what he might have done wrong and where he could drink some robust alcoholic beverage, look at the sealing and fall asleep.

With time, he became evermore weary of this dissociation between what he thought of himself and what others felt and could not envision any better escape than a peaceful and segregated retirement in the countryside. This is why Frank was the happiest of men when retirement day came and he had to lie no more. He rather thought of himself having coffee in the veranda each morning, looking at birds and flowers, enjoying the breeze and listening to the interminable repetitions of the ocean's breakers – all affairs that were indifferent to him and his actions and carried no judgment upon him so he could unwind without having to pretend and act ever again.

On retirement day, his chairman gave a big party. The room was full of colleagues, disciples, students, pupils, friends, and even strangers, who came to bid him farewell. Women cried. The chairman chocked at his own remarks, and the room stifled in the warm moisture of excess people and tears.

In that occasion, he had, of course, to give a speech, which he anticipated with pleasure as being the last one of his life. For the first time in a long time, he felt that he spoke sincerely, thanking everybody for their support and friendship for so many decades, the kind of support and friendship bequeathed so unconditionally even though undeserved.

***

Then, the morning after came.

The alarm clock went off at 5:30 am. Frank stretched and automatically rose from bed. He went to the bathroom and brushed his teeth. He shaved and, as he was about to enter the shower, he reckoned that he had no place to go. He had forgotten to reprogram the alarm clock.

With a sigh of relief, he reminded himself that he was retired. He turned the warming shower jet off. He redressed in his pajama and went to lie in bed for a well–deserved extra sleep in. As soon as he lay in bed, he noticed that the first sunrays forced their way through the curtains, reminding him that it was, in truth, time to rise. Upon scrutiny, he realized that in fact, the idea of sleeping till late in his retirement days was a delusion since he had never done it before, even when there was no pressing need to wake up. Once again, he recognized that he had deceived himself by forcing a pretense of happiness constructed on false grounds.

Nevertheless, he decided to doze a little longer because he could not accept that this pleasure he coveted for such a long time could not concretize. After a quarter of an hour passed with Frank laying rigid in bed like a mummy with his eyes wide open, and his cat purring on top of his chest, he took another big sigh and, without realizing it, a few moment later, he found himself in the kitchen preparing coffee.

It was at that moment when he reckoned that what he had really been coveting was not oversleeping but the privacy and seclusion that could be enjoyed in various forms, including a peaceful morning in the veranda with a cup of coffee in his hands, listening to the magic power of the ocean waves. In fact, he was now free to enjoy whatever he wanted and nobody was there to judge whether he had slept long enough or whether he was taking too much time in the veranda. He simply was a free man!

Therefore, at the dawn of his new free life and of rebellion against his lifetime compulsions, he forced himself to forget about showering, he put on some casual clothes, added low–fat milk and a half package of sweetener to his coffee and settled in the veranda, trying to focus on the perfection of the morning birth and, therefore, enjoy the fruits of his lifetime's pursuit of happiness.

***

As he brought the first sip of coffee to his mouth, he took a big sigh as to reaffirm his expectation of unending happiness. But it was then when he realized that he did not exactly know what happiness meant. No matter how creatively he forced himself to experience that rewarding feeling so coveted by all humans, he could not remember what it was, he could not relate to it nor reproduce it. In his vague memory, he seemed to remember moments as a child when he had experienced something of that kind, but now, it was just difficult to replicate it on the spot.

"Oh well, I probably do not deserve to be happy after all! But who cares? Nobody is here to judge whether I am happy or not, so I can feel the way I want!" was what he thought and he shrugged his shoulders.

"The good news is that I am alone now and I do not have to pretend to be anything including being happy." he continued, but even the concept of being alone, so anticipated in his previous life, did not seem that exciting anymore.

"I believe I fooled myself with this idea," he thought, and he remembered the days when he would sit with his wife on the same terrace to share coffee and thoughts with her. Sure, it did not seem that pleasant then, in fact, he even resented some of their early morning arguments, but at least they kept his mind busy, while now, he could only argue with himself, and no matter how judgmental his wife must have been, she, at least in retrospect, had been definitely much nicer to him than he probably deserved and nicer than he was to himself.

By 6:30 am, Frank was already tired of his retirement and had given up on the idea of fulfillment, concluding that he did not have to fake the pretense of happiness anymore.

Since it was too early to engage in any undesired social activity, he went for a walk along the beach to give himself a purpose.

By 7:30 am, he was back home and coincidence wanted him to receive a fateful phone call exactly at that moment.

It was a cordial conversation with a longtime acquaintance and illustrious scientist, who informed him plainly, and without preambles, that Frank had been elected as the winner of the top prize in the world in his field for his outstanding contributions to the solution of one of the major problems of science.

"Frank, this is a big honor for me to tell you," said the voice "you really changed the way we are doing things with your critical perspective and your humility that allows you to look at problems as nobody else does."

Frank politely thanked his longtime friend and colleague, emphasizing his surprise for a recognition that he truly did not deserve. On the other hand, he had no good reason to refute it, and as he was accepting it to become part of history, he consented to give an acceptance speech.

The phone call left him ambivalent and in a status of agitation. He realized that his retirement dream had evaporated and he could not judge whether this was good or bad.

As he was musing about the repercussions of this unexpected twist to his life story, phone calls started to come in as the announcement of the award spread quickly among colleagues at work, then, later, among friends and acquaintances who learnt the news through social media first, and then the newspapers and by mid–afternoon. The phone did not stop ringing for a single moment.

Among those phone calls was from his ex–wife also called to congratulate him.

"I am proud of you! I always knew that you would be deservedly recognized!"

"Then, why did you leave me?"

"Because it is impossible to live with you! I explained it to you many times. You have such a depressing personality! Nothing is good enough for you. Anyways, this is not the point of the conversation! I just called to tell you that I am proud of you!" and she hung up the phone.

Then came the time of the children. They were all proud, and he did not do anything to dissuade them but, with complacence, he humored them because in the end, it was rewarding to be appreciated by your kindred.

By the evening of his first day of retirement, he was way more exhausted than after a regular day of work.

He sat on the veranda and looked at the sunset right on the ocean and began to wonder what would be next.

***

What irritated him the most was the acceptance speech. He could not bear it anymore to propagate lies. He ran through his mind all the steps that brought to his "major discovery". It was clear to him that in the end, he had gathered the fruit of so many people's work that led to the said discovery and his seminal paper. It was obvious that that recognition should have gone to the many more people who had contributed to the discovery, of which he was only a messenger. Therefore, without being disrespectful to the nominating committee, he thought that he would emphasize in his speech how unworthy he was of the recognition or at least, how his contribution had only been incremental to the massive work of the academic community that led to final success. In the delivery of his speech, he focused on presenting an accurate historic recollection of the discovery that led to his humble increment.

This idea pleased Frank as he vouched never to lie anymore and to return to his coveted peaceful life after the acceptance of the award.

But in spite of the exposes and caveats, the speech had reaped the opposite effect: it was a great success. It was such a success that one of his estimated colleagues, who had flown across the ocean just to be present at the ceremony, told him at the reception:

"It is wonderful to see such a great scientist recognize so thoroughly the community that nurtured his work, you should have received the peace price just as well!"

***

So, life never returned to "normal" and Frank started to receive invitation after invitation because of the inspirational aspect of his speeches that powerfully enhanced the impact of his scientific achievements.

***

At the beginning, Frank was at peace with this new success because, at least, in his speeches he was not detracting others' contributions and, therefore, he was fairly representing the work of an entire community and could not be blamed for being self–serving. Gradually, however, the exaggerated success of this adjusted storyline made him uncomfortable and he wondered whether, in reality, his humility was just a pretense and an affectation and whether the excessive recognition of others' work was more a contrivance to manipulate audiences to gain their sympathy than a truly meant and genuine disclosure. Thus he started to feel embarrassed about his own magnanimity, as if this was just one more facet of a preposterous existence. Yet, what could one have done? Change the story and claim that he deserved the prize all for himself? Wouldn't that volta face appear awkward?

The more he thought about it, the more he convinced himself that, in fact, his contribution had not been that negligible and, indeed, there was some substance in other people's appreciation. But that also did not calm him down because it was clear that some of the original work was derived from discussions with his peers and with his trainees, whom he had neglected to acknowledge and who will remain buried in anonymity for the rest of history. The truth was that those incidental contributions were too disperse in his memory to be accurately recollected since (his mistake!) he had never conformed to the discipline of taking notes.

Of course, he could have declined to give more speeches and accept more awards, but wouldn't that be strange? Wouldn't people think of him as an arrogant and egotistic prick who thinks of himself too good to bother?

Thus life went on and Frank never retired but became increasingly involved not only in his own scientific pursuits but also in broader aspects of societal life against which he did not have the resolve to escape.

***

One day, several years later, one of his grandchildren asked:

"Grandpa, is it true that you are very famous?"

"Yes, but I want you to remember that it is not my fault!"

A few weeks later, Frank had a heart attack and died.

***

A few moments after passing away, Frank found himself in an anteroom that resembled a dentist's waiting area except that there were no newspapers or magazines, since nothing happens in Heaven and, therefore, there is no need for news. Even the weather forecast does not pertain to those altitudes where light permanently shines.

The room was occupied but not packed with souls awaiting judgment. Some were looking at their hands as if they were holding a mobile phone, others were talking to themselves, as if they were wearing a blue tooth, others where dozing off or staring at the ceiling, and the there three women who made a new acquaintance were agreeably chatting in a corner about their children.

The wait was considerable, but it did not matter because in eternity, time is of minimal if not of no consequence at all.

An Angel clerk stated at a certain point with indifference:

"Recently, we had a lot of complicated cases that take longer than usual." but nobody seemed to take notice.

When Frank's turn came, the Angel accompanied him to the boardroom where God's Council was assembled.

***

God was sitting at the head of a large mahogany table and looked nothing like they portray Him on Earth. He wore casual attire and looked like a Silicon Valley Tycoon, smiling amicably and encouragingly. At His right sat a balding Saint

108

CAT BEHIND THE WINDOW

Peter, who wore a more conventional suit, donned spectacles framed on top by severely arching eyebrows. His posture was straight and stern, making him look like a statue that deserved a place in the square named after him in Rome. He was twirling a pencil in his left hand as he was keeping it warm in case he had to take down notes. The rest of the Council consisted mainly of Apostles that gained their ranks during God's earthly experience. Among them was John, who was jolly as usual smiling affably, while Saint Thomas, playing the role of the Devil's advocate in the Council of God, kept shaking his head in disbelief. Saint Francis, who had been summoned to the Council *ad hoc* because Frank happened to be named after him, winked at Frank when he entered the boardroom and showed him encouragingly a thumb up.

Close to Saint Francis sat Frank's dad. The dad was dressed just as he always used to, with a double piece suite, an Ermenegildo Zegna tie, golden cufflinks and a pocket watch. Intermittently, the Dad pulled out the watch by the silver chain to check the time. Of course, it was out of habit since there is no need for it in Heaven where the only time zone is Eternity. The dad did not smile upon Frank's entrance but arched the corner of his left eyebrow, which, as Frank very well knew, was a good premonition, an impertinent movement that he not control when his son's outcomes were irreproachably perfect. The Dad had also been summoned courtesy of the Council for the very special occasion of the ascent of his only son to Heaven.

God was the first to talk. Irradiating His already beautiful smile, He said:

"Sit down, my good man. Sit down. Although I do not expect this case to take much time," and He gestured for Frank to sit at the end of the table opposite Him. "you have always been a decent person. You never hurt anybody on purpose. You were a good son and took good care of your family. You were a public servant who did a lot of good to your fellow citizens in your professional life and afterwards. You worked without remuneration after retirement and you recognized and mentored young people. Everyone loved you. I have nothing else to add, if the Council voices no other opinion, you are admitted into Paradise!"

God looked around to solicit opinions. Nobody opined any concerns and even Saint Thomas stopped shaking his head for that special occasion.

"OK then, case closed! Congratulations to you Frank, you are accepted in Paradise to be happy for the rest of Eternity" and turning to the Angel Clerk, He said:

"Bring in the next case, please."

But before the Angel had a chance to excuse himself, Frank spoke:

"My God, My Omnipotent God, Master of the Universe, if you believe that I deserve Paradise, who am I to argue with you? But let me plead for you to intercede after I have a chance to explain my point if You will allow." After God nodded in approval, Frank continued:

"I am not sure that I am suited for Paradise and for eternal happiness. You see, I do not remember ever being happy and I am not even sure about what happiness truly is; it would be unnatural for me to fake it. I feel more comfortable when criticized, when I have to apologize for something and offer explanations."

"My father, who loved me dearly" Frank continued, turning to his father searching for corroboration, "always found something wrong in what I did. Bless his soul, he wanted me to become even better than I already was and nothing I have done was ever done satisfactorily. He clearly showed me that under the surface, things are never as they may appear at first sight, and the more somebody knows you, the least likely he would be to like you. My wife could also always find something wrong with me. Maybe I came home too late, and that was because I did not care enough, or maybe I was too aloof to even know how to care. She said that I did not know how to listen, or that I could not relate to others including my own children. Friends also found me impassive, I believe. And what about all those reviewers of my papers? They send back comments that were longer than manuscripts! I never knew that I could make so many mistakes in a single endeavor, and not to mention all the committees, the bureaucrats, the ethicists with their misgivings, who made me fill out mountains of paperwork to prevent any wrongdoing– all the criticisms that occupied my life and kept me going. What am I to do without them? They distracted me from my worries. I felt that I was preventing castigation from a known evil, which is so much better than fearing unexpected lightning on a clear day, anticipating chastisement from the unknown.

Therefore, I beg you, my God, sentence me to Hell! There, I would be at comfort with my peers. I will continue to scrutinize my acts, I will try to justify them to others and to myself, and will repent over and over. I will continue to strive to become a better being for the rest of Eternity."

God looked at Frank with sympathy. He stopped smiling and assumed a pensive expression:

"Hmm..." He said, "that is an unusual request," and scratching His head behind the right ear, He looked around to examine the Council's reactions.

Saint Thomas was shaking his head even more vigorously than usual. Saint Peter, who had removed his spectacles to clean them with the whitest of Heaven's handkerchiefs, checked for their transparency by looking at the pencil tip through one of the lenses, puffed some extra moisture with his Holy breath on it, rubbed the lens a little longer and checked again. Finally satisfied with the outcome and noticing that everybody was staring at him expecting his words of wisdom, he simply shook his head. That is what Saint John did too. Even Saint Francis' eyes saddened and His smile waned. Then, turning to God, he nodded positively in disapproval. Everybody knew that there was no chance.

"I am sorry, my good man, but I cannot grant you this wish. You see, I have to be just! This is my job! While we all agree that you deserve to be in Paradise, you have no credential whatsoever to go to Hell. The souls who are there have done horrible things to get there! Inane crimes! Most of all, they did not repent! But

CAT BEHIND THE WINDOW

you are just their antithesis. You repent for imaginary misdeeds that you have never committed. You go around searching for faults that do not exist, you are repentance's antonomasia! Besides, Satan would not accept you either. With all His defects, Satan has done a great job at managing his Kingdom, punishing those who deserve to be! You would destabilize the principles of Hell. The Devils would not know what to do with you! And they would think that there is no more religion in Heaven! I am really sorry, my good man, but I cannot grant this favor to you! Please be happy for eternity in Paradise."

In a last attempt, Frank turned to his Dad:

"Dad, can you help? How could this be possible? The Council of God might have missed something! With all due respect, they do not really know me that well! They just met me only now and they must have been too busy to actually follow the progress of my life. They may have a general impression of me, but I am sure that under the surface, something is there to disqualify me! Only you could uncover it, only you know me that well. Please dad, intercede for me"

As the dad looked pensive but was not speaking, Frank added:

"Like, remember that time when..."

And the dad opened his mouth in one of his rare beautiful smiles:

"My beloved son, I am sorry, I deceived you all along by making you feel inadequate. I did it because I wanted you to be better than me. You know, I was not a good person on Earth: I cheated on your Mom, I conned at my work, I led a deprived life outside the family and I did not want for my son to be like me. I was so busy entertaining myself that when I died, it did not even occur to me to repent and now, I am condemned for Eternity in Hell. But you, my wonderful son, have been perfect all your life, you never did anything wrong, it was just me who made it harsh for you to make sure that you would never deviate from the right path. And you didn't. I am so proud of you now, on this day, in front of God and the Council of Heaven." and, turning toward God and the Saints, the dad added with pride:

"Yes, this is my son! He deserves Paradise, if anybody does".

As the dad was concluding his last statement, he took out once again his pocket watch and looked at it intensely, as if it was time to go, though it was only to avoid his son's eyes because he knew that he would never see him again and he did not want to show his tears.

 God smiled and pronounced:

"You see, my son, even your strict dad thinks you deserve Heaven. You are a good person and there is nothing I can do to change it. You will be in Paradise per My dictate."

And Frank lowered his head and said:

"I understand my God, and I appreciate that You took my request into consideration."

Then, sluggishly, Frank rose from the chair and proceeded toward the opposite side from which he had entered. With his shoulders cowered, shuffling his feet, Frank crossed the magnificent golden gates that opened into the pastures of Heaven, condemning him for eternity to be happy in Paradise.

The Speech

It was around sunset. One among the last sunrays pierced through the rarifying branches of a very old oak tree and came all the way to shine for a few seconds over Martin's tanned and thickened skin. At the same time, it irritated his eyes.

Martin squinted, looked away, cleared his throat, and began his speech:

"I have a dream,

...Yes, like Dr. King ...I have a dream too...

...I dream of a humanity that communicates through a common language called empathy, a language that is listened way more than it is spoken, and I dream of people who are powered by gratitude rather than envy, revenge and selfishness...

And in my dream, I see people walk at dusk along the riverbank and turn their heads in silence to observe on the other bank folks just like themselves, who are walking in the same direction, and those people feel happy because, while divided by the river, they know that they are not alone for they share common goals.

And I see fathers holding tightly their nipper's hand, happily protecting the same child that will one day stand by them as a grown person when they could no longer walk.

And I see women who follow their husbands with devotion, not because they ought to, but because that is all they want, and those husbands care for the women for no other reason than the one voiced by their hearts. And there would be no divorces because there would be no marriages – just eternal unions governed by the joy of faith in each other."

Martin paused and looked around, he corrugated is eyebrows, grimaced into a scornful smile, chuckled even, and then composed his posture and expression. He also took a deep breath in a dramatic pause and then resumed...

"Beware Fools! Everything flows as Heraclitus said long, long time ago.

Do not be misled by expectations of perpetuity. The subtle motion of time deceives the traveler but life is short and its product is only a baggage of memories.

And I see the dying old man holding in a tight grip the hands of the survivor. I see the old man smile, and that smile is a promise for a reunion in a better world where there will be no beginnings nor ends, where the rightful will repose after a lifelong journey, the longed paradise for the believers in a freshness that cannot be found in ordinary life...

There, the Savior, the Omnipotent will be waiting with His open arms!"

And so on and on...

***

Around the time when Martin had paused momentarily to clear his throat, a gentleman who had just rushed across the street, noted the orator and, in spite of the hurry, walked directly toward him.

A cat that was dozing at Martin's feet, put asleep by his speech, was alerted and it opened its eyes. Simultaneously, a pigeon that had been waiting for something more substantive than words from Martin trotted afar as it was just about to give up anyway.

The gentleman opened his wallet and took out a five–dollar bill:

"Take it, good man. Go home, it is getting chilly here!"

And even Martin's deranged brain understood that the five–dollar bill could do some good on this Earth. He started, therefore, to walk toward the shelter with the intent of stopping on his way somewhere where he could buy a beer because they do not serve alcohol at the homeless place.

The Homeowner
(Formerly: Children's Wisdom)

Miser Catulle, desinas ineptire et quod vides perisse perditum ducas.

Fulsere quondam candidi tibi soles...

Gaius Valerius Catullus, Carme VIII

Miser Catulle, cease to waste time and that which you see has died – consider it gone.

Bright suns once shone for you...

***

The sign was pragmatic:

"For Sale – Lendel Properties

Open Saturday – Sunday 11:00 am to 4:00 pm"

Therefore, each Saturday and Sunday at 10:30 am, after feeding the dogs, John left the house, where he had lived for the last 30 years, and walked for about a mile along the familiar road to retire at the closest Starbucks. He carried in the backpack a relatively new MacBook Air, a notepad, a bottle of water, and a foldable umbrella. In the front pocket of his flannel–checkered shirt, he carried the loyal Montblanc pen that had accompanied him since his retirement party and a short and colorful ruler that dated to the times when he read manuscripts in his office in between meetings.

This ceremonial had turned into routine – since the home had been on the market for quite some time, undoubtedly on account of an inflated asking price. But John was in no hurry, in fact, that half concocted procrastination suited him quite well, balancing the logical decision of retiring in an assisted living facility with the irrational determination of deferring the execution of the verdict for as much as possible.

A few agents, turning impatient, became bold enough to suggest alternative strategies revolving around price reduction, but John had easily solved such nuisances by firing them one at a time. Amusingly, an amateurish negotiator had even proposed a price below the expected selling value with the preposterous strategy of attracting prospective clients and letting them bid against each other like chickens establishing their pecking order!

"Where is integrity these days?" John thought, and with a gesture of a hand, he escorted the clumsy intruder to the door without bothering to say goodbye.

115

Surely, it was not debatable that the time had come to move on. But in John's subconsciousness, the exact timing of such "time" remained vague for the time being. In fact, he had just as much contempt for the concept as he had for the word "time" – an indifferent observer of things that cannot be changed!

That's all it was! His wife had left him a few years before and her memory rested peacefully in a corner of his wakefulness during the days, and it visited occasionally during sleepless nights interrupted by rare dozing moments.

His three children had also moved away, one at a time, to college first and then to the broader reaches of life to reliably return once a year for Thanksgiving, thus preserving a long established family tradition.

How all of this ("this" being his own life) happened so fast, and why it happened at all, was beyond his ability to comprehend. In fact, after much pondering, John had settled with the conclusion that things in life do not happen for any good or bad reason. They just simply happen – and all of those retrospective explanations with whom one tries to label the process of life, are just mere rationalizations to reassure oneself that there must be a meaning to existence.

***

The property was vast for an older man who could not take care of it, and its maintenance was costly. Not that he could not afford it, but it was wasteful, self–indulgent and even irresponsible to keep the whole enterprise going from one Thanksgiving to the other, just to avoid the pain of severing that umbilical cord that was carrying memories from each corner of the estate like oxygen to his fading brain.

***

After buying with a five–dollar bill a Grande Latte, enriched by two puffs of Hazelnut, and depositing the rest in the gratuity box, John walked to the stand to enrich the concoction with a sufficient quantity of whole milk and half a bag of Splenda, just exactly as he had done in the same shop for the last few decades, rain or shine.

He elected to sit indoor since right after Thanksgiving, the cool autumnal breeze was turning into a winter chill. He turned his computer on and logged in, waiting with soothing melancholy for the disorderly appearance of the various windows. He took the notepad out from his backpack and the ruler from its front pocket, laid them orderly on the table and exhaled a deep breath. Then came the turn of the Montblanc: he twisted it open and wrote the date on the notebook in such good calligraphy and with voluptuous pleasure, as this was the only sensuality that survived from the old times in his currently monastic life. It seemed that those gestures reaffirmed consistency by defying all other changes and that illusion gave him just the sufficient amount of relief he needed to carry on another day and another week.

Just as each time before, memories kept creeping up.

...Like, for instance, that time when his little daughter, Rachel, squatting on her tiny legs and with a finger pointing at the swimming pool, had realized in a magical moment of innocent thoughtfulness:

"A pool is an ocean ...for an ant".

That little girl, so considerate, so eager to understand and empathize since the time she could express herself with a smile, so avid to learn...

...Like that time in the car when Rachel begged her mom to let her listen to the deep tones of National Public Radio, debating about Microsoft antitrust litigation. That was firmly against the rules: no radio on in the car for the sake of good quality time together without interference...but that request, so innocent and stern, to listen to grownups talk, had won.

The little three and half year old listened pensively for a good quarter of an hour to the arguments raised, to points and counterpoints. And, at the end, when her Mom asked what she had learned, she said corrugating her blond eyebrows and nodding:

"Yes, very interesting ...only thing Mom, who is this Microsoft, is it a person or a dog?" Just a missing minute detail to produce a fair and cognitive judgment! But great scores for trying!

...And like that time when her Mom panicked upon entering an intersection, suddenly realizing that she did not know which way to go. The little voice from the back calmly reassured her:

"Mom, just look at the arrow on the dashboard! It will show you where to go!" How could you argue with such wisdom!

Life seemed so vast and unending then, so many years ahead, so many years that had vanished instead, no matter which direction the arrow pointed to.

***

Suddenly, he was dazed from his meditation by the voice of a little girl standing in front of him. She had a blond pony–tail just like Rachel's, and she asked him:

"Why are you smiling?"

"I was thinking of my own little girl." he justified.

"You have a little girl? But you must be older than my grandpa!" she said before her apologetic mom came to take her away.

"Do not worry, I probably am!" he said to the mom with an even bigger smile.

***

He struggled to write something, by hand first, then on the keyboard, but memories kept creeping in, diverting his thoughts. He would open the Zillow page to check on the value of the house, he would look at the details with fervor as if he was about to buy rather than sell. He would then shake his head more as an affectation than with purpose. Next, he would go to the real–estate page exploring the photos of the interiors. There, he saw what nobody else could see: that the kitchen and the kitchen table, where so many dinners had occurred with ten feet under the table and memorable interactions starting from...

...Those moments when Jamie, who had barely started to talk, would look at John after finishing the chocolate ice cream with a dazed expression from the highchair, with the spoon still clasped in his hand and shaking his head, declaring:

"All gone!" Yes Jamie, this is the way life works!

...Like when little Paula, complaining about a freezing winter day, said:

"It was so cold today, it was worse than zero! It was negative zero!" How can you correct that?

...Or when even younger, barely learning how to speak and referring to her authoritarian eighteen–months–older brother, Jamie, Paula mispronounced a recently heard expression:

"I think that Jamie is excessive compulsive."

...Yes, he was truly excessive in his logical processes, like that time when the family was going through the pre– dinner "grace" routine and Mom said:

"Grace! I am thankful because we have the best children in the whole world," to which sweet Paula replied in reciprocal gratitude:

"Grace! I am happy because we have the best parents in the world."

"Wait a minute!" wondered the distinguished statistician, "That would be an impossible coincidence! What would be the chance? Come on Jamie! Give us a chance!"

...And there were difficult moments like that evening when Paula had to explain why she had been referred to the school principal by her ten–year–old brother, who was serving as a patrol of the school bus. She had punched her best friend Sarah in the face and nobody knew why. The "excessive compulsive" Jamie had to report her behavior based on witnessed evidence collected in a summarily interrogation of little boys and girls. (A detail relevant to the story was the fact that Jamie was running for School Treasurer in those days!)

In the end, pressed by everyone to justify her behavior, Paula crashed in tears and sobbed the following punch line – so to speak:

"I punched her because she said that she would not vote for Jamie as Treasurer." There emerged the Italian genes! Good go, Godmother Paula! John was proud of her girl!

...And there was the time when younger Paula informed John that she had told their kindergarten teacher that:

"My Dad kisses people for a job!"

To her and John's defense, what Paula really meant was that when she would fall, John used to kiss the hurting site to make her feel better. At the same time, John had told her that his job as a doctor was to help people who were hurting: ergo the conclusion! How is that for deductive thinking?

More memories kept inviting themselves in John's mind like:

... That time when Rachel had done something naughty... so unusual for Rachel! John pointed the misbehavior to her and the poor girl burst in tears, sobbing so dishearteningly that John, to console her, said:

"It is OK Rachel, what you did was just mischievous, but not bad." to which Rachel, who had immediately stopped crying, asked inquisitively:

"What does mischievous mean?"

Patiently, John explained that mischievous meant being generally good but sometimes doing s things that are not proper without intending to, perhaps because the child has not learned as yet that they should not be done. Being bad, on the other hand, meant doing, on purpose, things that are obviously wrong.

As John was listening to himself, wondering whether that improvised explanation made any sense, Rachel thoughtfully admitted:

"I get it, I guess it is true that sometimes I am mischievous..." then, after further lucubration:

"...but Paula is bad!"

An intrigued John asked:

"And why would Paula be bad?"

"Because she said that I am a brat!"

Now we understand the subtle distinctions among misdeeds!

John had tried similar elucidations before but it was difficult to predict their effect when filtered through children's wisdom.

...Like when, on similar occasions, to console Paula after scolding her, he said:

"You did something bad, but it does not mean that you are bad!"

Paula had taken that to heart and, from then on, she would proudly and proactively mitigate any potential arbitration over her misdeeds, stating:

"I did something bad ...but I am not bad!"

Paula could definitely conveniently catch subtleties...

... Like that time when Mom had to run to the children's room summoned by screams of torture released by a little girl on top of whom Paula was sitting. Paula was trying to pull a toy out of her hands. After disentangling the two, Mom patiently explained to Paula that when friends are invited, the host should graciously "share" toys with them.

The consideration seemed to appease the territorial Paula on that occasion ...but the following day, when she went to another friend's home to play, as soon as she passed the threshold of the premise, she ran right on top of her friend and, pulling with might a doll from her hand, screamed:

"Share! Share!"

She had obviously understood that the concept functioned bi–directionally and was definitely more interested in the latter direction!

...Yeah, it was not easy to discipline those kids! It was impossible to know who did what, who initiated the problems, who escalated them!

Of course, there were occasions when it was obvious:

...Like that time when Jamie screamed because Paula had bitten him. Paula vehemently denied the fact till, upon intense investigation of the affected site, the parent–detective noted that the tooth marks missed just exactly the same incisor that was last seen under Paula's pillow for the Tooth Fairy's benefit two days before. It was a very strange coincidence!

John had tried different approaches to arbitrate discussions and discipline behaviors.

For instance, with Jamie, the first–born and by far the most behaved of the three, it worked very well to give points in exchange for a good action. Within the first three years of his life, the obedient Jamie had accumulated a large amount of fortune that would have probably lasted for the rest of his life including retirement. Occasionally, he would inquire about the amount accumulated, to which John would simply reply that he kept record in a spreadsheet at work and would have to calculate it the next day to give him an accurate report.

That approach worked well, till younger Paula, who had a different temperament, became old enough to be the target of the same deception. The first time John attempted his scheme on Paula, she straightaway asked:

"And what am I to do with these points?"

Good question indeed, but difficult to answer – and even more difficult in the presence of Jamie, who also for the first time looked at John inquisitively, wondering about the actual value of his accumulated fortune. But isn't it the way Wall Street works after all?

In the end, John learned that it was impossible to fairly discipline either of the two older siblings and resolved to give them a chance to sort things between them both with the threat of otherwise delivering long and boring sermons about proper behavior. That became, by far, the biggest deterrent to mischievousness because among all his strengths, John had an undisputable proclivity to deliver sanctimony in industrial amounts.

...And of course, there was positive reinforcement! When they both behaved satisfactorily, he would tell them:

"I am proud of you! Actually, I am very proud of you both, although I am just a tiny bit more proud of one and I will tell you which one privately!"

And when each one of them came separately to nervously inquire who was the champion:

"Which one Daddy, which one, is it me?"

He would say:

"I will tell you only if you promise to keep it a real secret, cross your finger secret!"

And Paula would nod thoughtfully while, when it was his turn, Jamie would look at the door to make sure that it was closed and nobody was peeking:

"Of course, I am proud of you the most! But really, I mean really, do not tell your sibling because she/he would be hurt." And that remained a lifelong well–preserved secret!

***

As the sun shone higher in the sky and the temperature rose, John, mostly to avoid the appearance of excessive loitering in the premise, resolved to take a walk down the road that brought him to the river. It was crowded during weekends by colorful bike riders, noisy motorbikes, SUVs carrying kayaks on their top and cars shuttling children to their soccer games.

But even that lively assortment of activities did not relieve John's dejection. Instead, those happy people reminded him of other times when all of that belonged to him, while now, they seemed only like a ragging remembrance of the time past.

How many soccer games did the whole family travel for, packed in the Suburban with soccer balls, shin guards, alternate–colored shirts and other infinite paraphernalia, including the not to be forgotten water bottles and peeled oranges?

And what about the ice cream shop, where they would stop, against the coach advice, before each game? Why would a soft and liquid treat hurt the kids' performance? Nobody knew. To his knowledge, no physiology textbook could ever explain it, so they laughed, ate with pleasure and went on. In truth, those naughty actions had no bearing at all on the game and, just the same, did not affect the rest of their lives, which kept progressing inexorably day after day.

...And what about that time when, upon taking Rachel back from a game, they stopped by McDonald's for lunch. What a painful moment it was when the innocent little girl, hungry after the game, exulted:

"This is the best meal of my life!"

What a humiliation to John's Italian pride! All those cooking fresh meals night after night for the family with the children circling around the isle where the professional stove emitted the most delicious fragrances, like little sharks around a school of sardines! And those special sauces! Those primi and secondi piatti! All that chef's pride washed down the drain in a blink of an eye!

...Paula had hurt him just the same years before, when she requested:

"Can you make a special pasta like the one I had at Sarah's last night?"

Upon inquiry, it turned out that she had been served pre–packaged macaroni and cheese pasta!

***

I know that as an author, I should be more structured but I am, instead, divagating unbridled spotting an empty canvas with the haphazard and epileptic movements of my brush. But in truth, this is not my fault; it is the way John's memories were rushing one after the other, faster than bikes and cars, up and down the familiar hills into his mind. And, what am I to do? I am just handing to the reader an account just as accurately as it might have happened in real life.

***

As John was walking one step after the other down the road, he started to think about those long car rides as they went back and forth to soccer games. The children were very good players, often playing in faraway places with their travel team. Often, a game took hours or even involved overnight stays. Lots of time to kill in the car!

So there came a guessing game that could keep them entertained for hours. It consisted of thinking of something and letting everybody else guess in turn what it was by asking questions that could only be answered by "yes" or "no":

"Is it alive or dead?"

"Is it bigger than a box?"

"Can you eat it?"

"Does it talk?"

Even those innocent games were not devoid of controversy. There were arguments whether that object was truly alive or dead, bigger or smaller than a box, and how big was the box to start with, and on and on with that competitive, excessively compulsive Jamie taking the game as seriously as if it was a thesis dissertation.

...This is how Paula, following thirty minutes of inquisition leading to inconsistent answers, once knocked poor Jamie out unconscious. Let me explain: after the rest of the family had given up long before, little man Jamie finally dejectedly admitted defeat and asked Paula:

"OK Paula, I give up. What are you thinking of?"

Little Paula, in absolute nonchalance, replied:

"I don't know, I forgot."

122

And she had probably forgotten all along– hence the inconsistent answers!

Upon recovering, professor Jamie scolded Paula for wasting everybody's time with her reckless participation. The scolding made her so nervous that the next time her turn came, she said:

"I thought of something..." and before anybody could ask any questions, she announced: "it is a dog!" just to make sure she would not forget it this time!

...And when it was her turn to guess, being afraid that Jamie would scold her for making an unintelligent conjecture ("Paula how could it be a train if I said it was alive?" "How could it be an elephant if I said it is smaller than a matchbox? Etc."), she would mitigate any possible reaction by qualifying:

"I think ...I am not sure, but I think it is a..."

And then Jamie and John, to make her feel better, pretended to think of a color asking her to guess which one, and whatever she would say, they would gasp in admiration:

"Amazing! How did you know" and that made her feel magic!

***

The walk back home was John's favorite part! He foretasted the handshake with the real estate agent. He would magnanimously console him for the few – if not absent – visitors and, patting him on the shoulder, he would reassure:

"You will see, next week will be much better. With the holidays approaching, people will have more time! Maybe some agreeable husband will want to make a nice Christmas present to his wife!"

And he would cordially put forward some other similarly improbable circumstances that would make the agent shiver while John would radiate in a patronizing smile.

Then, after the agent would leave, he would open the refrigerator, pull out a steak and a few vegetables, turn on the TV, prepare a fire and enjoy unpretentious cooking with a glass of Gin and Tonic as his loyal companion. Another week ahead to savor his routines, and another ahead and another and then another one, while the house would patiently wait to be sold and the benign ghosts of memories could continue to wander around undisturbed.

***

Getting closer to the house, he remembered little Paula running excitedly in the twilight of the evening, from one side of the house to the other, to confirm the presence of a big full moon at each side and then announcing excitedly to her visiting Grandma:

"Grandma, grandma: two moons!"

...And she would take Grandma by the hand to demonstrate how one could see one moon from one side and a second from the other. (Eventually, Paula did not grow up to become an astrophysicist and her astounding discovery remains a secret till these days.)

***

As he approached home with a backpack snug on his shoulders to keep him warm, John saw a black Mercedes pull out of the Gate of the property and pass by, driven by a suspicious character that looked more like a businessman than a person. (Do not kill the messenger, my dear businessmen! As an author, I reserve deep esteem for all of you and have no intention to offend, while here, I am compelled to report strictly what was taking place in John's mind).

The uneasiness created by that vision persisted all the way to the end of the driveway, where a jolly agent greeted him:

"Guess what! We DID IT!!!!"

"Did what?"

"We have a buyer! That guy who just left on the black Mercedes as you were coming in!"

"You mean that guy wants to buy the house? Why?"

"Because it is for sale!" mumbled the agent, who was getting nervous

"But he must be in his fifties!"

"So what? Do we have an age limit?"

"No," admitted John shaking his head "but I would have guessed somebody with young kids would want this huge property."

After putting down the backpack and sitting at the kitchen table, John offered a drink to the agent and grabbed one for himself. He definitely needed one!

"Does he know that it is sold "as is"? Did you make it clear to that guy?"

"Yes, he knows!"

"And absolutely no contingencies."

"No contingencies, in fact, he will pay in cash as soon as you sign the contract"

"And you walked him through the house?"

"Yes."

"And the pool house?"

"Yes."

"And the property all together?"

"Yes."

"Did you point out all the snags? All that needs to be fixed? Just want to be honest, you know?"

"Yes."

"And he still wants it "as is," without even bargaining the price?"

"No bargaining, I told him that you are inflexible."

John rose abruptly without noticing and, standing in front of the agent, asked:

"But what kind of a fool would buy this property "as is" for this price? Why would he do that?"

"He is a developer. He is planning to tear everything down, divide the property into lots and build new homes. He said that it is a good deal for him."

Relieved for having finally identified the glitch he was looking for, John told the incredulous agent:

"No way!"

"...No way am I going to sell the house to somebody who is going to tear it down. I knew it, I could tell right away that he was a businessman!"

***

There were some well–organized sheets of paper lying on the table and John saw that it was a preliminary agreement. He had an impulse to grab the paper and crumple it into a ball for kindling the fireplace to accentuate the irrevocability of his pronouncement. Instead, he sat at the head of the table, looked around as if the whole family was still there listening to the pater familias, and decreed:

"OK! I will sign the agreement."

What made him change his mind?

...A memory had surfaced from a long, long time ago.

He saw himself as a young boy at the side of Grandpa's bed.

Grandpa was telling him that the doctor, who just left, had pronounced a hopeless verdict on account of his bad lungs and that he would likely die sooner than he had originally anticipated. Grandpa also added that from heaven, he would keep a close eye on John since, up there, he would most likely continue the same slow–pace existence he had been conducting since retirement. He would, therefore, have plenty of time to check regularly on John and make sure that he would grow into a fine young man; that refined guy, who dresses properly with a tie, like city people do, who would salute passer byes politely and would hold the door open for young ladies. In other words, that he would follow all of those fine etiquette instructions that the rustic Grandpa had thoughtfully delivered day after day, along those walks to and from elementary school.

To console the sobbing boy, Grandpa smiled and, stroking with his peasant's hands the boy's curly haired head, said:

"Do not cry Johnny, I was lucky all along, I had all that a man could wish for, but "Quand l'e" basta, l'e' basta" (which in Milanese dialect means, "When it's over, it's over.")

125

John had forgotten that admonition for decades, but suddenly, those precise words echoed and, with soothing acceptance, he said:

"Quand l'e' basta, l'e' basta!"

And, while the agent was trying to figure out what was going on in his lunatic of a client's mind, he signed the papers.

In the end, he figured that it was so much better this way – all erased from the face of the heart ...a new development. This way, all those memories, all those precious moments would go with the house. Nobody could violate their sanctity and nobody could contaminate them with the stench of their ordinary life.

***

After the agent left, John rubbed his hands and whispered a playful tune to instigate happiness. Then, he removed a bottle of Prosecco from the cooler and opened it to cheer up. He poured a glassful and raised it in front of his invisible family audience. He swallowed it in one gulp:

"Salute!"

He then looked around at the familiar walls that did not belong to him anymore and, to shake off all that was in his mind, he mechanically started the Sunday evening chores. Those consisted of carrying the garbage and recycle bins down the long driveway to the street for the following morning pick up and, as the season demanded, starting a fire in the huge walk–in fire place.

After two rounds, back and forth from the house to the end of the driveway, John re–entered and stared at the fire and at the couch, where a long time ago, a teenager Jamie, on a similarly cool Sunday evening, was watching a football game. John, judging that his son was old enough to contribute to family affairs, tactfully introduced the idea that it would not hurt him to carry the garbage and recycle bins out:

"Kids should help their parents," he mumbled as he left the premise without receiving any satisfaction.

Although his behavior would not have suggested it, Jamie had absorbed Dad's comment. Therefore, when John returned to the house, massaging his triceps with his hands to shake away the cold, Jamie considerately said:

"Dad, I thought about what you said and I think you are totally right. Children should definitely help their parents! When I will grow up, I will make sure that my kids will take the garbage out!" and after a few seconds, he pensively added:

"And the recycle bin too." Yes, Jamie always took his dad's directions at heart!

***

After an uneventful dinner in front of the fireplace, John settled to go to bed. His conscious and subconscious concurred that there was absolutely nothing else to do. Therefore, taking the bottle with the leftover Prosecco in his right hand and the glass in his left, John climbed the stairs to the bedroom. He chose the stairs that went through the children's wing and, as he climbed, he heard Rachel's spirited footsteps up and down as she responded to her big brother's calls.

"Rachel...Rachel...Come up!"

"Coming, Jamie!"

There she was in Jamie's kingdom!

"Hey Rachie," Jamie would say "can you go down and, since you are going to be down there anyways, can you grab a Coke and bring it up?"

"Sure!" And down went Rachel, eager to please her big brother!

"Thanks, Rachie, but I changed my mind, I prefer a diet Coke. Can you go down again and, since you are going to be there anyways, you might as well get it for me?"

"Sure!" And down she went, eager to please her big brother again!

And down she went again and again, back and forth, over and over, never considering the not–so–remote possibility that her big brother was pulling her two little–but–athletic legs. Now, that was devotion! And she would probably still go up and down the staircase these days because she still loves her big brother unconditionally.

...Yeah, like that time when teenager Jamie had his friends over to play poker and the then seven–year–old Rachel came to her parents' room:

"Mom, can I borrow some money?"

"Why, honey?"

"Need to play Poker."

"Play Poker?"

"Jamie said I could play Poker with his friends!"

"How much?"

"I do not know."

"OK, I will give you ten dollars and that's it! When you are done losing them, you must quit!"

John and Elizabeth thought that it was a good teaching opportunity for the thoughtful Rachel. She would understand the futility of gambling. Except for...

...The morning after:

"So what happened last night, Rachel?"

"I won, Mom, I won! Sixty dollars!" And thus the life lesson went right into the trash! "Next time, Rachie, you should read Dostoyevsky's "Gambler". Maybe you could teach something to him! In reality, she never again played Poker with Jamie's friends: they simply would not let her. They were just too frightened by her.

...Then, John could hear Rachel running up the stairs shouting:

"Do dit to me! DO dit to me!" (Meaning: "Do it to me") because she had heard Paula's screaming laughs as John and Jamie were teaming up against her to play "unnecessary roughness," tickling and roughing her up in her room!

...And in those same stairs, years before, little boy Jamie had reassured her panic–stricken mom:

"Do not worry, Mom, you will be there!"

Elizabeth took great pride in always *"being there"*, in spite of her high profile full–time job, for any school event that involved the children. But in that particular morning, she had been caught unprepared by Jamie, who casually mentioned the soon to come event while having his cheerios with low–fat milk. She realized that she had missed a call and started fussing with phones and whatever was available at those times to communicate with the office and rearrange, given the "emergency", her tight schedule to "be there" for her son. But all that fuss appeared much unnecessary to Jamie, who reassured his mom that, based on her previous track record, he was positively confident that she "would be there":

"Do not worry mom, you will be there!" Thanks Jamie! That really helps!

***

After reaching the sleeping quarters, John went into the walk–in closet to fetch his treasured flannel pajamas. That was the same closet where Rachel told her mom, Elizabeth, who was getting dressed for a business event:

"Mom, you look gorgeous."

"Thank you, honey! You are so sweet!" replied her delighted mom

..."Mom?"

"Yes, honey?"

"What does gorgeous mean?" do not worry Rachel; mom knows what you mean even if you don't!

***

John was getting weary of these uncontrollable memories as the alcohol was taking hold of any relics of sagaciousness and the menacing image of the businessman hovered upon him.

"A business suite and a pen; that's all it takes to end it all!" he thought

.... And the emotions kept clattering.

In despair, he went to the bathroom as stormy brainwaves kept rushing uninvited from all directions. He blamed the alcohol, but his pain was deeper than that.

He became woozy. As a physician, he felt contempt for his own body; he scorned the predictability of neurophysiology and blamed that stupid Krebs cycle and all other biochemical nuisances that claimed control of his life. He tried to convince himself that the sensation of loss that he was experiencing was simply a chemical reaction that could be controlled by a good dose of aspirin. And so he untwisted the safety cap and swallowed a double dose.

As a physician, he also knew that all of this did not make any sense, that those unbridled thoughts were vapors of despair mixed with alcohol; that when the alcohol would dissipate, the anguish would still be there. He could not foresee relief to his torment as he tried to find refuge, like a hermit crab without a shell. For a few long seconds, the walls of the house disappeared, the sorrow became unbearable and he wished he had somebody to talk to. The grief grew heavier and he wished for a way out:

"They shoot horses, don't' they?" he declared remembering an old Jane Fonda's movie.

***

Gradually, the bathroom suite, with its familiar objects restored his confidence. The bright spotlights over the mirror revived his long–established routine and he found comfort in observing himself in the mirror.

He flossed his teeth judiciously to protract those habits that he did not want to let go; admittedly, not enough to forestall tomorrow, but enough to prolong today as indefinitely as possible. When the flossing was completed, he brushed his teeth to buy even more time, to reaffirm his presence in a home that no longer belonged to him.

More disorderly thoughts kept rushing in while he continued to nurture his routine: take the statins, and the antacids, and the vitamins, vitamin D in particular. Perhaps, this will fix it all.

***

Then, John noticed a guy in the mirror – just the same guy who had been flossing and brushing his teeth a few moments ago and just the same guy who had been conducting that neurotic routine for the last thirty years. The same guy who will no longer be there soon. John wondered what that guy was thinking and he empathized with him.

He thought it appropriate to smile in deference. That lifetime companion reciprocated with the same deferent smile.

He poured the last portion of Prosecco in the glass. The other guy did the same.

He inspected that guy carefully and he unearthed a young handsome prince that he used to be, full of dreams and energy. He mused that from the other side, that guy saw just the same in him.

He then raised the glass and so did the other guy. He touched the mirror with the glass and so did the other guy; the glasses clinked!

"Salute!" he said, gulping it all.

The other reciprocated.

***

Then, he turned the glass upside down. He looked again at himself in the mirror. The other guy was gone and only John's solitary reflection remained. And it was then that he said with a dazed expression, shaking his head and with the glass still clasped in his hand:

"All gone!"

Yes, John, this is the way how life works!

Tiger

(A tale of unspoken love)

No motion is as stealth as the cautious step of the tiger. Whether stalking a pray or playfully attacking a sibling, one will never hear the tiger till it is too late. On that night, the feline had managed to push aside the sliding door that led to the living room and noiselessly slip into the house. It negotiated the furniture, snaking its body with skill. In almost complete darkness, it swooped over an armchair, landing clandestine over a Persian carpet. The swinging of a pendulum of a newly acquired wall clock dazed the animal momentarily, but judging that it posed no threat after a few repetitions, the big cat proceeded into the bedroom through the open door.

There, it saw a sleeping woman lying, with her naked chest partially exposed. That vision perplexed the animal that squatted and, stealing cautiously, advanced one paw in motion at a time, toward the unexpected object. Prudently, it touched her body with its whiskers and sniffed her naked breast.

The tickling of the whiskers over her chest and neck awoke the woman to the sight of a two–quintal adult Indochinese male tiger staring at her in the moonlight.

The woman froze and held her breath. Then, she extended under the sheet her right arm to touch her sleeping companion, who was turned toward the other side. Firmly grasping his left arm, she whispered:

"Paul, Paul, the tiger came in, it is getting on me…"

Paul, who had more than a tinge of alcohol that evening and who was dealing with the much bigger problem of a pounding headache, had absolutely no intention of being bothered by such nuisance, and did not react promptly. Instead, with his left arm stretched backwards, he reached sluggishly for the woman and the tiger. As he recognized its familiar features, he gently slapped the tiger's snout with his index finger and mumbled:

"Come on RP, leave Isma alone." and clapping subsequently his hands on the other side of the bed, he intimated for the beast to come and lay down at his side.

Reassured that his master was still there, Richard Parker the Second stepped back from Isma's side of the bed and walked around to lay close to Paul with its back toward him, as all cats do, to feel protected.

Paul had attempted to wean Richard Parker from this and other bad habits such as licking his face in the morning with those sharp barbs to wake him up, but the tiger did not seem persuaded by the earnestness of Paul's resolve and, whenever he could, he would sneak in the house and comfortably continue its routine that was so dear to him.

***

The restored peace did not last long. As Paul was about to resume his desired sleep, Mimi, who had been patiently waiting for the morning by napping on Paul's head, erroneously yet understandably assumed that Richard Parker had come in the house with the specific purpose of entertaining her. Consequently, she swooped to the side of the bed and, reaching out of the edge, as if she was trying to catch a fish in the aquarium, began to jab at the tiger's left ear with her front paws as if it was a boxing bag. This resulted in an uncontrollable flickering of the target.

Encouraged by this rewarding result, the kitten dug even deeper into the auricle till Richard Parker, probably concluding that he had enough, rose and, turning around, returned the favor with his left paw that was twice as sizable as the whole kitten. That cautious tap was still vigorous enough to make Mimi roll over on her back.

Mimi had grown without ever seeing a domestic cat and, therefore, by logic of approximation, she equated herself to her closest mammalian acquaintance and suffered a feline delusion of adequacy leading to the conclusion of being a tiger herself. Consequently, she was poised to confidently defy any feline no matter the size.

In this occasion, lying on her back, kicking with her hind paws, then spreading her front claws and turning her ears backwards, she was exquisitely ready for combat. In response, Richard Parker placed his left paw on the bed, just on top of Paul's arm, to stabilize his posture and, with his right, he tentatively tapped the misbehaving kitten with claws retracted.

The weight of the tiger's paw on his arm irritated Paul even more, as he was still fighting his unfortunate hangover and, losing patience, he yelled:

"Enough the two of you! I've had enough! Stop it or I will throw the both of you out!" and, turning to the more mature of the two, he intimated:

"No!" in the third Chinese inflection, while tapping at the same time Richard Parker's nose with his index finger.

This warning sufficed to dissuade the well–disciplined tiger from pursuing further actions and he resumed his comfortable position at the side of the bed. But the stubborn kitten was suddenly afflicted with a loud–meow–attack intended to call his friend to resume playing. To calm down the kitten, who was by then laying in between his legs, Paul had no choice but to resort to pet her around the ear and neck, turning the meow into a laud purr. As all of this was evolving in the darkness of the night, Isma, who after returning to sleep had been aroused by the turmoil, approached Paul from the left side, sneaked under his arm to snuggle tightly and rested her head on his chest.

Trapped by way more affection than he could have ever bargained for, with a tiger on his right, a woman on his left and a kitten in between his legs, with two eyes wide open, the preferentially solitary man, who by then was completely awake, began to recount the series of events that converged into the current predicament.

***

Three years before, in his midlife, the renowned composer, worn out by the burden of his own popularity, had retired on an island in the Indian Ocean, off the coast of Thailand. I cannot recall its exact Thai name at the moment, but in my notes, I recorded that the name meant something like the "Mother of Paradise" in English. Therefore, the Anglo–Saxons living there referred to the place as either "Paradise" or "Mother" Island.

***

As a child, Paul had been a withdrawn character. He had few friends who were just as clumsy as he was. He shunned conversations and wandered silently around the house. His movements were naturally stealth and nobody knew where he was at any certain time, to the point that his mother often felt the need to check on him.

"How are you?" she would say, peeking at his room door.

"Fine." he would answer, continuing absorbedly to focus on whatever he was working on.

In school, he excelled in mathematics but struggled with anything that involved language, from spelling to composition. It took him longer than his other schoolmates to complete any assignment that comprised words. In the end, family and acquaintances accepted him for what he was and, without great expectations, they thought of him as a child with an agreeable temperament and gentle disposition.

When he refused to participate in any boys' activities, slacking instead in front of the television to watch documentaries, his dad would shrug his shoulders and say to himself:

"So what if he will never go far? He is still a good boy and he will be fine." and with his eyes, he conveyed the same feeling to his wife, who nodded and went to pat her son's curly haired head.

One evening, at dinner an old friend, who was an experienced schoolteacher, his friend made a comment about Paul after the then seven–year–old boy had retired to his room.

"You have such a nice son, so sweet and pensive."

"Do you think so? Sometimes I worry. He is so withdrawn and shy, so difficult to understand what he is thinking... if he is thinking at all."

"He is a clever boy, he just does not like to talk. I dealt with children like him before," and then she casually added: "you should have him take music lessons"

And so it was – a few weeks later, a vertical piano was carried into the family room followed a few days later by a scrawny Chinese teacher.

Before the first lesson, Paul did not try to play the keyboard but spent a lot of time observing the black and white keys, fascinated by their repetitive pattern.

He wondered what could all of this mean. What did mathematics have to do with music? Yet, that harmonic pattern with its predictability reassured him. By tentatively touching each key, it did not take much for him to figure out that each repetition corresponded to the same sound at a different pitch and he realized that the whole spread comprised a simple alphabet of 13 letters and infinite potential. Staring at the keyboard, he wondered what it would have been like to build one that continued endlessly in both directions.

***

Obediently, Paul sat at Mr. Cheng's side for the first lesson.

"No play before?" asked Mr. Cheng.

"No."

"Me show."

As Mr. Cheng played the beginning of Beethoven's "Moonlight", Paul stared at the teacher's fingers floating over the white and black keys. The most familiar messages kept emerging from the piano in the form of music that evoked well–known emotions that had carved his youth but had not, till then, found an identity. Paul was startled that one could talk with his own hands and, at that precise moment, he realized that he had found his language.

From that time on, Paul sat in front of the vertical piano hour after hour – till one Christmas when a grand piano landed in the living room. Music had entered his life. It was the only natural form of communication between him and the outer word.

He figured that life entailed the universal logic of mathematics, voicing itself in the form of sounds. Earth itself communicated through the most simple of instruments such as the whisper of the breeze, the murmur of water, the crackling of fire, the rustle of trees, the rumble of thunder and the blast of volcanoes. The universe echoed with the explosion of newly formed stars. The animals also combined their behavior with sounds to effectively communicate through that universal language where no words were needed.

He became fascinated by animals' behavior, by their ability to effectively communicate among themselves and with other species without words. He read all that Konrad Lorenz ever wrote; he read "King Solomon's Ring" and "The So Called Evil". He figured that words were not necessary, that language was just a human invention that complicated things, a language that separated them according to their origin rather than uniting them. Humans had become too dependent on words originally meant to expedite communication for practical needs, but incapable of describing the depth of emotions much better translated into the sounds of music. People had lost the ability to listen to the fragile vibrations of silence which, according to his ears, was never absolute but included amplitudes of undertones and cadences that framed the continuum of life's symphony.

He also became fond of cats. It seemed to him that they embodied the elegance of communication, balancing behavior with sounds in the leanest and yet most conducive formula. He raised kittens at home and watched the bigger cats at the zoo for interminable hours.

Among all books, "Life of Pie" left him with indelible awe. He read it time after time and, without even trying to understand the meaning, he vibrated of the emotions generated by the story. He imagined the vast solitude of the ocean, the distant sounds carried by the winds echoing in the emptiness, and the murmur of the waves caressing the boat, upon which communication occurred between Pie and the tiger through sounds and gestures. He thought of St. Francis who could talk to animals, reckoning that it was not such an unlikely miracle. It was just a matter of divesting oneself from the constraints of the human language to be able to listen and respond to the calls of Mother Nature.

***

When Paul turned ten, Mr. Cheng, after finishing their usual lesson, walked to the kitchen – where Paul's mom was fretting with dinner preparations – and timidly knocked at the door and said:

"Paul good ...Chinese boys good ...Paul more good!"

"Chinese boys good play," he said, rolling his finger over an imaginary keyboard. Then, pointing at his own forehead, he continued:

"Paul smart!"

"...Paul need teacher!"

Paul mom's smiled, dried her hands with her apron and walked toward Mr. Cheng.

"Mr. Cheng, you are his teacher."

"No, Paul need good teacher..." and again pointing at his head, "smart teacher!"

And this was how Paul went through a series of increasingly selective preparatory schools whose name I am not entitled to report.

By the age of seventeen, Paul had written his first symphony. When he presented the script to his teachers, it was a disaster. The piece was complicated and soulless at the same time. One of the teachers, observing his disappointment, summoned him to his office:

"Paul, you had the courage to assemble important work! Few students even try to do so at this stage. Do not worry if it did not get praised. First of all, you have to learn that you cannot always please everybody. Second, you have to please yourself in the first place. If you cannot create something that you like, how do you expect others to appreciate it?"

And the teacher continued:

"Do you like your piece?"

"No, Sir." responded Paul.

"Is there any part of the symphony that you like?"

"Yes, Sir."

"Then go back and get rid of the parts that you do not like. You have just done the first and most tedious part of composing – you built the infrastructure that sustains the building. Now get rid of the framing and work on the finishing! This is the fun part! The teachers gave you the tool to express your soul. It is up to you now to use them. You will not write music from now on to please anybody – not your teachers, nor an imaginary audience... but just for yourself, only to bridge what is in your heart with the harmonies of nature."

Months later, Paul presented his new script that was good enough to give him passage to an illustrious composition program.

By the age of thirty, Paul was already well known. He had composed classical and popular music, sound tracks for documentaries and then for movies. As they say, he was a legend in his own time.

On one Christmas, during supper, when just the three of them were sitting at the table, his dad said:

"I figured that we were so worried about you! Your mom, in particular, you know? But that old teacher lady understood you more than mom and I did! She could read your heart while we were looking at your lips. But at least, we always knew that you were a good boy. That, we always knew! And we have always been proud of you."

"Thanks, dad." said Paul, as he could not think of anything else to say. But that afternoon, he went to the old vertical piano in the family room, lifted the keyboard and played a melody dedicated to his parents that nobody had heard before.

Just the same, when Mr. Cheng died, he did not speak at his funeral but played a sonata that he had composed a long time before, when he was still Mr. Cheng's student.

With popularity came money. By the age of thirty–five, Paul, who lived a very simple life, had accumulated a fortune and, once, visiting Indochina and completing a tour around Thailand, he learned of an island ashore...

***

Paul moved to Paradise Island at the age of forty, compelled by an uncontainable urge for privacy. He just could bear no more harassment from those who asked questions for which he had no answer, their clumsy attempts to interpret his work, to identify meanings that were not meant to be in the first place, to attach words to emotions expressed by sounds – just exactly what he was not apt in doing. Queries were also raised about his secluded life, attempts to discover secrets behind his coveted privacy – all groundless inquires that were further ignited by the elusiveness of his answers. In the end, popularity was drawing him back to what he had shunned all along: reduce into words the universal language of sounds.

Thus, Paul moved for good to Paradise Island. Before moving, he established a fund where a great proportion of his royalties were directed – the fund aimed at supporting children with learning disabilities, but it was not because he felt he had been one of them. In fact, he grew up considering himself perfectly normal, thanks to the supportive attitude of his parents and teachers who had well concealed their concerns. It was only later on, after he attained success, that his apologetic father recounted all the worries and the apprehensions voiced by some teachers that he had a learning disability. Then, his dad told him about the prompting by an old teacher to introduce him to music that changed his life.

Listening to his dad, he considered how different childhoods were like in a less supportive environment. He fancied that the label of disability reflected judgment from preconceived societal expectations without appreciation for the richness of human diversity. He named the fund "Tiger," remembering the discouraging notion expressed by Pie's father that tigers could not be taught, as they were fated to follow their instincts. He wanted to vindicate the tiger against that notion and vindicate all children judged according to the rules of conventionality rather than their potential. He was convinced that learning is a bidirectional process through which either side can learn from the other: tiger from man, man from tiger, student from teacher and teacher from student.

He was inspired to establish the fund not only by altruism but also by a need to divest from the burden of wealth, directing most of it toward a good cause. He, of course, preserved a generous portion of the income to sustain the admittedly privileged existence that he had created for himself.

***

Paul owned a vast portion of the island, another bigger portion being dedicated to a national park, which was, in turn, surrounded by smaller properties scattered along the eastern and southern coast and belonging to other celebrities – who could reach their mansions either by boat or by seaplane for vacation – but who did not live there permanently. There was no paved road in the inland, which consisted predominantly of jungle and meadows.

Paul's estate spanned the northernmost part of Paradise Island, including a four–hundred–feet high promontory, on top of which the teak residence faced the oceanic winds. The eastern portion was fenced from each side of the house to a cove, where a pier extended into the sea with berths for boats and seaplanes. The fence was intended to keep wild life away from the port of arrival for the benefit of the unprepared newcomer.

The southern and western sides of the property were open to the island. About one hundred yards from the house on the west, stood a lesser promontory overlooking the deep blue of the Indian Ocean, where Paul had a cottage built. This was kept open in most directions during the dry season and was walled off with bamboo partitions during the wet one. There, he kept the old grand piano from his youth and spent long hours writing music and playing it above the changing rhythms of the oceanic roars. A third and lower hill parted the other two elevations from a meadow that gradually sloped on the opposite side, ending into the thick forest. On that hill stood an ancient teak tree imported only God knows when that had adapted egregiously to the marine climate.

Because of its seclusion, in the mid–seventies, Paradise Island was designated as a refuge for tiger repopulation. With its three hundred square miles of virgin territory, it could blithely host five to eight tigers that could feed on a dense population of deer and wild boars. Female tigers were originally brought in from the mainland, mostly as young animals rescued from poachers or left without territory after the destruction of their habitat.

Although the cats were left free to roam around the island, submitting to their unobtrusive instinct, they naturally established individual territories. One male was also introduced but, at the time of our story, only females were left as Old Jack had died at the age of twenty–two, just a year before Paul's arrival. When cubs became independent at around the age of two and wandered away from their mothers to conquer new territories, they were shot with tranquilizers by the rangers to maintain the density of tigers constant in the island and they were relocated to populate other sanctuaries.

All tigers were quite sedentary, as game was plentiful and, in any case, the rangers supplemented their needs by bequeathing food twice per week in predetermined areas to reinforce the stability of each one's territory. Tourists were allowed onto the island, disembarking for daily tours from a southern port and this left tigers with a preference for the more secluded central and northern part of Paradise Island.

***

About six months after Paul's arrival in Paradise Island, a ranger, who had assumed the habit of visiting in the evenings for a chat over gin and tonic, sat in front of him in the veranda of the main residence overlooking the valley and the old teak tree on one side and the ocean on the other.

The ranger was just as suitable of a company as Paul could tolerate. He was a buff middle–aged mix of British and local descent, with limited formal education but endowed with a wealth of colorful and exotic encounters. Together with Paul, he could sit contently in silence for prolonged spans of time to scan the ocean or, in turn, listen to the throbbing pulse of the jungle carried by the winds and commenting on their source. This activity was quite welcomed by Paul, who soon learned to recognize, among different calls, those of the tigers – from deterring roars to their pleas for companionship. The ranger, whose name was Rawan, dependably connected each reverberation from the jungle and its explanation to a past adventure, enriching the evenings with mysterious tales spoken in deep tones that timidly challenged the supremacy of the surrounding silence – natural melodies and harmonies that Paul would later conflate into symphonies.

"Last week, they rescued a young cub from poachers." said Rawan, who, after a significant pause meant to assess Paul's reaction, continued:

"It needs relocation. We lost Old Jack last year and we got to bring a new male for our ladies. But the cub is too young to survive in the jungle ...just two months old ...needs to be weaned ...to be prepared for the wilderness." And since Paul seemed captivated, he continued:

"Would you foster him? I can help you raise him".

It should be mentioned that Rawan's offer was at least partly inspired by a fancy he had developed toward a young and pretty servant in Paul's household, whom he considered to be quite suitable for him.

Dubious at the beginning, Paul stared at the muscular ranger. Then, comforted by his confident demeanor, he responded:

"I would love to."

By the time the cub was delivered, he was barely three months old and was still fully dependent on nursing. Paul named him Richard Parker the Second, in honor of his literary hero or, in short, RP – and he possessively took care of the cub under Rawan's supervision.

***

Like a kitten, RP soon became imprinted with his master, who fed him exclusively and spoiled him in any possible way, allowing him to sleep with him at night, walk in between his feet during day, jump on his lap when he would recline on the sofa at the cottage and nibble at his pants while he played the piano. A few times, Rawan admonished Paul that the beast was supposed to be gradually weaned from human company to develop its own independence, but neither Paul nor RP seemed to care much for that contrived idea, and the ranger soon gave up – with he himself becoming more interested in fostering the aforementioned relationship with the pretty servant whose human company came without reservations.

In a few months, a natural communication was established between the man and the tiger. Paul used simple words with distinctive intonations or just sounds and the tiger reacted with growls, snarls, rumbles, meows and roars, and a collection of variations around them that Paul, more than anybody else, could classify in his musical mind. The rest of the communication was left to behavior and soon, both animal and man lived in absolute consonance as if a solo conductor was holding the strings of both lives.

Like any cub, RP was mischievous and had to be trained not to steal the bottle of milk by jumping on the table, not to prowl in the kitchen to catch a fish that he would carry proudly to the terrace and deposit at Paul's feet or to grab a pillow from the sofa in the parlor and take it for a visit to the old teak tree.

These efforts by an apprentice predator soon became a nuisance for the servants, who had to lock up almost everything and Paul had to reluctantly restrict his access to the house, leaving RP free to roam around the rest of the non–fenced property.

RP had no choice but to industriously learn how to open sliding doors and windows which, in turn, triggered the ingenuity of the house tenants, who had to prepare special latches as a pertinent counter measure. The latter worked well when they were operated but there were too many doors and too little discipline on Paul's side to achieve complete success. Therefore, particularly at night, Richard Parker the Second sneaked in the house and jumped on Paul's bed whenever he could. Otherwise, after a few unsuccessful attempts, he would lay in the veranda just in front of Paul's bedroom waiting for the morning.

When the morning came and his master appeared with a cup of coffee in the veranda, RP got up and walked toward him to greet him with a few head rubs that were reciprocated by Paul, who then put the cup on the table and kneeled to less artfully bump his head against RP's growing one, caress his neck and smooth his whiskers. Then, RP would lie at Paul's side till he finished his coffee. RP would subsequently follow Paul to the cottage and stayed there till his master settled for work. Finally, at an undetermined time, he trotted toward the hill where he rested in sphinx composure under the old teak tree to oversee his future kingdom from the mound.

Paul could see RP sieve the air for scents and scan the sounds with his sensitive ears while his gaze was fixed toward the mysteries of the jungle. Regularly, RP rose from his contemplation and returned to the cottage for a few head rubs and hugs with his big paws that reached higher and higher on Paul's body as he grew up. Then he would lie belly up, with his front paws flexed around his head, expecting to be rubbed.

***

The biggest challenge consisted in teaching Richard Parker to play with care. He had not benefitted from the natural interactions with siblings or his mother and he had no awareness of his own strength. Rawan gave a stick to Paul to deter RP from biting or using his claws, but that did not work at all as the cub took it as a variation of the games rather than a deterrent, and he became even more aggressive toward the object and whoever was holding it. But Paul had, by then, learnt a better language: he presented the back of his hand to RP to suggest that he was not in the mood to play at that moment and pronounced simultaneously a firm

"No!" in the third Chinese inflection, while turning the hand around and pointing the extended index finger toward the snout of the beast and tapping it.

That association of a stern sound with unwavering gesture was instantly grasped by the attentive RP, who learned thus, the boundaries of respect. Eventually, Paul trained the cub to respect the same boundaries with others by simply confirming: "No!" in the third Chinese intonation, and Richard Parker the Second instantly knew what was a game or not.

Rawan also advised that RP should be encouraged to catch his own food, starting by presenting him live animals. The servants brought chicken, but that was no lesson – because RP first disregarded them and then enjoyed chasing them around for fun. Finally, when he realized that they were comestible and he happened to be hungry, empowered by a natural sense of entitlement, he effortlessly marched upon one as if it was served on a golden plate. The tamed chicken, naive to the threats of wilderness, squatted hypnotized by the subduing allure of the approaching tiger, which delicately grabbed it with his mouth and gently cracked its neck. Richard Parker the Second then carried the carcass under the old teak tree at the top of the hill and licked the feathers away. With the same sharp tongue, he would slurp the meat off the bones with composure till everything was gone and he would have to get up and go fetch another one. When piglets were brought in, he approached them with the same technique. Without stalking, he confidently came toward the victim, grabbed it by the neck and carried it away while the confused piglet squeaked its soul out.

Thus, disobeying nature's commandments, the young tiger had invented a new hunting technique that needed no stalking or hiding in the bushes. Whether that worked in the jungle where the wild animals lived, nobody knows. But as he passed the one year of age, RP started to catch, on occasional explorations into the forest, wild boars that he delivered quasi alive at Paul's feet. The servants quickly learnt to finish the prey and used it for supper, as RP seemed to value more the trophy itself than its taste.

When the time came to wean RP from human dependence by gradually rationing the food and encouraging hunting activities, Paul flatly refused.

"What is the point?" he said to Rawan. "If we can make him happy this way, why should we fix what is not broken?"

Since nobody could come with any cogent answer to this question besides some vague remarks about respecting the animal's freedom, no changes were made in Richard Parker's upbringing from then on and the tiger was left free to decide. Richard Parker the Second, therefore, sported happily around the island at his leisure, but decided to lodge where food and love were bounty and made Paul's home his den.

As the cub matured into a fully–grown male tiger, an additional pressing need to wander from the household intervened – a need shared by most teenagers among human cubs and by youngsters of other species in similar conditions.

Being about two years old and the only male tiger, RP had no territorial disputes to worry about. No tigress would dare to contrast the power of a male tiger, particularly when she was in heat and had no cubs to protect. So, Richard Parker the Second, like Old Jack before, became the undisputed monarch of tigers' dominion in Paradise Island. Paul could observe RP in the shade under the old teak tree. He saw him open his mouth and wrinkle his snout to enhance far away scents, or point his ears toward the jungle listening to sounds imperceptible to the human ear. Paul learned to anticipate RP's disappearance for a few days to return exhausted and hungry, and spend long hours recovering with a full belly under the old teak tree before resuming his usual routine.

Animal behaviorist may argue that this story is unlikely and I would not know how to defend it, except by simply reporting that this is what was gathered during my interview with Isma through her recollections.

A detail that did not come from my conversations with Isma but was reported by Rawan, referring to Paul's interactions with the complementary human gender in the years that preceded this story.

Like Richard Parker, Paul also occasionally wandered away from home. In his case, he took a seaplane to the mainland and there, he would meet with members of the other gender –. in particular, with a sweet Thai middle school teacher who loved him dearly and faithfully waited for him. With her, he would spend a few days exploring busy markets, strolling along beaches, and listening to her loquacious companion before returning satiated to Paradise Island.

On occasions, he brought his mate to the Island but, contrary to tigresses, women exercise the insupportable habit of unrestrained chatter, a plague afflicting exclusively the human kind. While Richard Parker rested peacefully under the old teak tree, Paul had to confront the vexing expectation by the woman to engage him in deep conversations about issues that mattered only to her. This resulted in the sole effect of frustrating Paul, who did not care to explain what plans he had for the future because he had none, including no plans to marry and have children. He had nothing against such possibility in principle but, as for himself, he listened only to the calls of the soul and respectfully followed their commands. As the woman kept talking, Paul reckoned that each person's essence resonates with ever changing sounds that some call emotions and carries the overwhelming power of dictating ones' life. But none had, for the time being, impelled him to move further in the process of life beyond the boundaries within which he was comfortably residing.

Drained by the woman's cacophonic sounds, he would eventually warmly kiss his temporary girlfriend in the forehead after breakfast in the veranda, cheerfully informing her that the seaplane was waiting for her at the berth. After she left, he would walk to the cottage, lie on a reclining sofa, take a deep breath and fall sleep for a whole day with the supportive Richard Parker at his side.

Life was thus flowing tranquilly for the two friends in Paradise Island and would have probably continued so indefinitely, but for...

***

Mimi was the first to perturb that harmonious balance. As we already know, she was a confident little kitten that sported a cotton white fur, garlanded with red ears and tail. Paul had impulsively bought the kitten at the market and carried her back from one of his escapades to the mainland. In truth, she had chosen Paul more than the other way around, when she tried to reach out to him with her paws stretched through the cage bars. When he took her out, she clambered confidently up his arm to his left shoulder. From there, she purred loudly and meowed at the same time; she licked and nibbled his ear, frolicked with his hair and fussed with his collar. It was only after asking for her price, paying in cash, putting some kitten food in a bag and walking toward the harbor that Paul realized that he had bought her and wondered how Richard Parker would react to her.

When RP first met Mimi, he cautiously prowled toward her, arising Paul's suspicion. As he came closer, Paul confirmed his imperious third intonation:

"No!" pointing his index finger toward RP.

The tiger understood and wincingly turned around. Two days later, while RP was consuming a chicken under the teak tree, Mimi trotted toward him with her tail straight up like a flag pole and, while the tiger turned to look at her, she jumped in between his paws and started sniffing and then licking his meal. Increasingly disgusted, Richard Parker stood and walked a few steps aside, pretending that he was not actually seeing what was in front of his nose.

After that, Mimi became a mixed blessing for Richard Parker, half annoying and half amusing him. She stalked him and pounced on him. She tried to nurse by knitting her paws around his belly, completely confusing the poor RP, who looked at Paul as if he was asking for advice. Receiving none, he would sigh deeply, turn his face toward the jungle and pretend he had nothing to do with all that nonsense.

Mimi became increasingly assertive, and grand were her expectations that Richard Parker, being her closest relative, should take the role of mother and sibling at the same time. Therefore, she kept stalking him, attacking him, hissing at him and doing whatever else to provoke the beast, which eventually, remembering his own youth, started to return the provocations with gentle and tentative aggressions, including stretching his big paw on Mimi and rolling her over while she would glue to it with her own four paws, nibbling at it before running away. In the end, Richard Parker the Second had managed to accept the intruder and let her buzz around him – much like how horses get used to horse flies.

Richard Parker, prompted perhaps by some arcane remnant of maternal instinct, also became protective of Mimi and he would not let her wander too far into the jungle. As soon as she would direct her steps toward the forest, he would stand up, follow her with his attentive gaze for a while and, when he judged that she had gone too far, he would speed with long tiger leaps toward her and pounce upon her. As he approached her, he would make her loose balance with a jab of his paw against her tiny body that turned her over, holding her down with the other paw and then grabbing her by the whole head rather than the nape, since that was just too small for him. Triumphantly, he would bring Mimi back hanging like a sack of potatoes with her head totally inside his mouth. He would then spit her out either under the old teak tree or onto the veranda, keeping an eye on her, as a cat would do with a mouse.

The first time Paul saw this scene, he was sure that Mimi was forever gone, but when Richard Parker dropped her on the veranda and she started licking and cleaning her fur, he wondered how big a tiger's heart could be. Meanwhile, the tiger watched the kitten attentively, encircling her with his two forepaws to prevent further escapes and hovering over her with his face. After completing the restoration of her fur, Mimi looked away, annoyed by that intrusive interference, slapping her tail nervously on Richard Parker's nose. As she grew smarter, she learned to pretend subservience till RP would become distracted and she could zoom away with the stubbornness of a kitten so that the "catch me if you can" game could be repeated over and over.

***

But Mimi was only the beginning of Richard Parker's troubles. As Eve took care of Adam in the pastures of Eden, a young tigress appeared to radically transfigure Richard Parker's existence in Paradise Island...

***

A young tigress, the youngest offspring of the late Old Jack, had been held in Paradise Island to compensate for the death of another female tiger. She was of lesser constitution, subdued in character and nethermost in the hierarchy of Paradise Island's tiger society. She had to search for a territory away from the prime mid–island real estate and thus settled in the northern territories shunned by other tigresses that were intimidated by Richard Parker's presence and by the humans who lived with him. By reverse logic, the tigress, worrying more about her direct competitors than the might of a male, sensed that what deterred the other cats could work as protection for her.

Thus, she appeared more often at the end of the meadow where a fresh water creek served to quench her thirst or was spotted at the side of the jungle, searching for a passage to the northernmost beach, just below Paul's cottage that attracted her for unknown reasons.

Richard Parker seemed oblivious to her, while Paul, captivated by the new acquisition, followed her movements with binoculars. Eventually, he had to bestow upon her a name. Going to sit close to RP under the old teak tree on a breezy afternoon and looking at the tigress imbibing at the creek below, he proposed:

"Nice looking gal, isn't she? Let's call her Bagheera ...what do you think?"

And receiving no objections from Richard Parker, who was also staring at the feline beauty, the matter was settled.

One morning a few months later, Paul walked out of his bedroom in his underwear with a coffee mug in one hand and a journal in the other. By habitude, he searched for Richard Parker to exchange morning greetings. This time, however, RP did not move. Without a glitch in his composure, he contemplated the hill on top of which the old teak tree stood.

Following RP's gaze, Paul looked down and, under the old teak tree, saw Bagheera comfortably lounging in Richard Parker's favorite place. Circling her were two playful cubs that chased each other in the shade at the repair of the early morning sun. Later on, when Paul walked to the cottage, RP followed him and stayed there with him all morning till they both returned to the veranda.

By the following day, Richard Parker had relocated the headquarters of his kingdom to the veranda, where he could oversee Bagheera and the cubs settled under the old teak tree. The good–natured Richard Parker the Second had come to terms with a compromise, conceding Bagheera the rights to his preferred spot under the old teak tree.

***

But as for anything involving females, things were not meant to be so simple.

Everybody knows that a nursing tigress needs plenty of sustenance. Perhaps sensing that she was, in the end, taking care of Richard Parker's progeny, Bagheera concluded that it was the father's responsibility to share chickens and piglets with the mother of his cubs. From her point of observation, she could see the fodder wander within a fenced yard, meant to confine piglets and chickens without limiting access to Richard Parker who could swoop in and out at leisure.

Bagheera had followed attentively Richard Parker's grocery shopping and she concluded that those were the easiest meals one could ever dream of. Therefore, a few days later, when nobody was disturbing her or the cubs, she stealthy progressed toward the pen, cautiously aligning one step after the other, with her tail abased to the ground and squatting her body – just exactly as any sensible tiger would do in the jungle. She then hid behind a fence pole surrounded by a small bush that barely covered a third of her body, waiting for the suitable opportunity to pounce on an unsuspecting victim.

However, contrary to RP's inconspicuousness, her behavior – so well suited for the hunt of wild game in the cover of the forest, so was her stalking and staring at the piglets in open space – unnerved the naïve creatures that would rather be slaughtered by the noblest oblige of the nonchalant Richard Parker than by an unsophisticated wild beast. Therefore, the closer she approached from one side, the more they made sure to stay at the opposite. Finally, upon losing patience, she leaped into the field to chase any of them; they managed to outrun the tigress, spreading in all directions, grunting and squealing and making enough fuss to alert the chickens that flew on top of the highest perches and the people in the house who came out just in time to see the defeated tigress looking around in total embarrassment.

After a few fiascoes, appreciating the unusual–yet–effective technique invented by Richard Parker, and yet being forbidden by her natural instincts to duplicate such civilized manners, Bagheera resolved to let the male take care of the hunt while she would wait to share the kill. When Richard Parker carried out of the enclosure a screaming piglet, she would approach him from as far as she could without stirring a reaction from him and then she would lay down to patiently wait for the remainders of the banquet.

Progressively, she inched a few steps closer, waiting for a dissuading reaction from Richard Parker, who instead seemed to ignore her. As his hunger subsided after a few slurps, the well–fed and agreeable Richard Parker, as he had done for Mimi before, moved away, leaving the catch for Bagheera. To those observing the scene from the house, it became clear that the simplest solution was to increase the number of animals in the yard as well as providing poor Bagheera, who was already corrupted by the leniencies of civilization, with a daily allowance of fresh meat.

By the end of the first month, Bagheera and her progeny were part of the family. The cubs were happily growing, their mother had consolidated the status of Queen of Paradise Island and Richard Parker had moved the headquarters of his otherwise undisputed dominion to the veranda.

***

Tiger cubs are just as mischievous as any house kitten. Bagheera was becoming increasingly accustomed to and comfortable with human presence, yet she maintained a prudent distance from the house and other places where humans might face her. However, the two female cubs, driven by curiosity, were attracted to the house and the cottage and she had no qualms about that.

Tina, being the more assertive of the two cubs, was the first to reach the veranda. She climbed the steps that lead to Richard Parker's new den. RP did not seem to mind. However, Tina had to deal with the not–as–friendly Mimi. The first time Tina stepped in, she was received by the most deterring hiss that made her retract promptly, losing her equilibrium and she rolled down the steps. As soon as she recovered, Tina came back to learn more about that strange kind of ill–tempered tiny and fluffy tiger... this time, she was welcomed by a menacing and prolonged high–pitched growl. As Tina's curiosity was mounting, she slowly approached Mimi with velvety stalking steps, trying to move around the kitten to surprise her from the back, with the obvious intention of sniffing her more directly. But Mimi was more experienced than the naïve Tina and kept turning around like a sunflower to face the inappropriately indiscreet cub and, ultimately standing up, she arched her back, hissed and spitted such a menacing foam that awarded the impertinent visitor with a most valuable lesson on civilized manners and conclusively convinced the cub that little white fluffy tigers have no sense of humor and are no fun to play with.

A few days later, Lilly, the warier of the two, received the same treatment. As the two cubs learned to ignore Mimi, the latter, in a role reversal and with a boost of confidence, became increasingly probing and, a few days later, Paul observed Mimi stalking Lilly, bouncing on her, hitting her from behind and then running away to find refuge on top of the furniture in the veranda behind Richard Parker, where the two cubs had already been trained to stay away from. How Mimi managed to survive and even play with two rough young tiger cubs is difficult to imagine, but she did so and soon, the cubs became part of the household and frequently dwelled in the veranda as both Mimi and Richard Parker had accepted them while Bagheera, from her mound, did not seem concerned.

***

Richard Parker felt increasingly uneasy about the distance that separated him from Bagheera. Was it curiosity? Was it desire? Was it attraction? Was it ...love? Who knows what animals feel? Each day, he took a few additional steps to challenge that distance. And while he would spend most of the day in the veranda, he occasionally stepped out and trotted toward the old teak tree, looking away from Bagheera as if he was interested in anything else but her. If with the corner of the eye he noticed that she was looking at him, he would stop and assume his sphinx position, staring toward the mysteries of the jungle. At other times, when Bagheera took the cubs to the creek for a drink or to the beach to play, he would timidly reach the spot under the old teak tree to judiciously sniff the site where Bagheera lodged and to leave the scent of his own by rubbing against the tree, squirting and rolling his back on Bagheera's nest.

By the time Bagheera was back with the cubs, there was no trace of him save for his scent, which Bagheera studied attentively before laying on top of it, as if they were news of no particular interest for an upper class tigress.

Slowly, the progression continued and, day after day, Richard Parker the Second patiently made headway. Eventually, he was at a distance just steps away from Bagheera, where he reposed in his elegant sphinx posture, chuffing intermittently or exhaling a sound reminiscent of a high–pitched meow mixed with a moo that Paul had never heard before. The closer he came, the more distracted Bagheera looked, as if she was not noticing Richard Parker's presence. In tigers' language, it was clear that Bagheera had accepted RP.

One morning, Paul saw the two cats stare at each other till Bagheera turned her gaze away. Richard Parker had won: not by the power of his muscles but by the invincible might of affectionate patience. Bagheera stood up, then rolled belly up and rubbed her back against the ground. She then rose and walked a few steps away in the opposite direction from Richard Parker to lie down and composedly look toward the jungle. Richard Parker rose and walked to the spot just abandoned by Bagheera, smelled it carefully, and then rolled on his back to reenact the ceremony. Then Bagheera rose and walked toward him, who was still laying belly up. She rubbed her head against his, opened her mouth in a grimace, against which Richard Parker responded with his own while with his left paw he gently tapped Bagheera's head. Abruptly, he rose, turned around and trotted back toward the veranda where he spent the rest of the day content.

From that day on, Richard Parker greeted Paul in the morning at the veranda. Then moments later, he trotted toward the old teak tree to greet Bagheera with an identical head rub , one that she reciprocated by raising her face toward him as to smooth her whiskers against Richard Parker's snout, in what we could imagine would be a tiger's kiss.

***

147

A few months after Bagheera and the cubs had settled under the old teak tree, Paul came to the veranda to sense tension in the air. He quickly realized that all four tigers were looking penetratingly at the same spot in the forest at the end of the meadow, about one–hundred–and–fifty yards away. Richard Parker from the veranda and Bagheera with the cubs from the old teak tree were motionless, as if made of marble stone. Squinting his eyes, he looked in the same direction but could see nothing. Yet, the four animals remained totally concentrated on that spot, while Mimi peacefully slept on a chair in the veranda.

Paul returned to the house, fetched an old binocular, and came out. The tigers were still motionless. Focusing the binoculars in the distant direction, Paul gradually started to recognize orange stripes meandering up and down at the verge of the forest that was nearest to the fenced field where chicken and piglets roamed.

Paul stood behind Richard Parker entranced. After an interminable wait, Bagheera slowly began to steal toward the challenger. She moved calmly and determinately, stopping every few yards and then resuming moments later at the same pace. The cubs did not move but straightened their ears while Richard Parker, descending the steps from the veranda and with his head cringed, hid behind a bush where he followed Bagheera's progression.

Within a few minutes, Bagheera was at intercepting distance and Paul saw, through his binocular, that the swinging movements of the orange stripes had halted. Richard Parker cringed his head even more, periodically adjusting the direction of his gaze between Bagheera and the intruder. Abruptly, he cocked his head and lifted his right forepaw as if he was about to advance, but instead, he remained in that statuary position.

Suddenly, the intruder came out of the forest and in a few pounces, attacked Bagheera, who responded with snarls and growls. The two tigers wrestled and within a few seconds, it became clear that the attacker had a competitive edge over Bagheera, who was forced to retreat and squat in submission while the newcomer stood menacingly in front of her.

As the challenger started to move forward for a second round of aggression against Bagheera, Richard Parker sprang. Within a few seconds, with the big leaps of a tiger, he crossed the meadow and without hesitation, pounced on the aggressor who, startled, responded with growls and grimaces that had no deterring effect on the determined male. With his enormous weight and power, he smashed onto the tigress, pushing her sideways with his extended forepaws and making her roll on her back. The tigress was squashed by the male forepaws against the ground and she froze. Richard Parker kept his snarling breath upon her neck.

There was absolute stillness for three interminable seconds. Then, Richard Parker moved away from the tigress, taking a few steps toward the forest to leave the defeated animal between himself and Bagheera. Bagheera, encouraged by the new state of affairs, slowly started to move toward the unfortunate visitor who clearly understood that she was not welcome in that part of Paradise Island.

Sensing that this was her last chance, the newcomer suddenly rose and rushed away after being chased by Bagheera for a few yards till she disappeared in the forest. Nobody saw that tigress again.

When the calm was restored, Richard Parked walked back toward the spot where the aggressor had been laying under him and sniffed the spot judiciously. Then, he squirted on top of it and with his back limbs, scraped the ground. Bagheera, limping, walked toward him and sniffed the newly marked territory. As she came close to her companion, he turned toward her and rubbed her head then licked her right shoulder. Then still limping, Bagheera trotted toward the old teak tree, where the cubs were waiting, followed by her mate who had taken her side against the competitor. As they approached, Mimi, who had been awoken by the clamor of the fight, arched her back, yawned and went back to sleep.

When Bagheera rested under the tree, Paul could see through the binocular that she had been wounded on her right shoulder by the claws of the aggressor and was still bleeding. Unsure about what to do, he dispatched Rawan. Later on, when Rawan arrived, the two men approached the tigress for the first time. Rawan carried a gun loaded with tranquilizer while for ultimate safety, Paul carried a loaded pistol. Bagheera, who had noticed them, did not seem alerted but continued to rest while the cubs were sleeping peacefully a few steps away.

Paul and Rawan came within a few feet from the tigress and at that point, hesitated – not knowing what to expect from a wild animal. But Bagheera seemed unconcerned and after taking another look at them, she stretched and lay on her left side, exposing her wounded part as if she understood what they were about to do.

At that point, Rawan spoke:

"The wound does not look too bad, I have seen worse, it will heal without us doing anything. I do not think we need to push our luck or to tranquilize her. We can just observe her progress."

And the two men walked back toward the house. In fact, in a few days, Bagheera was back in perfect shape, the limp was gone and the scar became well camouflaged among her natural stripes.

That night, however, Paul regretted that he did not have the resolve to go all the way to Bagheera. He would have risked dying for the excitement of touching her and he also knew that she would have let him close to her. By then, he had learnt to speak tigers' language fluently.

He confided this thought to Rawan at dinner and then wondered:

"What made RP take Bagheera's side, almost like a lion protecting his pride? Do tigers ever build clans?"

"Perhaps he was simply protecting his territory, nothing to do with Bagheera," responded Rawan without much pondering.

"Maybe, but then why didn't he chase away Bagheera in the first place. Why did he let her take over his spot under the old teak tree?"

"Perhaps Bagheera knew how to smoothly enter his life. Maybe some tigresses, like some women, know how to conquer one's heart," concluded Rawan philosophically... and then he continued:

"Talking about women, I need to talk to you about something else."

Paul turned his eyes inquisitively toward Rawan to encourage him to speak out.

After a few moments of hesitation, Rawan spat all in one breath:

"I'm asking your permission to marry Jasmine."

Paul scrutinized Rawan for a few long seconds, searching for any sign of ailment such as loss of weight, jaundice or a droopy eye. Seeing no objective evidence of a catastrophic disease, he shook his head and smirked:

"She is not my slave ...she is old enough to make her own decisions. It is fine with me if this is her wish."

Then he rose from the table and went to the railing, facing the old teak tree where Bagheera and the cubs were resting. He stretched his arms, pushing his body away from the balustrade, and tensed his muscles in trying to identify a most appropriate composure for the occasion. Then, he turned around and, addressing both Rawan and Richard Parker, said:

"You two! What's going on with the two of you? What are these women doing to you? They are playing you two like finely tuned violins! Men are supposed to be on the conductor side! Are there any real men left in this place?"

Not receiving any answer from either Rawan or Richard Parker, and noticing that the latter was ostensibly ignoring him by looking toward the jungle, he added:

"I am talking to you too, RP! Bagheera has wrapped you up around her fingers or whatever they are called for tiger paws. Do you have any self–respect? Look at her laying there under your tree and all you can do is watch her!"

Still not receiving any feedback, he shrugged his shoulders, sat in front of Rawan and, addressing both of them, said:

"Guys, if this is what you like, suit yourselves!"

Rawan, who by then had learned to appreciate Paul's awkward ways of communication in human terms, knew exactly what he meant with that disconnected pantomime and, interpreting correctly that it was Paul's tender way of manifesting with roars his unconditional approval, he smiled and said:

"Thank you!"

Meanwhile, RP, hearing his name and sensing anguish in Paul's words, lacking any formal psychotherapy training, did what he could do best: he rose, walked toward Paul, gave him a gentle head rub, then he put his big paws on Paul's shoulders and with his snout, sniffed Paul's face in what one could also consider a tiger's kiss.

Paul then turned to a servant, who had witnessed the scene from a corner of the veranda, and said:

"Hey Poom! Get everybody here and bring some Champagne. I guess these are the sort of occasions one must celebrate!"

When the whole household was gathered holding a glass in their hand, Paul turned to Rawan and said:

"You better hug your betrothed! Give a kiss to Jasmine!" making the poor girl turn redder than a ripe tomato in spite of her dark Asian complexion.

Eventually, Paul had a cottage built in the fenced part of the property for the new family as Jasmine managed the courage to articulate the legitimate concern that it may not be healthy to raise children in direct contact with tigers.

***

As for Adam with Eve in the Gardens of Eden, and for Richard Parker with Bagheera in Paradise Island, destiny was about to change the course of Paul's life...

***

Love takes unforeseen appearances and penetrates through the thinnest fissures – like the stealth steps of a tiger, it prowls onto the unaware, who will not know until it is too late.

***

One morning, Paul received a dispatch from a renowned publisher, who contacted him directly because he wished to publish his authorized biography. Paul reactively declined. The reason was simple: there was nothing remarkable about his life besides a piano and what came out of it. He did not want to be bothered with the wishy–washy rubbish that journalists scavenge to embellish the truth. All there was to say about him could be learned through his music.

But the publisher insisted. Paul did not need to discuss anything that made him uncomfortable. The publisher suggested a preliminary interview by a young yet experienced disciple of a famous biographer, who was gifted with very agreeable manners and could spend a fortnight in Paradise Island. All that necessitated was Paul's corroboration for the accuracy of the research. He would only have to say "Yes or No".

Paul retorted that he did not buy the notion that somebody would come all the way to Paradise Island just to give him a test – to which the publisher patiently countered that the biographer was experienced with celebrities and knew how to extract information without being intrusive. Therefore, no efforts were required from Paul's side, just a few interviews to clarify and confirm the research already done, leaving room for spontaneous disclosures should they emerge voluntarily.

Paul brought up the concern that his life, save for the musical aspect, had been a complete blunder. He had no friends, no family: his parents had died and he had no siblings or progeny. The only acquaintances consisted of an unsophisticated ranger who just got married with his servant, a Thai teacher in the mainland who was nice (bless her heart) but talked too much, a kitten, and a few tigers.

This latter's argument, rather than deterring him, intrigued further the publisher, who pointed out that tigers, granted that they are obviously less ferocious than critics and are definitely more tamable, still represent a respectable challenge and, therefore, his close relationship with a few of them could make a story on its own.

For the sake of argument, the publisher also suggested that Paul's music could not be completely dissociated from the rest of his existence, pretty much as the rain originates, in one way or another, from clouds. Even Paul might value a few unpretentious conversations with the young writer that may give him an opportunity to better appreciate the worth of his own life through its product.

In the end, Paul, caught in the debate and drained as expected by his hopelessness in sustaining it proficiently, gave in.

***

Around three in the afternoon, on a windy day, Paul went resignedly to receive the young writer at the berth. The wind was strong and produced a festive choppiness, causing the irreverent waves to resound under the berth with splashing sounds and gurgles. As the seaplane negotiated its route toward the downwind side of the cove, Paul turned toward the house to make sure that Richard Parker had not sneaked into the safeguarded territory. He had remarkable experiences before when unaware visitors were greeted by an approaching tiger. No matter what he said to reassure them, they froze at the end of the berth like caryatids of the Parthenon, till somebody returned Richard Parker to the other side and defrosted the visitor with a triple vodka[1]. A panic–stricken visitor even jumped at sea, missing completely the point that tigers are great swimmers. On that occasion, Paul concluded stupefied:

"I guess it takes time to get used to tigers," missing, on his own account, the point that there are ailurophobes, who wet their pants at the proximity of a kitten!

***

The door of the seaplane opened and the young writer was helped to disembark onto the pier.

As Isma lifted her face from the suitcase, holding with her hand her black hair against the wind, away from her face, and as she walked the first steps toward him, with her tiny body, her elegant and confident posture, an irresistible smile, and two big brown eyes gaped like those of a startled fawn, Paul freaked and wondered what could be summarily fabricated about his life that was worthy of such vision. Even more dreadful than having to talk was to have nothing to say.

By the time Isma reached the end of the berth and stretched her arm to shake his hand, Paul was ready to ask her to go back: he did not want to waste her time.

---

[1] In some occasions was a double shot of whiskey

Fortunately, the same shyness that made him lose opportunities with women in the past, came to his rescue this time by freezing his tongue. Therefore, he smiled, forcefully grabbed her backpack to transfer it upon his shoulders, and managed to put together a:

"Thank you for coming to Paradise Island."

"The pleasure and honor is mine," replied Isma and continued: "I have adored you since I can remember and I finally have the opportunity to meet you in person!"

Not knowing how to respond to such a touching comment, Paul spouted a deep sigh and replied:

"You know, I live with tigers, I hope you do not mind."

"I know, I read a lot about you! I am looking forward to meet Richard Parker the Second" and she added:

"You know, I did my research. I am not here to ask questions. I am here to listen to you, particularly to your silence."

By the time they reached the house, which was two hundred yards up the hill, Paul's angst over Isma had dissipated and, opening the entrance door, he said with a smile:

"Welcome to Paradise!"

***

The first encounter between Isma and Richard Parker was not ideal. As Paul took her to the veranda facing the ocean and the jungle, Richard Parker was absent because he had gone grocery shopping in the pen.

Therefore, Isma had the privilege of observing the gigantic animal step confidently toward a chicken perched on a wooden console. She saw the tiger leap elegantly onto the console and grab the bird that stood motionless, mesmerized by the allure of the tiger and subdued to his power. Richard Parker tightened his jaws and carried the carcass a few feet away from the veranda. He then slurped some meat with his rough tongue and left the rest for one of the cubs.

Isma, who thought she had prepared herself for the encounter with the beast, did not feel so confident anymore and turned her gaze away from that vision to encounter, under the old teak tree, Bagheera's eyes staring at her.

Isma vaguely recollected the reason she came to Paradise Island. Now all seemed so different and distant from what she had ever experienced before. In truth, what she foresaw in preparation for this encounter was not far from what she was actually experiencing, save for the fact that now, it was tangible and the scene was not projected on an imaginary screen but was being played live – and she was in it.

She turned to examine the hero of her youth: the great composer. He was tranquil in that feral environment. He looked so different from the person of culture depicted by the tabloids. Yet, as she looked at the actual man made of flesh and bones, she did not feel disappointed. In fact, she forgot about Paul's music and the buzz around it and instead, at that moment, she saw in Paul just exactly a man who was magnificently strange and enigmatic.

***

At dinner, Richard Parker came to the veranda to greet Paul with the usual head rub and he also greeted Rawan, who had joined. Like all cats, RP liked to listen to the soothing sound of human conversations. Rawan had instructed Isma to act naturally and to relax should Richard Parker approach her, adding that not feeling threatened, RP would quickly become accustomed to her. But even though the tiger had noticed the newcomer, he did not pay attention to her and rather retreated a few feet away to lie between Paul and Rawan.

Mimi, on the other hand, welcomed the female presence and, without preambles, pounced from a couch onto her lap, tapped a few times her necklace with her left forepaw, purred proficiently and, finding her velvety skirt quite suitable for a nap, kneaded for a little while, curved her body, wrapped her tail around it all the way to the head, closed her eyes and fell deeply asleep while Isma rubbed her ears.

Principally, it was Rawan, who always had stories to tell, that held the conversation. One joke triggered a cheerful laugh by Isma. That unusual high–pitched sound prompted Richard Parker's curiosity. He, therefore, rose, circumvented Paul's side of the table and went to check the source of that shrill call. As the tiger approached, Isma stiffened and tried to act as calmly as instructed, while Paul reassured her by touching her tiny wrist and gently squeezing it.

Richard Parker sniffed the newcomer a few times, starting from her hand all the way to her shoulder. With his cold and humid nose, he touched her forehead. Paul worried that RP may lick her with his rough and unpleasant barbs and, therefore, confirmed:

"No!" in the third Chinese intonation.

Richard Parker immediately stopped, turned toward Paul, walked to him, rubbed his head against his arm and then lay in between him and Isma, but not before sending a skeptical glance to Paul that appeared to say:

"If this is what you like...suit yourself!"

Evidently, that little human thing emitting strange sounds did not impress Richard Parker at all. Nevertheless, he acknowledged that Isma, for the time being, was going to be part of the family.

***

"Paul has done an incredible job with this tiger."

Interjected Rawan

"He is always aware of what RP is thinking and has turned this wild animal into a most docile pup. He can talk, mumble, whisper, hum, whistle, click his tongue, snap his fingers or simply budge and RP knows exactly what he is communicating to him."

"Can you believe it?" he continued, "Paul understands tigers so well that he knows what they listen to. He even wrote a song for them. It is full of strange rhythms and provoking sounds ...you have to see it to believe it ... Richard Parker, Bagheera and the cubs turn around when he plays and listen."

"Tigers crave noise and sound," intervened Paul, unexpectedly entering the conversation "particularly sounds that suggest motion or animal calls. When we think that they are lazily sitting in the shade and appear to be distracted, they are interpreting the voices of the jungle, pointing their ears to different directions and if one turns in the same way and redirects the echoes by caving the hands around the ears, one can catch the unceasing symphony of their life."

***

After dinner, Rawan left, the servants retired, and Isma and Paul remained in the veranda at the flickering light of a gas lamp that framed the silence within which the cats, the two humans and, in an ice bucket, a bottle of wine, reposed.

"This is so exhilarating," burst out Isma's mouth "to be with you in the middle of the Indian Ocean, with a tiger at my feet and with infinite time to listen to the sounds of the night." And reciting a quote from Paul, extracted from an old interview, she continued:

"You were so correct when you said: *the deeper the silence, the richer is the symphony of life*. I think I can now hear what the tigers hear."

By then, Richard Parker was wide awake, staring at the infinity of the night and surely listening to the concerto of the jungle.

Paul rose and held Isma by the arm. He guided her to the cottage under Richard Parker's attentive eyes from the veranda and Bagheera's from the old teak tree. By then, Isma was already relaxed about the animals. Carrying Mimi still sleeping in the cradle of her arm, she followed with a throbbing heart Paul – the most majestic among all the tigers.

As they reached the peak that overlooked the Ocean, Paul stood silent, listening to a myriad of sounds emerging from the darkness, which were crying to be heard. Then he said:

"You came from afar ...you must be tired. Do you want to sleep?"

Isma shook her head, looking up straight into Paul's eyes.

Paul felt uncomfortable at the stare and turned his gaze toward the ocean. Then, he continued:

"Should I play for you?"

Isma assented.

Sitting at the old grand piano and smiling, he announced:

"I will start with the tigers' song."

It consisted of a repetitive tapping on the mid–keys of the piano, as if wooden marionettes were dancing on a stage. The tapping was erratically interrupted by tweets, shrills and whispers, interpreted by higher notes, and rumbles and thunders deciphered by the lower ones. In its chaotic simplicity, the song was quite pleasant and could delight almost anybody age three and above.

As the notes floated, Isma reclined on a couch that faced Paul's back, the piano and the ocean in succession. Recollecting the purpose of the song, she lifted her body and twisted her waist toward the veranda and the old teak tree. In the splendor of the crescent moon's light, she could clearly observe both tigers listening to Paul, and even the cubs' ears could be seen at a shorter distance peaking as silhouettes in the darkness. Then, she saw Richard Parker rise and come confidently toward the cottage. He did not look toward Bagheera but leaped directly onto the stage where Paul was playing and Isma, reclining. Richard Parker continued straight toward her and she froze. Paul, turned toward the ocean, was concentrated on the music and could not notice.

In a second, Richard Parker stood in his monumental posture in front of Isma and looked at her half distractedly while she held her breath. She wanted to call for Paul but she did not have enough air in her lungs. Then, Richard Parker came closer and thrusted his head against hers, giving her a head rub before laying in front with his back toward Isma and facing Paul. Inadvertently, Isma had taken Richard Parker's place on the couch and, once again, the docile RP conceded – just as he had done with Bagheera before.

***

In the following days, Isma and Paul spent every moment together from morning to bedtime. Mostly, they sat at the cottage. In the evening, they favored the veranda, hosting Rawan and his stories. Part of the day was also spent on strolls along the western shore. Richard Parker would follow occasionally from a distance while Bagheera and the cubs did not seem interested.

Isma learned to listen to the kaleidoscopic reverberations of the echoes in the emptiness of the shore. Her ear adjusted to Paul and Richard Parker's awareness in the vast solitude. As Paul had told her on their first walk:

"It is not what you hear that matters but what you listen to."

She did not ask questions but silently accompanied Paul. The less she talked, the more words sprang out of Paul's soul. They arose in a melodious voice, mostly in low tones tuned to the surrounding hums from the ocean and the jungle.

Paul seemed more interested in her life story than his own. He maintained that there was nothing interesting about his and that was no affectation. He earnestly believed that besides composing music, he had nothing else to show. He did remember and talked with pride about the Tiger Fund. He thought that it could stand as a tangible outcome of a lifetime of self–indulgence. In the end, he was neither apologetic nor proud. He had just followed an internal voice that guided him from the day he sat at mister Cheng's side:

"No matter how hard we attempt to justify our existence, there is no true explanation for our actions and for their results. We follow our instincts and our fate. If it weren't for an old teacher, who suggested to my parents that I should study music, I would still be there... trying to learn how to spell "Conneticutt". If one wants to go into the root cause of everything, there is only the big bang to blame, for since then, everything followed the intangible process of cause and effect. We are no masters of our own destiny; we cannot take credit for our achievements. I did not choose to become a musician. Music chose me."

As he talked, Isma silently looked up into Paul's eyes that, in turn, became gradually less resistant to hers. Slowly, Paul was learning to look straight into Isma to discover that beyond those beautiful eyes rested an infinite horizon, over which sailed a sound of uncontainable beauty that was not played by vocals or instruments and could be heard even by the deaf.

On another occasion Paul said:

"I think humans have pushed evolution too far, complicating everything: their own life, those of brother animals, they ruined the environment... anything that belongs to Mother Earth is dismissed by our civilization. I believe we are pushing the evolution of our species too far. Now, civilization has reached a peak and we are testing how far we can go... but we cannot go an inch farther, and we should retrace our steps. We live a life dictated by artificial sounds that we call words, concepts, strategies, and goals, we call them key performance indicators and other stupid qualifiers what would mean nothing to those who, like tigers, know what they are looking for and how to get it.

All these things bring us nowhere, things that do not exist in nature and that detract from the spirit of our own soul. I was never truly happy till I moved to Paradise Island. Sometimes, I feel like going further: move into the jungle, live with the tigers, the boars and the deer, return to the rich life of our ancestors capable of listening and interpreting their surroundings, a life where everything counted in its simplicity. Life can be so interesting when we relieve ourselves of unnecessary distractions. Music is just the same; to compose a symphony, one has just to get rid of the background noise and let the overpowering logic of our internal music come to life."

Then, observing Isma's inquisitive silence, he added with a shrug:

"I have used such arguments occasionally. They are perfectly suited to extinguish annoying conversations as the debater invariably shuts up, not as much because my jabber convinces anybody but, rather, he figures that there is no point arguing with a lunatic."

And with a smile, he concluded:

"Do not worry Isma, I am not crazy, I am just pulling your leg. I am content where I am and I am not planning to take you into the jungle anytime soon!"

***

The next day, Richard Parker, Bagheera and the cubs were nowhere to be seen. Paul and Isma walked the usual path to the western beach where the white sand and the emerald sea were chiseled by coral reefs. The deserted beach spanned kilometers southwards with the jungle bordering it about fifty yards from shore. They walked barefoot along the backwash. Isma collected shells and organized them in little piles along the path to wait for their return.

In an impulse, she held Paul's hand, which, in response, tightened its grip on hers. They walked farther hand in hand, without words, listening to silence – that blank silence that no sound dominates, clearing space for thousands.

Suddenly, Paul congealed. Isma looked up and saw his unflinching gaze aimed at the distance and she recognized in his eyes the scrutinizing stare of a tiger.

"I cannot tell from here, but I think he is teaching the cubs to fish!" said Paul, "I have never heard of such behavior, but this is exactly what it looks like."

Following the direction of Paul's gaze, she saw in the distance the stripped orange of tigers mixing a few feet ashore with the emerald hues of the oceanic tide. It was Richard Parker with the cubs and Bagheera, who stood in her majestic posture at shore. As they approached closer, they were sure enough that is was exactly what RP was doing. He pounced in the water in different directions till he dove his head into the sea to come out with a fish in his mouth. Then, he carried it to the shore and let the cubs play with it.

"I have never heard of such behavior," mumbled Paul, and then he added, "I guess RP is not just a chicken stalker. I never thought of him as a skilled predator. He must have taught himself just as he has done with the wild boars ...or perhaps Bagheera taught him! She is the one who has longed for beaches since I have known her."

As they came closer, the tigers paid no attention to them but continued their play, fishing or chasing each other in and out of the water, jumping over the waves as if they were bushes in the depth of the jungle.

***

That night after dinner, Isma listened to Paul's music at the cottage. She reclined on the couch with Richard Parker at her side. It was a tranquil night with a gentle breeze and the murmur of the ocean that insinuated a gentle harmony like a lullaby, over which Paul's music danced. Everything was natural and relaxing, and as the night progressed, she transitioned into a dozing state.

From there, Isma saw the tiger swooping over the piano. The tiger then turned and came toward her, confidently aligning step after step as he had done with the chickens and stared right into her eyes. And, like a chicken, Isma froze, dazed by the hypnotizing power of RP's gaze. The tiger moved closer, aiming his predatorial eyes into hers. Isma was paralyzed and could not move or breathe while he came over her. With his mouth, he grazed her neck, with his paws, he grabbed her shoulders, and with his tongue, he licked her mouth while his body pressed against hers. And she felt the power of the tiger when she hugged his strong body, and then she felt the warmth of the tiger inside of her. Like the chickens, she felt that she was completely under his mercy and she reckoned that her acquiescence was not just for that moment but for the rest of her life – wherever the tiger might carry her.

When she recovered from her trance, she saw Paul holding her hand tightly and, without words, lead her to the house into his room where they slept together from that night on.

***

Following that night, and for the rest of her stay, Isma slept at Paul's side. In the early hours, they slept on the couch at the cottage with RP at their side. They woke up in the middle of the night under the silver blanket of the Milky Way. As the temperature dropped, they retired to the bedroom, and Paul made sure to latch the door each night, staring at Richard Parker's questioning eyes to warn:

"No!" in the third Chinese intonation.

***

He remembered to latch that door each night ...except for this last one.

It was still the middle of the night and Paul was lying in bed, fully awake with Richard Parker on his right, Isma on his left and Mimi in between his legs. That evening had been the eve of Isma's return to the world where she had come from. They opened a bottle of Champagne to cheerfully celebrate their unspoken sadness and, perhaps because of that, they loosened their spirit and had a little too much. Uncharacteristically, Paul had made vague promises about seeing each other again somewhere, someday:

"Will we see each other again?" he, against his nature, hesitantly asked.

Isma responded that she learnt all she needed for the biography and it would be unlikely that the publisher would sponsor another trip. That comment vibrated in very low tones in Paul's chest. He suddenly reckoned that he had so much more to tell... so much more to share... if he only knew how. Restlessness overtook his soul, something that could only be mitigated by another glass of Champagne.

Lying in bed, holding Isma with his left arm, Paul caressed her left shoulder, and at the pace of her rhythmic breathing against his chest, he recollected, moment after moment, the succession of events along Isma's stay till his thoughts stumbled into the image of her suitcase waiting for the morning. That image triggered the memory of Tango, the last cat he owned in the old town. Tango could sense his preeminent departure by sniffing his stocked suitcase and carefully inspecting each aspect of the preparations around it. He kept himself closer to him, walked between his legs and followed him till the door was closed. And he recollected the time when he left for good to move to Paradise Island, entrusting Tango to a friend. He wondered why he did not bring Tango with him: "Cats go with the house, not with the owner," they say. Perhaps Tango was happier now in the old place with a new owner.

That panicky sensation of loss, triggered by the image of her suitcase, gradually converted into a melancholic feeling of vanishing prospects as calm was restored in the peace of the night. Then, mysteriously, that deep emotion morphed into merry anticipation, like the one experienced at the tapping of the rain that ends a drought, or at the rustle of trees announcing a cooling breeze on a hot summer day, or at the jingling of bells proclaiming the advent of Christmas. It was a sentiment never felt that turned into a melody, a serenade made to accompany Isma wherever she would go.

That night, Paul composed and memorized a script, as he did not want to disturb the enchantment of the night by leaving his bed. As he was composing the serenade, he turned toward Isma, gently thrusting his head against hers in a head rub, to which the half sleeping woman responded with a similar gesture.

***

At breakfast, Paul mumbled something intended to convince Isma to postpone her return for a week: he had much more to reveal that was critical for the veracity of the biography:

"I can call your boss and he will agree for sure if I tell him that there is more for his book! Will you stay if he agrees?" and she answered:

"Yes!" in the second Chinese intonation, into which Paul could read all that he needed to know about that woman's heart.

At breakfast a week later, Paul asked Isma whether she could postpone her return for another week, and she said:

"Yes!" in the second Chinese intonation, into which Paul confirmed all that he wanted to know about that woman's heart.

***

Isma never left Paradise Island. With time, she bore two human cubs, which grew with generations of tiger cubs. When they became ready for independence, like the tiger cubs, they were relocated to distant countries, where prestigious colleges take care of human repopulation.

Paul never married Isma nor did he ever tell her that he loved her – he never knew that he did since he never learned how to translate his feelings into human terms. He only knew what his heart was saying through music that he translated into symphonies, ballades, serenades, sonatas and other pieces that I am sure my readers would recognize each time they are played around the world.

Isma was not only a writer but also a painter, and she dwelled at the cottage, capturing dreams inspired by Paul's music while keeping Paul company. In time, Paul observed that Isma needed space for a desk, for the easels, the tripod for the camera, the canopies, and the frames, so he had the old grand piano transferred to the veranda. There, he worked with Richard Parker by his side, right on the spot where RP had chosen after conceding the shade of the old teak tree to Bagheera. Rawan joined them at the veranda more often, to drink some green tea and listen to music. Jasmine had made it clear that he had responsibilities both

160

as a husband and even more so, as a father. Thus he should not wander unnecessarily in the jungle beyond what was utterly required.

From the veranda, the three old friends listened to the calls of the jungle day after day and remembered the times when those sounds were provokingly close, whereas now, they echoed obsolete memories that refused to die. At turns, to interrupt the monotony of the long day, one of the friends would take a break from the veranda to salute his respective *Cherie* with a head rub, a hug from behind the shoulders, a kiss on the forehead or to bring a glass of lemon mint, mango juice, green tea – cold or hot – according to season and preference.

Once, returning from the cottage where he had just kissed Isma on the lips, after bringing the mint and watching her paint, Paul observed his two friends waiting for him at the veranda and wondered what turned the three of them into such finely tuned violins, zealously waiting for the tapping of their respective conductor's baton. And he looked at Bagheera under the shade of the old teak tree; she was the one who started it all! And then she saw Jasmine, who had come to whisper something in Rawan's ear. That had been the second warning! And then turned back to look at Isma, at her beautiful slender figure, raised against the ocean, with a palette in one hand and a brush in the other – the queen of all the tigresses. But in the end, neither Richard Parker nor Rawan seemed to resent the situation, thus he repeated to himself:

"If it ain't broken, don't fix it."

***

One evening, Paul was sitting in the veranda with the loyal Rawan in front of him and Richard Parker dozing at his feet. Isma was still at the cottage, taking photos of a sunset that shone in a distinctive hue in a brisk October evening. Paul pulled from the front pocket of his shirt a sheet of thick and faded paper carefully folded into quarters, and meticulously opened it. Then, he read:

"The timeline of love...

Drop by
Drop, it
Falls from the
Stalactite of the
Future

Time
Fills the
Past

And you

Loved

Yesterday

Propose your
Heart
Again
Tomorrow

Love in this
Moment.

Crave
Love
Tomorrow
.
Drop by
Drop
Steal from the
Future this
Minute...

Existing
Comfort
Preview of
Your
Memories."

***

"An old friend wrote this poem some time ago," he explained. "He gave to me the original script. Here it is! It is beautiful! I like to read it once in a while; although I am not sure if I understand each concept, I like how it sounds. I have been trying to translate it into music but it is impossible."

He handed the wilted paper to Rawan, who took it into his hands and scanned it line by line to read exactly what had just been recited.

"Poetry is the de–evolution of culture." continued Paul, "Poets have figured how to use words to make music... and create beautiful lyrics that appeal beyond their significance ...but it is difficult to turn it into my kind of music. Perhaps I was wrong all along. Perhaps there is a limit to the power of notes ...of the alphabet of music... perhaps the deeper notes stirred by emotions expressed by words cannot be reproduced by other instruments. Here, Giuseppe speaks of love... what is love? I don't know! But whatever it is, this poem applies to the way I feel about Isma. I do not remember what my life was like before she appeared in Paradise Island, but now I know that she is my past, my present and my future."

Partly touched by the unexpected burst of loquacity from the former solitary man, Rawan looked at the piece of worn paper one more time, folded it and gave it back to Paul while saying with a big smile:

"If this is what you like... suit yourself." and since Richard Parker showed no objections, we may safely assume that he would have pronounced the same verdict if he only could speak.

***

Time passed... year after year. With time, Richard Parker and Bagheera became less dependent on the chicken coop and preferred to hunt. Often together, they disappeared for a day or two to return exhausted to their den where love was waiting. Richard Parker continued, of course, to entertain a few romantic escapades to keep the other tenants of Paradise Island happy and productive in the repopulation business, but Bagheera did not seem to mind.

Paul, on the other hand, did not go to the mainland for the old purposes. When he did, he went with Isma at his arm. They brought with them a collection of paintings and spent a few days in the mainland readapting to civilization. Jasmine and Rawan most often accompanied them. At the market, they collected as much paraphernalia as Isma or Jasmine deemed necessary. Once, they even bought a kitten to replace the departed Mimi. When they returned to Paradise Island, they consistently found Richard Parker waiting for them at the berth. The three of them walked the way up to the house followed by Jasmine and Rawan, and when they reached the door, invariably Paul would turn toward Isma saying:

"Welcome to Paradise."

***

When Richard Parker died, Paul had him buried under the old teak tree; and each evening from the veranda, he played the tigers' song. A young male cub, from the latest of Bagheera's litters was kept and trained by Paul to take his father's place at the veranda, and he was named Richard Parker the Third.

When the time came for Paul to also leave Paradise Island to relocate to another type of Paradise, Isma had him buried under the old teak tree, beside Richard Parker the Second and, each night, she listened to the tigers' song played by Paul's son, who had come for the funeral and stayed.

***

As the seaplane is leaving behind Paradise Island and I watch it disappear through the discolored window, I imagine my skeptical readers in the future shaking their heads, closing the book, putting it to rest on the coffee table, mumbling:

"What a superlative waste of time! This story is totally apocryphal, a nice tale but not meant to occur in real life."

And they might very well be right! But I encourage those who liked the story – and very much wish for it to be true – to search for Paradise Island in the Indian Ocean, or (why not?) in the middle of any ocean or other place on Earth because:

"One may never know!"

The Soldier

Contributed by Jamie Marincola

"No, that's not him."

"I thought you said he had red hair," her new companion refuted.

"He does, but that's not him."

Daria waited patiently for her love to return. It had been many months since he had last been home and she could hardly wait any longer. Her heart raced every time a new man in uniform revealed himself beyond the security threshold.

"Do you think you'll recognize him?" her chatty acquaintance inquired awkwardly. "I mean, do you think he'll look any different?"

"He'll probably have a nice, scruffy mustache." she responded, "He loves to grow it out while on tour." Though true, her answer was hollow. While waiting for him to come home, she had nothing but his face on her mind. Those slender cheeks, that tender nose, and those hazel eyes wished her goodnight every time she dozed off alone in their queen bed. Moreover, she knew that those cheeks would be even more slender than when they left and that nose would be a crisp brown from its days underneath the Afghan sun. And yet, his change in appearance didn't bother her, not anymore. She was ready for them. The one thing that she never quite could get used to, however, was the change in his eyes. For every month he was gone, untold years accumulated behind those pensive pupils. It was a subtle change that only she could see, but it was unmistakable.

"So, how long have you been doing this?" she asked the woman next to her, trying to be polite.

"Three years now. I make it out every time I can." she paused, but only long enough to start her next sentence. "You know, those soldiers are out there doing God's work, it's the least I can do to be here for them and their families..." she went on, and continued to go on, long after Daria stopped paying attention. This woman was part of an organization that camped out at airports with flags and banners in front of the doors of the International arrivals terminal to welcome home troops from combat. As the wife of a soldier, Daria felt it was her duty to make them feel valued, even when she wanted nothing more than to be alone with her husband.

"There he is," Daria whispered.

The woman paused, despite being at mid–climax in her story about how she once saved her cat from drinking the milk she had spilled. "What was that, dear?"

"It's him!" Daria darted forward towards her husband. When he caught his first glimpse of her, he revealed a hearty, familiar smile. It was not long before they embraced to a huge applause. It was as though the crowd around her felt what she felt; however, she knew that nobody felt how she felt, except perhaps the man in front of her. They pulled apart and embraced once again. "You came home to me," she mumbled aloud.

"And I would have been home sooner," he reflected, "but the pilot refused to go any faster! He had to put on the fasten seatbelt sign and had three of his stewardesses tie me down before I'd stop pestering him!" she laughed at his absurd story while she pictured the fictional stewardesses on top of her frantic spouse.

As they turned toward the exit, Daria nodded to her new friend.

"I hope I didn't leave you with them too long," Jeremy teased as they waved to the onlookers.

"Not at all. I was only an hour away from memorizing the lyrics to that 'U–S–A' chant," Daria teased back.

The reunited couple made their way to the parking lot as they squeezed each other's' hands and exchanged stories. When they made it to the car, Daria paused, "shit, I forgot to pay for parking at the machine."

"Damn it, Daria!" Jeremy retorted. The reaction was impulsive, but uncalled for.

"Sorry, I guess we'll have to endure a little more walking together," Daria apologized sardonically. She started her pace back towards the parking machine. Jeremy was quick to catch–up.

"I'm sorry, I didn't mean it," he fumbled, "I'm just eager to get home."

"So am I, but your snappiness isn't getting us back any quicker. What's wrong, did you not sleep on the flight?"

"Not really," Jeremy reflected. "It was a long trip."

"You only had one layover, not as long as usual."

"No, I mean the whole trip since I've been gone," he paused as though he wanted to elaborate, but instead steered the conversation in a new direction. "I could really go for a good meal tonight. What were you thinking?"

"Ravioli, your favorite!" Daria wanted to probe deeper, but was also a little relieved at the change of subject. Soon, their dinner conversation turned into a celebrity gossip debate followed by a full status update of their friends. "Jenna's pregnant again, can you believe they're having *another* one?"

"Another one? Seriously? *Banana*?"

"Banana" was Daria's genuine reply. Asking and replying with 'banana' was something they had started years ago as a way to indicate that they weren't just joking around, especially since Daria's deadpan humor was sometimes difficult to decipher. Although something along the lines of 'are you serious?' might have had a similar effect, a lot of times it would only serve to escalate a joke. Responding with 'banana' was sacred and could never be broken. It was sort of like a 'pinky–promise', but unmistakably more adult.

"Isn't that three now?" Jeremy continued.

"*Four*! Their oldest is barely out of kindergarten!"

"Jesus, they're going to be outnumbered two–to–one. I don't like those odds."

"It's more like four–to–one since Darren's never around. Jenna says he's working like a dog, but I think something else is up."

"Uh huh," contributed Jeremy, a sure sign that he had swiftly spaced out. Otherwise, he would have been grilling Daria on her suspicions.

"We'll never be like them, right?" she inquisitively declared.

"Drowning in kids?" he snapped right back, "I hope not!"

"I stopped taking my pill." Daria interjected with no hesitation. There was a long, uncomfortable pause. Jeremy could well have spaced out again; however, Daria knew he was contemplating silently. "We discussed this, are you getting cold feet?"

"No." his answer was as uninformative as it was abrupt.

"We're ready." she stated, gaining confidence. "We're *more* than ready. We've got a place, we still have four healthy parents; heck, we've even started a college fund already!"

"I know, it's not that..."

"Then *what*?" Daria was losing patience. They had been planning for well over a year about how this tour would be his last for a while and how it was time to settle down and start a family. After more silence, she tried once again to open up the conversation with, "What's gotten into you?"

"Nothing, I'm ready," Jeremy re–focused. "A hundred percent in. You know that." Jeremy's new zeal felt instantly reassuring.

"Ok." she nodded before letting out a smile. "I'm excited."

***

"Look at the skin around her eyes, you can tell."

"My god, shut your mouth Karen, she just needs a little more sleep," Jenna rebutted. "She looks stunning and, besides, she already told us: *she's not pregnant.*"

"I know that's what she *told* us, but it's been three months since he's been back and I'm telling you, *she looks pregnant.*" Karen hissed back.

"If you're so sure, why don't you ask her again?"

"Ask who what?" Daria chimed in as she entered with a platter of small triangular sandwiches.

After a sudden uncomfortable pause, Jenna was the one to pipe up, "Daria, you would tell us, right? If you were expecting?"

"You kidding? Of course!" Daria feigned shock as though she didn't see this line of questioning coming. "But I told you, these things take time. Not everyone can pop out a kid every year!"

"I deserved that," Jenna withdrew, ashamed to have sunk to Karen's level.

 Meanwhile, Karen tried to contain her maniacal grin while contemplating how to proceed with the questioning.

"I don't understand, Jeremy should be shooting liquid gold! Isn't he one of seven? Baby–making should be in his genes!"

"*Karen*!" Jenna barked as the adrenaline crept up her neck.

"Jenna, it's okay..." Daria was well–accustomed to their dynamic and decided to jump in before Jenna completely lost her cool. "First of all, he's one of *five*. Secondly, you are one to talk, Karen. The closest you've come to getting pregnant is when you hooked up with Davie Jennings while babysitting those poor Palmer kids junior year of high school." The insults bought Daria a little time, but she knew they wouldn't stop until she provided a more robust explanation. "Look, there are some things you just can't force. We've been together for over twelve years, what's a few more months?" Daria explained, as best she could.

"They aren't fucking."

Everyone turned their heads to the corner of the room where Olivia had been sitting quietly, watching the three of them go at it. She had only now stumbled upon something which caught her interest. The ensuing pause was enough to confirm her suspicion. "How long's it been?"

"It's temporary," Daria sputtered. She was taken completely off–guard. "I mean..."

"Not at all since he's been back?" Olivia observed. She was now settling into a role somewhere between facilitator and therapist. "Is the problem physical?"

"Did he get his dick blown off?" Karen couldn't restrain herself. Daria wisely ignored her.

"You don't understand. It's not like he's been off on some business trip: he's been fighting a war. He sees things every day that we've only seen in the movies. It's not like he can just come home and pretend none of it happened, it takes time." Daria reeled off the same script she had recited to herself over and over the last few months.

"So this isn't unusual?" Olivia queried, "Does it usually take time for him to warm up to you after being gone for so long?"

"Well, not exactly." Daria confessed. In fact, it was usually quite the opposite. The extended abstinence usually amounted to an intensified veraciousness in the bedroom. Something was clearly different this time. At first, she questioned whether it was her, if she had changed. She was getting older and felt less attractive, but she knew their bond was powerful enough to endure something as frivolous as a little aging. Then came the more serious concern about how their life paths had strayed and how they might not be as compatible as they once were. They had known each other since the eighth grade and started dating at nineteen. They were children when they fell in love, how could they have anticipated what they were to become?

"Sweetie, it hasn't been that long," Jenna had finally mounted the courage to jump into the conversation again. "After having my last one, Darren and I weren't intimate for almost half a year!"

"Oh, yeah? Then who's the father of this one?" Karen scoffed while pointing at Jenna's protruding tummy. Her attempt at comic relief was again not appreciated by the gallery.

"Have you considered seeking professional help?" Olivia was strictly business.

"Like a doctor? Or, did you mean, a shrink?" Daria questioned cautiously.

"Either." Olivia was content to keep the discussion open–ended.

"No, I really don't think I need that right now. I'm fine. Life is good; my husband is finally home!" Daria could have ended things there, but instead blabbered on, "Besides, I really don't know why you guys are in such a rush for us to have kids, or what gives you the right to march into my house and sit me down for an intervention like I was some sort of junky! *I don't need help!*" She was clearly ready for the afternoon session to be over as she withdrew in silence with her head pointed firmly towards the carpet.

"Honey, I think she was asking for Jeremy." This time, Karen wasn't joking.

Daria paced the family room as she waited for Jeremy to get back. It was completely dark outside now, much later than she expected him to return. He had gone off to the range with a couple of high school friends to teach them a thing, or two, while vacating the house for Daria to play host for Sunday afternoon tea. It had been hours since everyone had left and she had tidied up the place in their wake. Daria knew Jeremy wouldn't be eager to get back for Sunday chores, but she had expected him back for dinner at the very least.

'Be back in an hour. Don't wait up. Luv you.' her phone finally spoke, revealing that it wasn't as functionless as she was beginning to suspect. The relief of knowing her husband was alive and coming home was immediately usurped by a consuming rage fueled by incredulousness and suspicion. She wandered off to get ready for bed and eventually tucked herself in so that she could stare at the ceiling until he got back.

It must have been past midnight by the time he got home. The front door creaked open and closed as the sound of locks and keys got Daria's heart racing. Jeremy made his way straight for the bedroom. Not sure if his wife was awake, he kept the lights off and began to undress.

"Did you go out drinking?" was her first question. She didn't want to give him a chance to spin a narrative.

"No... I mean... we didn't go to Tony's."

"I didn't ask if you went to Tony's. Did you go out drinking?"

"We had some beers with dinner, sure..."

It was enough for Daria. Her tone mixed with his reply simmered in silence and produced the desired effect. He got ready for bed and snuck in behind her. He tried to put his arm around her, but was rejected forcefully. He turned over and joined Daria in staring into the dark.

Eventually, Daria's carefully assembled concoction boiled over and Jeremy could take it no longer. Despite having many minutes to formulate his story, he barely managed to articulate, "I just lost track of time a little bit. We went shooting. They asked to get dinner. I didn't realize how late it was!"

His explanation didn't really mean anything to her as she continued to punish him by not making a noise. For all he knew, she had fallen asleep on him instead of giving him the silent treatment. He wasn't sure which was worse.

"Look," Jeremy went on, "I just needed some time to decompress. I'm sorry."

"Decompress?" Daria was dumbfounded, "*You* need time to *decompress*? Has three months not been enough?!" Any uncertainty about her status of cognition was immediately clarified. "You've hardly had to report to work since you've been back and have accomplished nothing around the house aside from beating your own high scores in God—knows—what game. You've done nothing but 'decompress' since you've been home!"

"I know, I know," Jeremy wasn't in a position to deny any of it. He was searching for any sort of explanation other than the usual, but ended up finding no alternative. "I just need to forget about that place. I need a little time to myself to move on."

"Move on from *what*?" To say that Daria was getting frustrated would be an understatement. She had witnessed and supported Jeremy acclimating from his oversea trips many times, but she had never felt as distant from him as she did now. She had heard terrible stories of death and destruction from him over the years, but hardly anything from his most recent exploits. What could be so bad that he could not even get himself to confide in her?

"Jeremy: I think you need help." Not hearing an immediate response, she continued. "You've always been strong. You've been there for friends who have suffered the shock of war. Now it's your turn to seek support..."

"I don't have PTSD," Jeremy cut her off. She didn't want to label it, but her diagnosis was clear and he was having none of it. "Look, I just need a little more time to decompress. This will all blow over soon, I promise."

At that, he secured the confidence to face the night and shut his eyes. They didn't speak again until morning.

***

"I say fuck them all!" Darren blurted out comfortably while manning the helm of his own dining room table. Jenna buried herself into her wine glass. "They're all a bunch of jokers! What self–respecting person would ever become a politician?"

Daria knew better than to egg Darren on, but Jeremy wasn't going to let the opportunity pass. "And yet, we vote for them every time! How can you not help but to vote for the politician?"

"Ah, ha!" Darren had clearly already thought this through and was prepared with a response. "That's why I don't vote at all! Not since Reagan have I had a reason to vote!"

Jenna swallowed her wine in order to interject, "Weren't you only a baby when Reagan was elected into office?"

"And you weren't even born yet!" Darren seemed to have scripted the entire conversation from the start. "What does that say about our generation that we haven't even had a reason to vote yet?"

"What a shame." Jeremy wasn't going to let this go. "If only Arnold was an American, then we could continue voting actors into office instead of politicians!"

They went on like this well into dinner and through dessert. It was rare that they were all four in town, which was reason enough for Jenna to send the kids to Grandma's for the evening so they could enjoy a grown–up night. Jenna loved to host, but had a hard time luring over friends with four screaming kids roaming the halls. This was their first night alone since their youngest was born. It was also Jenna's first taste of wine for nearly a year.

"Did you need a hand?" Daria offered as Jenna started clearing the table. She got up and soon found herself keeping Jenna company as she started on the dishes in the kitchen.

"You and Jeremy seem so happy all the time, how do you guys do it?" Jenna's inebriation would oftentimes lead to unsolicited compliments. She quickly backed–off remembering Daria's struggles. "I mean, aside from the kids thing, you guys are just so close. Maybe you should forget about getting pregnant, keep things simple!" She was trying to be helpful, but realized she had once again bungled her intent.

It didn't take much for Daria to turn the conversation around. "What about you? Four young kids; how do you manage?"

Jenna put down the glass she was scrubbing and turned towards Daria. The anguish in her face gushed toward her lips. "We don't. *I* don't. Darren manages just fine."

"Oh, I'm sure it's nice to have a stabilizing husband to support..."

"*Support*?" Daria had said the wrong thing. "He manages just fine, but I'm not sure how taking the last lifeboat is supposed to help the captain of a sinking ship!"

"Jenna..." Daria knew where this was going and wasn't looking forward to the outcome.

"I found his condoms." Jenna paused and then continued, *"What the hells is he doing with condoms?"* Tears welled up in her eyes. Jenna wasn't sure where to look, though it didn't matter since she could hardly see anything anyway. She started to collapse within herself while silently weeping. Barely able to keep herself standing, Jenna was saved by Daria who, at just the right time, snapped out of her own stupor to reach out and stabilize her crumbling friend.

"Jenna, it's going to be alright, okay? I'm here for you. We're all here for you." Daria didn't know what else to say. A part of her wanted to know more, but a much larger part of her simply wanted to console her friend who was experiencing so much pain before her.

"I'm going to sleep. I need some sleep. Tell Jeremy goodnight." Jenna made her way toward the back exit of the kitchen. Daria hurried to catch–up and help her to the bedroom. Together, they managed to get Jenna tucked in. Before switching off the light, Daria gave Jenna a kiss on her forehead and a squeeze of her arm. She worked her way back to the kitchen and finished cleaning the dishes before heading back to the dining area.

"I'm telling you, my guy can hook you up! He's gotten me a forty percent return in the last year, over double what the market's done! The guy's a pro." Darren's glass of whisky was half empty, which was enough to merit a refill. He gestured to Jeremy's tumbler, which was still half full, "want some?"

"I'm good," Jeremy stated, waving off Darren who then decided to drain the bottle into his own glass.

"Hey Jer, time to go," Daria had no interest in sticking around and watching Darren clear out his booze.

"Where's that wife of mine?" inquired Darren playfully.

"She went to bed; wasn't feeling well." Daria replied carefully.

"Oh. Well, it was good seeing you. Jeremy, think about what I told you." He got up from the table to escort the couple to the door.

"I will." Jeremy responded, trying to be polite.

"Okay, take care then."

"See ya."

"Good to see you."

"You too."

"Alright then."

"Later."

The formalities were complete and the door was closed. Daria turned toward the car and was followed by her husband who paced after her, asking, "What's going on?"

"I'll tell you in the car, let's get out of here."

***

Olivia was the type of woman whose picture would make any man excited, but whose presence made his dick shrivel up out of fear. Although her existence was proof that she consumed food, it was nearly impossible to find her eating in public. It was for those reasons that Jeremy was both intrigued and terrified awaiting her arrival at *La Pomme*. She had made a lunch reservation for the both of them under the guise of wanting to catch up.

About twelve minutes after their reservation time, Olivia appeared. Despite her apology for being late, Jeremy suspected she was not in the habit of showing up early or waiting for others. The two of them sat down and began with the meal.

Jeremy and Olivia were friends through Daria, but this was their first outing alone. Aside from the expected awkwardness, things were going relatively smoothly. Over drinks, they exchanged commentaries about the waiters' outfits and when appetizers arrived, they moved on to funny stories about their mutual acquaintance. It wasn't until Jeremy's chicken and Olivia's salad arrived that things started to get interesting.

"I think I'm actually more worried for you than I am for her." she said, before even picking up her fork.

"Excuse me?" Jeremy reacted nonchalantly.

"Whatever this is that you're going through: Daria can take it. She's tough. If you want to be coy about it, she'll wait you out. But eventually, you'll break and she'll be there to pick up the pieces. The longer you wait, though, the more pieces you'll shatter into." Her words were direct and her tone pierced right into Jeremy's chiseled armor.

"Listen, Olivia, I appreciate what you're doing here..." He looked up from his dinner, and then looked immediately back down when his face met her staunch scowl, "but there are just some things that happen when you're on tour..."

"Don't give me this wounded warrior bullshit." Olivia wasn't willing to entertain his rhetoric long enough to even let him finish his first sentence. "You're not just scared; you're *embarrassed*. You fucked up, didn't you?"

"Ok, I'm not sure I appreciate what you're doing anymore..." Jeremy was now transitioning into being irritated and defensive.

"Look, Jeremy... I don't care what you did. I just care that you're bringing everyone down with you. Whatever it was, own up to it. If you did something you regret, it's never too late to apologize." she paused. "Even if you have to do it to their family."

Jeremy was silent. His face went from blood red to snow white as tears started welling up in his eyes. He didn't imagine he'd breakdown so forcefully at a stuffy French restaurant, even at the hands of ruthless Olivia. He didn't even attempt to formulate a sentence, opting instead to pick back up his fork and knife and continue prodding his meal.

Ultimately, Olivia showed mercy. "I'm sorry. You know I'm really just trying to help, right? If you want to talk, you know how to reach me." At that, she put forward more than enough cash to cover her portion of the meal, got up, and left.

She hadn't touched the salad.

***

"I'm so sorry, Jenna. I don't know what else to say."

"Then don't say anything else." she replied. Her shock was veiled by furry.

"I don't know what got into me. We just got carried away... I should have never..."

"I just can't believe you would do something like that to me and our family." She looked away, repulsed by the conversation. "Is it love?"

"No, of course not. It was a complete mistake."

"How long has it been?" Jenna inquired incredulously.

"A few months, but not very often."

A long pause ensued. Jenna still couldn't face forward. "I always knew you were rotten, intent on breaking up this family."

"I understand that you're angry, but that's not fair!"

"I decide what's fair!" Jenna exalted, invoking a chilling calm.

"What are you going to do?"

"I'm leaving."

"I'm sorry."

"Fuck you, Karen."

Jenna got up and returned home to face her husband.

***

"The world is fucked." Daria cried after turning off the election coverage on TV. "Is this really what the party has to offer?" Jeremy looked up from folding clothes to shoot her a smile. She went on, "Maybe we should move to South America. We can live in the jungle and not worry about waking up early or paying half a week's salary for a decent meal. I've even been practicing my Spanish!"

"Hell no, I'd never live in another county. You don't know how good we have it here." Jeremy indicated with no hint of sarcasm or satire.

Daria was taken aback. She was clearly joking about moving away, but was then surprised by her husband's firm position. "I didn't realize you were such a patriot, G.I. Joe." she jabbed.

"There's a lot of wrong with this country, but I haven't shed blood, sweat and tears so that I could move to Venezuela."

At this point, Daria simply couldn't tell whether she was being fucked with. "Banana?" she asked.

"Well, *maybe* I'd consider moving to Peru, but only if we can get a llama and live on top of an ancient Incan village." The tension immediately vanished resulting in a childish smirk across Daria's face. Jeremy, too, broke his composure to let out a little laugh. Then once more, things got serious – but this time, there was no joking.

"I shot somebody."

Shifting her tone appropriately, Daria needed to know more, so she responded with, "What happened?"

"It was stupid. We were doing a training exercise where our targets were mounted on a wooden wall. I fired a shot that went straight through and nicked a private in the arm." Jeremy paused shaking his head, still in disbelief.

"How is he?" Daria questioned, afraid of the answer.

"The kid was fine!" Jeremy blurted out. "Got a free trip home. Probably back out in the field already."

"Oh, are you feeling guilty about it?" Daria was grasping at straws, trying to get her head around the cause of his discomfort.

"Not really. However, after the incident, I was temporarily re–assigned to desert duty, pending the resulting investigation."

"Desert duty?" Daria still didn't understand.

"Yeah, it's what we called *lookout* in Tower Charlie. The tower's the only one not connected to the base. In fact, it was a good kilometer outside camp. It had been built back when the base was really just a series of towers on the main road. They built the base around the first two towers, but kept Tower Charlie as a lookout point. Eventually, the road was actually blockaded off by a checkpoint a few miles down the way, making the tower entirely obsolete. However, they kept the post manned as a way to break in the newbies... and punish the troublemakers."

"*You*? A *troublemaker*?" Daria empathized with her husband who must have felt humiliated and alone in the middle of the desert. This was one of many times she wished she could have been out there, by his side, but was instead on the other side of the world, stuck, only wondering what on Earth her husband was up to.

"Not exactly, more like they had nowhere else to put me and wanted to keep me out of the spotlight to let the whole thing blow over. My CO, on the other hand, was in serious trouble for the whole affair. Someone could have died over the makeshift bullshit they had set up." Jeremy kept going, "Anyway, they had us up there for twelve–hour shifts, two of us at a time."

"At least you weren't alone." The meaningless and obvious observation went ignored.

"The days I was up there turned to weeks, then months, as the bureaucracy slowly churned. It was unbearable," he winced. "the boredom was worse than any drill sergeant I had faced at the academy."

"Could you read or nap while the other guy was looking out?"

"Technically, no. We were on guard duty. We got a couple breaks, but had to be looking out the rest of the time."

"So *did* you?"

"Fuck no! It was the most pointless job ever. Pretty much just hung out with whatever poor soldier they sent up with me trying to forget how goddamn hot and muggy it was."

"Sounds terrible." Daria was then struck with a moment of whimsy, "Now you know how I feel when you abandon me for months!"

"Fair enough." Jeremy accepted Daria's reaction to make light of the situation. Of all the things to happen in war, it was a pretty stupid thing to complain about. He wasn't finished, however. "This one day, a particularly long and muggy day, the private I'm stationed with turns to me and..."

At that moment, there was a knock on the door followed by three chimes of the buzzer. Daria and Jeremy glanced at each other and exchanged a look signifying that neither was expecting a guest. "Hold that thought," Daria instructed as she jumped to her feet to respond to the summons.

She opened the door to find a distraught Karen and collected Olivia.

"Sorry to disturb you guys. I know it's late and we could have called, but we were in the neighborhood and thought we'd just stop by." Karen rattled.

"It's alright." Daria was more interested in facts than formalities. "Is everything alright?"

"Probably. We just wanted to come by to see if maybe..."

"Jenna's missing." Olivia chimed in, impatient with Karen's circuitousness.

"Missing? For how long?" At this point, Jeremy was also at the door asking questions.

"We're not sure." Karen again indicated unhelpfully. "Darren said he got home to find the kids all alone."

"Oh yeah? What else did Darren tell you?" Daria inquired accusatorily.

Karen blushed. She then hesitated before responding, "He asked us to try to find her and make sure she's alright, while he made arrangements for the kids."

"Have you tried calling her?" Daria continued, deciding to not belittle Karen too much in this state of emergency.

"Of course," Karen was quick to reply and move on from the uncomfortable topic of Darren. "No answer, goes straight to voicemail."

"We've got a few suspicions of where she might be." Olivia jumped in. "We were thinking if we all go together, we could hit each spot then fan out looking for her."

"Ok, let's go." Daria ran inside to grab her coat while Jeremy threw on some shoes. He almost tripped over his untied laces as they piled into Karen's sedan.

They had been driving around town for a couple hours now. It was nearly midnight and most of them had to be up early for work the next morning.

"Should we call it? Not sure there's much more we can do." Daria was the first to suggest giving up. "She probably just booked a room for the night in some random hotel out of town."

"Darren's already been on the phone with the credit card company and confirmed it hasn't been ran anywhere tonight." Karen piped up. "He's also been in touch with her parents who have no idea where she is either."

"Amazing how you still manage to find the time to keep in touch with Darren during this whole ordeal." Daria jabbed in jest, but also in earnest.

"That's enough." This time it was Olivia who was taking a stand. "Karen fucked up, but she's trying to do the right thing here. We all know this wasn't Darren's first transgression and probably won't be his last. This is something Jenna's got to figure out for herself and we've got to be there for her." She glanced at Karen who was behind the wheel and added, "If she wants us to be."

"Hold on, I've got an idea." Karen hung a quick and unexpected right at the light.

"Willow?" Daria questioned. "Wait, are we going to..."

"Southeast." Olivia snatched the deduction out of Daria's mouth.

"Our elementary school?" Daria's quizzical disposition made its way out of her lips. "Does it even still exist? Don't Jenna's kids go to Saint Joseph's?"

"Yeah, but when we were kids, Saint Joseph's was hardly more than a steeple with a couple of pews. Southeast is where we all met. It's where she met Darren."

"A little dramatic, don't you think?" Daria was startled by Karen's sudden bombast.

They pulled over and all four got out of the car. They hardly had to split up before finding Jenna rocking back and forth on the swing set, staring blankly at the sky. No one said a word. Only one person had the privilege to break the ice, and she was intent on basking in the crisp winter breeze. Finally, she spoke up.

"Remember when we used to huddle inside the playhouse and talk about boys?"

Daria nodded and looked up at the group awaiting a response, then realized there was no one to respond but her. Olivia hadn't moved to the area until high school and Karen was currently much closer to the doghouse than the playhouse, so kept her mouth sealed tight. Daria responded as warmly as she could, "Yeah, of course."

For the first time, Jenna looked down from the sky and fixed her eyes on Daria. "Do you remember when we swore we'd never kiss a boy? That if any of us were kissed by a boy, the other two would be there to get her to the hospital as soon as possible?"

"Yeah, that sounds like us." Daria expressed a grin. Although she didn't really remember, she wasn't about to interrupt Jenna's train of thought.

"Darren's a good person. The kids love him." Jenna was now staring back into space. Her voice was calm and pensive. "He's not perfect, but he pays the bills and treats me right when he's not out and about."

Daria moved to voice a dissenting opinion but Olivia stepped forward instead, "How can we help?"

Jenna looked back down from the stars, this time towards Olivia. "Sweet Olive. Always so serious! Sometimes not even you can fix a problem. This is entirely my cross to bear." She scanned the small crowd and fixed her glare on Karen, who was knocked aback by the unexpected eye contact. "I'm sorry, Karen."

"Sorry?" Karen was shocked. "I'm the one who is sorry. I didn't mean to hurt you, Jenna."

Jenna went on as though Karen's sounds were those of a flea pleading for its life underneath her fingertip. "I'm sorry for you, Karen. The emptiness inside you aches to be filled with validation from anyone who will give it to you. How did it feel when my husband would fill you with validation before abandoning you to sleep with his wife?"

Jenna's unnecessary tirade was beginning to lose her sympathy from the crowd. Daria pleaded, "it's late, Jenna, let's go home."

"*Home*?" Jenna got up from the swing and walked towards Daria, who was now standing directly in front of her. "Where is *home*? No amount of children can veil what that place has become. It's a *prison*."

Daria wasn't dissuaded. "Jenna, come home with Jeremy and me. You can stay with us for a bit."

At this point, Jenna shifted her weight towards the lone male on the playground. "This must seem so silly to you." she sneered to Jeremy. "I'm sure the tragedies you have witnessed make my charmed soccer mom predicaments seem like a dull episode of *Desperate Housewives*."

Jeremy's conspicuous silence was broken by Daria's defensiveness, "You lay off Jeremy. He has nothing to do with this and you don't know the half of what he's been through!"

Jenna turned toward Daria, relieved to finally have some energy to feed off of. She lifted her finger and gestured at her fortified friend, "Oh? And you do?"

Daria was furious that Jenna would go after her and Jeremy, especially at a time when Jenna's marriage was so clearly in shambles. "I may not be out on the frontlines with him, but I can sleep easy at night knowing he's pointing his weapon across enemy lines and not between a woman's legs. Jeremy is suffering from *post–traumatic stress disorder*, he has every symptom in the book. We all need to be there for him as he stands up to this terrible disease."

Again, it went quiet. Even Jenna felt bad for belittling Daria so gratuitously.

"I fucked a dude."

All faces turned toward the startled Jeremy. Not even he could believe what he had confessed. "In the tower, in the desert... I fucked a dude."

Although this was hardly anyone else's business at the moment, Jenna felt a certain entitlement to the evening, and so led with the questioning. "How was it?"

"I don't know, what's it matter?" Jeremy took the opportunity to face away from his wife who was in a state of shock and approached the questioner. "I felt terrible afterwards. Immediate regret."

This time, it was Olivia who chimed in, "Are you gay?" Even she hadn't seen this coming.

"No, I'm not gay. I was just *bored*." Jeremy was getting agitated. He hadn't anticipated telling his wife amidst such a large company, but couldn't let her weave this lie any further. "Look, isolation does some funny things to you. It was never something I had wanted to do... it was just *there*."

"What about the other guy?" Even Karen was gaining the courage of voice. For once, she wasn't the biggest fuck up. "Was he a fag?" Jenna and Olivia shot her a look, which caused Karen to awkwardly backtrack. "Er... I mean... was he *queer*?"

Jeremy had no interest in playing twenty questions, but still couldn't muster the courage to face his wife. "Probably, yeah. It's sort of a don't ask, don't tell thing out there."

"And it was only once?" Karen continued.

"Yeah, of course. Only once." Jeremy insisted. He turned away from the crowd and suddenly, it was only him and Daria. Everything else faded out of view. He would never forget the contorted expression on her face. Every emotion that had built up within her was trying to escape, causing a traffic jam on her brow.

"Daria, talk to me." Jeremy's plea elicited no response. Daria's focus was on something far beyond the man standing in front of her. At this point, Jeremy was inches from her face. He was tempted to kiss her, if for no other reason, to invoke some sort of reaction. "Daria, say something!"

That was enough to pierce Daria's trance. She slowly raised her gaze up to the object before her. Collectedly, she moved her jaw to inquire, "Banana?"

Jeremy closed his eyes hoping the night would end then and there. Outing the truth had done little to assuage his guilt. When he finally had to open his eyes, he was met with the unfortunate reality before him. There was one last thing Jeremy needed to do to cleanse himself of this lingering secret. He leaned forward, put his lips to Daria's ear, and whispered: "Banana."

The Art of Gardening

Contributed by Catterina Coha

When my mother died, a dear friend gave me, according to tradition, a nice vase with a plant. There was nothing special about the plant, and it did not bear flowers, just pleasant green leaves. Separated from my mother's grave by an ocean, it was not possible for me to bring the plant to her. Initially, I did not care that much about this plant, but I grew fond of it with time and ten years later, it is still with me. It does not really grow bigger, but seems to change very little with time. Once, the handle of the vase broke and now, it hangs sloppily on top of it, but this does not bother me, it gives it character. Perfect things are all alike, but they break in unique ways.

Some years ago, in May, the month when my mother was born and died, my little plant produced a single white flower. It was amazing: even though if it was not the most beautiful flower, it was such an accomplishment! Since then, I grew even more attached to the plant. Then, one summer, I went away with my daughter, and for the first time, without my by–then–grownup son. He stayed home with his father. When I came back, just as he was assuring me that they took care of everything, I saw the plant with its beautiful green leaves resting on the floor, lifeless. They forgot to water it. They just did not see it coming because it meant nothing to them.

My son assured me that the plant could be resurrected, that it was not too late, probably equally motivated by the urge to get out of trouble consoling me...and he was right. The plant came back to life, perhaps to symbolize the unwavering nature of motherly love: between my long–gone mother and me and between my forgetful but optimistic child and me.

***

There was a really pretty plant, with lots of flowers, which a lonely man was charmed by. The plant was in an abandoned corner of somebody's garden, and he made an effort, whenever possible, to pass by and look at it. Finally, one day, he thought that he had an opportunity to get it for himself and he took the risk, entered the garden and gently picked it up. The neglected plant thrived in the hands of the man, who for a short while, gave it a lot of attention and care. But with time and watering regularly, the plant became a burden. He still liked it and in those rare occasions, when he was in a good mood, he reminisced happy times and the day he brought the plant home. But most of the time, he was too busy or concerned with more pressing issues that even the little effort of bringing some water to the plant seemed a superfluous distraction. He would look at the plant and, shaking off the unpleasant feeling of guilt, would feel somewhat angry at it for looking "needy," with her leaves bending down. Every time that the thought "I need to water the plant,"crossed his mind, he would promise himself that he would do it the next day but end up forgetting it.

One day, while waiting in the lounge of an airport in a faraway city to board the flight that was going to take him home, the man nostalgically thought about the plant. He reminisced its beauty, and this time, he committed to take care of it as soon as he returned home. He kept thinking about the plant even in the taxi that was taking him to the doorsteps of his house. Right after entering his apartment, he rushed with a sense of happiness and a water–filled jar to attend to the plant. But the leaves were dry; nothing was left of its original beauty. He anxiously watered it anyway, hoping to resurrect it but in the coming days, the water only accelerated the decay of the dead plant.

Hotel Room

Contributed by Catterina Coha

When the alarm woke her up at 6 AM, Madeleine could not think of a good reason to rise from bed. Nothing pleasant was waiting for her that Saturday morning. She did not merely feel tired; she felt an underlying anxiety, and a burdensome feeling of inadequateness pervaded her.

Slowly, she dragged her feet to the bathroom and went into the shower without looking at herself in the mirror. Automatically, her mind was rehearsing the script of the play about the routine of her life: make coffee, put few things in the bag, do not forget the phone charger, get out of the house by 7 AM to make the 7:30 AM train, and so on. The entire daily schedule was planned with tasks to complete during the train ride, meetings and presentations, business dinner and eventually her night alone in an empty room with all the comforts of a luxury hotel, which she profoundly loathed.

The early spring morning was glowing in a clear blue sky and the fresh air felt energizing. Perhaps influenced by an old nostalgic song that was played by the car radio, Madeleine momentarily conceded that she liked her life.

After all, she was busy because she was successful, and she was travelling to so many places in the world just as she had often fantasized in her youth. But the sense of excitement that used to accompany each minor success in the past did not complement even the biggest of successes now. She had become used to failures and setbacks just as much as she was to triumphs, to peaks and troughs seen more as an observer from a distant post.

That same indifference saturated almost everything. She knew that it was important to celebrate accomplishments for those, who worked for her, and she did it in apparent enthusiasm, but deep inside it felt like a play in which she had become proficient as a stage character. In truth, there was no other reward for her soul beyond the recognition that she had survived another day.

While the train was running its course, making all planned stops to reach the final destination on time, it occurred to Madeleine that there was always a choice in life not to follow the predetermined path, not to labor through time to reach on schedule the final destination. Why not get off earlier, at a random station? The unexpected thought felt liberating in the powerful light of the morning sun. The welcoming world out there made irrelevant the worry about the consequences of getting off and about the nature of any haphazard place.

Madeleine's mind quickly ceased wondering when she reached her destination for the day.

Entering the convention center was like entering the scene of a theater. The show was starting and Madeleine almost effortlessly transitioned into her character:

an enthusiastic, energetic, curious and intelligent scientist; and she performed well all day long.

After the business dinner, she had a drink with a colleague. They both needed a break, but a well–controlled one: one drink, not two.

"I have to go finish some work" was the standard parting excuse.

"Me too," replied Madeleine with a big sympathetic smile that looked sincere.

Walking away from the bar, she looked sexy in the black skinny pants, almost teasing, and she attracted the attention of a couple of men who were hanging out at the bar looking for an opportunity. Yet, the message was clear about what Madeleine's confident gait meant:

"Do not follow me."

***

Once in her room, she felt oppressed. It did not happen right away. The view of the downtown skyscrapers glowing in the night was nice but totally neutral, like a picture hanging on the wall. When she was younger, the prospect of colorful big city life outside of the window was associated with excitement, but now it did not even occur to Madeleine that she could have gone for a walk along the beautiful river flowing not too far from the hotel.

Although she was tired, an unsettled anguish prevented her from relaxing and falling asleep. Following habit more than necessity, she sat at the desk and opened her laptop, trying to work. There was a long list of overdue tasks, but she knew that none of them would have been accomplished in the late evening after that long day, when she could not focus to write even the shortest paragraph that could make any sense.

After the botched attempt to work, she looked for a distraction in the room. The coffee was her default choice; perhaps some caffeine would sharpen her mind and make her more productive. With disappointment transitioning into deep irritation, she discovered that the coffee maker was broken. A couple of swearwords later, she opted not to call the concierge, considering that it would be too much aggravation for a cup of bad coffee. To counter the growing anxiety Madeleine opened the minibar, which was congested with all sorts of drinks, including a large variety of hard liquors.

Her first reaction was to close it again; she would be charged a ridiculous amount for opening one of the bottles. And the drink she had at the bar was already giving her a headache. She went to the bathroom to get a couple of pills, forgetting that she had already taken a couple only an hour earlier. She resolved that the only thing left to do was to go to sleep. The big comfortable bed, however, made her feel very lonely; it seemed wasted for a single person. Unable to lie down and relax, she finally decided that for once she would break the rule and take a bottle, have a drink just to get sleepy.

The port wine was smooth and pleasant, and after a large glass, the mellowing power of the alcohol was slowly dissolving some of the walls that kept each compartment in her consciousness sharply separated, and unlocked doors that had been untouched for a long while.

She thought of people she had loved and of one person whom perhaps she still loved. He had reciprocated her love with genuine passion in the brief days that they spent together. They dreamed of plans for the future. His enthusiasm seemed genuine, and Madeleine truly believed him, for it had the power of a commitment. But soon afterwards, it became obvious that he would never make any room in his life for her, a fact that was perfectly rational in a world where even love is subjected to professional standards. It was clear that the priorities were non–negotiable, and that he expected her to feel the same. Madeleine could not hold it against him. It was somewhat silly of her, even childish, to expect something else.

Each glass emptied made it easier to fill the next one, until the whole bottle was gone. But, rather than sleepy, Madeleine felt in a trance, a feeling that was familiar yet unknown. And in the midst of the trance the thought of that morning subtly insinuated into her mind. It had been transformed, however, by the darkness of the night into something quite somber.

It occurred to Madeleine that there was always a choice in life not to follow the due course, not to labor through time to reach on schedule the final destination. Why do not get off earlier, at a random station? Why wouldn't she hop off the train right now? Madeleine reasoned that any station was just the same, just an early exit, to challenge the compulsion of reaching that final destination. Because the final destination with its darkness, which appeared sinisterly luring, was a place where the unsettling pain would be gone; it represented eternal peace sitting in the middle of the maelstrom toward which she was ultimately attracted.

It was not a conscious resolution that drove her back to the minibar, but the plea of ending her pain. In a way, she felt that for the first time in her life she was exercising her own will, rather than following her duty. In the growing fogginess of her mind, a funny thought emerged and made her smile: she could drink the entire stock of liquor and not worry about the cost and the embarrassment of presenting the expense listed in the hotel receipt to the administration for reimbursement. It would not be her problem anymore.

After several glasses of cognac, she sat on the floor, with her head resting on the bed. A blues song was playing in her head, together with blurry snap shots of her childhood, but everything was surreal: any recognizable image and sound was dissolving in a shapeless haze until her consciousness dissolved too.

***

The call caught Juliet by surprise. It had the startling power of changing her life. She realized it immediately, but she could not accept it for a while. The explanation provided by the hospital officer was clear, and Juliet responded on the spot with a composure that surprised her.

After putting down the phone, however, she found herself in a state of numbness, dominated by the desire of reverting to the reality that just few minutes before preceded the ring of the phone. She had experienced this feeling once before, when she was much younger and for the first time had to face an irreparable break in the harmony of life: the sudden death of her father in an automobile accident; that phone call that had shattered the serenity of a perfect day and a perfect life till then like a stone that brutally perturbs a lake's smooth surface in a windless summer day.

She did not allow herself to dwell on her feelings for too long. When her wandering gaze paused on the watch, she swiftly returned to the current status of affaires and concocted an action plan. After all, her sister was not dead "...yet". There may be hope. She needed to get to Chicago as soon as possible, and at least say goodbye to a warm body. The importance of this she had learned the hard way, by feeling the lifelessness of her father's cold corpse, which could not be warmed by any amount of love flowing from her parting hug.

Juliet decided that for the time being she should not inform anybody in the family about the tragic event. As she was accustomed to do, she took it upon herself to worry about the downfall that such news might have on the people close to her, and the least painful way to deliver them. In addition, she needed to protect Madeleine from unfair judgment, whether she would live or die. Making up a plausible excuse, she arranged for a colleague to cover her for the next two days at work. She then ran home, without forgetting to buy the Russian newspaper for her father–in–law and the cereals for her daughter. The feeling of following a mission – a mission dedicated to Madeleine – had a comforting effect. It was like playing a make–believe game, as they used to do in their childhood, and gave Juliet the strength to lie to her inquisitive teenager daughter about the reasons for her urgent departure without raising suspicions.

During the flight, the hum of the engines sung a lullaby for Juliet, who exhausted by the intense day, became drowsy, closed her eyes, and went into a semiconscious sleep, populated by vivid images. She saw the bedroom that she had shared for so many years with her sister, in the house where they grew up. Her desk was a mess, and she was anxiously looking for something important but could not find it, and the more she looked frantically for it, the more the objects, books, papers, brass jewelry and other strange stuff kept accumulating on the desk, making it more and more difficult to look for it. She felt the gaze of her sister: her blue eyes with an ironic expression, looking at her with amused criticism.

The scene then changed abruptly. Madeleine was in a bus next to Juliet, both of them dressed up, going to a party, and there were two boys, who looked familiar next to them. When they reached their destination, they found themselves in an ice skating rink, and Madeleine was helping Juliet get on the ice, holding her hand... and they were much younger, just kids, perhaps eight and six year old. It was snowing, and they were trying to imitate the figure skaters they saw on television watching the winter Olympics. Other girls came, who were friends of Madeleine but did not pay attention to the younger Juliet, making her feel jealous and deserted. But that childish feeling metamorphosed, and Juliet, now an adult, saw a grownup Madeleine parting from her. The ice skating rink became surreal,

CAT BEHIND THE WINDOW

the falling snowflakes were now a fog that swallowed Madeleine, and an imperceptible barrier prevented Juliet from following her sister. She saw Madeleine disappear and in desperation called her, tried to run after her, but to no avail: she could not find her way in the fog, a virtual space that that she could not cross.

The feeling was so powerful that Juliet woke up, her heart beating fast, her consciousness struggling to regain control of reality. Shivering, Juliet feared that perhaps her sister had died just at that moment. Then she tried to convince herself that it was just her fear reflected by the dream. The plane was about to land, and Juliet settled like a soldier resigned to face the inevitable battle he would rather avoid. Soon she walked the path to exit the plane, then the airport, eager and afraid at the same time to reach the hospital and find out the truth.

The fading light of dusk welcomed Juliet to Chicago in a warm late spring night.

***

Juliet sat in the dim light of the intensive care room, staring at Madeleine heartbeat on the monitor, the regularity of which was reassuring. Because of the heavy traffic from the airport, it had taken longer than expected to arrive to the hospital, and the attending physician taking care of Madeleine was gone. Juliet had spoken briefly with two house staff doctors covering the night shift. She had learned that Madeleine arrived comatose at the emergency room early that morning. The diagnosis was "acute alcohol intoxication" because of the high BAC, or "blood alcohol level" as Juliet had summarily learned. Her sister's BAC did not reach the "dangerous" level of above 500 mg/dl associated with risk of death. However, the two young doctors cautioned Juliet that there is a lot of variability among people, and they had just witnessed an amazing recovery in a homeless dude, who had a BAC above 1000 mg/dl. He was a drunkard accustomed to tolerate large doses of alcohol, but her sister did not look like one, so she may be less tolerant.

Juliet's perception of tolerance to alcohol had been shaped by her teenager experiences. In her mind, Madeleine had high tolerance, at least compared to her. Juliet thought of the disastrous nights when she attempted to keep up with her older sister and ended up vomiting just about everything inside her but her soul. She recalled waking up in the morning, feeling lousy and with strings of long hair clumped by dry puke. Madeleine never vomited and would know when to quit, unlike Juliet who would be distracted by people who caught her interest and in whom "she saw more than was there", at least according to Madeleine. But after they had moved on to their adult lives, Juliet and Madeleine had not seen each other often, and Juliet did not feel qualified to express a current opinion about Madeleine's tolerance to alcohol, or anything else, for that matter. It occurred to her that she knew very little about the person who still remained in her heart and mind her closest life companion.

In the long hours spent at the hospital that night, Juliet thought about the unique bond that siblings have. The shared genetics is often redistributed in random ways among the children, giving rise to people who can look either very similar or so different that one would not assume any relationship. Madeleine resembled their mother far more than Juliet, and at least in Juliet's perception, she had always been more beautiful than her. When they were teens, Juliet, striving to catch up with her sister, had grown almost to the same height; they would often dress in identical clothes and pretend to be twin. It was a game, but Juliet deep in her heart, truly desired to be identical to Madeleine.

But more than genetics, it was the memory of early life experiences that merged into a sense of shared fate and identity, into a unique bond. Together they had experienced the oddities of their family, the reassuring sweetness of the happy times, and the anxiety of the unhappy ones, when the parents quarreled or worried about finances or other matters. And given their small difference in age and the fact that Juliet followed Madeleine like a shadow, the two sisters had lived common social experiences: friends and disappointments, boyfriends and betrayals. Facing together the early challenges of life had made it easier, at least for Juliet, who felt that she had an unwavering advocate in her sister. Madeleine, perhaps because of her beauty and sharp intellect, as well as her rank of first−born, grew into a confident and dominant personality. Juliet, on the other hand, born to a world where the spotlight was taken by the sister whom she adored, and naturally more inclined to please than to impose, developed a personality rather submissive to Madeleine.

Memories of childhood kept surfacing from the corners of Juliet's brain that had been put aside in storage for many years. Juliet had been so busy, especially since the birth of her children, keeping up with her own life, and years had passed before she hardly noticed that she had not seen Madeleine more than once or twice. Time contracts and expands in our perception, so that the first twenty years of life occupy the same space as the rest of it, no matter how long that would be. Juliet indulged in recollections of the past, like a rainy autumn day when she saw Madeleine emerging first on the last stretch to win the race. She was so genuinely happy for her sister's unexpected triumph. Madeleine, on the other end, then 11 year−old, swore that she would never do it again; she hated the mud where they had to run. This was Madeleine: the strong−minded and stubborn child that was turning into a difficult teenager, and then into a young woman "in control of everything"!

Madeleine's early teenager years challenged their tight partnership, as Juliet struggled to understand the transformation of her sister. The beautiful large breasts grown on Madeleine's chest were loathed by the girl, causing Juliet to feel lucky and even guilty that her own had not grown as much, a perception that of course would change with time. Madeleine went through a period of withdrawal, during which she appeared to be fighting with nature over the control of her own body. She often refused to go out, gained weight by eating chocolate all day long, then lost it, becoming almost anorexic. Poor Juliet was so concerned about her sister that she had no time to worry about her own physical transformation. For the first time in her short life, she had to get her own friends, as Madeleine had none anymore. The more Madeleine refused to ski, skate, run, swim and do all of the activities that they used to do together, the more Juliet became active, to compensate for her sister inactivity. The high school gym teacher loved Juliet: one year when there was a shortage of girls involved in track and field, she had Juliet compete on all possible games, taking advantage of the inability of Juliet to say no.

But in her late teens, the intelligent Madeleine emerged from her fight with nature as a winner. Struggles are necessary to give depth to our confidence and test the sturdiness of our resolve. Madeleine's confidence grew, fueled by her academic success, and the acceptance of her body gave her a new sense of power, realizing that she had become a beautiful young woman. However, she rarely found satisfying relationships, despite the many suitors. Her high standards, challenging intelligence and intransigence made it difficult for her to find a mate that she admired enough to fall in love. On the other hand, Juliet was tolerant, adaptable, energetic and keen to please, and such a comfortable partner that her boyfriends would never want to leave her, and she had to scramble out of relationships she had grown tired of. As time passed, Madeleine left home to study at the university and became absorbed by her passion for science and a successful but demanding career. Juliet, who was equally intelligent and successful in school, gave up potentially more rewarding jobs to accommodate the needs of the man she eventually married.

Juliet's thoughts slowly dissolved in a dreamy haze while her eyes closed, and she fell asleep, her chin resting on top of her crossed hands resting on the back of the chair near the bed where Madeleine was still fighting for her life.

Madeleine was sitting in her office, overlooking the East river, shades lowered to reduce the light coming through the windows. She was looking attentively at graphs and numbers that were flowing through the screen of her computer, trying to find an answer to a puzzle. But each time she saw a glimpse of a solution, the screen would change; new shapes, colors and numbers appeared, and she had to start over and over to try to make any sense of them.

She knew that there was a clue, somewhere: a clue to the portal that she was looking for. She had been searching for it for so many years since the first appearance of the clue that had come in a dream: a memorable dream that she had a few days after her father's funeral. The portal was the path to her father, who was now secluded in a parallel world, inaccessible to her. In that auspicious dream he would be able to communicate with Madeleine and let her know about that secrete passage to his world.

Years had passed since that dream, but she felt that now it was the right time, her chance to find the portal, her chance to visit her father. Driven by the intellectual challenge like a chess player, she pursued the goal with unfettered focus and with lucidity blocking any distraction. She had never reached such absolute concentration before, and she was aware that something strange was happening to her, but her own personal circumstances did not concern Madeleine more than such. She was unaffected by the sense of frustration that grows when we repeatedly fail despite increased efforts, and kept analyzing screen after screen, image after image, for what must have been a very long time, an immeasurable time. As living creatures, we measure time according to our needs, to eat, to sleep. Madeleine, however, did not feel hunger or tiredness.

Suddenly, the clue came in the shape of a plane. It occurred to her that the key to the portal was embedded in an old science fiction movie that she had watched a long time ago. This was the clue from her father! Unfortunately, when she woke up in the morning, only the vivid recollection of the dream was left, within which she could not remember the title of the movie. Oddly, no other person could remember ever watching such movie, although she was sure that she had watched it with some of her acquaintances.

But now all was clear. Triumphantly, Madeleine recalled that in the movie, the plane accidentally went through a portal to make it to the other side while the passengers were asleep.

Suddenly, she was no longer in her office. She was walking on a strange, hostile planet, over a rocky desert. Like in the movie, crevasses would suddenly appear, forcing her to jump aside to avoid falling in. Then she encountered the monsters: mechanical monsters that destroyed everything in their path. Madeleine did not experience fear; her analytical mind was driven to remember every action that the characters in the movie performed to overcome the monsters. She knew that the hostile planet was an anti–world that she had to cross to reach the parallel world where her father was waiting. After making it through the last challenge, she found the passengers whom she remembered from the movie. They were ready to board the plane, eager go through the same portal to return to Earth. But Madeleine was determined to proceed to the parallel world that she had come so far to reach. One of the stranded people seemed to understand how the portal worked. To go back to their compatible world, they had to cross the portal while asleep. Although there was no guarantee, being awake would probably lead to the parallel world Madeleine was seeking, but nobody knew if there would be a chance to return from there.

Like a movie director, Madeleine produced the script for the next scene. She should pilot the plane and keep an oxygen mask on to stay awake while she dropped the oxygen pressure in the cabin to make everybody else on board fall asleep. The switch was programmed to restore oxygen levels immediately after crossing the portal, so the real pilot would then take control while she would have disappeared, just like it occurred to the character in the movie whose role she was now replacing.

It all happened swiftly. Madeleine was now flying in a space without boundaries, and in the distance she saw a young man in a suit and tie, standing on top of a monument with a confident relaxed stance, one hand in the pocket of his trousers. He seemed to be looking towards her, and his features were familiar, but the image was blurry. Madeleine recalled her mother telling her that her husband had come to visit in a dream right after his death in the appearance of the young man he had been when they married. With amusement and anticipation, Madeleine approached the man. She looked into his eyes to recognize the warm loving eyes of the old man she knew as her dad the last time she had seen him, few months before the accident that took his life.

Communication did not need spoken words in the parallel dimension of memories. Their physical forms had somehow vanished but thoughts and feelings were present and intense. Madeleine felt comfortable in this place outside of the physical reality of the living. She revisited all of her past life, feeling free and open to a dad who had been at times strict and demanding but never judgmental. The dad had a new respect for his adult daughter and admiration for her accomplishments. It was like continuing a conversation abruptly interrupted fifteen years before; that was how long ago he died! In fact, in their last phone exchange, Madeleine's dad had asked if things were good with her. It was not the usual predictable question. Instead, the dad seemed genuinely concerned and wanted to be reassured before leaving for a far away trip that his children were capable to take care of themselves, as if he intuitively knew that he would soon die.

Now he was proudly pointing out that she had accomplished far more than he had in his lifetime. In his youth, full of hopes and energy, he had dreamed of accomplishing something great. He bred rabbits and sold them to pay for his education past elementary school. Grounded by an unbreakable sense of duty, respect and love for his parents, he never deprived them of the support that his work away from the farm was bringing, or the help he could give in the fields when he would return home. His intelligence and initiative eventually landed him in the city where he started his own business and built a family. And adventures in the free time were exclusively devoted to field trips back to his root in the countryside, where he would make up fun stories for his young children. Madeleine still remembered them fondly.

He mingled wisdom to drollness within his stories... and he taught her that knowledge, not material goods, was the outmost attainment, as nobody could take it from her no matter what adversities and instabilities could supervene. Madeleine had followed that advice passionately, but lately she started to doubt the significance of what she was doing. Were her lofty goals corrupted by the pervasive hypocrisy of successful politics, her work just an empty chess game driven by the ambition to win? Her dad could not possibly judge the importance of what she was pursuing, but his advice to her was to be honest with herself:

"We cannot always be right, but we can always be honest, and while it is sometimes necessary to lie to others, we cannot lie to ourselves. This is why I loved mom so much," he said with affectionate humor. "She was like clear water: when she was caught taking the last piece of cake, she would feel so guilty that she was unable to make up any excuse... not for lack of creativity, she just could not hide from others what she could not hide from herself."

He continued, "As you know, Maddy, this made life difficult for all of us, as her criticism was sometimes abrupt and unfiltered, and..." he paused, "she was not always right, but she was always damn honest!"

That intimacy of the family's memories, spiced by her dad's benevolent sense of humor, was sweet and healing for Madeleine's brittle soul. She realized that her biggest doubt was not about the worthiness of her professional accomplishments and goals, rather about the choices she had made in her personal life. She felt lonely. Her dad understood her pain and explained that her expectations of sharing her soul with a mate were unrealistic. She was too intelligent not to know this, but had never accepted this imperfection of human beings.

Despite his love for the wife and the children, he confessed that he had been alone for most of his life, but this did not prevent him from enjoying deeply the occasional connections he could develop with others. Sharing years with his wife bore several memorable moments when companionship could be felt. And then, it was also entertaining to share just a few moments with a fellow passenger met in the train, or a conversation with acquaintances as they dropped in the evening for an aperitif at the neighborhood café. Finding commonalities, small and big, with all sorts of people gave flavor to daily life and a momentary illusion of companionship that bore its own value. Madeleine's mistake was to perceive as worthless the simple pleasure of sharing a bit of oneself with others, no matter how insignificant they may be. In the absence of deeper connections, she missed the pleasures of the simple presents of life.

Madeleine admired her dad's wisdom; this was what she had missed more than anything else since his death. It was so nice, so reassuring to communicate with him. She felt relaxed for the first time in the fifteen year as orphan.

"And Maddy," she heard him say, "do not forget that you have Juliet."

***

Tears were pouring from her eyes, not from sadness but from the relief of letting go her defenses.

She felt a caressing hand on her hair, light and gentle.

"Don't forget that you have Juliet," she recalled.

***

"Maddy, Maddy, can you hear me?"

Madeleine opened her eyes and saw Juliet's face. She was bending over to look at her, with an expression between joy and disbelief.

"Maddy? Are you here? Are you awake? Can you hear me?" Juliet was now talking louder and louder with excitement.

"Yes, Juliet, you do not need to scream."

Juliet smiled and asked her:

"Maddy, where were you? The doctors could not understand why you would not wake up..."

***

Two years later, in a hotel room in Chicago,

Madeleine was sitting at the desk, but she was not working. The room lights were off, and the room was illuminated only by the glow of the surrounding skyscrapers that came through a beautiful glass wall window. The candid rays the full moon, which dominated the sky with a cold hue, entered the room to highlight the contour of a person sleeping in the bed.

Madeleine was holding a glass of white wine, sipping it slowly, avoiding any noise that could disturb the sleeping companion. The memory of her past binge drinking was surfacing. Despite the awfulness of that moment in her past, she looked sadly at the cabinet filled with liquors, which was there, in the room like in any other hotel room, to tempt its guests. Madeleine did not long for alcohol; she had almost none in the past two years, and it did not take much effort to stay clear. But she had a deep desire to go back in time, not on account of the death wish and for the loneliness of that dark moment, but rather for the joy that she had experienced in her dreams and most of all, for the delight of seeing Juliet sitting at her bedside when she had opened her eyes.

Madeleine reenacted the events that had followed, as to make sure to never forget any details about her sister, her expressions and her voice.

After leaving the hospital, Madeleine spent a few days at Juliet's place. The small apartment was a bit messy but colorful and welcoming, and the crowded Russian neighborhood, where Juliet had moved with her husband years earlier to be closer to the ageing father–in–law, shared the same characteristics. Juliet liked it and decided to stay there even after the separation from her husband, who was vexed by the place and preferred to go to the quiet suburbs. Madeleine had been there before, but never appreciated the good sides of it, letting her be distressed by the inconveniences of the place. Now, "rebooting" the spirit after two days spent in a coma, her attitude had changed.

The two sisters spent hours chatting and sipping coffee in the kitchen, while Juliet was preparing an old family dish that they did not have since childhood. It was improvised, like many things Juliet did in contrast to the careful planning and perfect organization of Madeleine. But it came out fine, seasoned by laughter, which was pouring spontaneously and almost uncontrollably from Juliet and Madeleine, who were both exhilarated by having survived the dangerous event. Laughter is contagious, and soon the thirteen–year–old Svetlana came to join her mother and aunt.

"Svietka," ordered Juliet sweetly, "please set the table".

The young girl sighed but obeyed, looking inquisitively at the two women, sensing that there was something unusual beyond the sudden appearance of the aunt in her home.

"Hey Maddy," she asked her aunt with a slightly impertinent tone.

"You aren't usually this fun... What happened to you? Did you win the Noble prize?"

Madeleine smiled and quickly replied in an amused tone:

"No, Svietka! I leave that task to you!"

As a response, Svetlana showed the tongue to Madeleine in a sweet, childish way, and they both smiled.

The dinner was nice and the simple food seemed so much more appetizing to Madeleine than the sophisticated cuisine she had at restaurants around the world in her business trips. Svetlana had to go to sleep early because it was a school night, and the two sisters were left alone in the late hours after a long day.

"You know," Madeleine said, "I could not help but notice how Svietka spontaneously organized by color the napkins and the little forks, and..."

"Yes," Juliet interjected, cutting off her sister as if she could not hold the words any longer. "She looks so much like you! Perhaps not physically; her hair is dark like mine, and she has the eyes of her father... but it is her behavior. I sometimes think that she is more like you than me..."

Juliet paused, and then continued in a reassuring tone, "Nothing bad. She is super–smart in school, like you, she gets all top marks."

"But," Juliet continued after another pause, "I must confess that I am a little concerned about the way she is taking puberty... remember what a mess you were?"

"Oh yes, sorry..." was Madeleine's answer, and feeling an impulse to be useful, she added,

"Maybe I can help her."

"Yes, if think you could," replied Juliet, and went on to explain how Svetlana was missing her brother who had gone to college. He was sort of a second dad for her, given that the actual dad was not much part of the girl's life.

"You are the determined, assertive person," explained Juliet, "whom she needs, and I am not."

***

In the following months, Madeleine managed to find the time to visit Juliet more often than she had ever done. She invited Svetlana to visit her research lab, and sparked an interest in science in the soon–to–be high school freshman. But the best time they had together was a short vacation in Italy. An old colleague and friend of Madeleine let her use a house she owned in the hills of Tuscany. Madeleine had been there a few times, the last time with the man she had loved and perhaps still loved: the man she was thinking about on the fateful night of her acute alcohol intoxication.

Madeleine loved the place, but after that romantic relationship ended, she could not go there again, but with Juliet's family with her, there was no more sadness, no longing for a lover. Madeleine felt happy and meaningful. They went there with the two kids in late summer, just before Victor had to go back to college.

There was a piano in the house that Victor played, and they all sang old songs in the evenings, when the air of the darkening valley was rising to refresh the hot hilltop. The sun was retiring behind the silhouette of the far away mountains, leaving a last present to the clouds by dressing them for the evening in an intense orange hue.

One morning, after dropping off Svetlana and Victor at the beach, the two sisters were driving towards a little town in the hills to do some shopping. For the first time Juliet felt the urge to ask the question that had been lingering in the back of her mind since the night spent in the hospital at Madeleine's bedside.

"Maddy, can you tell me why did you try to kill yourself? You pretended that it was a mistake, that you were exhausted and sleep–deprived and had made accidentally some bad decisions, but I know that it is not true."

Madeleine sighed and replied with a resigned tone.

"I know that you were going to bring it up sooner or later..."

And after a long silence, she continued:

"You may not believe me because, like everybody else, you have idealized me as a perfectly balanced and self–confident person, who always knows what to do."

Juliet tried to protest, but was quickly stopped by her sister who continued:

"I felt tired of life, but I guess not the way depressed people do. I was tired of having created a trap for myself, in which everybody expected for me to be strong and rational all the time, and ...

"I wanted to scream, to let out a huge pile of feelings that I could never openly express."

Madeleine paused for a minute, and then she continued:

"But, I just did not know how to do it."

"So?" asked Juliet softly.

"So, so, so..." replied Madeleine, "so I rebelled for once and did not follow the script, did something outrageously stupid, and what is worst is that I did not have the courage to face it, so I tried to make it... hmmm, final..."

Madeleine, who was driving, turned towards Juliet for a moment to check her reaction. Juliet was pensive, looking at her hands like if there was something interesting there that attracted her attention away from Madeleine's confession. Then she said:

"Well, Maddy, I am relieved. You are still the same person I have always known."

"What do you mean?" asked Madeleine, caught by surprise by her sister's reaction.

"I mean that you simply rebelled against the trap, and I disagree that this was cowardly. I think it takes courage to accept death."

Then Juliet's tone changed into a more cheerful one. Her voice went up an octave, and she declared:

"But I am so very happy that you screwed up. You did not succeed in making it final!"

***

In a hotel room in Chicago, two years later

Madeleine's memories of the time in Tuscany with Juliet and the children were so vivid that for a moment she forgot the present. A groan coming from the bed brought back reality abruptly. After checking to make sure that the person lying in the bed was still in a deep sleep, Madeleine finished her glass of wine and sat in the bed. Aware of all she would have to take care next morning, she was hoping for some sleep. But when she closed her eyes her mind went back to the unfinished business: remembering the sequence of events that followed the vacation with Juliet in Italy.

In our life, there are days that stand out from the background noise of daily routine and of those days each detail remains forever sculpted in our memory. October 29 had been such a day. On that day Madeleine was riding the subway, looking distractedly at the ads in front of her. One carried a sentence written in glowing letters

"When diamonds do not last forever" advertised a divorce lawyer.

Next to it there was an ad about bankruptcy, followed by another one directing toward the agency to contact on the verge of homelessness, and showing a woman with a sad expression while holding the hand of a small child. Madeleine wondered if the person, who put up the ads, wanted to suggest that divorce brings to bankruptcy and eventually to homelessness. Usually the ads in the subway cars were about fruit–flavored juices or home–delivery food services. This unusual disaster–focused sequence made her think of an Italian college friend, Carmela, who would have commented with her thick accent and wide–open vowels:

"What a Jella[2] these ads!" probably followed by a couple of colorful dialectal curses that most likely Madeleine would not be able to fully understand but that sounded passionately hilarious. Madeleine, of course, did not believe in luck, good or bad, but the thought of Carmela made her smile, and she felt the urge to move to a different spot in the car, facing more mood uplifting ads. Unfortunately, the ads were foreshadowing a somber conclusion of that day.

Several small aggravations had lined up Madeleine's morning at work. One had a bigger impact on her mood. It was an unsolicited gossip from a colleague about Madeleine's former lover. The man she still cared for was going to marry his secretary, with whom he had a secret relationship for many years.

Madeleine did not have the energy to sort out the complexity of the feelings elicited by such news. Nevertheless, a deep disappointment controlled her mood.

---

[2] Italian slang word suggesting bad luck

Although she had the discipline to be rational and not to expect anything from this man, deep in her heart the feeling of love for him had been a pleasant companion for years, enriching her life. Now she would have to dissociate from the news, so that the feeling could stay pure and beautiful, while the object of it suddenly appeared so inadequate. He had plunged in mediocrity, unworthy of any interest: just another self–centered middle–aged man skilled at the art of seduction, incapable of being honest and settling for a care–taker as he aged. For a brief moment, Madeleine conceded that the man she had fallen in love with never existed; it was a creation of hers, and she was the one to blame, not him, for the inevitable disappointing endings. Then she thought that perhaps the faceless secretary was an exceptional woman... but no, she had actually seen her once, a pretty dull person... go figure! Her storm of thoughts was interrupted by the sharp sound of the Google meeting reminder, and she refocused her attention on getting ready for an important discussion in the five minutes left.

The sense of irritation did not fade as the workday was approaching its end, and was still shaping Madeleine's reactions, when she received a call from Juliet in the late afternoon. Juliet wanted to talk about something, but was not getting to the point, which was probing Madeleine's patience.

"Sorry, Juliet, I have to finish some work. Can you tell me what are you calling me about?"

The rude tone of Madeleine elicited a confused statement by Juliet, whose voice was shaky and sad, reaching more than her words into Madeleine's heart, thus changing her irritation into concern.

"I am sorry, Juliet. Do not mind me. I just had a bad day. Please tell me what is going on right now? I do not want to wait until tomorrow... work can wait."

"Well, it is that..." said Juliet shakily, "I have cancer, and it is a bad one."

***

It was indeed a particularly aggressive and relatively rare form of breast cancer, showing up suddenly and without a discernable reason, no family history, and no risk factors. Juliet was just a statistical accident, as several cases of cancer are; somebody has to make them up. The ordeal challenged Madeleine's perception that substantial progress had been made in the treatment of cancer. All of the discoveries made by Madeleine and her colleagues that looked so meaningful, so important, so close to the cure of cancer, now were dwarfed by the realization that she could do nothing to help the person she loved, her little sister.

Excessive rationality can turn into an enemy in these circumstances, and Madeleine, who became the optimistic captain of a sinking ship carrying Juliet's family, abandoned it. She turned into the cheerleader, mastering at her best the difficult art of infusing hope without deceiving. One day, after a visit to her physician, Juliet went home with Madeleine. The doctor was a good and warm person; he had tried, perhaps too obviously, to be optimistic. Juliet, who was seating quietly in the passenger seat of the car, suddenly broke the silence by singing, with a voice that was weak but still beautiful, a phrase from *La Traviata*:

"Oh bugia pietosa, ai medici e' concessa[3]"

This was Juliet's favorite opera, and she knew it by heart. Art is more helpful than medicine when life gets really hard. It provides the only way to cope with tragedy without losing the best part of our own humanity. The words sang by Juliet revealed that Juliet was fully aware of the fact that she did not have much time to live without the need for more trivial and painful explanations. Juliet started to plan for the future of her children without her. The first concern was Svetlana, who was still minor.

When the two sisters arrived at Sergei's house, Juliet's former husband was standing in the porch, waiting for them, with a golden retriever lying at his feet. Seeing Juliet the old dog immediately went to welcome her, showing in any possible way his affection. Madeleine could not help noticing how lucky the dog was compared to the man, unable to show the love that he still felt for his wife. He was standing firm in an effort to withhold the tears that he believed would make everybody uncomfortable.

The man who had always been so critical of everybody now was visibly hurt by Juliet's request that Madeleine be the guardian of Svetlana after her death. He felt that this was another way for Juliet to show distrust, lack of confidence in him, unwillingness to understand him. But in the end Sergei had to concede that, although he loved his daughter very much, he did not know what to do with a 14–year–old girl. An acceptable compromise was attained, and they parted, having missed the last opportunity to absolve the past.

***

The trip to Chicago had been initially a trip of great hope. Madeleine succeeded in getting Juliet enrolled in a clinical trial of a new treatment, one that had shown unexpected great results even in advanced cases. A relentless advocate for her sister, Madeleine had leveraged all of her knowledge, all of her connections to fight for her. Even Juliet seemed to have recovered some energy, perhaps because she was so happy to see Svetlana looking cheerful, blooming with the contagious energy of youth. Together they celebrated Svetlana's 15th birthday in that hotel near the hospital.

Ironically, Juliet was in the same hospital where Madeline had been wearing off her intoxication just two years earlier. Now Madeleine was sitting at Juliet's bedside.

One evening, Juliet confessed her fear of death.

"I imagine it as a dark tunnel, cold and dark, and bare and lonely. The only place where death seemed not only acceptable, but almost inviting, was Tuscany…"

Juliet continued as in a reverie:

"…The warmth and beauty of the landscape, those immortal hills gave me the strange desire to fuse with earth, to join the thousand of souls, who lived and

---

[3] The charitable lie is the privilege for doctors

loved and created in that land before me... I guess that if I was buried in such place, I would not feel lonely."

***

Madeleine dozed off, and it took her a while to understand where she was and return to the hard reality: her sister had died that afternoon. Victor asked to be left alone with his mother for the night. Madeleine had spent the evening trying to calm down Svetlana and help her deal with the unbearable pain, the anger, the despair, until the exhausted girl had also fallen asleep.

Madeleine gently caressed the long brown hair of the girl lying in bed near her. Then she closed her eyes. She had a mission the next day: taking Juliet and her kids for a last trip together to Tuscany, to bury Juliet in a place where she will never feel lonely.

The Box

Contributed by Catterina Coha

Suddenly, the realization that there was no urgent matter to deal with felt strange. Joseph searched in the corners of his mind to make sure that nothing was forgotten. The car needed inspection, but it was not urgent and, strangely, this irrefutably critical responsibility that had triumphantly taken priority before in his mind at the top of any list did not seem that important anymore.

He inspected the house, searching for misdeeds he could feel proud to discover and find satisfaction by blaming somebody for them. But the housecleaner (how bad she was, he could not believe it!) had not been there for a while, and there were no toys, books, jackets or socks lefts around, where they should not have been, by the children or by his wife.

The house was empty. This was not the first time that Joseph found himself alone. It had happened almost every summer, but for the first time, he felt that he had lost a sense of purpose. In the past, when his wife and children were gone, he usually had no trouble justifying the undeniably important reasons why he could not go with them, and running between work and taking care of home repairs could fill the time sufficiently with worries that left no time for anything else, not nostalgia for the family.

Sensing a growing sadness that evolved into regrets and even an uneasy perception of guilt, Joseph reacted instinctively the way he had been primed to react in his early youth, when his body and pride were threatened by a gang of street boys searching for a victim to drown their own dreadful sorrow in racially fuelled hate. He fought back, with the determination needed to survive in a hostile environment.

Quickly, he reassured himself that he was a blameless man, that he had always done what was important for the family, despite being little appreciated. Of course, his wife spoiled the children, with her excessive understanding and forgiveness while applying a dismissive attitude towards him. Thanks God, they still turned out to be good people! It was largely because of his determination to take upon himself the difficult job to always tell them the truth when they were not doing well enough. Joseph even felt in reassurance even a subtle feeling of heroism.

Like almost every boy, Joseph always wanted to be a hero, and this is what motivated him to get others' attention and admiration: whether it was for drinking more than others, seducing girls, telling the funniest jokes, or withstanding the pain of a wound without leaving the battlefield during the war. The quick rewards of immediate popularity had been inebriating and consumed to some degree his talents in youth, but did not distract him from pursuing the ambition of a serious career. He was accepted in the best schools and universities, and graduated successfully.

But adulthood was not as easy, and success became a moving target creating a growing sensation that he was back into confronting a hostile gang, this time bigger and more vicious than the street boys, a mix of hypocrisy and unspoken social rules that he could not grasp, or simply refused to care for. Rather than trying to understand what was wrong, Joseph reacted to growing disappointments by retracting into a personal shelter and preparing to fight back. Living with a perpetual sense of being in combat, he ended up shaping much of his relationships accordingly. He had no inclination to make new friends, and no time for old ones; he was mostly in hiding. His priorities were clearly set: there was no distraction worthy of letting down his guard. Joseph felt almost as if everything else had to be postponed until the end of his personal war for the conquest of his ambitions and preservation of his self−esteem.

In the meantime, children had grown and were living lives about which he knew very little and about which he rarely wondered. Joseph reckoned that he was busy with critical tasks, and everything else was going to be taken care by others. Of course, he had done a few important things for the family, and his wife could take care of the other trivial details. It was annoying that she did not seem to recognize his undeniable contributions.

Lost in these thoughts, Joseph did not realize that the sun was setting down on that autumn day until it was dark. At this time of the day, he was longing for companionship, to share a glass of wine and have some food on the table. His wife had fulfilled at least this need for a long time, despite the frequent and sometimes unbearable bitching. He had often felt irritated by her lack of satisfaction, her incomprehensible unhappiness. Joseph did not quite know what the hell she wanted from him, and did not give too much importance to her changing moods, as soon as he felt sure that she was there, that he had a wife.

He was confident that he loved her and this was good enough for him. He had avoided pondering the question whether she loved him. After all, she seemed so committed to the family, and he did not mind letting her go on vacation with the kids and her siblings' families.

They liked to travel and be outdoors, and he was happy not to be dragged into these foolish activities. He recalled how the children would annoy him with their enthusiastic and chaotic stories about lizards peeing in their cousin's hand, jumps into the sea from the rocks or hikes to the top of a mountain. Joseph's window on the world had been narrowing down, over the years, to the size of his computer screen, where he spent hours reading and watching what was happening out there to see what people were doing. He would find there such interesting things that he sometimes felt the urge to share them with his wife. This was often unrewarding as she would barely look at him and keep running up and down the stairs with laundry in her hands, or tell him it was getting late and she had to prepare dinner.

There were still happy times when they had some real conversation, often when the whole family sat down for dinner and the children were active participants. Joseph would get everybody's attention with his stories about youth adventures;

he knew that he was a good storyteller as he had in the past successfully entertained many audiences. But other discussions about decisions and problems of the moment would usually end up in disagreements, if not quarrels. So Joseph preferred not to discuss most decisions with his wife, but just decide by himself and often he did not bother informing her.

Now Joseph was feeling really hungry. It was late, and he was appalled that his wife was not home yet to prepare the dinner. Where did she go anyway? He recalled that she was trying to talk to him that morning, but sensing that it was an unpleasant matter he had told her briskly that he had no time to listen to nonsense, a trick that usually avoided him the aggravation.

He called her cell phone, just to discover that "this idiot" forgot it at home! She *could not* call him to let him know that there was a problem.

"Maybe she had a car accident!" He started to panic. After more time spent reviewing all possibilities that he could imagine, Joseph decided to call the police to ask if there were any reported accidents in the area. There were a couple but clearly unrelated. Becoming restless, he walked down to the garage and was astonished to find that both cars were there. He was relieved that obviously the cars were fine, since he would have been the one to take care of fixing them. But how did she go? She liked to walk, but all day? And where? Surely, one of her stupid friends must have picked her up, and they probably were late chatting or having coffee somewhere.

Joseph's wife had a couple of chatty friends, who unfortunately were such bad cooks that he hated to be invited for dinner at their premise. Joseph had told his wife many times that it was not fun but agony for him, but she selfishly did not care and insisted on having some sort of social life. Joseph considered calling one of the friends, but was unsure about what to say, if his wife was not with her, it would be embarrassing. Calling the husband? He did not have a particularly good relationship with him either; they could have a laugh together, but had never discussed personal issues. While Joseph was pondering if and who to call, additional time passed, and now it was decisively late enough to realize that there was surely something wrong. A dreadful feeling was growing inside of him, and he walked to the bedroom to get the phone, determined to ask the police to start a search. A noise in the heating system, probably some air bubbles, attracted Joseph's attention and made him turn his head towards his night table. It was then that he noticed the box.

It was made of a nice polished wood, with golden corners and a few hand–drawn music notes in the front. Joseph recognized it immediately as one of those old music boxes that were popular when he was a child, and often part of the artifacts you'd find in the living room of a nice home in his natal town. Without thinking, he opened it, expecting a graceful ballerina to start dancing to some soothing tune. He was surprised to see instead the statuette of a faceless woman, turning around while a dissonant tune played. The statuette was holding a piece of folded paper, carefully stuck under one of its arms. Puzzled, he carefully pulled the paper out, and unfolded what appeared to be a hand–written note. It was from his wife:

"When I met you more than twenty years ago, you once confessed to me that you would have liked to keep me in a beautiful box, like a precious jewel. I was so naïve then that I thought it flattering and inconsequential, but I was wrong. You clearly meant it; I have been not a real person, but just a decoration for your own ego. Living in a box has not been easy or rewarding, and my feelings have become so inharmonious, that I have to get out of it."

At first, Joseph felt a surge of contrasting feelings rising, and soon enough they were dominated by anger.

"She went mad! What is this absurdity? How did she find the time to get this box? What is this garbage that she made up, about a jewel? She is mad and trying to stick it on me, like it is my fault!"

He walked to the kitchen, cut a slice of bread and ate it voraciously. The next day, he went to work, still angry, believing that it was just one of his wife's scenes and she would come back eventually. But as the days went by and she did not come back, did not call, did not write, Joseph felt abandoned. He had to face the reality of making his own coffee in the morning, buying food, preparing meals, doing laundry, and paying bills. It was unfair to be abandoned like this, after all these years, after all he had done. Somehow he did not worry about her; he was sure that she was with friends or relatives, but was too disgusted and offended by her behavior to go search for her. Surely she would come back because she needed him.

In the next year, unavoidable practical issues forced Joseph and his wife to communicate directly or indirectly with each other. Joseph was eager to give his wife the chance to apologize, and she had an unrealistic expectation that he would finally acknowledge his unfairness and her hardship, but neither happened. Joseph was firm, as he had to be, and attempts by the children to mediate invariably hit a wall. He expected more support from his children, and yet felt bitterly disappointed by them. Bitterness and loneliness dominated Joseph's later years: this was a battle for some recognition of righteousness with no winners; they both had lived for too long in a box.

Untranslatable Communication

Contributed by Catterina Coha

Guia lived in one of the largest human camps for most of her adult life. Each day life was perpetual and predictable in these well–organized areas. They were clearly separated from the natural resources camps, where only a few were allowed mostly to check on the artificial intelligence systems that ran them. The global government had been successful at controlling most of the planet, focusing first on highly populated areas and then areas suitable for growing food or producing energy.

Emerging from an era of separatism and violence, when fierce competition for resources had polarized the exploding world population along ethnic, cultural and religious lines, the new world order had been established by erasing any divisive concepts and beliefs. The Equalizers, faced with the task of saving the planet from sure demise due to pollution, global warming and use of nuclear weapons, had implemented an emergency plan to bring the situation under control, by developing technological advances that could provide solutions to the greatest problems.

The spread of technologies, which now provided not only information but also an interactive system to organize all activities, had been relatively fast and easy, even in the most underdeveloped societies. What had proven to be a greater challenge was the inability to control human irrationality, which had, in fact, found a new channel through the interactive systems of the global communication network.

After intensive investigation, the task force created to identify solutions to this problem came to a consensus: human nature was not clearly definable or *intrinsically changeable*, but the vehicle allowing the irrational impulses to transcend the individual and catalyze the diffusion of unhealthy ideas to large groups of people was *language*. The latter was actionable.

***

Guia was born in the middle of the Transition Period, when people had become used to rely almost entirely on electronic personal devices for any form of communication. The benefits were multiple in everyday lives. It was easy, convenient and less intrusive to send a message rather than talking. Confrontations were avoided, since this form of communication was free of the signals that accompany face–to–face exchanges, and raise strong emotional reactions such as the tone of voice or body language. It also decreased racial tensions, since it avoided reactions to accents and appearances by separating personal contact from communication. Similarly, sexual harassment and illicit affairs, the cause of conflicts big or small since the antiquity, as exemplified in the epic history of the Trojan War, were minimized in the absence of the seductive allure between people of different sex, which was often an inevitable component of social interactions.

This form of indirect communication through personal devices did not only govern the work place, but also pervade households. Children informed their parents about their school and play schedule by entering the information in the shared family calendar, reducing chances that they forgot to tell parents about something important. In fact, for small children, this was done directly by the teachers. Calendars eventually became public, so that employees did not even need to inform their superiors about needing to leave early to attend a school game or take a child to the doctor. Everybody found the system convenient: everything was transparent and followed the law. Employees could not take unjustified time off, but did not need to ask permission for the justified leave, and employers had an efficient system to plan coverage always knowing ahead of time who was available and who was not.

Overtime, the language that was still used in the beginning of the Transition Period evolved into a form better suited for communicating via personal devices and for the fast pace of life. Words were substituted with graphic symbols: simple ones with universal use, such as a smiley or a sad face, and a few other variants to express basic human emotions. A heart symbolized love, coin money, wavy lines the sea, and so on. Symbols had multiple advantages: faster to read than letters that make up words, no chances for misinterpretation due to incorrect spelling or grammar, and, most importantly, they removed the barriers between more and less educated people, and between people speaking different languages.

As communications were reduced to the simplest form, the new generations easily adapted, and resistance came only from the older people who wanted to add qualifiers to their thoughts. They protested that the culture of the past centuries was wiped out by this trivialization of human communication; they upheld the complexity of the human soul, the inspiring dialectics of philosophers, and the poignant lyrics of poets.

When the Equalizers challenged these old culture lovers to agree on matters of religion, political and social structure, or on the definition of beauty in poetry, however, they could not agree with each other, and it became easy to dismiss them since activities fostering disagreement were illegal. So it happened that a generation of grandparents found themselves unable to communicate with their grandchildren and transmit to them their knowledge: the youngsters were educated from pre–school by a well–organized system, in which the pre–existing multiple languages of the world were no longer taught.

The Equalizers had achieved the original objective of creating a more homogeneous society, one with a common communication system that gave every citizen equal opportunities. Entertainment was widely available at home via the web, which provided endless options, or in public places. The new cafés were equipped with tablets showing all available food and drinks, and the customers could order what they wanted with a click, thus avoiding the inconvenience of waiting for a waiter. They could listen to music using headphones so that customers with a different taste would not impose on each other. Couples could go out together, but did not need to agree on what to do, eat or watch. Each one was free to choose what they liked, which avoided quarrels. In fact, each individual was enabled to be equally self–centered, and divorce became extremely rare. Young people in search of love through "match makers" used special programs. Every characteristic of the potential partner could be specified, and the search was open to the entire world, providing thousand of options to choose from. Other programs were used to identify the top candidates within the selected pool, and in the end, when a match was made, people were sure that they had found the very best and had no regrets.

***

On a warm November evening, Guia found herself in a smaller human camp, in an area of the planet that she had never visited before. Since all human camps looked alike, people would not experience curiosity or anxiety when they traveled. Everybody relied on their personal devices to keep connected to family and friends or watch the same show they had been watching at home. Thus, nobody raised the gaze from their personal device to check the surroundings, or look at the people near them.

But Guia felt an inexplicable impulse to look at the horizon as the vehicle was landing. The sun appeared as a huge orange ball of mesmerizing beauty. It was only a glimpse before the windows were closed, but that image made a strong impression on Guia's heart. She felt a mixture of excitement and sadness, and was inebriated by a magic feeling. She had no vocabulary to name that feelings though, since she had never learned a language, but from the deepest memories of her childhood sudden words came out in a language that she once heard:

"Mais il est des villes et des pays où les gens ont, de temps en temps, le soupçon d'autre chose. En général, cela ne change pas leur vie. Seulement, il y a eu le soupçon et c'est toujours cela de gagné."

She heard these words in her mind, spoken by the voice of her grandmother.

Guia had lost her parents as an infant, and was raised by her grandmother until she turned five. The grandmother lived in a remote area, in the mountains of what had been once called Southern France. In this remote and quiet location, the Transition Period had been slow to come, and authorities forgot about Guia so that she had entered the school system later than she should have had otherwise. Her grandmother, secretly an old culture lover, had made her best efforts to teach the little girl the language she knew and adored, reading to her as many books as she could, until one day Guia was taken away by authorities to a large and advanced human camp to get a 'proper' education.

The words in French were playing in Guia's mind like music, but she was not completely sure about their meaning. Yet, this memory awoke an awareness that she could not remember feeling before. Automatically, Guia followed the flow of people walking near her, and entered the first café to eat something, as she was hungry. The café was ordinary. She sat at an empty table and scrolled the tablet to order some food. But while she was waiting for the food to be delivered, Guia did something unusual... she looked around. She looked at the people in the café.

People were not interesting; everybody was transfixed by their personal devices, checking messages or watching a video. She looked at her personal device, to find a standard message from her husband, asking if she had a good trip. She replied quickly that everything was fine.

Everybody had their headphones on, but Guia did not want to listen to music or block the background noise. She felt that she could be missing something... something interesting... an expectation forecast by the image of the setting sun.

Then, a man came to sit at the other end of the table. She felt an urge to raise her gaze and look at him. He had dark curly hair sprinkled with gray strands and dark warm eyes. And to Guia's surprise he was looking at her. He smiled, and she felt her heart racing faster. She never looked into a stranger's eyes so deeply, and the way he was looking at her was hypnotizing. They sat together for a little while and ordered the same drinks. During this time, he never looked at his personal device, and neither did Guia, which was very unusual. Then, unexpectedly, he asked her:

"Tu aimes ton mari?"

Guia felt confused, but she understood the words, and she knew the answer right away... and it was:

"No!"

She could hardly remember her husband's voice, since they never talked. In contrast, the voice of this man was warm, sensual and enticing. Nothing else happened that night, but they exchanged their electronic addresses. Guia could not sleep; she was overtaken by a desire she had never felt so strongly before.

In the next few days, Guia and the man met again in the same café. Although the two of them knew only a few words in a common language, they communicated with all of their five senses. The delicate and almost timid touch of their hands gained a growing strength, and became a passionate grip, and then an embrace. They made love for hours. Intimate relationships had always been bittersweet for Guia's. Even with her husband, she was relieved when the lovemaking was over. For the first time, she could not get enough of it. Lovemaking with this stranger was a completely different experience. He seemed to know her better than anybody else. For once, her mind, body, heart and all of her senses were in harmony with the lover.

It was simple and pure love. Guia wanted to share everything she could with this man, and the physical communication, so deep, so intimate, was the only vehicle to compensate for all of the thoughts she had no words to express.

Soon, the time came for both of them to leave the small human camp with the big orange sun. They parted with a passionate kiss. Guia felt the memory of his touch on her skin for months to come. She saw his warm eyes in her dreams. Now that she had experienced real love, a real human interaction, she could not accept her previous life. She had never really been happy, but did not know what happiness was and could not miss it. Now the balance was broken, and her mood went from joy to deep sorrow. Of course, she communicated with the man using the personal device, but without words and without symbols to express, but the trivial superficial nature of her thoughts. The communication had become shallow and frustrating. Perhaps this same sense of frustration was the reason why he seldom replied. Years passed and Guia kept thinking about the man, whom she still deeply loved and missed. She often wondered where he was and what he was doing. She wanted to let him know that she would do anything to be with him again, but there were no symbols for such an irrational emotional concept in the personal device symbolic vocabulary.

One day, Guia learned that the man was going to be in the same camp, where she had to go for business. She was excited and could hardly wait for the moment where she would see him. She anticipated the sweet pleasure of the warmth of his body, the magic touch of his skin, the desire to exchange her body and soul with him again. But most importantly, she hoped to be able to communicate to him her commitment to find a way for them to be together. She wanted to change her life, and hoped that he would want it too.

When she walked into the café, she expected that it would be easy to find him. He would be the only person whose eyes were not empty, who would look at her rather than see through her as everybody else would by focusing on their devices. With growing anxiety, Guia walked along rows of tables, and finally saw a man who looked like him. Approaching him, she became sure that it was the right person, but something was wrong. He was not looking at her; he did not raise his gaze; when he did his eyes were not warm; worse, he did not even smile. He had the same expressionless face as everybody else in the café. He recognized her, and politely made place for her to sit near him, but communicated with her not with words or touch, but through the personal device. His messages were short and shallow for he was busy with work.

In a last desperate attempt, Guia tried to talk to him:

"Je t'aime"

But he did not seem to understand her.

Guia's heart sank. How could she translate to a person who lost the ability to recognize words, to look into one's eyes, to hold one's hand? Her feelings and thoughts become untranslatable. Guia stood up and walked away. Her steps felt heavy, very heavy, and so heavy that she could hardly walk. It was the weight of solitude. The last person who knew how to talk and love had been re–educated: the human being within was gone.

A WALK IN THE PARK

I RICORDI

Unpublished original poems by GV Masucci

Vengono alla mente

Poco a poco

Prendono forma
Lentamente

Ridanno sensazioni già
Stampate nella mente
E

Improvvisamente
Tutto è lì
Vicino e vivo
Come se fosse ieri

Rimangono fino a quando
Ti rendi conto...

Non sono il tuo presente
Solo un pezzo del passato

MEMORIES

*This poem is published in "Dry Petals" by GV Masucci (2017)
and is herewith reproduced in this book with his permission.*

They come to
Mind
Bit by bit

Take form

Slowly

Giving the best
Feeling
etched in
Mind

And

Suddenly, everything is there

Near and alive

As it was so
Yesterday

They stay
Until one realizes that

They are not the present

But just a piece of the
Past

On a cloudless April 1ˢᵗ of several years ago, Luca, or more precisely, professor Leoluca de Mirafiori, was taking a stroll across the Giardini Pubblici[4] of Milan. With both hands in his pockets and being about five in the afternoon, Luca had nowhere to go nor did he retain a precise recollection of where he was coming from.

Suddenly, the professor interrupted his meditative saunter. He sat on a bench and, intertwining the last three fingers of both hands, he joined the palms, opposed the thumbs against each other to hold his chin, and applied both index fingers to gently massage his upper lip all the way to the base of the nose, dislodging upwardly the heavy framed glasses. Having satisfactorily completed such ceremonial, he began to recall.

***

We all experience occasions when the past appears livelier than the present itself, which, in turn, seems breathless and inanimate. At those junctures, we witness events that happened a long, long time ago as they materialize in front of us, while we discreetly stand aside as silent bystanders.

Of lately, Luca, who was experiencing dissociation from his own surroundings, had been living by default, as if he had no other practical alternative. It appeared to him that reality belonged only to his mind, while what was out there was just a distraction, a realm breathing an autocratic and autonomous existence that had no impact on his own being. It seemed that he was transiting life as a tourist who roams a notable place to which he does not belong; a site from which one would accumulate assorted images to be deposited in the baggage of memory for an undefined subsequent use. Just as we are unsure about what to do with the heap of photographs that sit on our desk at the end of a journey, he did not exactly know how to exploit that mélange of recollections – save for, perhaps one day, conflate them into a disorderly catalogue, a jumbled memoire for an inexistent audience.

He had tried in the past to apply the power of concentration to trap the ephemeral progression of events. By enhancing life's corporeality, he fancied that it would be easier to get hold of its parts, but this effort could not slow the process. This attempt to capture experiences could not stop their motion by turning them into still objects. Contrary to photos, life could not be framed, and he eventually conceded that it was to no avail to attempt to catch the moment while the present wiggles away and turns into past right before one's impotent eyes. As a consequence, through a process of reverse logic, he had taken to disregard the flowing of current events as if they were just momentary illusions not worthy of consideration.

---

[4] Public Gardens

Yet, depending upon the direction we face in a moving vehicle, we may judge that we are staring at the future when facing forward, or to the past otherwise. In reality and independent of our perception, our movement makes no difference to the stillness of inanimate things that, indifferent to time and motion, dwell where they are, save for the imperceptible ethereal motion of the universe to which we all abide unwarily. But, engrossed by the illusion, we wonder whether we could reverse the course of our own life by simply turning back to stare in the direction from which we came.

Accordingly, Luca, dismissing his skepticism, and uncharacteristically engrossed by the moment, scrutinized his surroundings as if what had intervened in the last decades constituted only a dream from which he was awakening just now to realize that his past – in the form of centennial horse chestnut trees orderly aligned along the pebble paths, the conceited pigeons, the pond with its boring carps, the lovely mallards, the elegant water striders and the lilies, the monumental fountains, the artificial miniature hills, the Museum of Natural History, the Planetarium, the austere statue of Antonio Stoppani [5], and all of this – was still there completely unchanged. Contrary to the rest of his life experience, time had miraculously halted exclusively in these gardens; a natural preserve against the extinction of moments. All of it was still there unchanged while, for the rest of his world, several things had come and gone in the progression of time.

***

It was, therefore, natural for him to rewind at leisure the footage of life while resting on that bench. And as Luca was going through these meditations, he looked around baffled to see that, after enduring many winters and summers, what had been long gone was still there – unchanged, including this old bench where he used to sit with friends when they skipped school in similarly bright days of spring... and that old horse chestnut tree, oddly–shaped like a humongous diapason with two parallel branches departing from each other a few feet above the ground, where, a long time ago, he had kissed Sleeping Beauty.

Some coquettish classmates had persuaded him on a purposeless afternoon to reenact Perrault's tale by impersonating Prince Charming. When the moment came to rouse from her slumber, Clara, who was acting as Sleeping Beauty, lay with shuteyes in the embrace of the tree's branches. He cringed toward her and, with the gentlest motion, grazed her lips with his own. Two immense blue eyes opened in front of him, of an infinite color and of the loftiest freshness; and she smiled and flushed simultaneously. Without hearing the giggles of the girls and the squawking of the immature boys, he lifted her from the tree and, holding her in his arms, walked away bequeathing another gentle kiss that, this time however,

---

[5] The author of "il Bel Paese" a best-selling book published in 1876 celebrating the beauties of Italy and became the name, decades later, of a brand of a very popular cheese product.

resulted in a bit of a warmer and velvety contact between his two slightly open lips and her upper one.

***

On the following day, as Luca was approaching the school entrance, a scrawny boy with red hair and freckles, and a noticeable pimple on the left cheek, placed himself sturdily with legs wide apart pointing his index finger straight at Luca's nose. Although it was Luca's fourth year spent in that high school, he had never taken notice of the minuscule creature and, without imparting him the satisfaction of paying any attention, he swerved to avoid him. But the stranger stepped closer, and as Luca was about to overtake him, he delivered a girlishly controlled punch right to the side of his left lip that, without truly hurting, obliged Luca to acknowledge the existence of the annoying adversary.

Luca, who was a youngster of athletic built but of agreeable personality and respectable upbringings, abiding to the Milanese upper class' etiquette of polite debate rather than contentious disagreement, did not know how to react against this adversary of miniature proportions but of sedulous temperament. Therefore, proactively, he turned his chest toward him and, to avoid further embarrassment, held the red–headed boy with his two arms and lifted him up to look straight at him in the face:

"What the hell is wrong with you?"

To which the read headed boy, who was already shaking, then answered:

"I was told that you kissed Clara at the park yesterday... don't you know that I love her? For you...for you, these are just... they are only games." he stuttered.

Luca held the wiggling worm a little closer and, with tightly closed lips, he kissed him just to the side of his pimple and then whispered:

"I am sorry, do not worry, she is all yours."

Then he dropped the boy with his far–apart legs frozen in the same position as before he was lifted and Luca left him there with his arms resting flaccidly along the gaunt torso.

Following that episode, Luca noticed Clara more often in the crowded school corridors, with her royal blue eyes shining like sapphires amidst her unnoticeable friends; and when their gaze met and he kindly smiled at her, she blushed. But he never came close or talked to her. An inexplicable pride to honor his commitment to the freckled boy forced him to pretend that he was occupied; he quickly corrected his gaze to look over her as if something behind her was distracting him.

Days passed, as did the months, till high school was over and they both moved on along the distracting paths of life for which all they needed was a tiny suitcase to carry their hopes and dreams in. But her gentle demeanor, her sweet smile,

215

her elegant countenance never abandoned him, and those transparent blue eyes with the clarity of Ceylon sapphires kept staring at him wherever he went and made him wonder how it would have been to have known her better. Even years later, he thought of Clara with regret, like an omen of lost opportunities, of dreams that do not materialize, of voices fading into echoes in the irreversible mystery of time until...

Now, when, sitting on the bench, with eyes closed and forehead reposing in between his palms, Luca could see her clearly smiling as if he was just now taking her away in his arms from the embrace of the tree.

***

It was then when his trance was interrupted by the voice of a man asking him:

"Who do you think invented marriage?"

On his right side sat an aging gentleman of the finest Milanese breed, who had blighted unannounced on the bench. He wore a twit jacket with an elegantly folded pocket square and an azure and thinly striped shirt where the finely woven initials "LM" stood at the left side of the collar. He wore a thick tie that could have been of the Marinella brand[6]. His trousers were of premium wool and they were short enough to expose two skinny ankles covered by lightly colored silk and cotton socks that connected the body to a formidable pair of leather–woven Moreschi[7] shoes of impeccable elegance. As a result, the stranger's demeanor appeared immured within his own attire, although of these constraints, as for most aristocrats, he did not seem to take notice.

The stranger held his left arm along the backside of the bench as if he was about to offer the comfort of an embrace. His hair was flickering under the breeze and it was of a chestnut color that shone under the oblique sunrays, heightening two green and penetrating eyes with which he inspected Luca as if he was reading a treatise, while his words melted in the northern breeze to pleasantly caress Luca's cheeks.

Luca had turned to verify the source of the voice. But rather than questioning the stranger of his identity, satisfied after a preliminary glance at his decent appearance, he turned his attention back toward the diapason–shaped tree, relaxed his body over the backside of the bench, corrugated his eyebrows, pursed his lips into a curious shape that resembled a duck's beak and admitted to the tarrying stranger:

"I have no idea!"

Encouraged by the admission of ignorance, the stranger crossed his right leg over his left, reached with the right hand the left one that was hanging free from the

---

[6] Classic fashion brand from Naples producing mainly ties

[7] Top brand of Italian shoes for men

arm and, interweaving the fingers of both hands, embarked into an impromptu dissertation.

"Plato imagined that humans originally existed as hermaphrodites, conceitedly autonomous in reproductive needs. At last irritated by their arrogance, Zeus split them into two parts, with each complementing the other. This is why humans, now torn in their essence, wander the world seeking to reunite with their match. Thus, love is the longing to retrieve what we have lost, the instinct to restore the unity of our spirit... some may argue that this is the justification for marriage."

"Yes, but how does this myth relate to the institution of marriage as it is inflicted upon us by society? How does this allegory advocate for the exclusivity of a lifelong relationship?" wondered Luca, still staring at the empty embrace of the tree.

"According to the Christian faith" continued the stranger "God instituted the covenant of marriage by uniting Adam and Eve. *'It is not good for the man to be alone. I will make a helper suitable for him.'* God said and, while Adam was asleep, he removed a rib from his body to form his eternal companion to complete His own creation. Even though Adam and Eve were two separate creatures, God called them as "one flesh", thus becoming the Minister of the first marriage ceremony."

"But one could say that the Devil contributed his own part through Eve." the stranger reasoned.

"There was Adam! The poor guy was innocently enjoying a carefree life immersed in the beauties of the Garden of Eden. Then, the Devil, together with Eve, plotted his curse, gifting that unfortunate prototype of mankind with a conscience. It was a diabolical deception to bridle him like a draft horse... the curse of Eve: to be lashed for the rest of eternity by the whip of guilt, the rules of conventionality that traveled beyond East of Eden to become universal. And from then on, men are expected to follow, among other moral constraints, the rules of monogamy – though they still cannot quite understand its reasoning. In other words, how come we can hold with our fingers as many roses as we want and can eat as many candies as we please or ride as many horses in the big prairie, but we are supposed to share our life with just one woman, for better and for worse... and mostly for worse? Who set this rule and why do we have to abide by it?"

It occurred to Luca that the stranger's words resonated as familiar concepts that must have been dwelling in the meanders of his subconscious for a long time without answers, for he had never managed to articulate any of them on his own initiative.

"Of course, in Adam's times, it was easier to be monogamous because there was only Eve. There were no distractions, no subtle touches of the hand in moments of unhappiness, no understanding of smiles or compassionate eyes to compensate for one man's loneliness. There was nobody to turn to when Eve had her premenstrual syndrome or other oddities of women's behavior that remain beyond any man's ability to comprehend."

As the stranger kept talking, Luca noticed two mallards: a beautiful male and a not so pretty female silently parting the still surface of the pond, tranquilly paddling toward their future and unwarily leaving behind an imperceptible wake as a fugitive memento of their recent past.

"But the instinct to multiply, to propagate the reach of the human species complicated things. Men became bewildered, juggling the instinct to procreate against constrains imposed by their wives. While they generously tried to satisfy as many women as they could, women took the Bible's directives literally, turning the covenant of marriage from the original allegory into a firm commandment: *'thou shall not covet other's men wives!'* says the commandment! Thou shall not covet other's women at all – save for your proper wife, was the interpretation!"

"Why do people get married in the first place? Who started this unfortunate practice? Who invented marriage? Was it a man or a woman? Did insecure women create this covenant because they wanted to preserve their possession coveted by other competitors like growling dogs defending their bone, or did men, just as insecure, trying to guard their wife from predators with this virtual boundary? Who invented marriage? Was it a man or a woman who drove a covenant meant to control the uncontrollable?"

At this point, Luca started to feel kinship for the stranger who had risen by then to a friendly accomplice.

"But it is understandable for men to view monogamy as a part–time engagement, pretty much like a professor taking a sabbatical away from routine assignments. And it can be expected that men can be serially monogamous, having different women in separate and discreet moments to adapt their behavior to societal views. Thus men can devote themselves all heartedly to one woman at a time by looking straight into her eyes and momentarily forgetting about all the other ones. It is like our beloved Italian strikes that are programmed by the hour; you can have a life–long hunger strike that is planned in between meals. Just the same, men can be comfortably monogamous in multiple relationships by genuinely devoting heart and soul to one woman at a time, just like hermaphrodites with multiple personalities searching for various selves."

"Marriage is not an institution of nature. The family in the East is entirely different from the family in the West. The institutions are society grafts, not spontaneous growths of nature." continued the stranger, paraphrasing Napoleon[8].

***

---

[8] Napoleon Bonaparte's speech in front of the Conceil d'Etat on the Civil Code and subsequent quotes from Honoré De Balzac: "The physiology of marriage"

"What about those men like me who have never learnt to love properly?" interrupted Luca at that juncture

"Is this logic stipulating a pretext for all of them? Is this all intended to rationalize depraved behavior? Are you telling me that my conduct throughout my life was not as debatable but the result of a legitimate rebellion to conventionality?"

"Well, that could be the topic for a whole novel," answered the stranger with a composed smile.

Then, he cordially shook Luca's hand and departed stating:

"I hope to see you here again."

"When will I see you again?" asked Luca.

"When the appropriate time comes," returned the stranger with a bow of his head.

***

Following the stranger's departure, Luca also rose and began to walk distractedly toward home. He thought about his wife, or to be more precise, his former wife as he had been divorced for some years. And that thought made him turn toward the mallards that were still cruising along in harmonious peace:

"Those animals are together for a lifetime. There is no rule or covenant to force them to linger together yet they do not part. Have they learned what I have yet to grasp after all these years? Are love and companionship a given for them?" and at that same time, he remembered a remark offered by a woman once dear to him:

"You are like a leopard... powerful... beautiful... smart, whom we all adore and admire – but which nobody can own or control because it thrives on freedom."

It was getting late and the breeze was getting cooler. Shrugging his shoulders, Luca went home, musing over a seemingly trivial question:

"Which is happier, the leopard doomed to follow its lifelong solitary trail or the gregarious mallard? Why was his instinct, like that of the leopard, programmed to dismiss love? Don't leopards ever encounter blue eyes like those of Clara? And if they do, would they take notice? And what about his own story? Would Clara have made a difference by turning the leopard in him into a happy mallard if he only had had the courage to give it a chance? Or, as for Clara before, it was in his nature to shut his heart to the joys of a lifelong companionship? What drove him to the solitude that was bearing on him now with the overpowering weight of regret? What waited ahead for him and for the solitary leopard, now that the vigor of youth was languishing and loneliness was becoming a reality rather than a choice?"

Walking out of the park, he ignored a beggar by turning his gaze to the opposite side of the sidewalk. But after a few steps, he stopped. He put his hands in the pocket and found a few coins. He retraced his steps to deposit the little fortune into the beggar's hand without looking at him and without waiting for signs of gratitude. He did not feel he deserved any; he had done it only for himself to temporarily quench a troubled conscience, to perform an act of goodwill, to symbolically compensate for much harm imparted to others along years of self-absorption.

It felt even cooler in the early evening and he dug both hands in the pockets of his trousers, hastening his steps toward home. So many memories of women suddenly flocked to his mind: beautiful, warm, intelligent, and generous companions, who had by turn, performed love dances around the path of his life. Women he had mislead with temporary attention; with whom he had never been able to establish a reciprocal relationship; a procession of vanished opportunities that had left him ultimately alone like an odd and thirsty plant desiccating in the rain forest. And on that cloudless afternoon of April 1st of several years ago, he suddenly missed each one of them, including the most important: the one who used to be his wife, the one from whom he had parted for what it seemed to him now as for no apparent reason.

***

Luca lived in an elegant apartment within the meandering of streets that carve a path between Via Monte Napoleone and Via della Spiga. It took him about a quarter of an hour to reach home from the Public Gardens, snaking through the crowd of shoppers. By then, it was dusk and the streetlights gleamed and, along with the elegant shop windows, enlivened Corso Venezia. A few drops of rain started to fall despite the cloudless day, and soon it was pouring:

"Aprile, ogni giorno un barile![9]" he recounted.

By the time he reached home, his clothes were sopping. He did not look for the key but rang the doorbell. He needed somebody to greet him as a reassurance that he was not totally alone.

"Good evening, Mister Luca."

Sabrina came to the door dressed in her servant uniform. Luca inherited her from his Dad who died a week before. She had no job and nowhere to go. She would stay with him for the time being.

Luca looked at the minute Filipino woman and smiled at her, making her blush.

"At least I am not entirely alone!"

---

[9] April, each day a barrel (of water)! – Expression suggesting that rain storms are common in the month of April

And he recalled the times when the cat came to welcome him before his divorce, before his wife took it with her without any thought of joint custody. Even that had seemed trivial then.

Sabrina took his jacket and disappeared in the laundry as he walked to the bedroom to take the rest of his clothes off. He piled them on the bed and redressed. Then, he called Sabrina and handed the pile to her and, while she was attentively organizing them into the laundry basket, he felt warmth in his chest: a familiar sensation triggered by the presence of a pretty woman that had opened the door to so many adventures in the past, a tender feeling that knows no boundaries.

"Sabrina?" he said.

"Yes, mister Luca?" she replied

"I want you to eat with me this evening...and, by the way, can you just call me Luca?"

***

That night, Luca made love to Sabrina for no really good reason. He simply did not want to be alone – just as when he was a little boy and did not want to be left abandoned in the dark and so he sneaked in his mom's bed. Since then, he had never been without a woman in his bed for too long, and it did not matter which one, as long as she was pleasing and with an agreeable disposition, and like a kitten, he would purr in response to any kindness till the flow of life would attract him elsewhere.

Later on, in the silence of the night, as Sabrina's head rested on his chest and her pretty shoulders were rhythmically rising with each of his breaths, Luca stared at the ceiling and momentarily forgot his solitude, his grieving over his Dad's departure, his angst for the lost opportunities that had tormented him that afternoon. Once again, he had yielded to the ephemeral illusion of companionship that the contact with a warm and naked body can offer to a solitary leopard. Then, deeper into the night, as he still could not sleep, he saw Clara's eyes, those big blue eyes of infinite color, staring at him in mysterious silence.

The Old Boys Academy

Now, Sabrina turned out to be quite an exceptional woman. Her existence perfectly balanced Luca's needs. She was well educated. She spoke Italian and English fluently besides her maternal Tagalog language, and whenever she pronounced "Mister Luca" with her purring Filipino accent, his ears pricked up like those of a kitten.

Sabrina took the initiative of answering the phone, taking accurate messages in both languages and orchestrating with pride Luca's personal life. She took care of his wardrobe with zeal and, as if a magic wand had been waved on Luca's life, soon everything around him became well–ordered as fussy as a spinster's closet. Luca discovered shoes, ties and shirts in the armoire that had been buried in drawers and cabinets for decades, waiting in vain for his occasional returns to the hometown. He lifted an old pair of shoes dating back to his high school days that had been polished as a vintage Ferrari. He noticed on the medial side of the right shoe, an old scratch that had survived with dignity for the last thirty years. After turning the shoes a few times in his hand, wondering what to do with that testimony of youth, not having the resolve of putting them down to rest for an indeterminate number of decades, Luca decided to wear them. In the end, they looked quite the same as his current loafers as he had never changed his preppy style all along those years.

Promptly, he reassumed and even enjoyed the orderly life that had been put aside after the divorce. Without pampers from his attentive wife, he had discovered then that laundry could be hung around the house right out of the washing machine and shaped by his own body at the time of use. Sabrina instead ironed everything she could get hold of, including curtains, sheets, socks, handkerchiefs, towels, tablecloths, napkins and ties, and washed them with compulsion after each use without giving them a chance to get dirty. Conforming to the craving of an art collector, she would bolt out of the house on her free time to scavenge for any possible permutation of absorbent, cleaning, softening, moisturizing, refreshing, or aromatizing equipment to be applied to the prince's clothing, and Luca ended up walking out of the house smelling of talc powder like a pampered toddler fresh out of the tub. She would admonish him about correct combing strategies and adjusted his tie to be properly centered and all of this was done with such a delicate touch that progressively Luca not only renounced to resist by even became dependent upon such attentions.

She cooked meals of several denominations searching the Internet. And she accepted Luca's criticisms with grace and his recommendations as Gospel. She enacted requests verbatim without need to be reminded. She had an iron memory and a sharp intelligence that was applied with ardor to all domestic matters as if they were of cosmological relevance without expecting more than receiving a modest check at the end of the month to be sent in almost its integrity to the Philippines.

Above all, she did not interfere with Luca's life, whether it was about professional or personal matters, and she let Luca free to continue his dissipated existence without questioning. She even served with deference occasional lovers, whom he brought home inconsiderately for a dinner and overnight stay. Afterwards, upon Luca's request, she even offered comments on those guests' qualities that not only demonstrated how much she understood her master's nature but also made him laugh in good humor.

 In conclusion, Luca had found in Sabrina the ideal companion to meet his self–indulgent expectations and, therefore, after a few weeks of such coddling existence, being impressed by her talents as a servant and as a woman, the professor's subconscious started to recognize in Sabrina some sort of human being. As a consequence, he retained her for the time being as his servant concubine: a reasonable prerogative for a spectacularly privileged person.

At this juncture, I warn the readers, who may start to dislike Professor Leoluca de Mirafiori's character, that we should not hasten to judge others and that Luca was in truth not such a despicable narcissist as this preamble may suggest. Rather what we are observing in this moment of Luca's life represents a downfall of destabilizing circumstances that concurred to shape a naturally withdrawn personality just as much as our reflection in the mirror summarizes a composite of long gone events of which the image portrays the outcome.

In reality Luca, being far from cynical, was a profound and decent character worthy of empathy, if not sympathy, when judged from the perspective of the path that had been tossed to him.

As we previously mentioned, Luca lived by default and his detachment toward Sabrina or whoever else was roaming in and out of the outskirts of his existence paralleled his own disengagement with the affairs of life. In the back of his mind, he very much appreciated Sabrina's fervor and even envied her energy. He would be the first to agree that she deserved more than she received. But how could one blame a cadaver for not rising to water a thirsty plant?

Yet Sabrina seemed to understand, and no matter how gloomy her master returned home, she welcomed him with a smile, with warm meals, and other joys that were only for him to choose. And she did it in good humor and with cheerfulness since she was thankful for all she received that consisted of a decent salary, a comfortable room in an elegant neighborhood, a few books to read and an old computer to connect by video with her children whenever she wanted to. That salary, in particular, was good as she had two young children in the Philippines and a husband, who waited for the monthly transfer sufficient to take care of so many things in that faraway country.

***

To better appreciate Luca's state of mind, it is therefore sensible to retrace his story a few years back when, still trusting that he had a happy family and a decent future ahead, he was returning a day earlier from a business trip to his apartment in Park Avenue and was greeted by the bell boy with a hand–written envelope freshly dispatched from Italy.

It was an eccentric note from Tullio, an old friend with whom he had shared the pains of growth in high school and with whom he studied medicine at the University of Milan before moving after graduation to America. It said as so translated from Italian:

"Distinguished Gentlemen,

Following an extraordinarily high level discussion, Prof. Zamponi and I decided to establish the Old Boys Academy (with special emphasis on the "Boys" rather than the "Old" element).

Membership is highly selective, arbitrary and admittedly self–indulgent.

Currently, the Academy has no bylaws and none are foreseen neither in the near nor in the distant future.

The intention is to provide a forum for jovial and pleasant exchanges. Professional discussions are discouraged but not completely forbidden, provided they do not generate severe spells of boredom measured as yawns or more flagrantly snores among the participants.

Gatherings can be held monthly in any agreeable and conducive ambience in the presence of plentiful chow.

In relation to the latter point, we propose to hold the first gathering at my residence in Milan on November 15, …

Wives or significant others (more or less significant that they may be) are not only discouraged but also strictly prohibited!

RSVP directly to me (no assistants need to be involved)"

Folding the letter and returning it to the envelope, he smiled, shaking his head and wondered how to decline politely while the old wooden elevator was still sluggishly climbing toward the 36th floor:

"Nice of them to remember me! I will send the apologies tomorrow to steadfast Tullio. I wonder whether Giuseppe was invited. Would he go to Italy just for that?" For a second he entertained the prospect of joining his old friends.

***

Holding the envelope with the left hand and unscrambling the keys with the right one, Luca judged that by then his wife should be home and reactively rang the doorbell. By the time he had managed to open the door and pull the rolling case through the door, Christina was staring at him, impassive without attempting a smile. Instead, George, the house feline, came to rub his feet, attempted a crowing meow and dropped belly up, expecting some reciprocity. Luca bent and rubbed his soft tummy in silence.

"I thought you were coming tomorrow?" Christina managed to say.

"Got done early, caught an earlier plane. I thought you would be happy. We can even go out for dinner so we do not have to cook and wash dishes!" mumbled Luca while still looking at the cat.

At the rhythm of silence, he rose and walked by Christina, dragging the rolling case and he bent to kiss her somewhere in the face. She did not resist but also did not respond to his gesture as if she was trying to convey some news. Moving toward the bedroom and passing by the dining room, Luca saw Jonathan, a longtime common friend sitting at the head of the table, with an elegant meal for two, a bottle of Champagne and a lit candle to complete the scene.

Jonathan got up and stood motionless, incapable of finding a word. Luca helped by releasing the grip from the case and in apology stated:

"Sorry for interrupting you guys! I can just go to my room."

Just then Christina came out of the kitchen with a set of plates and cutlery that she reposed on the side opposite to her and to the left of Jonathan, who was still standing at the head of the table.

Smart people cannot lie; not to themselves, not to others; it is just in respect of one's own intelligence. Luca did not ask for explanations and nobody offered any; it was clear that the marriage was over ...no other explanations were necessary.

The old friends continued the dinner that had to be consumed for the sake of decency. In particular, the recovered Jonathan identified topics to fill the time, and all managed heroically a labored conversation. Luca noticed the food prepared by Christina. It was his favorite meal: rosemary flavored standing rib roast with baked potatoes. But tonight, it was insipid and so was everything else. He shuttled into his mouth a piece of meat, alternating with a piece of potato and a sip of wine, while Jonathan was reporting on the financial crisis. He was a businessman in Wall Street and Luca pretended to listen with temperate interest but as soon as the dinner was over and the plates were adequately emptied, Luca rose.

"I am tired. I am going to bed. Do not let me bother you any further."

Dragging the rolling case, he reached the bedroom. He noticed that the bed was perfectly done and wondered whether they had been already sleeping together or it was soon to come. He looked with marvel at himself in the mirror, at his statuary appearance, at the face of a man known for his good looks of which he had been made aware by so many women and pondered:

"What does she find in that plump and bald slug? Only notable thing is the flashy Rolex."

It should be noted that Luca took for granted his appeal to the other gender without any special pride, just as a matter of fact as if it had been imposed on him by fate just as a life on a wheelchair is imposed upon a handicapped person. Yet, with his analytical mindset, he entered with objectivity his charisma into the algorithm of his existence leading to the proprietary assumption that women existed exclusively to complement his being. But now, what was wrong with his wife?

Poor Luca! How could he have known that Christina had tried so hard to be close to him for all those years! That only in the end, when she could bear no more to compete with the furniture for attention, as a pretty decoration, a picture on the wall, only then she fell for the seduction of being solicited, being cared, being told of her beauty, of her intelligence, of her qualities as a caring mother, as a woman, of her entitlement to be loved.

How could poor Luca know? In fairness, he had praised Christina on occasions, but rarely, never spontaneously, only when objectively demanded by a conversation of substance. For a scientist, things do not need to be repeated once the truth is established; when a statement is made, it should hold forever; an ascertained truth is a step from which one moves forward. He knew how good of a person his wife was and he had told her once and for all. But this is not how women's minds work: they need reinforcement for their insecurities, they need nurture like an indoor plant, and they need fertilizer for the flowers of their heart to blossom and water to keep them alive. But emotions are difficult to express in scientific terms: it was too difficult for Luca to translate feelings into words – it was logic without metrics, calculation without integers. He knew that he should have told Christina that he loved her more often than he did, but that word, that concept seemed so empty, so vague, and so intangible to be used with ease.

"Am I over–reacting? Am I over–interpreting?"

He questioned as he walked to the marital bed. There, he lifted the sheet, reached for the pillow, put it under his armpit and walked to the den. After turning on the light, he looked at the familiar objects and wondered what they knew that he did not know. He then rested the pillow on one arm of the couch, took of his shoes and dropped them on the floor, removed his pants, undid the tie and opened the shirt, sliding out of it and letting it fall onto the ground. Finally, he lay down, adjusted the pillow and stared at the ceiling.

Like a cat listening to a mouse behind the wall, he heard the two lovers whisper a few words and soon the latch of the door was secured. Jonathan had the decency to leave and Christina came right after looking for Luca. Not finding him in the bedroom, she walked into the den, just as beautiful as she had been since the time they met thirty years back.

Christina did not talk but looked at Luca, who bitterly smiled and asked:

"Do you love him?"

"Yes!"

Luca felt the urge to ask:

"Why?"

But at once, he realized that many more questions would follow without answers: questions referring to times past that should have been raised then not now, when it was too late. Instead he looked straight into Christina's eyes:

"Do you still love me?"

Christina, who had been unnaturally self–contained and distant throughout the evening, burst into tears. Without answering, she came toward him, kneeled at the couch, put her head on his chest, the left cheek down with the face turned away from his and sobbed:

"I am so sorry!"

Luca lifted his ataxic hand from the floor at the side of the couch where it had dropped and delicately caressed Christina's blond hair. It was a strange feeling. It had never occurred to him to wonder what would feel like to be deserted by a woman, a companion, not to mention by his own wife and he found himself surprised by the feeling. Staring at the chandelier, he reckoned that, without admitting it, he had loved this woman throughout those many years. In spite of differences and difficulties, unspoken grudges, resentments, misunderstandings and rebellious actions, they had shared so much together, raised beautiful children, who were now gone along their successful paths. He felt no anger, not even sadness; just only profound tenderness. He thought of his wife as a teenage daughter searching for new horizons, exploring the unknown, cutting the umbilical cord that had kept them united for all those years whether they liked it or not, and he realized that if he really cared for her, he had to let her go. This is what true love was about. In the end, as he had learned raising his children, one cannot control others' wills; one can only try to understand them.

Eventually, her uninterrupted sobbing distracted him, and he said to his wife:

"Shush, stop crying. All will be fine, do not worry; everything is going to be fine. Go to sleep now, we can talk tomorrow. I just cannot talk anymore; I would not know what to say."

Christina rose and without turning hurried to what had been for decades till that moment their bedroom. She accosted the door while Luca kept staring at the ceiling.

"What a strange feeling it is to be alone," he reasoned.

He realized that he had never experienced the sentiment of being earnestly alone. Throughout life, he always had a companion at his side, mostly by default, girl after girl, woman after woman, affair after affair till his marriage; each departure had been just a door opening the path for the next one to come in. But now, for the first time, he savored loneliness: that immeasurable emotion, so limitless and impalpable, that comes without sadness, or joy, without despair or hope, but presents as dry and absolute emptiness as the eternal motion of stars and galaxies along their solitary journey in the darkness without hope for encounters in the millions and billions of years to come.

About to close his eyes, Luca remembered Tullio's invitation. He thought it such an odd coincidence – an omen. Far from believing in supernatural powers, he perceived the note as a forewarning of change, a harbinger of resolution, and a leap into the future by retracing the old. I took it as an invitation to revisit the dated path searching for the crossroad that led in the wrong direction, to restart anew if it wasn't too late. Thus, he told to himself:

"See you Old Boys! See you in Milan!"

***

When Luca woke up, it was still early and the dawn projected just enough light to let him explore the surroundings and recall the events of the night before. He recognized the den and that vision reminded him of the new predicament. Luca scanned the familiar objects that enlivened the room in the past, while now they were framing its emptiness. He thought of the quote:

"If a tree falls in the forest and nobody is there to hear it, does it make any noise?" And he recited:

"If a man cries in the forest and nobody is there, does it really matter?"

Indeed, for the first time he finally understood what it meant to be alone, to be on his own, not just for that day, that week, that month, but for the years to come.

He rose, tiptoed to the bathroom to clean and shave without disturbing Christina. In a rebellious act, he decided not to shave and by seven thirty he was walking out of the house, having a free day ahead. Before leaving, he returned to the den, picked up the note from Italy, put it into his pocket and repeated:

"See you, Old Boys! See you in Milano!"

***

The air was crisp under the canopy and Luca, exiting the building, insentiently aligned his spirit to it. He discovered that he was just as free as the breeze that was lifting his soul, and he felt relief, if from nothing else, from the burden to please. He considered that throughout life, he had been curbed by the fear of upsetting others: his parents first, then his wife, and the relatives, particularly those on her side, even his children. Averse to confrontation, he avoided arguments, conceding to the will of a strong woman rather than arguing, pursuing nevertheless his wants in subterfuge according to the tenet that, when caught, it is easier to ask for forgiveness than for permission beforehand.

This caginess lead to confusion and distrust, mostly for petty reasons: coming late from work, finding excuses to avoid family gatherings or dinners with acquaintances about whom he did not care, performing otherwise innocent activities that she disparaged. All behaviors innocent in their motivation but that lead to suspicion on the receiving side.

The more Christina reacted with rage to the subterfuges, the more he, like a reproached cat, withdrew. He mastered progressively deceitful talents, figuring out how to avoid being caught the next time. He persuaded himself that Christina would never accept the truth, no matter how innocent. All happened instinctually, without a good reason, and with naïve maliciousness, the deceptiveness of a child who does not want to study or of a puppy that steals a cookie. But these actions were not perceived as such by his companion and gradually, almost inadvertently, this misbehavior dug, drop after drop, an abysmal valley between the two, and the only comfort in the relationship progressed to rely only upon seclusion.

But today he was free! He owned the world, with all its prospects and he had nobody to please or be accountable to.

As the fresh air was seeping through the skin of the forehead to refresh the mind, he crossed in high spirit Park Avenue proceeding toward Fifth Avenue in search for a place to buy a cup of coffee: the first accomplishment of the new life! And that elation... that refreshing joy lasted indeed for a while... but a very little while, just until the middle of the crosswalk. As he approached the other side, looking at the warning countdown of seconds by the stoplight, he felt sadness. He reckoned that what he had been misrepresenting as relief and freedom was in reality a reaction to profound anguish, and that the momentary happiness was only sugarcoating over a rotten apple.

By the time the sidewalk was reached, happiness was replaced by bereavement. He reckoned that the momentary relief was harbinger of hopeless loneliness, while his existence was turning into a meaningless vegetative state; nobody to please, nobody with whom to share successes or seek comfort. Luca wondered what would be life about now. What was the purpose of all? Did he really care that much about his profession? Or were his achievements solely aimed at impressing his wife, at making her proud? Admittedly, his profession was useful and, therefore, in some sense important but now his existence had changed flavor, his own identity was gone, now that the wife of so many years was not in the picture. There would be no mirror to reflect the fruits of his successes, not even a smile to compensate for unending streams of frustration. In truth, he was the tree falling in the deserted forest where no one can hear or see.

Yet, his determined logic did not intend to concede to emotions. He turned to an objective analysis of the current predicament and he questioned himself:

"How did all of this happen? How could have happened?"

Not finding a clear–cut answer, as he crossed Madison coming from Sixty–First, he resorted to more tangible reflections:

"She loves him. She is unhappy with me. I love her, and I want her happy. Ergo, I must let her go! This will be my happiness and purpose from now on!" Thus he recovered, with such contorted formula, a vestige of purpose to his life.

By the time Fifth was reached, he had pledged to sacrifice his life for his wife's contentment, and this resolution gave him peace ...for a while ...just until another thought arose:

"Wait a minute!" he said to himself

"Why should I worry about her happiness? I did nothing to deserve this. I worked throughout. I provided for the family just as much as she did, if not more. I worked weekends and nights. I did not play golf or fool around with friends, no nights out, nothing of what I was accustomed to as a bachelor. Why am I so sorry for her? I should be angry instead!"

But even the concocted wrath did not last long. No matter how hard he tried to picture his unfaithful wife lustfully enjoying life at his own expense, his imagination kept carrying back those moments when they met decades ago, the first communications in broken languages, that mélange of Italian, French and English. And the same vexing imagination could not be controlled and kept dumping a plethora of unnecessary images from the time when the children were young and life was joyful and enriched by unbridled expectations and sweetened trepidations.

In the end, he concluded that there was no reason to bear resentment toward Christina just as much as there was no reason to blame his own self. To every action there is a reaction; any effect derives from a cause but too often causes are vague and mishaps are downfalls from remote and negligent choices of which we bear no memory. Yes! Uncountable had been the wrongs from each side, reactions to poor choices that spawned chains of counter–reactions, an endless stream of mistakes to which there was no determinable beginning, whose initial perpetrator was hidden within the oblivion of time.

Many had been the circumstances when she could have acted in a suitable way to save their relationship. But just as many chances had been given to him to do better: to hold her hand instead of walking away, to look into her eyes instead of turning them away, to listen and respond considerately rather than dismissing her worries with superficial accusations or patronizing comments.

A well–known defense mechanism called repression came to assist Luca in this predicament when circular and unproductive thinking overtakes the conscious mind. Incapable to find closure by solving the current quandary in which he had been thrust so unexpectedly, Luca reframed his thoughts on the Old Boys Academy. And he fancied his old friends sitting around the poker table at night. Some of them were focusing on the game, others were annoying the players by introducing distracting thoughts about the Vietnam War, Bob Dylan, The Band, Woodstock, the cultural revolution in China, and other concepts that the professors did not discuss in class but that were in their minds at those intense times when they were youthful and in so much want for adulthood.

He thought with a smile of Gramsci[10]'s "Lettere Dal Carcere[11]" and his Cultural Hegemony theory; so much debate around lofty topics that he could barely remember now. Heated discussions erupted while Tullio attempted to herd the focus on the game to quench the juvenile wrath of the friends. But they all cared about distant events, remote in time and so far away from their town, where they were cozily sitting around the table in the cold winter nights, and while the hosting mothers, who could not refrain to check on the boys, sneaked in occasionally with the excuse of checking on the guests at the cost of irreparably embarrass their respective sons.

And those preferred evenings when safe sex was anticipated as they converged to a friend's home, whose parents were out of town; those evenings when girls were allowed to decorate the room as three–dimensional holographs.

He recalled "La Candela[12]", so called because she stood on top when she made love, like a candle on a stick. She spent the night in the guest room, passionately hosting in turn the one who needed a break from the game or who had become weary of politics. And she was so proud of such privilege to serve! And she loved them all, thankful to be accepted like an abandoned bitch that has found a home.

"Boy was she fun?" he smiled. "What happened to her? I wonder; I wish I could see her again."

And he thought of the alcohol. It was hard liquor that they drank to be like the grownups: whiskey, vodka, and Cognac, taken out of the parents' cabinets. He recalled the crystal chalice of Cognac held by the handsome Tullio, who had given up herding his friends into the game, and had retreated to the armchair, posing in mockery of his distinguished ancestors' portraits that were hanging on the walls just above him but making nobody laughed because by his own nature, Tullio somberly looked just as stale and stiff as his departed relatives did a century before.

***

---

[10]Marxist theorizer and founder of the Italian Communist Party

[11]"Letters from jail"

[12] "The Candle"

Along Fifty–Second, Luca notice a street artist, who was painting with pastels a portrait on the sidewalk. She was a pretty oriental woman, focused on the ephemeral work, barely aware of the passersby. That vision of the beautiful stranger toiling so hard early in the morning distracted him further from the current predicament. That vision of youthful enthusiasm offered a serendipitous albeit temporary relief to his loneliness.

Luca accosted her and his own shadow covered the art to distract her momentarily. She turned her face to look at him and smiled: a beautifully simple and innocent smile. He wanted to talk to her, to tell her about his current predicament, of his pain, of his guilt, and of his remorse, of his certainty that he would never repeat the same mistakes, that he would be a better companion from now on, and that he needed somebody to believe in him. He wanted to tell her that her tiny body reminded him of a sparrow sipping the water from a puddle created by the recent rain and that her smile forecasted a beginning, it was the first sunray after the storm.

But those chaotic impulses clogged his throat and he said nothing. He reciprocated the smile and went on along his path.

After a few steps, he turned and saw her still busying over her decidual masterpiece meant to last till the first rain. He almost went back to introduce himself politely, to offer to buy a cup of coffee, but instead he shook his shoulders and moved on:

"I can always talk to her when I come back."

***

Several miscellaneous and disconnected thoughts, emotions, and arguments continued to crowd his mind for the following steps going from the infatuation with the pretty artist to the opposite resolution of sacrificing the rest of his life for Christina's happiness, to rather despising her and all members of that gender, or to revenge his pain turning against Jonathan by telling of the affair to the banker's wife. Finally, he considered the ultimate drama: a suicide that would make both perpetrators repentant for the rest of their lives. In the end, he got bored of all that nonsense figuring that none of those contemplations yielded any actionable resolution worthy of an academician on the account of their lack of originality. Therefore, he decided that life in its multifactorial essence was way too complicated to be repaired with simple measures and, incapable of balancing with logic the thrust of his emotions, he once again shrugged his shoulders and moved on toward the Plaza.

By the time Luca arrived at The Plaza Hotel, he had forgotten about the troubles with his wife, he had forgotten about the Old Boys and forgotten about the street artist, and instead he asked himself:

"Why not? I will treat myself with a cappuccino at The Plaza."

In the end, this was the only sensible action he could find the resolve to complete.

***

Entering the coffee shop, he noticed a rather minute woman of remarkable contours, dressed more like a cowgirl than a New Yorker, who stared and addressed him with the sweetest smile:

"Audi partner, what're you up to?"

Stupefied by the insightful comment, unconcerned about its sincerity, he looked straight into her eyes and gently squeezing her right shoulder, he answered:

"Don't know... Actually... to be frank... I feel just a touch lost, just a little bit more than a touch in fact sort of dumped if you allow...not that you would care anyhow."

"Why shouldn't I care? Don't we all feel lonely most of the time? You looked distraught indeed!" she replied, following him with her big eyes as he proceeded to the counter to order the cappuccino.

While waiting for the cup, he turned around and noticed that she was still looking impertinently at him with a mischievous expression. As she moved closer toward him, he asked:

"Do I know you?"

"Probably not... but I do know you, Professor!" and nodding her head, she added thoughtfully:

"All women in campus with a good vision know you for sure!"

Then realizing that her cheerfulness did not steer much of a reaction in the Professor, she touched his right elbow and, turning pensive, she corrugated the forehead and asked:

"What makes you so lonely? I am sorry, I was jesting before!"

Flattered by the pretty woman praises and in much need to examine his thoughts through a conversation, Luca impulsively opened the heart to a total stranger:

"My wife is cheating on me... after thirty years." Then, listening to his words he thought it better to temper with:

"She is in love with someone else."

The pretty woman did not say a word. Her stern look turned into a tender smile: a maternal act of woman's dexterity.

"I came home a day earlier from a trip and I found her having a romantic dinner with a common friend. Candles, Prosecco or may be Champagne, whatever! All the nine yards! And when I asked her whether she loved him, she simply said 'yes'. What bothers me the most is that the guy is bald and fat, and to be honest I do not think he is that smart either. He is just a businessman."

"Do you still love her?" She asked at the first break.

"Don't know! I wonder if I ever loved her to start with, but I spent all of my life with her, all that I can remember. I never asked myself whether I loved her... I guessed... I assumed that I did. But now, to be sincere, I miss her whether I love her or not. Isn't it what love is all about?"

"Did you tell her?"

"Tell what?"

"That you miss her."

"Why should I? What would she care? She loves somebody else!"

"Oh dear! I guess you really do not understand women, do you? By the way, aren't you jealous? Aren't you going to smash the lover's face? Just a curiosity, not a suggestion!"

"Never been jealous! Thought one should earn one's love each day anew, not take it for granted. If a woman does not want to be with you, what's the point of cursing, yelling and screaming? In the end, if deserts you, it is because you failed to keep her. I have no control on how a woman feels. Only control I have is of myself! I could have tried to improve if I knew, but I guess it is too late now.

"This is the way I feel. But I do not understand what is that I did; I thought that I was a good husband. Maybe she just grew bored of me... By the way, can I get you a coffee or something? My name is Luca. What's your name?"

"Valentina," said the pretty woman and with overstated affectation she added:

"Extremely honored to meet you, Professor de Mirafiori!"

Luca talked a lot that morning to the pretty stranger and Valentina listened thoughtfully, looking straight into his eyes with her own that barely blinked, crossing her leg occasionally and arching her back to emphasize her bosom that was admittedly remarkable.

Suddenly, Luca remembered that he had planned to call Giuseppe, who by then must have been awake in Palo Alto. Therefore, he excused himself after exchanging contacts by thanking Valentina for the patience prodigally offered to a serendipitous encounter.

"No problem at all, Luca. I enjoyed talking to you! Your wife is a lucky woman. You are a good person, not a good communicator maybe and definitely a little too self–absorbed, I must say. Go back home and talk to your lovely wife and you will see she will forget about the chubby banker!"

"But in case she does not... you have my number!" she added.

To that last comment, Luca reacted by approaching the petite woman, circling his arm around her waist, lifting her up, giving a hug, and kissing her gently on her closed lips.

"Thanks!" he said and away he went towards Central Park.

***

"Hey Luca, what's up? Long time, no hear from you!" said Giuseppe

"I am getting divorced," said Luca impetuously, forgetting that he had called Giuseppe for the entirely different purpose of asking whether he was planning to go to Milan for the Old Boys' get–together.

"Congratulations! It was time finally!"

"What do you mean?" asked Luca, totally dumbfounded

"Come on, you two have been the oddest couple for a long time. You acted around Christina as if she was your dentist about to pull a tooth as soon as you opened your mouth. We all wondered when Christina would get tired and leave you. Who wants the divorce? Do not tell me that it is you because I would not believe it. You would simply be too spacey to even think about it."

"She is having an affair with Jonathan, you know, the banker? You know who I am talking about, that fat guy with the Rolex... And how do you know that she is the one to break up?"

"Because she told me last time I saw her. She said that she was unhappy with you. That you couldn't care less about her! That you had completely dissociated your life from hers, always away, not involving her with your work, avoiding vacations together and fooling around with women. She is not a stupid woman. In fact she is a great woman."

"How would she know about women? And how would you know?"

"I do not know, but Christina is not stupid and you are still so naïve on these matters! When will you ever grow up? We are not in high school anymore! That was decades ago! You cannot have one affair after the other, no matter how insignificant you may deem it to be, and expect that your wife would not at least sense it."

"Then what about you and Shirley?" Luca retorted vindictively.

"That was a long time ago and in any case, I guess I am better than you at keeping discreet about my affairs! At least I do care enough about my wife to make sure that she does not feel completely neglected and does not look around for other men... at least that I know of. Anyways, I am not the one divorcing."

And noticing the silence from his friend, Giuseppe added:

"Come on, man! Cheer up! You must have sensed what was going to happen. Don't tell me that you are completely surprised, are you or not?" Because there was still silence, he added:

"I can't believe this! The guy is really surprised! Come on! This guy really is the dumbest self–absorbed son of a bitch that I ever met! Come on, Luca! Cheer up! You can find as many women as you want or otherwise just go back to Christina and tell her to forget about that hot air balloon and that you will take good care of her from now on!"

"Anyway, this is not why I called you," interrupted Luca, who by then was confused to the brim and worn by the stern logic of his friend.

"I called to ask you whether you received any message from Tullio recently."

I should note at this juncture that Giuseppe, a fellow that some of my readers might recollect as the main character of *The Wise Men of Pizzo*, was not from Milan but from a little town in Southern Italy. Therefore, not being originally part of the old clique of high school friends, he had been adopted by the Old Boys who appreciated his skeptical demeanor and ironic wisdom. Giuseppe had befriended them by spending long stretches of time in Milan during college breaks when he needed a respite from the American life.

Hence, Luca meant to tactfully test whether Tullio had included him in the reunion.

"Yes, I did. That old archimandrite of Tullio! Of course I got it! What a crazy idea, but you know what? If you go, I will go too. We live only once, don't we?"

And before hanging at the end of the conversation, Giuseppe concluded, "By the way, my regards to Christina."

***

On the way back, Luca retraced his steps towards home and walked to the place where he had left the street artist, but the object of his infatuation was not there anymore. Her masterpiece was completed and a few casual admirers were standing around it. She had collected her belongings and she had gone forever. The sparrow had migrated to a more welcoming territory, and in her flight, she had dissipated that sunray of genuine smile that had pierced momentarily beyond the clouds. Luca felt a pang in the heart, a forgotten feeling that came together with the vision of two beautiful blue eyes of an infinite color that had been fated to follow him silently for the rest of his life.

***

"Christina, are you up? Sorry for bothering you. I just wanted to know if you are busy today."

"Of course I am up. I did not sleep all night! Then, I could not find you and I was worried. You did not even leave a message. Nothing! How are you? Where are you?"

"I am OK, just went for a cup of coffee. You busy today? Are you going out with Jonathan?"

"No, I decided to take a break. I am confused. I need some time alone. What about you?"

"Nothing... I mean, not much... actually nothing, I mean completely nothing to do. I guess I could work. I do not think I could focus... What do you think? Should we go for a walk together? I am still in Fifth. I could come to get you or I can wait for you."

***

The river in which one steps is not the same. More and yet more waters keep flowing on.

Into the same rivers we step and yet we do not step, we exist and at the same time we do not exist.

After all, one does not step into the same river twice. Waters disperse and come together again ... they keep flowing on and flowing away.

In the end, there is only flux, everything flows,

Everything is in flux and nothing rests,

Everything flows and nothing remains,

Everything constantly changes and nothing stays the same.

The River – Heraclitus

***

Luca rested on a familiar bench in Central Park. Sitting on that same bench, where he used to wait for Christina when, coming back from work, they would get together to go grocery shopping on the way to their apartment or they would instead look for casual dining before wrapping the evening up. It was an ancient routine that lasted for decades and intensified after the children had moved away.

So he settled on that bench once more, waiting for his Christina, rehearsing meanwhile the most sensible strategy to confront her. As a matter of fact, there was no strategy at all; what Luca was imposing upon himself was a pretense of logical considerations that unconsciously reflected the simple desire, even fervor to see her again. Instinct had compelled him to call her in the first place, a need to come to a resolution either through forgiveness, or anger, but a resolution nevertheless. He feared belligerence and prepared with angst for the worst because he could not cope with the swiftness of her arguments in moments of

238

wrath. He just wanted peace. He had to convince himself that decades of living together could outweigh any challenge brought by the current predicament.

...Or at least, he was hoping for a truce. He recollected Valentina's admonishment that reverberated in Giuseppe's words: "Amend the past! Open the heart! Just tell her that you care and that you do not want to lose her."

He also vouched to listen with care and empathy. He wanted to acknowledge. Perhaps for the first time in his marriage, he willed himself to understand Christina for the sake of love, or at least this is what he contemplated.

But even such noble resolution came in Luca's style. His apathetic mind had finally identified Christina as a problem, an interesting problem worth of investigation and he gave permission to his heart to lucubrate and dissect. It was a primordial form of affection, a difficult one to explain in comprehensible terms to those who live a normal life: those who experience the freshness of spring water when they submerge their hands in it and do not have to explain to themselves why they should sense and perhaps even enjoy that simple sensation.

Luca was not like them. He was not familiar with spontaneity and he experienced only second–hand sensations. He processed and fabricated into emotions the messages imported from the exterior by his senses, a contorted exercise that demanded explanation for things that could not be explained. It was the best he could do because it had never occurred to him that there is no reason to explicate everything... that humans are impetuous and their deeds are irrational. Rationality is of use only retrospectively to justify one's own actions.

Resignedly waiting for Christina like the respondent waits for judgment, he held the empty cup of cappuccino, turning it clockwise and counterclockwise over and over. He observed distractedly the assortment of park dwellers and, tightening the grasp on the cup at intervals, he found reassurance in doing so as if he was keeping hold of a handle that connected him to the practicality of existence. Realizing that he had been tormenting the empty cup for more than an hour and that such occupation had no intelligible purpose, he stood and walked toward a bin to deposit it with satisfaction, upon careful selection of the appropriate container, as a token of a deliverable that could be completed in defiance of the overbearing apathy of the morning.

Mission accomplished, he looked toward the direction from where Christina was expected. Not seeing her, he returned to the old bench. But it had been already occupied by a young couple tenderly holding each other's hand and basking under the occasional sunrays that descended from an otherwise self–absorbed sky occupied by churning and digesting strata of grey and white clouds in its turbulent stomach.

***

Christina came with a light gait and approached him with a smile. Luca walked towards her, touched her left shoulder and kissed her on both cheeks, the Italian way.

"Should we get something to drink?" he offered.

"Sure!"

They walked purposelessly and indefinitely up and down the park without managing to get to the substance of the conversation. They recollected distant episodes that had nothing to do with the current predicament and they laughed. They walked off the path and through the grass. Then, he climbed a miniature hill as the children used to do and waved at her from the summit. They admired a few reminders of the late fall in the shape of colorful leaves that carpeted the grounds. They stared at policemen riding the horses and asked a passerby to take a picture of them under an ancient tree. To immortalize what? They would not know. He attempted to hold her under his shoulder but she declined politely. He grazed her hand with the back of his but she withdrew it hastily. When they set on a bench he tried to kiss her but she said:

"I do not think it is the right thing to do, Luca!"

Then he asked her:

"Are you happy with Jonathan?"

"Yes! I have not been this happy for a long time. We spend time with each other whenever we can and he does all he can to be with me. He has given back to me the self–esteem I lost waiting for you day after day... he makes me feel that I am worth something." And then she continued:

"I do not know what happened! You know, I loved you so much. I did all I could do to make you happy, hoping for you to want to be with me. I could have never imagined a life without you. But then, I realized that it was not up to me; that you were not happy with me no matter what I would do; that you were with me because you did not have the courage to leave me and there was nothing I could do to change it. I had to do it for both of us."

"What about his wife?" interrupted Luca, mostly to deflect the sequitur onto something he did not have to confront. You may call it dismissive but in reality, he truly did not know what to say.

"He told her last night after he left our home. He has moved out. He already has a flat downtown. He had it for a while."

"And our kids?"

"They are all grown up They will understand!"

"Do they know?"

"Of course, they don't!"

"Who is going to tell them and what are we going to say?"

Silence ensued. Christina was turning stiff. Her eased mood was gone; she assumed a defensive posture by settling her joined hands in a crevasse between her knees and looking into the distance; yet they were not arguing:

"So are we divorcing?" asked Luca mechanically as if he was about to summarize a scientific discussion at a journal club.

"Yes!" pronounced Christina.

Luca looked towards the pond at the lovebirds, those mysterious monuments to eternal love. He recollected the reason why he had asked Christina to come. He thought of the intent to ask her to forget about the whole thing, to forget about the bald banker with his fancy watch. He thought that it was time to tell her that he loved her; that he cared more than anything else; that he was sorry for his dismissiveness in the relationship; that he was repentant for all that had gone wrong no matter whose fault it was. But he did not say anything. Those words of hers ("I have not been this happy in a long time!") had created an insurmountable barrier.

He told himself that he had no right to interfere with her happiness. How could he expect to deliver what he had failed to give decades before? And he gave up. This time he relinquished not for a vane principle of martyrdom but because he genuinely felt that he did not deserve her.

"OK!" he said then clasping his hands against each other and reposing his mouth over them.

"OK!" he repeated. "I guess this is the right thing to do."

Practical as usual, Christina had already worked out all details. The divorce would have been easy. The children were independent. They both had similar assets and made about the same amount of money. They could have gone to a mediator and have it executed friendly. Soon they would both be "free" to pursue their own happiness.

At the word "free", Luca looked at a hawk hovering over Central Park and wondered about the meaning of the semantics. Are those unbridled creatures free? Aren't they slaves of their own nature? Is freedom something we can take advantage of or it is just another way to subdue ourselves to our instincts?

His subjection encouraged her to talk, and she vented what had been interred for years. She confessed, as if she was talking to a brother, that she had another affair before Jonathan, a brief and casual relationship some time ago when he was gone for a business trip. She narrated that the relationship with Jonathan had been going on for months. She explained that it had started with a casual comment after a business party that she attended alone because once again Luca was out of town. Jonathan had invited her out for dinner afterwards and said that he was in love with her, that he had been in love for a long time. Of course, he was not expecting for her to act on it as long as she was happy in her marriage; he just wanted for her to know. But she, under the seductive fumes of alcohol, confessed that she was not happy: her husband did not love her, and he was having affair after affair. Jonathan listened with empathy and while she talked, he grasped her hand. Not long after, they slept together and they did it again and again with passion, whenever Luca was out of town or during the day in Jonathan's flat.

Luca listened to all in admiration. He could not figure Christina, his proper wife and the mother of his children, to behave with such creativity and rebelliousness. She appeared to him as a different woman. He listened attentively, trying to imagine the scenes that she was describing and wandering what was he doing at those moments...and he did not say a word till a sudden thought interrupted his train of thoughts and consequently interjected hers:

"But then, what is going to happen to us?"

It had occurred to him that this was not just an academic discussion. It was not a journal club. He reckoned that fate was knocking at the door; that his life was about to be turned upside down, and he continued:

"As far as I am concerned, I just do not care about all of this. You are still my wife and you will be forever. We can divorce. You can get married again and sleep with whomever you want, but I do not care. In my heart, I will be your husband forever and one day, when you will need me, I will be waiting for you. See those mallards out there? They live together without need for covenants or legalities. They are bound together forever by their own natural disposition. I do not know what law of nature keeps them loyal to each other for a lifetime but there they are, united forever!

"Christina, I will be your lovebird and you will be mine no matter what we will end up doing for the rest of our lives. My dream is that there will be happiness when we think of each other, that there will be pride for all we have achieved during these years and, when possible, there will be love and not hate or resentment. There will be intelligence and understanding. In the end, what else is left but hope through a glimpse of wisdom that there will be respect among the characters of our precious story? I think we have lived long enough to know that mistakes are nobody's fault but the consequence of careless choices whose accumulated burden cannot be reversed by regrets. I do not know what lies ahead of us, but for me, a lot of solitude. In the end, perhaps this is what I deserve and need. Solitude, like silence or darkness, enhances the senses and makes you feel and see what you could not see before."

It was Christina's turn to listen silently. She listened voraciously with tears in her eyes till the tears turned into a sobbing cry:

"You see? I love you so much. I miss you already but you... you sound already relived. You already look at the future. You are doing nothing to gain me back. You are not fighting for me!"

Yet Luca did not understand. He wondered:

"What have I been doing till now? I listened to her, I tried to tell her that I love her forever and she told me that she has not been as happy as she is now with Jonathan for a long time? What should I fight for? To make her unhappy?

"You just told me you are happy as you have not been in a long time. Why should I change that? What right do I have to make you unhappy again?"

Christina looked at him, admiring her husband whose passion and resolve had awoken lost emotions.

"Would you want us to go back together? Would you really want for me to leave Jonathan?"

That question confused completely the already perplexed Luca, who was sitting in front of a wife that had turned from the faithful long–term mother of his children into a vibrant sexually active and romantic person. He nimbly questioned what would be like to go back to her and whether it would be possible to reassemble from thousands of pieces a broken crystal. But seeing no impediment to giving it a try, he said:

"Of course, I am open to it. Let me think about it. What you just told me about yourself has confused me quite a bit, but I am open to the idea."

Poor souls! Why did she miss the fact that what he actually meant to say was "I have not been this happy in a long time!", only tempered by an instinctual tinge of caution meant to preserve a façade of dignity. Why didn't he simply answer "yes", which was all she needed to hear from her handsome husband of so many years?

I am puzzled myself as the author of this story. I wish I could change the events with a simple stroke of my pen, but that would not be realistic. There is no such thing as benevolent authors, who can correct the course of actual lives; who can suave with their wisdom the faulty logic of our choices and temper with the pastels of hope the wilting canopy of solitude. I wonder why we cannot recognize the root of our feelings till it is too late. Why we entangle our decisions with the twisted logic of a conversation that dissipates our will, while we forget to listen to the depth of our soul? I do not know how to answer these questions. Perhaps, somebody else could. Yet, these few misinterpreted words had a determining impact on these two decent people's lives.

"See?" almost screamed Christina, "You do not really want to go back together. Enough with the bullshit about the lovebirds! You have no clue about what you are talking about." Without further said, she stood up and left.

Luca looked at her disappear in the distance, wondering about what had gone wrong. Trying to summarize in his mind the various pieces of a puzzle he could not ensemble, he told himself:

"I better let her go. She would never be happy with me!"

***

Pigeons are not known for their intelligence but perhaps they are not as stupid as we give them credit for. This particular one landed just at Luca's feet and stared inquisitively at him with his left eye first and then, twisting the neck, with the right one as to get a second opinion. Was the pigeon questioning his acumen? Wouldn't be great if in moments like this, a pigeon, an angel, a God or whoever from up there could descend to reprogram our thinking? To tell us what we should do? To make as notice what is standing right in front of our eyes when we are too confused to see? Perhaps, the pigeon was trying to tell something to Luca with its perspicacious stare as it circled around bending and bobbing its neck. Finally, it gave up and walked away in dignified steps.

The instinct of self–preservation comes within the enclosure of one's ego. One wants to perpetuate that collection of embodiments through which the identity mirrors. But at that moment, Luca had lost any sense of belonging. Nothing that he could recognize in his visual field or beyond it that was familiar. The world around had nothing in common with him; it was a world that belonged to another person who was now gone; a married man with a family and a future ahead, a person whose soul had walked away following Christina's steps. It is in those moments that a person gives up.

Luca rose to leap out of that torpor. Mechanically, he walked toward home. But then he realized that it was not home anymore. He then turned hundred and eighty degrees towards the opposite direction where the rest of the world was waiting. But that seemed to overbearing in its boundlessness. He then turned ninety degrees to the left as to halve that infinity and indeed, he saw something concrete. Just a few yards away there was the pond with the lovebirds... and he walked toward them... and he observed them for God only knows how long till he realized that companionship did not pertain to him: not now, not for the time to be. And so it was that Luca began his journey as a solitary man.

***

Odi et amo. Quare id faciam, fortasse requiris?

Nescio, sed fieri sentio et excrucior

I hate and I love. Why do I do it, perhaps you ask?

I don't know, but I feel it in me and I ache

Catullus – Carmen 85

"Time flows. So does everything else. Only I persist; dammed to judge into Eternity what's evil and what's not because of the Omnipotent's wish... but I question why. I judge petty human affairs in their ephemerality and I marvel why should I care. People are reactive, their decisions are casual, and one gives them too much credit to believe them capable of willful sin. They do what they do out of compulsion, sloppiness and instinct. There is no premeditation even when it may appear so. Why would one kill the lifelong companion to collect life insurance? This comes from a well–thought compelling and logical decision? Or isn't this action a superlative example of absolute madness? Believe me, they are all incontrollable ancestral instincts. Only instincts govern human actions and their deeds result from egotistic subjection to their chaotic fate. One's life is a prolonged struggle at mastering the pseudo–logic of rationalization.

"Yet, I must judge the indecipherable enigma of the human mind and, when all is gone, when only memories remain to witness a purposeless life, I sentence for eternity. I judge based on memories that will be obsolete in a generation or two! Life flows and soon it's gone, yet I judge from the perspective of eternity the perpetrators of this tedious and insignificant flash of existence. I judge the path of lightening querying why it struck one rather than another tree as if it is the result of willful causality rather than a combination of chances. What is the purpose of all?"

A lanky and gaunt gentleman of elegant composure was standing at Luca's side, talking to himself, yet cognizant of being heard. When Luca turned towards him, he twisted the neck like an eagle without other motion and looked through Luca's eyes as if he was staring at his mind. Just the same, Luca saw through the gentleman's eyes, beyond a crystal gate, an impenetrable abyss.

"Most misdeeds committed by humans come from thoughtlessness, but the worst come from false morality. Some humans are compelled to justify their actions with a sort of distorted logic, and they become master at this. Most atrocious choices are made because the faulty mind asserts control. In fact, most dangerous are those with strong beliefs, the moral among humans, those that rationalize their impulses with faulty reasons," the gentleman continued emphasizing the world "moral".

"Now I ask you, what kind of human are you?"

Luca shook his head and guessed:

"I do not know, perhaps a little of both?"

"Yes, correct answer! All of you humans are."

By the time the intrigued Luca was ready to pursue the conversation, the stylish gentleman had vanished, and he was left wondering.

Meanwhile, a new sentiment was dawning.

"A tree falling in the forest, that's what I am. I carry this weight in my chest! I would have never imagined that it would hurt so much! But does it matter in the end? If nobody can share my pain, does it really matter?"

This time he earnestly fancied to end his life.

"It is easy for a doctor. It can be done inconspicuously."

But then he thought:

"Not worth it! Too many people would hurt because of my stupidity, my Dad, the children, maybe even Christina... not worth it. Sadness is subjective. I should not take my feelings personally! Better stay silent like the tree in the forest. If I am the only one to know, my desperation may not be true... it might just be the fruit of my imagination."

So arguing with himself, Luca shrugged his shoulders and strolled along recollecting the lanky gentleman:

"Who was he? Why did he question what kind of human he was? What had the question to do with what was going on in his current predicament?"

As he walked further, sadness turned into wrath. For the first time in his life, he experienced anger. Till then, all had rolled peacefully. Day after day, life had been still in its motion and the slow flow of time reaffirmed its stillness. Yes, the children could have won a few more soccer tournaments, and definitely, reviewers could have been more lenient about his science. They could have saved a little more money if Christina had been more parsimonious; they could have even bought a little cottage upstate. But overall, he had been very lucky. Nothing ever shook his privileged and fortunate experience. Years after years, building a block after the other, he had erected a palace of apparent professional and personal achievement. But now, all of a sudden everything had crumbled.

It wasn't just about Christina. It was about all that she represented. It was the vicarious life he had breathed through her. Luca realized that his life had been a fake, a castle made of cards, and a drama put up to please those who could not accept the emptiness of his soul. He also reckoned that he had never been sincerely happy, even once in his life, particularly on those moments of youth when he should have been. He truly did not know what true happiness was but he had learned to fake it in physical appearance. He had learned to cope with the emptiness of the spirit by manufacturing emotions.

Christina, with her constructive attitude, had naturally guided him through the murk. She had been the lighthouse in the stormy obscurity. Perhaps, more than a lighthouse, she had represented a docile firefly in the depth of the night with the reliable reappearances of its placid light.

He reckoned that he had loved her through the good and the bad times, and what she had interpreted as disengagement was only fear to displease; it was embarrassment of sort, an impression of inadequacy in front of the beautifully opinionated and strong–willed companion. Like cats often are, he had been misinterpreted. Cats are social and affectionate animals but they respect other's territory and do not intrude. They approach only when they feel unquestionably welcomed.

He did not feel welcomed by Christina. He had learned to observe her from the distance, from the corners of life fearful of unpredictable burst of anger, as she was capable of. Christina had never understood that those moments of impatient wrath only distanced him from her because like a cat he could not understand her words or appreciate her motives; he could only sense the rage.

But now, Christina was gone! She had abandoned him for no good reason, just out of an impulse, like the gentleman said, an arbitrary decision rationalized by a faulty logic. And he... he was left impotent, clasping the winds of his vanishing past, like a child thrusting the hand toward the balloon that inexorably climbs the sky.

And he hated Christina. He hated her and loved her; he hated all those preposterous rationalizations of loneliness and neediness but he loved all the rest. Once again he thought of the gentleman, and he thought:

"Nothing we do come from selflessness, and we rationalize our impulses to deceive others and ourselves, while nothing we do origins from a sound reason."

Then, recognizing the tastelessness and vulgarity of his turmoil, his embarrassed id forced him to camouflage the anger as indifference for the future to come.

***

As we previously implied, Luca, perhaps to compensate for his instinctual detachment, had no familiarity with physical solitude. From the nurturing arms of his mother, he naturally transitioned to the arms of one girl after the other, and then a woman after the other. He barely knew what was like to be in bed alone without a warm body to comfort the night. Women were transitional objects toward which he held profound affection. So, one at the time, each woman temporarily carried the baton of his hollowness till exhausted she unloaded it to the next one. This reaffirmed Luca's impression that relationships are transient and thus justified his casual attitude toward the other gender.

The day ahead was still long and without his wife to tell him what to do, Luca did not know how to organize his next steps. So he did the most obvious of all things: he pulled out the piece of paper where Valentina's number was waiting and dialed:

"Hi, it's Luca..."

"Well, it did not take too long!" answered Valentina. "Do you want to come over or do you want to meet somewhere?"

***

Valentina's studio was tiny and luminous. There was a miscellaneous collection of art on the consoles and on the walls: photographs and paintings, little statues and colorful marionettes from all over the world; an obsessive collection of lighthearted beauty that probably compensated for a harmonious melancholy. Valentina described everything with forceful enthusiasm that made everything appear more tangible.

"I did not come here to make love to you."

Preempted Luca considerately, in an effort to break the ice:

"I just came here because I could not think of anywhere else to go."

"I know," replied an understanding Valentina with her mischievous smile.

"In any case," she continued, "everybody knows that a proper girl would not make love on the first date. First date: one exchanges pleasantries; second date: the first kiss, only on the third she is supposed to yield. This is my resolute etiquette!"

Needless to say, within half an hour they were making love. Luca could not resist the beauty of her delicate and athletic body capped by the most flirtatious poses. He sat on the couch and drew her to him. After a preliminary kiss he started to fondle her, to which she replied:

"I am not very good at saying no!"

"Sorry, I cannot resist touching your ass."

"Am I stopping you?"

"I thought you said you do not make love on the first date!"

"Yes, but if we count this morning... this is already the second... one and... by the way... you kissed me this morning... so that anticipated... the second date! It can be argued that... this is in all practicality... the third one," said she in between kisses.

It was so mechanical, so technically proficient and irreproachable. So they made love. Luca concentrated on her beauty, on her passion and responsiveness, on her orgasms. Luca tried hard to focus on what a man should focus on in similar circumstances. And he tried even harder to forget Christina, and not to think about how she might have enjoyed Jonathan's attentions. He tried to repulse the image of himself impersonating Jonathan making love to Christina. He tried very hard, also in respect of Valentina's sweetness, but in the end he turned upside down in the bed, looked straight at the sealing and did not say a word.

Valentina rested her head on his shoulder and gently caressed his hair. Then she followed with the index finger the contours of his silhouette from the forehead, to the nose, the lips, the chin and further, further down. She kissed him a few times, and then she told him:

"Do you know that I love you? I have been in love with you for a very long time. You have been always in my dreams since the first time I saw you giving a talk. You were so handsome under the deem lights. Your eyes were so bright and dilated, your words so passionate, your person so charismatic.

"But I know that you do not love me. I was just lucky to have you here for a fleeting moment, and I thank you for this," she added.

"I want to go!" said Luca impulsively.

"I am sorry, but I need to go," and he began to put the clothes on with determination as if he was in a rush. But as he was about to leave the room, he turned back, walked close to Valentina, sat at her side and kissed her gently on the forehead stroking her hair.

"Thank you. You offered shelter when I needed it. I will not forget it. I am just not ready for you or anybody else. You are really sweet and you are so beautiful! Sorry if I leave, I just need to go, not sure where but I need to be alone."

"You are like a leopard... powerful, beautiful, smart, whom we all adore and admire. But nobody can own or control because it thrives in freedom. You can only follow your instincts that are solitary. Like a leopard you cannot share love but momentarily before moving toward the next catch. But I love you for what you are, for what you can and what you cannot give, because I know that deep inside, against all your instincts, I know you are a decent and caring human being."

As he was about to exit, Valentina called him:

"Luca, I want you to know that I love you, and I will be here for you whenever you need me."

***

That evening at home, Christina was waiting for Luca with a simple dinner and a bottle of chilled wine. They ate silently, and then Luca thanked her and went to sleep in the den while Christina washed the dishes and dignified herself with a few more chores. When he was about to fall asleep, Christina tiptoed into the den, bringing an extra blanket. Believing him asleep, she sat close to him, caressed his hair and murmured:

"Be well, my Luca. You deserve to be happy. Who knows who will snatch you? Do not fall for just any woman. You deserve a good person, better than I was." As she was saying this, she started sobbing, but Luca did not move. He pretended not to hear. Once again, he just did not know what to do or say. This is simply why he pretended to sleep.

***

Tullio came to the door, wearing his preferred attire for casual events, consisting of the wool vest reserved for home occasions, the customary velvet trousers and

249

soft leather loafers. Standing stiff like a flagpole in a peculiar aristocratic posture, donning the usual charming smile best suited for toothpaste commercials, he opened the right arm to greet Luca. Nothing had changed in those decades! Truly nothing had changed!

Luca smiled and offered his right hand. Then, he changed his mind and thrust his arm around his friend's waist and lifted him up in a tight hug that lasted beyond necessary while he revitalized the past into his veins through the embrace.

As he was about to say something, Luca felt a punch in the back and heard Roberto's jovial voice:

"Look who is here? The little scoundrel! The ladies man! Hei Luca! Any virgin left in the USA?"

Roberto, who was even taller than the other two, piled on the embrace, sticking a bottle of chilled Prosecco in Luca's neck that gave him, together with the goose bumps, a refreshing sensation of the disordered and unpredictable ways in which things evolved in the good old times.

Then, Tullio's mother, who had managed to resist the not–so–subtle encouragements by her son to vacate the premises, came at the door eager to play once more the role of the magnanimous mamma–host. In fact, just like decades before, the dinner was planned at Tullio's parental apartment partly in respect of history and partly to circumvent potential disputes with his better half at home.

Tullio's mom always retained a maternal affection, if not an obsessive infatuation, for Luca, and she had been anxious to see him again after so many decades.

"Dio Mio[13]! You look even more handsome now than you used to! What a distinguished gentleman! But still with those *biricchini*[14]eyes!"

Then, the mom took Luca by the hand and, utterly disregarding Roberto, the little woman carried her catch to the sofa in the living room:

"Accomodati, accomodati bello mio[15]! Tell me, how are things going with you in America? Nuova[16] Yorka, isn't it? How is the family? Did you ever marry? Who is the lucky woman? Do you have children? Do they look like little Luchini?"

That was not exactly how Luca had intended to start the evening. As he was about to offer the standard "all is fine" answer and a few generalities about the children, Giuseppe, who had already arrived and was coming out of the kitchen with a few

---

[13] My God!

[14] Mischievous

[15] Make yourself comfortable, my handsome boy!

[16] New York in some sort of Italian!

pieces of Grana Padano[17] in one hand and a little plate with slices of soppressata[18] in the other, deposited the goodies on the coffee table and sitting close to Luca, put an arm around his shoulders and stated:

"His wife is giving him trouble; she is getting rid of him!"

Why would a smart man like Giuseppe trespass any sort of privacy rule by making that blunt statement? Well, that was the point of the Old Boys Academy: no beating around the bush, "*unus pro omnibus, omnes pro uno*[19]" they were just there to share their lives for better and for worse like in the good old times.

"I think I am divorcing!" Luca admitted, and that confession, for unclear reasons, took five hundred kilograms off his chest.

"Because his wife has a lover," added Giuseppe free of charge.

"That is no problem at all! I can find you a lovely woman any time," interjected Roberto's mouth that, like its owner, always bore a paternal instinct toward the friends.

"There are corsages of good–looking young chicks around who would love to make your acquaintance! Milano has become cosmopolitan! Lots of models from all over the world! There is just *l'imbarazzo della scelta*[20]."

Wearing his imperturbable smile, Tullio interrupted:

"Come on, Roberto! If there is somebody who does not need your help to find a woman, it is Luca!"

But it was Tullio's mom to take control of the conversation and, waving her tiny hand to demand silence, she posed to have the last word on this:

"Luca, that woman... I mean your wife, whoever she is and whatever her name is... does not deserve you! How can a woman leave you unless she is a complete fool?"

"It was partly my fault, I guess. Christina is not a bad person," whispered Luca, looking elsewhere to find inspiration for a diversion away from the topic.

"The divorce is very painful to me. Although I have not been getting along with Christina, it is difficult to do without a person with whom one lived almost all of his life. She became worn of my apathy and found somebody else. He is an old friend and they are happy now. In fact, she told me that she has never been that happy. I am happy for her, but still I feel desolate thinking about the past. All seems to have vanished all of the sudden. It is a strange sensation of disappearance! It is like the fog that hangs over the rice fields and erases

---

[17] Brand of Parmesan Cheese
[18] Spicy sausage from Southern Italy
[19] One for all, all for one
[20] The trouble of making the right choice

everything. One wonders whether everything is truly gone or it is just out of our eyes as a momentary illusion. But then, when the mist dissipates, one realizes that indeed all is gone! I wonder whether even I will disappear into the haze. May–be, I am the fog myself."

He continued, "You know, I feel exposed now as if I am walking on a tightrope without a balancing stick. Christina was my balancing stick! She is the only woman who truly knew and understood me!"

"And this is probably why she left you!" interjected Giuseppe sympathetically!

***

At that juncture, the intercom rang and Tullio announced:

"Enrico is here!"

"Is he still a communist?" questioned Giuseppe, affecting some interest on the subject. In reality, Giuseppe carried an inborn antipathy for those who identified themselves with any ideology and, as much as he respected Enrico as a friend, he felt contempt when it came to politics.

"Is he going to bore us to death with his Gramsci rubbish or did he finally get over it?" continued Giuseppe who was starting to feel comfortably at home.

"Of course, he still is!" proclaimed Roberto. "But no more Gramsci! He made a career out of it, but now he has real problems to deal with! He is now the mayor of... and he goes *pappa ciccia*[21] with all the politicians whatever their colors are."

"And they say that he is even good at it!" intervened Tullio. "They even say that he is "honest"! As if honesty has anything to do with a politician's prerequisites. Wouldn't you rather go for somebody who is effective and can solve problems than for an "honest" guy? Who cares if he gets a cut as long as the trains run on time? But Enrico still carries a monastic life breathing the socialistic spirit. He lives in his one–bedroom apartment with his wife and drives the same old Fiat that you probably remember from before you went to America with all the stickers attached to it that are probably the only thing keeping it together! His favorite hobby is to add cold water to the engine before it's going to melt! But anyways, there is nothing you can do about Enrico. Boring but honest, he really can't do without integrity! It's not his fault. It's in his genes, and there is nothing you can do about genes, isn't it true, professor?"

Turning toward Luca, Tullio added:

"Any gene therapy to correct the "honesty" problem?"

---

[21] Hand in hand

"Well, perhaps he is both; just because he is "honest" it does not mean that he cannot be effective!" concluded Giuseppe, who was starting to regret his original burst also in consideration of Enrico's preeminent appearance at the door.

But in all events, the conversation took another turn before Enrico's arrival. The mom had not fallen for the diversion and, keeping focus on her prey, she did not relent. Holding Luca's hand, she continued:

"Luca, listen to me... You have always been the sweetest among all of your friends. They are all wonderful including my son, but you... you are special. Since I can remember, you were always humble and even shy, with so much inner depth. You never believed in yourself and you always looked for affirmation. Handsome and smart, you never had a thread of arrogance. You were so charming in your simplicity, and just looking at your eyes, I know that you still are. But, no matter how many girls loved you, you never learnt how to understand women. I remember those times when you confessed to me your affairs! You were always so panicked about those who loved you! The more a girl loved you, the more scared you were and the more you ran away from her! What was that? Did you ever figure it out?"

***

Enrico came in, and after the customary hugs and handshakes, he set at Giuseppe's side. He was the image of Saint Francis: not an extra gram of fat, simple but ordered attire, piercing eyes mitigated by a sweet smile, and no words to accompany his presence, but a genuine inclination to listen.

The mom continued:

"Luca..."

Tullio came to his mom's side and, gently tapping her on the shoulder, invited her to leave as she had promised, the mom waved him away.

"Just one more word and I will go. Let me finish!

"Luca, listen to me. You deserve to be loved! Stop running away from those who love you and believe a woman when she tells you that she loves you. Women do not use this world as lightly as men do!"

At this point Tullio took the bottle of Prosecco from the table, poured a glassful into his mother's crystal glass and gently, lifting her by holding the fragile body under the armpit, he walked her away while she received hugs and kisses from each of the Old Boys along the path pretty much like the statue of the Madonna is venerated in Southern Italian processions. As she was about to disappear behind the fixture, she turned around and waving at the Old Boys, she concluded:

"Thank you for coming! I missed all of you during these very long years! You are one of the best memories of my youth, and your presence makes me feel young again!"

***

"I guess your Mom still has a crush on Luca!" Roberto smirked after she disappeared.

"Maybe you should take her to "Nuova Yorka" with you," smiled Tullio. "She would definitely love it!" Then he added:

"I love my mom. She has been more than a mother, a sister to me! After my dad passed away, she clinched on me and my sisters, spending all her energies to convince us that she is the luckiest of women, telling us how wonderful her husband was, and how great her children and grandchildren are. I never heard her complain of anything in all of my life, and in so many ways she is much more of a companion to me than my wife. This is why we have the reunion here... So, I guess what I am trying to say is, forgive me for her intrusion, but I did not have the heart to keep her out completely. She really wanted to see all of you."

"No problem, Tullio! Of course, we love her! We all remember how hospitable she was! No apologies." reflected Giuseppe, who was gradually returning to his natural disposition of a moderate and nonjudgmental wise man.

"Yes, nice woman!' confirmed Roberto. "A little too intrusive sometimes, like that time when she walked in the bedroom and found Luca with La Candela on top of him while we all thought that she had gone out to La Scala!"

"You mean, Luisa? What happened to her?" asked Luca, suddenly awakened from his trance at the mention of the old girlfriend. "What a nice girl she was! I never met anybody sweeter than her!"

"She is married now with two children! She is a different person now!" answered Tullio defensively.

"Don't get any wrong ideas! Besides, she has aged. She is not the way she looked before."

"Her husband is sick, he has terminal cancer," interrupted Enrico who among all was the only non–physician.

"What cancer?" ask Giuseppe who was the authority on the subject.

"Don't know. In the liver I believe."

"Most cancers go to the liver eventually! Do you know where the primary was?" Then recognizing that it made no difference for the purpose of the conversation, Giuseppe added:

"Sorry, never mind. He is probably in good hands at the Institute, and in any case I barely know Luisa. I guess she goes back to your depraved high school life, which I did not have the privilege to share. Anyways maybe Luca should consider reactivating the relationship. She may need some support and Luca definitely needs somebody to talk to. Maybe he can take her to "Nuova Yorka" together with Tullio's Mom."

"Maybe Luca should have married her to begin with, instead of going to America," added Tullio sarcastically, who was getting bored of the conversation and sported a portentous yawn.

"She would have cheated on Luca just as much as she would have with anybody else," commented Roberto, who had been silent way more than he could bear.

"Don't be so cynical," Tullio intervened. "You never know women, and in any case, pretty much all women cheat on their husband at one point or another, and this is good! The ones who don't become a pain in the neck with their righteousness, and they are generally, and not surprisingly, the ugly ones!"

"So your wife is cheating on you, isn't she?" surged from our friendly Roberto.

"None of your business," intervened Giuseppe, but Tullio, calmly and aristocratically, stood up towering over his friends:

"She is! So what? With all the times I cheated on her? How can you blame her? Since she found this guy, she is leaving me alone, and this is good enough for me. Cheers!"

And the old boys lifted the glasses of Prosecco for a toast:

"To our wives and their happiness!" exclaimed Tullio, staring at Luca and expecting a positive reaction from his phlegmatic friend:

"Come on, Luca. Loosen up! See, we are all on the same boat!"

"You see, Luca? You should learn from Tullio! If you lose your wife, you can just take it easy and compensate with high–class young lovers," concluded Giuseppe.

***

"I am going to call Luisa," Interrupted Enrico, but once again the intercom rang, and Marco was announced.

"Let's wait for Marco," said Tullio. "He is the last one we are expecting."

"What about Mario? Is he coming?" asked Giuseppe.

"No, he is having troubles in Rome where he is now. He called to say that he cannot make it."

"What kind of troubles?"

"Not sure. Marco knows since he is a surgeon colleague and they are quite close."

"Well, let's call Mario then at least to say hi."

The doorbell rang and Marco came, carrying a load of bottles and dessert boxes.

Marco was the most jovial and wittiest of them all. He was a short, skinny character with a composed and dry demeanor. He wore formal but not elegant attires, regardless of the occasion to the point that it was whispered that he would go to bed wearing a tie. Even worse, the rumor was that he wore calf suspenders to support his socks, which he did not take off till he was in bed. However, such debasing gossip had been never substantiated since none of his friends had ever seen him naked nor any relevant woman ever offered to testify on this delicate subject. Thus, since nobody could prove otherwise, the Old Boys assumed for practical purposes that indeed, Marco was the kind of guy who would wear calf suspenders even in the shower. Just like his posture, dry was his humor; sharp like a Chinese knife that could cut through bones as if they were butter.

"Hello, everybody! What a pleasure it is to see my Old Boys again! Where have you been for all these years while a poor guy had to take care of all your relatives?"

In fact, Marco, among various talents, was the doctors' doctor. With a terrific common sense, he was taken advantage of by all of his friends, in particular by those living abroad, who made sure that he would intervene. Whenever a problem arose among their relatives, Marco would be at the forefront.

Turning toward Luca, Marco gave him a big hug:

"How is your dad doing? How is his heart? is the A Fib[22] controlled?"

"Fine! Thanks for taking care of him. Yes, he takes his Coumadin and Digoxin religiously, if not for other reasons, just to make sure that you do not scold him. Thanks for checking on him often."

"So what happened to Mario?" asked the inpatient Roberto.

"Do not know for sure! I believe he has some problems with the administration in Rome. I have no idea why he left Milan and his unbelievable cardiac surgery program to go there!"

"Obviously, it must have been for a woman!" interjected Roberto, receiving unanimous assent from the complete audience.

The phone was put on speaker mode and, after a few rings, Mario answered:

"Hei! It's us, the Old Boys! Sorry you could not make it!" opened Tullio.

"We wish you were here" added Marco. "Everybody is here! Including the "Americani"! What is going on with you? I heard a lot of bad rumors! Did you get in trouble for taxes?"

"Sort of! Well, guys, it's a long story. You know, people are jealous and they would do anything to get rid of a successful guy, but I did my part to help them on this! In the end it is always about women. I used some grant money to pay for a pied–a–terre where we could meet and then deduct from taxes from the payments as

---

[22] Atrial fibrillation in doctors' slang

a business expense. At least this is what my detractors say. Now they are forcing me to resign to avoid a bigger penalty. You know, it is a Christian place, so they worry more about the image than the facts. Who can blame them?"

"Wow, is she beautiful, at least? Is she worth it?" asked a fretful Roberto, who was earnestly more concerned about this latter aspect of the problem. How could somebody blame Mario if the prize balances the cost?

"Of course, she is! How can you even ask something like that? What do you think, that I lost it? She is amazing, her skin is so smooth, you see, not that cold and frigid slickness of marble, but the grainy smoothness of silk that sticks to the pulp of your fingers and penetrates the skin into the blood... if you know what I mean. You can go up and down her body with ease and yet, you feel you are touching an angel who is made of real flesh!"

In the silence that followed, several heads nodded their endorsement:

"How could anybody argue with such well–presented and compelling argument?"

"Is she Japanese?" asked Enrico all of a sudden, interrupting the meditative moment.

"No! Why do you ask?"

"Japanese women have that kind of skin!"

That was an unexpected poser! Everybody wondered how Enrico could come up with that conclusion. It was Roberto who recovered first and asked:

"I think you are thinking of their kimonos, and in any case, how on Earth would you happen to know anything about Japanese women's skin, or for Christ's sake, any woman's skin?"

"I heard it in a movie!" answered Enrico factually.

"Ahh, now this explains it! Anyways, sorry, Mario for the interruption, so what is going to happen to you?" resumed Marco.

"I think I will have to resign!"

"Well," interjected Marco, "you remind me of Al Capone. After killing all of these people with your cardiac surgery, they finally got you for tax evasion!"

"Wow! With a friend like this, who needs a mother–in–law?" exclaimed the disgusted Roberto.

The proper Enrico had to add his part:

"I am sorry, Mario. Is anything that we could do?"

"No, do not worry, guys, I will be fine, and I can always make a lot of money by going private. I know that this is not what you want to hear, but you know what? Lovers are expensive!"

 Even the prude Enrico assented with a smile.

"Do me a favor, guys! Keep me in mind for the next time, and I will be there for sure... if I am not in jail!"

***

"Wow! That was interesting! Are we all this rotten? Is any of us straight at all?" commented Giuseppe not without a subliminal sense of pride.

That was a good question, and each of the Old Boys considered it thoughtfully. As they were going through this introspective moment, considering their existence and wondering about their friends, automatically all the eyes converged toward the honest Enrico. If there was hope for redemption among all, he was the one would who could save the pack of wolves from perdition. So Enrico saw a myriad of eyes staring at him over this very special kind of inquisition:

"Come on, Enrico! Do not tell us that you never cheated on your wife. Got to be some woman who loves your pimples!" attacked Roberto.

Now, you ought to know that Enrico did not smile that often; neither frowned easily nor exercised in extravagance any connection between the frontal lobe and the mimic muscles of his face through the facial nerve. Most importantly, he did not blush at all or behave like octopuses or chameleons that change colors in response to environmental pressure. But all of this happened at once as the aftermath to Roberto's question. While the honest man was blabbering some disconnected excuse, everybody understood that even the honorable Enrico failed to carry the lantern of purity for his profane friends, and they all lost interest in the matter:

"Yes, obviously we are all rotten! So what? Let's move on with dinner!" concluded Tullio. But this caused Roberto to claim proudly:

"Wait a minute! I am the only one who has never cheated on his wife!"

"Of course, you have never been married!" pointed out Marco.

"Hey, whatever works!"

***

Dinner started with a clap of hands and Tullio announcing:

"Que la fête commence!"

Simultaneously, a blond woman of the kindest manners and a charming smile emerged from the kitchen with a steaming bowl in her hands. The latter emanated a fragrance reminiscent of Alpine forests and contained a consommé

258

of Porcini mushrooms.

Upon first inspection, tacit exchanges conceded in unanimity that the woman was endowed with a great body. This first impression was confirmed by subsequent inspections carried discreetly with the corner of the eye by each member of the audience that was obediently taking position around an ancient mahogany table. A tablecloth laced by the hands of some grandmother a century before and concealed by all sort of hors d'oeuvres covered the latter. There were typical Northern and Southern Italian cold meats such as Prosciutto di Parma wrapped around breadsticks and hot soppressata reposing over dried tomatoes. There were grilled vegetables drizzled with balsamic vinegar and virgin olive oil and decorated with fresh rosemary twigs, bruschetta with basil and vine–tomatoes, chunks of parmesan cheese, baccalà[23] soaked in pomegranate–vinaigrette topped with black olives and ginger flakes, smoked lox with capers and lemon cloves, goose liver pate and, right in a middle, a big bowl containing gigantic prawns that sat prostrated toward the center in reverence to a porcelain basin from ancient China filled to the brim with cocktail sauce. Such cornucopia was sprinkled with delicious, thou often underappreciated, pickled gherkins. At the center of the table also sat a crystal bowl, where colorful and fragrant camellias floated on rose water: an elegant touch emblematic of Tullio's mother, who wished to remind the guests of her tactful presence.

In the absolute silence, the woman approached the table, deposited the soup close to the crystal bowl and, progressing guest by guest, she held a ladle with the right hand lifting with the other a plate at the time and pouring a generous amount of consommé. All was done without spilling a single drop on the tablecloth. At last, she reached Tullio, who, as she was pouring the concoction, put his hand around her waist, just on top of what technically should be referred to as the junction of the gluteus maximus with the iliac wing, but is more widely known as the rump. Tullio smiled at her and softly stated:

"Grazie Martina."

Martina responded with a submissive smile and a subliminal bow of the head, and for the first time she looked around. When she sighted Luca, who was, like the others, staring at her, Martina, as most women did at such occurrence, radiated a graceful smile while Luca appropriately pretended not to take notice.

As soon as Martina disappeared in the kitchen, Giuseppe asked:

"If Luca takes your mom to *"Nuova Yorka"*, is Martina going with them?"

Simultaneously, Marco interjected:

"Let me say this to you, Tullio if you do not mind: did you really have to screw up the dinner with this woman? Nobody is going to focus on anything else now!"

---

[23] Dried and Salted Cod

"Come on, guys! Grow up! She is just my mother's help! A woman from Ukraine! She just offered to help!"

"And what was that caress to her butt about? Come on, do you think it went unnoticed?" added Roberto. "Be honest! Tell us the truth! Did you do it with her?"

"What kind of question is this?" the proper Giuseppe intervened to protect Tullio, who did not seem the least fazed by the comment and continuing to smile enigmatically, lifted the cup of Prosecco for a toast:

"Welcome, all of you! Welcome back to the Old Boys Academy! *At Maiora*! I already see that in spite of the decades, little has changed in our spirit! *Unus pro omnibus, omnes pro uno!*"

As they all raised their glasses and gulped down the nectar, Luca nodded and thoughtfully offered his expert opinion:

"She is indeed a beautiful woman!"

"Thank you, professor, for pointing it out! We would have never noticed," added Roberto, while Tullio interjected:

"Guys, let's forget Martina! Can we just move onto something more interesting?" leaving the audience wondering about what could be more interesting than the aforementioned miraculous apparition.

I forgot to mention that sitting at the table, as part of the Old Boys ensemble, was Tommaso. I forgot to mention him, because frankly he was the least notable creature. He rarely spoke and, therefore, all friends fondly regarded him as part of the furniture, taking no further notice beyond such generous concession. He was a stocky and buff figure, exaggeratedly tanned, donning gold watches, bracelets and heavy necklaces that shone over the hairy chest from the open shirt in utter dissonance with the subdue elegance of his friends. Yet, he had been a legitimate constituent of the Old Boys Academy since high school days, simply because his congeniality deflected any questions about his belongings. He studied briefly in America, accumulating just enough credentials to elevate him, upon his return, to a prominent gynecologist with mixed academic and private practice. He was seen consistently with spectacular women hopping in an out of his red Ferrari with stunning legs veiled by black stockings and supported by laced garters that transpired at the verge of vertiginous miniskirts. Allegedly, he was married; in fact, a plump and unrefined woman, introduced as his wife appeared on a few occasions at his side, but, like him, she never took the initiative to begin a conversation and nobody ever felt the compulsion to compensate for that shortcoming.

As the Old Boys were about to move away from Martina's subject, unexpectedly, Tommaso pronounced:

"I agree with Luca. She is really beautiful, she is just perfect!"

This further blow disheartened Tullio, who had been trying to elevate just a notch the conversation directing it away from its repetitiveness.

Meanwhile, Giuseppe, overtaken by a philosophical attack, shared this hypothetical scenario:

"Think about it! Luca goes back to America with your mom, Luisa and Martina. What a trio! Maturity, affection and attraction! Commitment, companionship and passion! The perfect relationship built around three women!"

"Yes... till the three of them start plotting together against him! Then the poor Luca is kaput! *Unus adversus omnibus, omnes adversus uno!* Excuse my Latin!" reflected Marco.

"He can then find a fourth nice woman!"

"Till she also joins the pack!"

"It will end like Christopher Columbus, who had to run out of the Old Continent! Believe me, he discovered America by accident; the issue about the Earth being round was just an excuse. He was just in trouble with a bunch of women and needed a pretext to get out of town and refurbish in the New Continent," mentioned Roberto scholastically.

"And where did this notion come from?" asked Giuseppe, who was the most versed in historical matters.

"I read it in Wikipedia."

"Didn't know you were a Wikepedophile! Great for you to keep up with high standards!"

"That Wikipedia sounds good till you look up topics about which you actually know something about. Then you will appreciate how inaccurate it can be."

"Glad we are moving away from the Martina subject!" sighed Tullio in relief just before Martina returned. This time she was carrying a copper pan filled with searing rice colored by saffron and smelling of white truffle that had been freshly grated on top.

Martina, repeated the ceremonial of the consommé around the table, offering, in addition, to grate on the rice extra truffle from Alba or Parmesan cheese with the premonition, however, that truffle alone should do for taste.

As she approached Tullio, all eyes pointed at his hand, but the experienced Tullio, preempting the inquisition, maintained composure by leaving this second passage uneventful.

A few bottles of Barolo were brought in that had already been opened and vented, and the friends poured generously into each other's crystal chalice. Roberto took the bottle from Tullio's hand and studied the label. Then nodding his head in approbation, he returned it to Tullio, commenting:

"Wow! You must have put some overtime for this stuff! Hope the quality does not compromise the quantity! You know, these "Americans" suck wine like sponges when they get a chance to return home."

"Talk for yourself!" grunted Giuseppe. "Come to Napa sometimes, and you will crawl on your fours within an hour."

Tullio reassured that a rich patient donated a case of the precious Barolo, and added that there was plenty of white wine in the cooling cellar and of liquor of any color and vintage dispersed in his mom's home that had been waiting for the Old Boys' return.

Again, Martina smiled at Luca, and again he pretended not to notice. But after she left, he reinforced his previous statement:

"She truly is a beautiful woman!"

In answer to this comment, Roberto emanated a big sigh, and in agreement with Tullio, mumbled:

"OK, let's get over this!"

But Tommaso muttered:

"Yes, she is just perfect! Just like my wife."

I admit that it would be an exaggeration to state that a clank caused by the Old Boys' jaws dropping on the floor could be heard from miles away. So be it! It still provides the reader with an approximate idea of the magnificence of the Old Boys' reaction! After Roberto had a chance to recover his own jaw from the floor and reattach it to the temporal mandibular joint, to test his regained verbal skills, he asked:

"What do you mean your wife looks like her? If I remember correctly, your wife looks... looks... looks just... different, I would say. May–be a different kind of beauty?"

"You are talking about my other wife," reacted the inflexible Tommaso, while he shoveled a forkful of rice in the mouth, raising the glass of Barolo to facilitate the progress of the chow.

"Sorry, I did not know you were divorced!"

"I didn't."

"I am sorry. Let me get this straight and sorry again if I may sound brash, but... did your wife get a total body replacement recently? That is what you mean by your new wife?"

Tommaso was not only quiet but also exaggeratedly slow. He could make a sloth look like a cheetah. But eventually, as everybody was about to give up, he mumbled:

"I am talking about my other wife!"

I assure you that this is what emerged from Tommaso's munching mouth to everybody's disbelief.

The friends looked around to confirm consonant reception. Then, they waited for a volunteer to carry the sequitur of such strange conversation. Nobody came forward and the curiosity mounted. Finally, Tullio reluctantly felt the responsibility, as the host, to initiate the impromptu interrogation:

"Tommaso," he calmly opened, "we do understand that this is none of our business, but we are friends and we do care for you. Did we understand correctly that you have two wives?"

Trying to coordinate talking with munching, Tommaso intercalated:

"Yes, I know that you do not consider me a genius, but you should concede that even I could figure out that one plus one equals two!"

"But, do you understand that, at least in Italy, no matter how permissive our beloved country is, polygamy remains illegal?"

"This is why I shared this information with you guys in confidentiality, and please keep it for yourselves." Then he added:

"It is not the law that I am concerned about. I do not want for Isabella to know about Jasmine and the other way around. I would not want for either to be hurt."

"Now, this is what I call being considerate!" commented Giuseppe. "We cannot take good care of one wife, and this guy here sports the energy to worry about two!"

"And how did you even get married? Don't you need a license or something?"

"Listen, guys. I know that it is none of your business, but I am still compelled to share the story with you all. I met Jasmine at a strip club. She was a stripper and I had a dance with her. Next thing I know, she tells me that her husband is a drunkard and abuses her and their child. What's a man to do? I felt bad and decided to marry her. The husband comes to beat me up and kill me. He was the bouncer at the same club and he was huge: he could kill an elephant with one stroke but, I tell him, 'Listen, she is not happy with you and you have a lot of debts. I will pay them off and you let her go.'

"We both agreed that it made perfect sense and, therefore, we shook hands and from then on, we have been good friends. Now we jump on a plane to Las Vegas and we marry on a wedding chapel with bouquets of plastic roses in the background. She is moved and cries and next she falls deeply in love with me. She wants kids from me. I want them too because Isabella can't have any. God knows how much we tried! Later on, during a romantic dinner, I get drunk and when I do, my imagination unleashes. I tell her with tears in my eyes (not sure where it came from) that my Isabella died a year before in a car crash, and Jasmine cries in empathy, isn't she sweet? And we both cry, though I reckon with relief in another part of my brain that Isabella is alive and well. We ended up enjoying the sweetest honeymoon. Now she is pregnant with my first baby! It's going to be a girl! She wants to call her Isabella but I think it would be too much."

"And what about Isabella?" interrupted a suddenly interested Luca.

"She is happy. She doesn't know about Jasmine. Meanwhile, I have never been as kind to her as I have been since I married Jasmine. I spend two weeks with one wife, alternating with the other for the other two weeks. I told them that I took a missionary project in Rwanda, requiring two weeks on site each month to help women with difficult pregnancies. I learned everything about endemic problems there. You won't believe how primordial conditions can be in that beautiful country devastated by fratricide. I feel ashamed for the way we carry our life of entitlement. How can we complain about anything? Sometimes I feel that I should go to Rwanda for real, but then, how can I if I have to rotate between two wives?"

"They both admire me for this Rwanda thing, and now I am addicted to it. I am a victim of my own success. I go from one to the other and narrate great stories about rescued pregnancies and miracle babies and, as I polish them, I start to like the stories myself. I know that they are apocryphal, but so what? They seem to enlighten and mature them into better persons. After all, does is really matter what's real or what's imagined? Isn't the message that counts?"

"God save the King!" concluded Giuseppe, lifting a full glass of Barolo. "As long as you can deal with it, it certainly takes a lot of planning and coordination; not something for everybody. Your next job might as well be an intelligence agent for the C.I.A.!"

But the usually reticent Tommaso, under the influence of Barolo, was relentless and could not bridle the mouth from its momentum:

"Well, it wasn't always that simple. This is when a friend's help is critical. Once, I was almost exposed to Isabella. I was in a faculty senate meeting when I got this call. I went out of the room to answer it, and it was Isabella. She was yelling:

"'WHY IS THERE A PHOTO OF YOU IN THE INTERNET MARRYING ANOTHER WOMAN IN LAS VEGAS?'"

"What? I said, pretending to be surprised... and I was! My dear gentlemen! What did Jasmine think? Why did she post the photo without first consulting me? Well, I cannot tell you how much I hate social media; they just complicate a poor man's life. Anyways, I say in a whisper as if I could not talk:

"'Can't talk to you now, I am in a meeting. I'll call later!' But as I returned to the room and I sat down, I can't focus and kept shaking and tossing on the chair till Professor Salimbeni, who was chairing the session, noticed me and asked, 'Something wrong?'

"I cannot hold myself! I keep shaking, and I have no clue about what to do. I am not concerned about the faculty senate. I care about my wonderful wives! And how could I be blamed? How could I have predicted that my little Jasmine would do something so naïve in her sweet spontaneity? This is what I recounted in front of them!

"Anyways, Professor Salimbeni listened pensively to my executive summary, nodding his head at intervals and in between scratching his temple with a pencil, which otherwise he kept twisting in his nervous hand. Promptly, the astute academician reckoned that this was no ordinary senate matter; this is a real problem! Therefore, he said:

'There are a lot of superbly practiced men in this room, who survived the turbulent waters of academia, which are almost as bad as dealing with two wives. Any suggestions from the audience?'

"Prof. Gasparoni, who is the Chair of Ethical Studies in the Department of Philosophy, had no doubts:

"'Buy a luxuriant bouquet of red roses and go home. There, you tell your wife...' Then upon reflection, he specified, '...I mean the wife, who just called... tell her the truth and plead for her pardon. We all make mistakes, but true love should overcome minor setbacks. Tell her that you did it out of generosity for an abused woman. Women like candor; she will forgive you if she loves you. If she does not forgive you, then it means that she does not love you and then... forget about her!'

"Then Prof. Lentini, Chair of Civil Litigation, interjected:

'With all due respect for my distinguished colleague, I would have to humbly disagree. Philosophers are often naïve in practical matters.'

'Never admit any fault unless you talk to a lawyer first. You have to understand the extent of the consequences of confession in the court of law!'

"'Then what is a poor man supposed to do?' I asked".

"'I know what you are going to do!' said Prof. Leoni, Chair of Humanistic Studies, who had recently published a treatise on the aftermath of the feminist revolution in the Western world, demonstrating that he knew just enough about women to possibly endure them.

'You tell her that this was just a prank! A set–up to protect the poor woman from an abusive boyfriend, that you pretended to marry her to discourage him, but it was just a farce, a joke pretending to be in Las Vegas, thanks to Photoshop. Kind of thing anybody would do with friends when drunk! In the end, she knows that you have... an active life, so to speak. Only thing she cares about is reassurance that you do not leave her for another woman and, most importantly, that you keep bringing the dough home!'

"I turned to look at our chairman Prof. Salimbeni, wondering whether he would call for a vote. But he simply nodded his head and said:

'Great idea! This is why we should support humanistic studies or, as they call them now, Science of Antiquity! It is the evolution of civilization, the survival of the human species against the odds, the fortitude of manhood before feminine hurricanes. If I were in the same predicament, I would definitely follow Professor Leoni's advice. Any further suggestion?'

"Nobody said anything, so Prof. Salimbeni continued:

'OK then, you proceed and let us know how it went at the next meeting. Let's move ahead with the agenda. By the way,' he said, turning to the assistant, 'it goes without saying that this confidential matter does not need to be included in the minutes!'"

"And so what happened?" asked Roberto for all.

"Well... Isabella was touched by my munificence. She told me that she always knew I was a good man, and that she was proud of me for helping the poor woman, and for the Rwanda thing as well. Both corroborated each other as evidence of my compassionate metamorphosis. She cried and even apologized for accusing me. I gave her a big hug and forgave her. She never talked about it again and never looked me up in the Internet."

"Wow, there is always something to learn from those scholars. I guess it helped that Prof. Leoni spent most of his life scratching his head over Macchiavellis, Ciceros and Descartes! *Cogito Ergo Sum!* And he was really something to figure that out in the spur of the moment! A tribute to the senate of our glorious University! Sometimes, something of substance can come out of it!" said Tullio, raising and drinking in immediate succession another glass of Barolo.

Silence followed. Then Giuseppe, who, in spite of his successful career held a grudge against the academic system and its overbearing bureaucratic aspects, lifted the impasse.

"Perhaps, the faculty senate of the University of Milan is more practical than in other places. Academia in America is now under the hands of bureaucrats, so much posturing about doing "good" for people's health, but little support to move forward with programmatic studies that could fulfill the promise. Bureaucrats run the show: people that justify their existence claiming a need to solve problems that would not exist if they didn't create them in the first place. A bureaucrat is somebody who can find a problem for any solution, but for sure cannot find a solution for any problem! Bureaucrats will do anything to convince you that you do not know what you are doing, and that they are the only ones who can help you fix what they know nothing about. They will drive you crazy with "strategic planning" trying to package creativity and intuition into a box! What kind of strategy do you think Heraclitus, Socrates, Plato, Pythagoras needed? And what was Newton's strategy? Keep walking under an apple trees till something would hit his head and teach him gravity? What about Copernicus, Galileo or Einstein? What about Vera Rubin, who described dark matter? What was her strategy besides sitting for endless boring nights taking notes behind a telescope? And what strategy followed Beethoven when he composed "Moonlight", and Albinoni composing the "Adagio"? Did any of these creators need a strategy or they simply needed to be left in peace without interference from idiots?"

Giuseppe continued, "For example, in the institution where I work, there was an escalator that carried from the ground floor to the second floor cafeteria. I took it each morning to fetch the habitual cup of coffee... each morning except for when it was out of order, which was not so rare of an occurrence. The poor escalator was out of service every other day, and one could observe two or three maintenance guys musing over the dismantled steps in awe as if they were Japanese tourists facing the Grand Canyon. It vexed me so much, but I sucked it up, mumbled something about raising a complaint about it to some unknown entity while I climbed the stairs and, by the time I was up, I would have forgotten about it. Then one day, I received the honor of being invited to be part of a prestigious panel of scientists assembled to discuss strategies to advance the treatment of cancer. It was indeed a great honor to be included in this distinguished group of experts put together by our administration with the specific purpose of demonstrating that they were doing something to earn their salary. But it was also utterly boring to trail all day along pompous presentations that emphasized how, coincidentally, the protein, the mouse model, the new gadget that each expert happened to be working on, stood as a portentous solution to the cure of cancer and perhaps anything beyond that including possibly global warming. Therefore, money should be thrown at it! By the end of the day, everybody around the big table was worn out. Some were even dozing off, except for the bureaucrats, who were frantically typing notes to justify their existence as if they actually understood anything that was discussed. It was then that a ruinous idea assailed me: I switched on the speakerphone that reached up to my mouth like the leg of a big daddy spider and, when my turn came, I said:

'Maybe we should consider a feasibility study. We should try to fix the first floor escalator in this building once and for all! Then we can worry about curing cancer. I mean, Macys, Bloomingdale (for the Italians, UPIM and Rinascente) and all other big department stores manage to assure that each day, stacks of escalators reliably elevate common people to the altitudes of consumerism while we cannot even get one to work for our scientists to get a cup of coffee in the morning! If we cannot match that, how can we deal with complex problems like cancer? Conversely, we could ask Macys' managers to help us here!'

"It was obviously meant to be a lighthearted comment at the end of a draining day, but it did not go well. Even from the 20th floor, where the meeting was held, one could hear the crickets chirping cheerfully from the gardens below. Nobody laughed!"

"And then what happened?" asked Roberto eagerly.

"You mean, to cancer or to the escalator?" asked Marco sarcastically.

"Well, a few days later, my Chief summoned me to his office after he heard of my unsolicited remarks and warned me to watch my tongue in the future. Meanwhile, the escalator was removed forever from the premises, and that took care of it! Of course, cancer is still there for the next strategic panel to contemplate."

"Yes, sounds exactly like our administration: feed the bureaucrats with chatter and they will be content, but do not challenge them with real problems, except, of course for Tommaso's case which after all was handled by bonafide academicians!" summarized Roberto.

"Well, it must have been quite embarrassing. I hate when I throw a joke and nobody gets it," commented the astute Marco.

"Tell me about it! But it can be even worse! Talking about embarrassing situations in academia!" interjected Tullio.

"Do you know what happened to me? I was at a stage of life when I was happily trailing along my existence on the passenger seat. Wherever life wanted to go, I docilely followed. My only goal was to inconspicuously carry a lifeless body around in the form of flesh wrapped around a beating heart... and that was fine with me. But my wife insisted that I should see a shrink."

"That's called depression, nothing that Zoloft can't take care of," interrupted Marco, who like Tullio's wife, was rather inclined to turn philosophical matters into practicality.

"That's exactly what the shrink prescribed, but only after I dropped five hundred Euros in his piggy bank. Next time I will come directly to you, Marco. Anyways, I started taking the pill that did almost nothing except for forcing me to produce superlative yawns. You have no idea what kind of stretches of the jaws were involved. They would last a minute, and I was at constant risk of dislocating my mandible. I could barely breathe in between yawns, and I had to wipe tears from my eyes. It was embarrassing! It was the worst nightmare... like when one dreams of having a boner in a public beach while wearing those "dental floss" swimsuits so popular in the Riviera. I am sure that you can empathize with me."

Tullio continued, "Anyways, it was a minor token to pay to restore one's sanity, one would say! That was also what I thought till I had to listen to a presentation from Il Rettore Magnifico[24] of the University, who gave a forecast of the strategic development of our research program: a highly selective audience pretty much like Giuseppe's for the cancer panel. Well, I sat right in front of Il Rettore, forgetting about the Zoloft and its side effects. Few minutes into his talk, I was

---

[24] The Magnificent Director (name used for the Provost or President of the University)

overtaken by a yawning attack that was completely incoercible. As I became unnerved, I started yawning more repetitively, with small enough pauses in between to wipe the eyes from the tears and take a deep breath. The problem is that yawns are contagious, and mine must have been particularly compelling since in a short while, the whole audience was yawning uncontrollably, with stretched mouths as big as those of caged lions at the zoo. Our Rettore Magnifico, as you know, is a very experienced person with infinite public speaking practice. Therefore, he courteously pretended not to notice and carried on trying to finish as soon as he could till he himself was overtaken by a yawning attack that was just as incoercible. Fortunately, the speech was meant to be short, and at the end, he thanked all for enduring the wearying presentation. He, more than anybody else, was well aware of the unpleasantness of strategic mumbo–jumbo, though it's a tenet in academia. In the end, Zoloft had a group therapy effect, a pharmacological peer pressure on our Rettore Magnifico to keep the BS to the least minimum denominator. Unfortunately, I am quite aware that this episode did not help my career and my prospects to rise upwards in the ranks of our esteemed faculty senate."

***

"It is heartbreaking to see how funny life can be sometimes. It is deceiving; it makes one believe that it is worth living just because of these rare exceptions springing occasionally along an otherwise meaningless existence!"

Luca's comment interjected amongst tearful laughs befell as a cold shower. Everybody realized how dejected the friend's mood was, but nobody reacted.

"Well, talking about yawns and embarrassing situations, I will tell you what happened to me. I would love to know what you would have done in my shoes," Mended Marco, who was trying to recover the good humor for the benefit of the gloomy friend.

"Of course, needless to say this is highly privileged information that cannot go beyond these walls!" he continued.

"There was a young intern at the hospital. She was tiny and pretty. She had a reserved personality that a radiant smile, like a pulsar in the deep sky, dependably enlightened. Often, she sat by herself at the cafeteria in between surgical cases, reading a manuscript or a book with delicate eyebrows that when corrugated looked like little exclamation marks. She wore nerdy spectacles that were bigger than the face and made her look just irresistible. One day, after a long case, I believe it was a hepatic resection, in which she helped me as third assistant, I noticed her at the cafeteria sitting by herself as usual behind the spectacles with the corrugated eyebrows and munching chips. I asked for permission to sit beside with the excuse of gathering her thoughts about the case that we had just completed. She smiled, and after a little while we were talking about anything but medicine. Turned out she was recently divorced and lived alone. To make it short, we met in the cafeteria together a few more times, then we started to go for walks in a nearby park, and eventually we ended up having dinner on a night when my wife was going to be late due to her own commitments. It came after a romantic rainy afternoon. We had walked in the park and visited the museum of Natural History. There was nobody there, save for the stuffed creatures that looked resignedly at us with their glassy stares. When we walked out of the museum, it was still drizzling, and she rested her weight on my arm that was carrying the umbrella, pressing her little body against me. We went for dinner at a bistro close to her place, and we had a bottle of good wine. When it was time to walk her home, the rain had subsided, but my arm was still warmed by her embrace. At a red light, I kissed her and the kiss lasted for a few cycles of greens, yellows and reds whose reflections took turn on the wet street. We walked for a little longer and we kissed again... and again till after a few more stop–and–go, we reached her place. She asked me:

'Do you want to come up? I live by myself. It is a little but cozy place, we can have a drink before you go home.'

"Her apartment was more like a studio. It had a kitchen–dining–living room unit and an adjacent bedroom in which a matrimonial bed peaked from the open door with enticing warmth in that cold night. Needless to say, it did not take long to adjust to the coziness of the warm embrace, and soon we were making love while the rain was tapping at the window. With astounding efficiency within a few minutes, she sported a spectacular orgasm. That encouraged me to persist on my duty to provide further opportunities for pleasure. But she appeared excited no more. You very well know that it takes delicate moves and gentle persistence to go over the refractory phase of a woman. So patiently, I rock my body with grace and continue to kiss and caress her till I notice a periodic huff. The latter progressively turned into a clearly detectable rumble till it matured into a flagrant snore! The gentle soul had fallen asleep and, while I was still inside of her, she was detonating thunders that were worthy of my late grandpa, who was relegated in exile by my grandma to the basement in safeguard of her sanity.

"Now, it had never happened to me before, and I felt both hesitant and embarrassed! What is a man to do in such circumstance? Have you ever encountered such case in any textbook? Never knew that narcolepsy could affect pretty women, or maybe it wasn't narcolepsy at all; it was just my uninspiring presence? Good news, for the sake of my ego, that at least she did not yawn away like Tullio. Anyways, I could not lie down to sleep beside her because I was mindful of my wife waiting at home, so I tried to wake her gently, just to say 'good night', let her accompany me to the door and latch it from inside... but to no avail! Sleeping beauty was resistant to any attempt from Prince Charming, and I am glad it was not she in the fable because I am sure the poor Prince would have had quite a hard time to fulfill the happy ending. Anyways, I kissed her and I shook her softly. I repeated a little less softly. I even checked her pulse that was beating regularly in restful rhythm while she lay like a baby, who had fallen into a solid sleep after gorging on a bottle of formula. In the end, I gave up and I left her sleeping. I accosted the door and walked home with the tail between my legs, not knowing what to think. I am sure it would not have happened if Luca were there instead of me. So Luca, do not complain life is beautiful and although you worry about Christina, remember: each end is nothing more than the beginning of a new journey. Be happy, my friend. There are lots of Sleeping Beauties out there that are waiting for their Prince Charming to awaken them!"

Needless to say, at that juncture everybody was wondering whether Marco on that occasion had been wearing his infamous calf suspenders that certainly might have had something to do with Sleeping Beauty's detachment. But nobody dared to question.

Instead, at the conclusion of the heartfelt confession, another round of wine refreshed the throats of the Old Boys.

This not–so–hilarious story conformed to the calando of the friends' mood in an increasingly somber atmosphere.

Then, Roberto offered:

"Well, I will tell you my embarrassing story! Not so bad actually but interesting! It shows how semantics can change a life. In my bachelor routine, I frequently invited pretty women for dinner at my place. I let them enjoy the meal and a good bottle of wine, and then after dinner, with seat on the sofa where we fondled a little till we progressed to the bedroom. Believe me, guys; with the right selection criteria it works just about 95% of the times. But this time, I invited this middle–aged spinster, who had an interesting body but turned out, as the discussion evolved, to be a virgin! Who knew that they existed anymore? That, of course, in some ways excited me even more but it also enthused my sense of responsibility. I wanted for her to experience a memorable first time, so I took it slowly, letting her relax according to her tempo. While I was at it, I was thinking:

'How can a woman with such a great body be still a virgin?'

"Meanwhile, little at the time, intercalating with – Oh Gesù e Maria – Oh Madonna Mia – and other such pleas to a greater authority, she let herself being fondled at relevant trigger points. She held the wrist of my hand as to control the progression of the fingers along her legs, but without demonstrating any earnest intention to halt the inevitable. Instead, all of a sudden she was taken by abrupt resolve and with crazed movements, she stretched her arm toward my crouch, opened the zipper and extracted from the underwear my masculine attribute. She started caressing, rubbing, stroking, squeezing and ravaging over it, as if she was a witch manhandling a ladle into a boiling potion. Then, she suddenly froze and looking at me with grazed eyes and in complete embarrassment, she questioned:

'I do not know if I can handle this!'

"What a strange selection of words! In fact, she was doing a great job at handling the aforementioned object. So I reassured her:

'Dear, I promise that, having quite a lot of experience on this matter, you are doing a fabulous job at handling it!'

"Well, that was just exactly the encouragement that she had needed to move on with her life! Maybe before that night, nobody took her as literally as I did!"

The Old Boys cheered again and again as they got drunker and drunker with the dinner.

"Yup, semantics can be crucial," added Marco. "I recollect this young woman, whom I examined in the emergency room. She came with belly pain. I asked her if she was sexually active and whether she could be pregnant. She sternly denied, but the pregnancy test came positive.

"'Why did you lie to me?' I asked empathetically. 'You should trust your doctor! I am not here to judge but to help,' I said.

"'I did not lie to you,' she replied. 'You asked if I was sexually active, but I am rather not! I lie passive in bed, and let my boyfriend do his part!'"

More cheers ensued and wine washed the throats. Then that Jiminy Cricket of Enrico had to ask:

"Why are we doing this? What is this obsession? Why do we have to run after women that do not belong to us? Why do we have affairs? Why do we enjoy so much recounting them? Are we never going to grow up?"

"Why should we?" exploded Tullio. "Aren't we beautiful people ninety–nine percent of the time, perfectly fitting the cage of conventionality? Why can't we be childish at least when we get together? Life has taught us a lot of lessons, but above all we learnt how dull it can be! We all know how to harmoniously cradle in the arms of high society and its expectations; we can go through its conformities smoothly but... is it really us? Where did the spontaneity go? Why did the mischievousness of youth abandon us? Can wisdom be derided at times? Are there ways in which a man can feel alive simply by rebelling against the predictability of a prefabricated life? We are not bad people; we pay our taxes, take care of our families, stop at red lights and obey speed limits. So, should we talk about our perfections tonight? Should we discuss how we could be better than perfect? Or should we just forget about it for a night? Should we rather follow the Peter Pan's spirit that is still in our heart?

"I do not know, maybe it is just boredom dumped upon us by conventionality. Some people rob banks, or drive drunk. Others take drugs or do any crazy thing just to feel that they are different from their neighbors, that they are colorful pawns in the chessboard of life. To play with consenting women is safe and legal. What is the harm if they enjoy our caresses? And it is interesting too. I have affairs because I like to hear the women's stories, particularly those of the married ones. Why do they cheat on their husband? What do they think of the men who cheated on them? Maybe I will learn something about myself," concluded Tullio.

"You remind me a lot of Alessandro," interjected Giuseppe. "He was like this. For him women were just a learning experience, a curiosity. The closer we became, the least I could understand this part of him."

"Oh yes, Alessandro, your compare[25] from Terronia Beach! What happened to him? Didn't he die of AIDS? I always thought that he was kind of weird. Was he gay?" Roberto remembered.

"Yes, he died of AIDS but he was not gay. He got it from an infected woman, but does it make any difference?" asked the annoyed Giuseppe. "Alessandro was the finest man, and he ended up where all of us could end up one day with our degenerate existence, except that for us it is more chatter than reality. For him, promiscuity was a modus vivendi."

***

The turn of momentary exhilaration into depression is a well–known aftermath of excess alcohol consumption. After inciting euphoria and excitement by dampening the grey matter restrains on our behavior, ethanol reaches subsequently the mood centers converting unbridled joy into gloom. So it was to be expected that from the playfulness of the early dinner, the evening landed into a sedated atmosphere.

To restore the sobering mood, Tullio resurrected the inspiring idea of calling La Candela:

"If I recall correctly, this is the moment when La Candela lifted our mood with her cheerful personality. I wish she were here now! I should have invited her. She is part of the Old Boys! Who cares about her husband and about the fact that she is not a man?"

Therefore, Enrico extracted the phone and dialed the number:

***

"Luisa, it's us! The Old Boys! We are having a reunion. We wish you were here!"

"No way!"

The Old Boys could hear her voice from the speaker.

"Why didn't you tell me! Really? All of you? Even... even the bratty boy? Even my Luca?"

"Yes, all, except for Mario, who is having some troubles in Rome! And yes, here is Luca! Come on, Luca! Say something!"

---

[25] Compatriot

"Hi Luisa... your voice hasn't changed at all. I hope you are well. Your husband is sick?" came out of Luca's mouth as he was searching for something to say.

"Yes, it's sad. I can tell you all another time. I love him dearly, a good man, but nothing like I loved you all. You filled my life with excitement. Those times were magic! And I was the only girl that you allowed in your circle! All of you so handsome and smart, unconventional, crazy, inspiring! I miss you all. And I miss my Luca, so gentle, kind, unsecure, needy and yet, the most autonomous of all; a tiger that roams the forest camouflaged among the leaves and invisible to the eye but whose presence anybody can sense. I miss you my Luca! I think of you every night my prince. I hope you are well!"

"His wife is cheating on him! He is available now!" offered Giuseppe magnanimously.

"I wish we would have invited you here," added Tullio, "but honestly I did not think of it. I guess I felt in my subconscious that you are a married woman, and that after all you belong to the opposite gender. I guess we still think of a married woman differently than of married men. And I am sorry, we did not know about your husband. Enrico just told us this evening."

"No, do not worry. Perhaps it's better that you did not invite me. It would have been too much of a temptation. I would not have come though, nothing to do with the fact that I'm married, but just because I am an aging lady, a faltering gardenia. You would not care for me anymore. I do not want to disappoint you with my gray hair and the wrinkles."

"Don't say that, sweet Luisa! You are going to be always the same for us! You are the nicest woman I ever met," interjected Luca, who had finally managed to find something appropriate for the occasion to say.

***

After the phone was silenced, Luca commented:

"Life resides in the impalpable essence of a future and past that are tenuously stitched together by the thread of the present, which distracts with its permanent illusion of corporeality. Each end marks the path toward the beginning of a new journey, you say. But, what I know is that I had a wife and now I have none! I had a family and now I have none! I had a dream and now I have none! I had a future, which is now buried in the past. Luisa was sweet, beautiful and creative; it was the embodiment of our future then, and that's gone like Christina is gone and like everything else. What will be the next future to be soon gone?"

"You know, she still loves you!" Enrico interrupted Luca's soliloquy

"She may, as many women claim they do. But I do not believe that love exists in the end just because nothing else exists save for the permanent illusion of the present, as I just said. This is why I do not like to talk about love. I avoid telling a woman that I love her. Funny thing is that when I told my wife that I loved her, just once or twice in my life, just one crazy once, I really meant it. I felt a lifetime commitment that was inspired by an incoercible hope springing from a person's heart... but she didn't believe me. Why should she with my track record anyways? But I swear that I did, just once, only once or twice in my life, and I meant it, but that was not enough for her. And now... now I just miss her. We have been talking about affairs and sex all night. But in the end, sex is just a distraction like most other things; perhaps real life is made of love, and you realize it even more so when you are alone, when you dream of it and you miss it.

"I wish one could crafts emotions, tune them up or down at will. But that is not possible! We can describe how we feel, but in the process, we cannot change what happens inside of us. Semantics do not help in my case! For an artist graphics is about geometry, music is about mathematical harmonies, photography is about light and angles, poetry about verbal consonance, narrative about dynamics of flow because the content is wrapped in form and that is what the artist cares about. The emotions that the artist bestows and that admirers covet are a given reality shared by all humans upon which the masters base their work. They are the dough that allows the chef's masterpiece. We all can experience at times fantastic feelings, emotions, and thoughts. They are no different from what a poet experiences, but we do not know how to translate them into a universal language as well as the poet can. The reason why we can relate to great artists is because they describe just exactly what we are feeling. Artists do not invent emotions; they cannot create or change them! They can only describe them better than most. I am no artist, and I wish I could better explain to all of you what I feel tonight, but perhaps you can imagine it if you ever went through the same. And I wish I could be empowered to change my emotions together with my semantics, but how can I if even a poet can't? And I am sorry if I am spoiling this beautiful party."

"Dear Luca," interjected Enrico, "we do understand! In fact, what is unfamiliar and new to you is common knowledge for most. You never had to conquer a woman: no flowers, no poems, no good words or gallant gestures. For you women have been a given; apples that wait to be picked from the tree when they are ripe. Who can blame you? We can only be sorry for you because in the end, you never had to work hard enough to covet your prize. It's only now, when for the first time you lost what was bequeathed to you by fate that you are discovering what most of us have always known."

***

"I need to go to pee," said Luca, who had regained color and initiative at least when it came to bodily functions. So he stood tall and turned around, sporting a controlled gait, and approximated the direction that leads towards both the kitchen and the guest washroom while his friends continued to chat.

As he disappeared behind the door leading to the services part of the apartment, Roberto questioned:

"Should we trust him? I think he is going to "make friends" with Martina: il lupo perde il pelo ma non il vizio![26]"

"He is just drunk and sad, he is not even thinking of her," sentenced a defensive and confident Tullio.

But as time passed without evidence of Luca's reappearance, the suspicion grew.

"I think we should go check on him before your mom finds him with Martina on top of him," suggested Roberto.

As the friends were inquisitively looking at each other waiting for some resolve, Martina appeared with a big platter in which a Tiramisu Milanese style filled with true Mascarpone cheese was standing.

"Where the hell is he then?" jumped up Marco. "He cannot have been peeing for a quarter of an hour." Leaving his friends, Marco rushed to the rest room, and from there the friends heard him gently knocking at the door at first and then more vehemently.

"Luca, what are you doing there? Come out, it's no time for jacking off! You are too old for that."

But still nothing could be heard. By then, the other Old Boys were assembled around the door.

"What is going on? I swear to God, the guy waited to come here to kill himself in the embrace of his friends. He was in that foul mood all night, and we kept jerking him around with our stupid comments! Come on, you idiot! Open the door!" concluded Roberto, summarizing the thought that was in everybody's mind.

"Or maybe he is just having a heart attack. We are not that young anymore," added Marco optimistically.

"Luca!" screamed Marco again. "Get out of there!" And turning to the others, he said, "We should do something to open this door!"

"I will take care of it," offered Tullio, and as he was about to kick the door, it opened, and a wobbling Luca came out:

"Sorry guys, I fell asleep on the toilet. The jet lag, I guess, or the wine. I haven't slept much recently."

Tullio sighed and hugged his friend. Then, holding him by the arm, he walked him to the couch. There, in turn each friend approached, touched his forehead to check the temperature, read his pulse, and looked at his pupils.

"Luca has more doctors than he needs here. Just let Marco do his job! He knows better than any of us," concluded Giuseppe.

---

[26] The Wolf sheds to fur but not its habits

"Maybe we should give him a thorough check up since we are all here. Tommaso may even give him a gyne exam. We should at least give him a rectal exam... with two fingers," offered Roberto.

"And why that?" asked a perplexed Giuseppe.

"So we can offer a second opinion!" Roberto exulted, for catching a sucker with his joke. "Don't they teach those things in America?"

"That is an old and disgusting joke," retorted Tullio, while Roberto, followed by the others Old Boys, started to dress up and to leave after patting Luca, who was by then laying semi–conscious on the couch.

"A bien tot... and to the next time. Next time, at my bachelor place!"

After the Old Boys left, only Tullio and Giuseppe remained at Luca's side:

"How are you? You better sleep here tonight. Martina can keep an eye on you," And turning toward Martina, who had been observing the scene from a distance, he said:

"I will call his Dad, and you take good care of our Prince!"

"How are you Luca?" asked a concerned Giuseppe. "You are not going to do anything stupid, are you? Remember, you have kids, you have your friends, you have your dad and, after all, you still have Christina. She loves you, you know that, and she needs you more than ever."

Luca opened up:

"I wish I could use better words to describe my feelings in the hope that a different connotation could quench the pain, but in the end, I am just a sad and lonely man no matter how I label it, but do not worry; I am not contemplating anything that would embarrass any of you. I am fine, I just need to sleep."

"Be well, my man. If it is of any comfort to you, consider that you are getting what you deserve: you have been a real bastard with your wife, and you are now receiving the just punishment. But look at it as a new start, a catharsis that will make you a better person. This is healthy sorrow, the bitter pill that will cure the ailment. I will go now, and you sleep in peace. Nothing is ever lost in the matters of love. Trust me. Sleep well and we will check on you in the morning."

And having so spoken, both Tullio and Giuseppe left, while Martina closed the door with care and locked it from the inside.

***

Around three in the morning, Luca woke up in the profundity of darkness. It was dark to the eyes because the face was squished against the back of the couch and it was obscurity into the mind because he was lost in space and time.

"I wonder if this is what afterlife is like: awareness of emptiness," he thought,

CAT BEHIND THE WINDOW

while he endeavored to reposition himself within the coordinates of existence.

As he turned his face away from the couch to facilitate breathing, hints of lights appeared through the curtains, compliments of the street lamps. Luca recognized the surroundings and recollected the latest events. He noticed also that he was wearing only underwear and that a flannel blanket snugly covered him. He rose and walked toward the bathroom to relieve the excess fluids from the bacchanalia. In doing so, he stepped into a body. The legs were stretched from the armchair to the coffee table, where the naked feet were resting on a pillow. In the silence and among the shadows, Luca identified Martina, who was sleeping in restful peace with her head reclined to the side and with half of her body exposed from a dropping blanket. Before continuing, Luca seized the blanket and readjusted it thus covering the beautiful woman.

A few hours later, Luca was awoken by a soothing massage to the shoulder. When he opened his eyes, the morning was tentatively trying to break through the curtain, and the light was just sufficient to recognize the face of Tullio's mother smiling at him:

"Martina slept at your side all night because she was worried about you. I just sent her to bed. How are you?"

Luca appreciated with gratitude the maternal attentions, but he had no intention to engage in an early morning conversation and thus responded:

"Much better! Thank you so much, but I am still sleepy," and pretending to be still in the twilight of consciousness, turned around, pulled the blanket over his head and fell asleep again.

Two hours later, his shoulder sensed again a soft tapping. The day was by then irrevocably established, and his eyes could see the brightness of Martina's eyes:

"La Signora went out shopping and she asked me to keep an eye on you. Would you like coffee?"

Luca pulled himself up, thrusting his back against the armrest of the couch. He bent his knees, resting the arms on them, and massaged the eyes to wake up once and for all. He looked at Martina with curiosity at first, then with affection.

"What a nice woman!" he thought. "Yes please, I would love coffee."

After Martina left, he put the trousers on and followed her to the kitchen after refreshing in the powder room. Martina was fretting with the aftermaths of the chaotic night that had been mostly cleared to restore the luster of a pristine kitchen. Luca walked to the kitchen table, drew a chair and sat waiting for the coffee and staring at Martina.

"So your wife left you!" started Martina, continuing her chores without turning.

The espresso mumbling on the stove appeared to assert in displeasure its opinion about the predicament and, for a few moments, Luca listened to it while waiting for inspiration.

"Yes, she did!" He finally spewed. "Believe it or not, she said that she did it for me! Can you imagine? She said that I did not have the courage to leave her, and she had to take the initiative to break the marriage, to relieve me from my unhappiness! How convenient! Don't you think? Would anybody leave their companion for love?"

Martina did not answer, but she poured instead with meticulous care the coffee into two cups, brought them to the table, returned to a cabinet, took out a sugar bowl, opened the refrigerator and poured milk into another bowl. Then, she came to sit, placing them, in front of Luca. Suddenly, she got startled, rose, went back to the same cabinet, opened it, found a colorful box, unwrapped it, unloaded the content on a plate and returned carrying the biscotti to the table.

"Yes!" she picked up the conversation, "A woman would do anything for the person she loves. This is exactly what I did."

Luca put a spoonful of sugar in the coffee and then some milk, stirred pensively the mixture, raised his eyes to encounter those of Martina, and offered:

"Would you like milk or sugar?"

Martina shook her head.

"OK then, tell me your story, Martina. I want to know about you."

"I was married once in Ukraine. I married my high school sweetheart. We loved each other and we married as soon as we were old enough. He was a handsome, hardworking, gentle and cheerful man. Life was paradise for us... for a few years. But then we dreamed of children. We fantasized, talked about, imagined them, counted them with our fingers, and he could not stop smiling. He would push me from the back on the swing to make me dangle higher and higher in the sky and when I would finally scream he would laugh and say:

'You are such a baby; our child will be fearless!'

"But the children never came.

"Finally, I went to see a renowned expert in Kiev, and after a lot of tests, he told me plainly that I would never bear children. I went through all these analyses by myself in secret, hoping to surprise my husband with wonderful news, but instead, when I came back that evening from the big city to our little town with empty hands, I could only hide into the kitchen. As I was cleaning the dishes from the previous evening, I reckoned that I needed to tell him the truth: plain and simple as the doctor had done with me. When he came in from the field, I set in front of him and opened my heart.

"He had tears in his eyes, but he told me:

'Do not worry, Martina; it is not of the essence. We will be happy anyways, if this is our fate.'

But things changed after that day. He continued to be the same handsome, hardworking and gentle man, but the cheerfulness was gone. So, one evening I prepared a pleasant dinner. I put in front of him all the delicacies that he liked. We ate and drank cheerfully, we smiled and we laughed, recollecting the good times. But, after he went to bed, I left the house forever... And I came to Italy. Here I am now, a few years and a few jobs later!"

"And what happened to him?"

"I asked for divorce. He could not understand, and I did not want to explain the reason. If he had known that I was leaving him for the sake of his ability to become father, he would have never agreed. Eventually, when he finally believed that I did not love him anymore, he agreed to divorce, and two years later he married another woman from the same little village, a very nice girl in fact, and now he has a little daughter. My friends tell me that his beautiful smile is returned to his cheeks, and that makes me happy. So, you see, one can leave somebody for the sake of the other person's happiness. Your wife might have been earnest when she said that."

"And what about you? What's next for you?"

"I have been going from job to job because sooner or later, somebody tries to have sex with me. It is the course of being beautiful. But I am happy here now with La Signora and, when he visits, with Tullio, who is a true gentleman. I am a very low maintenance person. I do not expect much. All I want is respect and a tad of care."

"At least you did not run away with somebody else!"

"Does it really matter? Maybe for your wife was easier this way. It would have been too painful otherwise!"

Luca rose, took the cups, brought them to the sink and rinsed them.

"I better go now! Thanks, Martina, for last night... thanks for caring... Your husband lost a wonderful wife. You know, you are a beautiful woman and, just looking at you, one would imagine quite different stories in your past. Isn't it strange how different we are from what we appear to strangers? Thank you for sharing your story."

"And you are a very attractive man, not just handsome! Attractive! There is something about you that sets you apart. You deal with women with spontaneity. You seem sincere in each gesture and word. I can see why women love you. I heard so many stories about you from La Signora. She also loves you! You very well know that!"

"And what about you? Would you love me one day?" jested Luca, smiling.

"Maybe I would! This is why I would not sleep with you. You are too special for that. I would not want to trivialize what could be... one day."

"I really think... I should better go!"

After putting on the rest of his garments, Luca hugged Martina, lifting her up from the waste and left:

"Say good–bye and thank La Signora for me," he yelled from the stairs as Martina was closing the door with care.

***

During the rest of the morning, phone calls poured upon Luca from all of his friends, who were checking on him, save for Tommaso, who, recovered from the fumes of alcohol, had resumed his verbal parsimony. However, when Luca arrived home, he found at the entrance a bouquet of white roses and a note from the latter that said:

"Be well, my friend! You are not alone!"

The dad welcomed Luca in good humor and, with some ancestral pride around the masculine attributes of his son, he mumbled:

"I guess you are still young! The small hours of the night suit you best like when you were a man apprentice. You have good genes and you know whom to thank!"

"Did anybody call?" asked Luca without preambles and pretending he did not hear the distasteful comment.

"Yes, the cleaning lady did. She will be late today because she has to take her son to the doctor."

"Great to know! That's exactly what I was wondering about!"

Luca went to his room, sat on the bed and began to read the walls as if he was there for the first time visiting the childhood home of another person.

"Something wrong?" asked the Dad.

"Yes, Christina and I are divorcing!"

And sensing the father's shock, he explained:

"She found somebody else: a bald guy with a Rolex."

The Dad recovered his composure and walked to him. Placing his soft hand on the son's curly hair, he said:

"Well, if you think that's all it takes, you should shave your head and buy a golden Rolex too!" said the Dad, extracting a smile from his prodigal son.

"She didn't even bother to call. She knew I was coming here! She could have called... just to know how the trip went!"

"Why don't you call her?"

"No, I do not want to make her feel stalked. She is probably pleased with her lover! Why should I bother her?"

***

In the afternoon, Luca received a call from Martina:

"Say! Do you want to go out for dinner this evening? La Signora gave me the evening off. I can show you around Milan! It will be my treat. No expectations, just some fun. It will be amusing to go around in Centro for the two of us. With a hunk like you at my side, people will think of us as celebrities!"

"No Martina, I am sorry! I am not in the mood today. Maybe another time soon? Maybe before I go back to New York?"

***

Later that night, Luca and his Dad were sitting at the table after a simple but cozy dinner. It was not a talkative time, and the two sat side by side with the background of the television in front that informed them about irrelevant events occurring somewhere out there in the vast world.

The Dad did not initiate any conversation of substance because he knew his son. He knew that he did not like to talk about failures, and that he considered the divorce a letdown particularly in front of him. In the end, they were Catholics, weren't they? An eccentric version of agnostic Catholics that carry in the subconscious guilt without hope! For sure his mother would not have wanted to hear about divorce. Thank God, she had graciously departed a few years before! Of course, Dad wanted to know more to provide comfort, but he let his son take all the time he needed.

Indeed, after dinner, Luca seized the remote and silenced the television:

"Dad," he whispered "of our existence, days are like leaves shedding one at a time from the old horse chestnut trees at the Giardini Pubblici, lying on the ground wherever the wind scatters them as a testimony of a gone life. The rain, the wind, the sun mark the passing of the seasons that are left to live, and the tree can sprout more leaves for them to fall into the ground in this meaningless cycle. I am confused about what lies in front of me. But I will certainly accept what's to come: the joys and sorrows, day after day, as I am expected to do. I will follow the path of the life you gave to me, just as any man has done before. I will, but it won't be trivial, I believe, and I need your guidance. I ask for your blessing before I embark toward the unknown."

And the Dad replied:

"The future! We all obsess about the future and do not live the present! Your Mom ate only rotten fruit to save the good one for the next day, when it will be rotten and she could eventually eat it without feeling guilty. Just the same for bread, she never ate the bread that I bought that day, but the stale one for the day before and, in a lifetime, I could not make her understand that it made no sense! That she could break the cycle just by skipping a day only. When she died, there were so many beautiful dresses left in the closet that were never worn waiting for the right occasion. In the country, we had two dogs. One came to me, when it saw me arriving and waited at the gate, till it was open and with the car I continued all the way to the end of the path to park it. He followed me, wagging its tail day after day for all its life. The other dog, after a few repetitions, figured it out and when he saw me, he ran to the end of the path where he knew I would park the car, stepped out and greeted me. Which one was right? Which one understood the difference between the present and the future? Which one was happier? We will never know.

"In the beginning, life is a journey filled with hope. Without it, there would be nothing, not even your childhood so full of fragrance. As a youngster, I had no time to worry about the future. My present was hard enough to distract me from other worries. I just tried to survive the miseries of the war and its collateral damage to our family. Besides, I had nobody to talk to. I had no dad, my mother was too busy making ends meet, and my brothers had either died in the war or had gone far away to build a new life... and you, of course, you were not there as yet. So I learned to carry on without asking questions to others and to myself. But now, you ask for your father's advice. You ask questions that I never dared to ask myself! What can I say? Maybe I could tell you what life is for me.

"I remember, if I am not mistaken, that life begins as a dream when as a boy one plays around the mother's skirt. But soon it turns into a troubled battle, and one soon realizes that, child no more, he is walking a solitary journey of fear of what's to come and what may not. While one fears the future, nostalgia of the time past hovers like fog upon a deserted path.

"It is toward the end of this path that I suddenly see in front of me my son, pensive and hesitant just as I was then, and I wonder what his future will bring. Why would it be any different than mine? You would not know, but when I observed you as a child and listened to your loquacious dreams, I said to myself, 'Perhaps I accomplished something!' But now that your life is rapidly streaming gradually equating to mine, now that your dreams are resting in the casket of memories together with mine, I ask myself, 'What did I do?'

"But listen at least to this advice: life goes on at its own pace and will. You do not worry! Live in peace as much as you can, do not hurt anybody and hope for the best. What is to come is not under your control, and because of this the future is not your burden. Soon a day will come when your own son, in a quiet night like this, will come to ask the same eternal questions as you are doing now. I cannot guess what you will say, but I imagine that you will recollect this night. Enjoy the moment now, the quiet night appears still, and yet it will soon be gone. Observe carefully because one day you will relish each gesture... each word of mine.

***

In his room, Luca sat on the bed, connected the phone to the charger and as he was about to rest it on the bedside table, he checked one more time at the list of missed calls, just in case. He checked the mail too, just in case. Then, he took a deep sigh, turned off the light and lay in bed, looking at the dancing lights from passing cars.

A few hours later, Christina set on the bed, connected the phone to the charger and as she was about to rest it on the bedside table and we will never know if out of curiosity, or perhaps out of nostalgia, or perhaps sadness or even despair, she checked for the list of missed calls, just in case. She checked her mail too, just in case. Then, she took a deep sigh, turned off the light and lay in bed, looking at the dancing lights.

***

SABRINA

(Or where Luca inadvertently finds himself
entangled in a thorny conundrum of women's wisdom)

Piano piano, little by little, delicately, tactfully, tacitly, and perhaps even a touch insidiously, Sabrina turned into what professor De Mirafiori never had: she became Luca's soul. Like the majority of Filipinos, she was Roman Catholic – yet she nurtured her own interpretation of what the illustrious denomination stands for. For her, religion was rather an overture toward a dialogue with an entity that would patiently listen to her monologues in the comfort of the penumbra of a church. Therefore, Sabrina spent a significant portion of her free time in a Romanic basilica, talking to a painting of God that hung in a recessed transept or, for more sensitive matters, to a statue of San Francesco standing at its side and sporting an empathetic smile that trembled over his lips at the merci of some impertinent reverberations bestowed by the flickering candles.

Such conversations progressed without a need for verbal validation from the listeners who, in turn, having been dallying at the site for the last few centuries, had no precise business to attend to on their own and, therefore, held no specific qualms against prolixity. Neither was Sabrina expecting their endorsement, as she was confident that whatever she proposed was of obvious consequence. Therefore, it did not need formal ratification and their silence could be interpreted as assent. Fortunately, Sabrina was a most sensible and practical person and, therefore, her assumption was, most of the time, correct and I am sure that if you were God or Saint Francesco, you would have also regularly agreed with her resolutions and supporting corroborations.

The substance of the matters was largely practical, since Sabrina judged that she lacked adequate sophistication to talk about anything that transcended daily routine. Conversations pertained originally to distant family matters but increasingly, her attention turned to Luca. Within a few months of coexistence with her master and commander, Sabrina reckoned that his perfection detained also what others would refer to as imperfections. And about those, she felt the obligation to debate in the presence of an objective third party, circumventing the impropriety of confronting the master directly. Therefore, she confided to God or Saint Francesco according the sensitivity of the subject to return home with the presumption of confronting mister Luca in accordance to a mandate conferred by a higher authority. As a consequence, while he was at the University giving lectures or listening to others' views about the future of mankind, the unaware professor had his existence dissected, judged and, in accordance, readjusted in the eloquent silence of a church.

A vexing and recurrent quandary addressed Luca's recklessness in abiding to a dress code proper for his status. No matter how compulsively Sabrina fussed to perfect his attire for the morning, Luca could always figure out creative ways to alter the masterpiece. Ties not properly centered or loosely tied, ruffled collars, inside out pullovers, mismatched buttons and respective buttonholes in the placket of the shirt, belts skipping loops, insufficiently tucked shirts were of the order. Worse of all, incompletely zipped flies became frequent accidents that stressed the poor woman. And no matter how mundane such consternations might appear to the unaware, they carry legitimate significance for those who, like Sabrina, devote their life to the appearance of their beloved masters and retain a chauvinistic attitude toward tidiness.

She was also concerned about Luca's reserved demeanor. Often, she observed his gloomy days, particularly during weekends, when he walked purposelessly back and forth in the living room, sat amorphously on an armchair, staring at the ceiling without saying a word till he fell asleep – even though he had just woken up.

From the verge of the door she would ask:

"Mister Luca, are you OK?"

He would reply waving his hand:

"Of course! I am fine!" or sometimes he would not reply at all.

Sometimes, he would take her for a stroll in the park as if she was a bitch that needed to be walked, but even then, he would not talk much. He would pace at her side, supporting her arm, opening doors and paving the way or summarily brushing off leaves from a bench where she was about to sit. But no conversations of substance ever came out of those moments.

And she would ask God:

"What should I do?"

Receiving no answer and having none to propose on her own, she sighed and lit a candle.

For Saint Francesco, she reserved more sensitive flaws that would not be properly conveyed to the Omnipotent without informed consent from the master. She felt that the experienced Saint could oblige as an ambassador by conveying those matters in confidence better than the muttering of an unsophisticated woman – not to say that God wouldn't understand in any case! God forbid that! But surely the Saint could unearth better words to soothe the message!

Such sensitive issues related, for instance, to excessive consumption of alcohol: not that Luca was an alcoholic, but for the abstemious woman, even a glass above the ordinary raised a flag. She was also stressed by Luca's refusal to go to church on account of the persuasion that any matter related to religion was a superlative waste of time. Luca told her that he was an agnostic and when she figured out what that meant, she considered that, in the end, she also did not know for sure whether God existed or not. Yet, there was no reason not to pay Him a visit, talk to Him and ask for advice. What was there to lose? In any case, it was up to the Saint to figure out how to present this quandary to God because she did not want to hurt His feelings, particularly in the case that He did indeed exist. In other words, the poor woman was trying hard to deal with the inconsistencies of existence, when one wants to follow some sort of logic that resonates within oneself and, at the same time, wants to protect and respect the logic of loved ones even without totally understanding it. Luca's agnosticism was, in her practical estimation, just a preference, a fad, perhaps just a fondness for a particular flavor such as one would choose linguini over spaghetti at a restaurant; and who was she to argue against it?

But the most serious of all matters, deserving the highest of the Saint's discretion, pertained to Luca's affection for women, particularly for two of them: an aging pretty woman whose name was Luisa and a beautiful Ukrainian called Martina. Both of them had increasingly taken a dominant role in her master's life, alternating their presence at home at the expenses of other occasional mistresses. Both of them, in turn, sat at the dinner table on the same chair to the right of Luca, unaware of each other's existence, while the discreet Sabrina would serve warm dinners and clean after them. Of the two, Martina was self–conscious and could not restrain from fighting with Sabrina for returning dishes and serving plates to the kitchen and it was only Luca's imperious gaze that forced Martina to sit at his side so Sabrina could accomplish her duties undisturbed.

Luisa spent long evenings and nights sitting on an armchair in front of Luca or cuddling at his side on the sofa but rarely did she cross the threshold of his bedroom. It was not because she did not wish to, but because most of the time, Luca did not seem interested in moving in that direction. He rather kept extracting from his friend everything that she could tell about how women think. It was an obsession and he would often bring up Christina with the lame excuse of having her serve as an example. Luisa, in turn, listened patiently and empathetically to the young sweetheart with the maturity of an experienced woman, and she reckoned that her beloved Luca was still, even after all these year, the same insecure boy who, in spite of all the fortune that had been bestowed upon him by destiny, particularly in gallant affairs, had learned nothing about women or, perhaps, even about life. Thus night after night, a sense of maternal instinct overwhelmed her and all she wanted to do was to hold in her arms that handsome, lonesome, and clueless man.

In time, Martina and Sabrina grew closer; it is not that Luisa was an insensitive concubine – not at all – in fact, she was the warmest of creatures but, belonging to the Milanese high society, she had a special affectation in dealing with Sabrina, bringing her presents and giving her gratuities substantive enough to be appreciated by a woman who had a family far away and who could use any penny to make her loved ones thrive till she may be able to reunite with them one day. But Martina had taken Sabrina's affection because she was a servant just like herself and could thus empathize by admiring in her what she could never be: the enchanting Cinderella worthy of Prince Charming.

Martina, who increasingly spent nights sleeping at Luca's side, seconded by the encouragement of her Signora, reserved the mornings to confide with Sabrina when the professor had left for the University. It should be clarified that Sabrina was the most selfless of people and therefore, the Saint did not have to worry not about comforting her feelings or emotions over this strangest of predicaments. Moreover, she had never confessed to the Saint the extent of her relationship with the master, particularly the carnal details and, although she implicitly talked about Luca as one would represent a lifetime companion to a marriage councilor, she never put her personal relationship on the table for discussion. Therefore, at least officially, Saint Francesco could tactfully disregard this facet of the matter. Rather, the Saint was summoned to worry about the potential effects that such dissipated life could bear on Luca's well–being and increasingly more on Martina's. Sabrina, in fact, was increasingly more concerned about the latter. She felt that Luca did not appreciate the depth of Martina's love for him or the beauty of her loyalty to him.

Others shared Sabrina's concern. Tullio had approached Luca with a benevolent scolding:

"I think Martina is getting too attached to you! I believe that you are misleading her and you should let her be – unless you really do care for her... but I doubt it! Not to be a snob, but why would you want to tie yourself with a nice but unsophisticated woman, who has nothing in common with you?"

Tullio's Mom bore another opinion in line with her resolve to find, once and for all, the perfect match for the Prince:

"Martina is the perfect woman for you! She is beautiful. She is nice, hard–working, and capable of attending without judgment to all that you need. You do not need another Christina or another high achiever. Those women eventually go on their own and you will be left alone in your old age! Martina will take good care of you just as she has been doing for me!"

But it was Luisa who broke the camel's back.

"I heard..." she said with a mischievous smile as she was sitting one evening after dinner on the sofa in Luca's arms, looking toward a turned off television: "that a beautiful woman has been spending quite a lot of time in your arms on this same sofa."

Luca did not answer but simply caressed Luisa's black hair dyed to perfection.

"I know everything about this Martina: Tullio told me and Sabrina confirmed. Do not be mad at them; they did not mean to betray you. They are both concerned about you and certainly about Martina."

"It is none of their business," mumbled Luca who, taken by surprise, had otherwise no deeper words to package into a cogent sentence.

"Just as it is none of my business either!" replied calmly Luisa. "But still, you better listen to those who love you." and rising from the sofa, she went to sit on the sofa's armrest, putting her delicate feet on Luca's abdomen and, looking straight into his eyes, she continued:

"My dear Luca, you cannot do this to Martina. I do not want to sound like a snob, but we – I mean you and I – and the Old Boys, and the people you are used to, belong to another social status, another cultural background. No matter how liberal we think we are and how sensitive to the world we pretend to be, we have been raised by the cynicism of sophistication! Words like love, commitment or care are just concepts to us: an intellectual exercise. We are like politicians sitting at a table, discussing the pros and cons of commencing a war. They drink coffee or tea around the table and do not smell the stench of rotten bodies, nor do they hear the cries of mothers for their shattered lives; they do not see the dust of destruction rising from the fallen homes that made for familiar surroundings to thousands just moments before. It is just a game for them no matter how thoughtful they pretend to be... and it is just the same for us. We can filter words according to modern or ancient philosophies, we can coat them with existentialistic shadows, and stick them against nihilist walls as two–dimensional graffiti. We can turn upside down and dissect the meaning of any word, interpret its impact on our or other's speculative existence, wonder about the weight of its relevance in the context of universal truths: the big scheme of things! We are trained to look at concepts as if they, in the end, meant nothing at all in relation to our daily life. But people like Martina are different; they come from the countryside where culture has not yet spoiled their dreams, where they have not been indoctrinated by skepticism and cynicism, and it will take a long time for their souls to be proselytized, if ever, by the cult of futility, pointlessness, senselessness in which we comfortably thrive. Martina carries dreams that are as fresh as the spring waters of her mountains, she believes in suns that are meant to shine forever, in crisp autumn breezes... in the whispers of the night. If you would ever tell her that you loved her, trust me, she would hang her life, her future, every drop of her energy into a dream that you cannot even conceive from your nihilistic bubble."

"Let me ask you something that may seem trivial to you but means a lot to a woman: have you ever told her that you love her?"

"Yes! I have. As you said, I am not sure what I meant, but she asked me once. I did not think too much about it. I just simply said: *yes!* We were making love and

I felt a deep affection for her then. How could one spoil such a moment? I do not think that this should count!"

"But it does, no matter what you think! By the way, do you know that you have never told me that you love me in all these years? And do you know why? Because I never ask you if you do! Probably, you would have said 'yes!' just the same to me, in a sweet, intimate moment. But in my case, you would have known comfortably that I was well aware that it would not have counted. And this is why, I never asked you."

"So what's your point?" interrupted Luca, who was listening attentively to Luisa's sermon. He felt that there was something in it that transcended Martina's issue and had more to do with Luisa's ability to articulate the roots of his emptiness: a self–centered and narcissistic existence.

"I think that you should pick a choice. I think that you should either leave the poor woman alone or commit to her. You know that you will always have me as your off–the–shelf, platonic soul mate and you know that you will always have the harem of women who care for you, but you have to learn to make at least one of them happy! If not for any other reason, just at least for your own edification! Women will sacrifice a lot for the one they love, particularly when they feel that their sacrifice will not be wasted. But it is not rewarding to take advantage of them without returns. If you love her, marry her! If you do not, don't mislead her any further!"

"I was already married once! I thought I was a good husband and look where it went. The truth is that I cannot make any woman happy... 'truth is that I am not meant to be a good companion. I am a leopard, as somebody told me. I roam without any purpose the Savannah, hunting when I am hungry and finding a mate when I need one; but besides those moments, I wander without purpose, hopelessly listening to distant calls and searching from scents of novelty, harbingers of deeper meanings that transcend the futility of our existence. You are right, perhaps education has spoiled our lives. We cannot take anything seriously and what may appear grand to others may mean nothing to us! How could Martina understand any of this? How could she comprehend our unspeakable secret?"

***

A few days later, Sabrina was lying in bed and in Luca's arms while he was staring at the ceiling and caressing her shoulder. Luca gently pressed her shoulder to make sure that she was awake and asked:

"Do you think I should marry Martina? Everybody seems to want me to marry her! Am I missing something? In the end, you are the only one whose opinion I care about."

For the oddest reason, Sabrina, who so much had concocted in her dreams a positive outcome of Martina's story, felt a deep pain, an overbearing weight in the depth of her chest that stopped her breathing. When she could talk again, thinking of Saint Francesco as a beacon in the middle of a stormy night, she gasped:

"I do not know, I think I will have to think about it."

***

The next morning, the temperature was biting in the basilica and the Saint's smile wasn't welcoming. In fact, at closer look, Sabrina noticed that the Saint wasn't smiling at all, and that he probably never did. She recognized that his benevolence had been an illusion all along, produced by the flickering of the candles. To persuade herself, she approached the statue from the side and looked at it, carefully squinting her eyes. The Saint continued to display an austere expression as if he already knew the terms of her imminent confession and was already considering the elements of its extreme quandary. It also occurred to Sabrina that the Saint was well aware of the unspoken truth that he knew about her affair with her master and that, likely, he was disgusted by her promiscuity. Perhaps he was looking down at her as a vulgar prostitute, an indentured servant for sale to support her family! Wouldn't it be just exactly what anybody would conclude? How could the Saint swallow the pretense that she truly loved Luca? What a convenient conception! Was it really love… or just convenience? The Saint was right to look down upon her: she had no right, no entitlement for sympathy and she reckoned that she should return home without wasting more of his precious time.

But she also considered the tenets of Christianity that include forgiveness, charity and compassion. She recalled that a preacher once told her, when she was a young woman, that Christ listens rather than judge. Turning to the painting of God, she sensed the same. She recognized very well that she was far from perfect like most people, and that her sin was grave, but courage rose out of her despair and she began:

"Dear God and dear San Francesco, I am talking to you both because I need all the help that you can offer! I am an unsophisticated woman. There I was, it seems so long ago: just a schoolteacher… but the money was not enough to raise my family. I came from so far away because I could not take care of my children in the Philippines. My husband was lazy and he was a drunkard. Job after job he lost. He would not show up at work when he was supposed to. When he did, he argued with his boss or coworkers till he was fired. I left my boys with my parents. They are good children. They want to study so they will have better lives than their parents. They want to become respectable people, people whose words count in society. Children now know that there is a big world out there, a world of opportunities and they want a chance to be part of it …I came here and worked hard. I never asked for anything more than what I was offered.

291

But then Mister Luca appeared into my life. I never dreamed of being close to him. I was just his father's servant. When he visited from America, he seemed such a gentle and quiet man, a devoted son. He was patient with his dad and was nice to me. When my master died, he decided to move back to Italy, to his childhood home and he retained me. He said that he did not have the heart to leave me without a job. I stayed with him because he was a good man and he respected me. He was a quiet man and he looked sad and solitary. He barely talked and whatever I did, he thanked me for it. He never criticized, was never upset and his few words were always encouraging. Sometimes, he would say soothing things like:

'Sabrina, can you please make sure that next time, the wine is chilled for dinner?' It was because I had put it out too early when a friend visited – and that was as bad of a criticism I have ever received.

Whenever I wanted to go somewhere, mostly going shopping for the house, he never denied. And I was so grateful to have a safe job, with no expenses in such a comfortable and luxurious apartment that is warm in the winter and cool in the summer. I was even proud of belonging to it as if it was part of my own life. Meanwhile, I could save my entire stipend for my parents and the sake of my children. And I came here regularly to thank you both for my blessings... and I could not think of anything else to hope for. At least this was what I told you and repeated to myself but... inside of me... inside of me... I loved him. I wrestled with my mind to keep the thought away. I kept telling myself:

'Sabrina, mister Luca is not for you. He does not even see you, he is circled by all these beautiful and smart women and such elegant and smart friends who are 'accomplished' as they say. You simply do not exist!'

Yet I waited all day long for him to come home and rushed to the door when the bell rang, hoping to catch a smile. I would prepare meals the best I could, anticipating his fancies and I wished to be his servant for the rest of my life. I was so happy to be by his side. No matter how many women came and went, I was the one who took care of him day after day and he showed me his gratitude.

But then one evening, he came home and asked me to call him Luca. He made me sit at his side at the dinner table. He held my hands after dinner and took me to his bedroom. I should have resisted, I know, my God, but I could not. I loved him so much and I knew that I would do anything he would ask me to do... then and now."

Sabrina stopped to consider her own words and anticipate the icons' questions, and then she continued:

"How could I say no when he took me by the hand? How could I say no to my dream? I did not even know whether what was happening was true or just a fruit of my imagination! I was recapping, in actuality, what I had lived so many times in my fantasies. I am not ashamed to tell you that I love him even more now. I love him with the unconditional love of a woman who wants her man happy. I want you to know that I am not here on my behalf. I am here for him. I am not asking for your forgiveness or understanding. I am not asking for your support. I just came because I need your advice for my advice. He asked me... he asked just me... his humble servant... he asked for advice. He wants to know whether I think he should remarry.

They all want him to marry Martina, a lovely and beautiful woman, much prettier and younger than I am. She is a servant just like me but she is tall and of natural elegance. She has a beautiful smile and a sweet voice. She is nice to everybody – including me. She tries to clear the table and to help me with the dishes when she is a guest for dinner. She talks to me and asks for my guidance, as if I was her older sister.

And Mister Luca asked me, as I said, if he should marry her. He told me that he cares about my opinion most, more than that of anybody else. Do you understand? He said that he wants my advice – the advice of a humble servant counts more than that of doctors and professors! Do you see how great my responsibility is? I ask you both: what should I say? How would I know what's right for him?"

Sabrina paused waiting for an answer. In turn, she queried the painting and the statue, but nothing happened. The silence echoed within the recesses of the basilica and only a soft litany could be heard from a few benches afar. Gradually, Sabrina reckoned that there was not a thread of communication between her and the icons and that she could sit there all day and night but would receive no word, no movement, and no suggestion that would come to appease her anguish.

So she looked at her hands that were resting on her fragile knees. She stared at her feet reposing on the footrest in a pretty pair of red moccasins that she had found on sale a few months before. She rubbed her calves with the palm of her hands to provoke a resemblance of purposeful dignity, buying time while she was deciding how to extract herself from that impasse. She looked back toward the origin of the litany wondering what she was doing there. Was it all a superlative waste of time, as Luca would have sentenced?

A few benches away sat an old woman with a rosary in between her thumb and index finger, mumbling Ave Marias. Further apart was a young man, likely an expatriate like her, kneeling in front of another statue of an anonymous Saint; another pariah that could find acceptance and comfort only in the darkness of a church.

It appeared to her that those two, like her, were talking to a mute listener and she concluded that this time, she was on her own; that, as for when she made the decision to leave her children in the Philippines, it was only in her hands to choose the path. It was for her – and only her – to decide what was good for Luca, for Martina and for herself.

So she turned around, walked out of the church where the sunshine blurred her eyes and resolutely walked home. She had made up her mind on how to proceed.

***

That Friday evening came and Luca retired late after dinner with the Old Boys. It was not particularly late, yet he did not ring the doorbell, choosing to quietly unlock the door of the apartment, turn on the lights and hold his breath so as not to disturb Sabrina. In his hand was a handwritten envelope addressed to him, one that he had collected from the mailbox. He removed his coat, rested it on a chair in the entry hall, quietly moved to the den and sat in front of the computer.

A few minutes later, Sabrina knocked on the door, sneaked her head through the opening and asked:

"Mister Luca, may I come in?"

Luca raised his face. The dim light coming from the computer screen drew a ghostly appearance of his features, and from the distance, his eye sockets seemed recessed and empty, like those of a cadaver.

Luca stood up and walked toward Sabrina, who had turned on the lights to return Luca to a human state.

"Sit down please." said Luca, taking his place in the meantime on the armchair in front of her.

Then proffering a gracious smile, he said:

"Sabrina, Sabrina, how many times have I told you to just call me Luca?"

Sabrina did not answer. Instead, she kept staring at her knees. Then she spoke:

"I came to give the answer to your question."

"What question?" Luca asked distractedly.

"Last night, you asked me if you should marry Martina."

"O yes! I see, sorry I sort of forgot about it! So what do you think?"

"I think you should."

Luca corrugated his eyebrows and looked straight into Sabrina's face to engage her eyes, but she stubbornly kept looking at the floor.

"Sabrina, do you mind looking at me when we talk?" and he continued:

"And why do you think I should marry Martina?"

"I am not sure. She is beautiful, she is considerate and I believe that she really loves you. She told me so many times! She is very loyal to you, do you know? She is an honest woman. I do recognize that she is just a servant like me and she has no proper education, but what do you care about it? You have plenty of that around you but you seem bored of it. She, instead, could take care of your needs, could anticipate your desires, could stand by you unconditionally without questioning – just waiting for you and loving you. She could also take care of your clothing, your meals, the house... or maybe she will not. After being married to you, she will need a servant for herself and will just be your devoted wife. Maybe she would retain me. I could serve her just as I do with you. I do not mind. I am a poor woman with children far away who need to survive. I will continue to serve the two of you, but please do not ask me to continue our relationship. I am asking not just for myself, but for Martina. I could not do that to her. I know how painful it will be for me to sit in my room at night without hope of being close to you, but at least, there would be the comfort of knowing that I did the right thing. Otherwise, it would only be wrong and painful for us all.

I do not know what makes you happy, Mister Luca, but it seems to me that when she is around, you are as carefree and playful as I have ever seen you. But I agree with Signora Luisa: you should either marry Martina or let her be. She really believes that there will be a future for the two of you... maybe even children and... a new life for you, Mister Luca... I am sorry... Luca.”

“Martina cannot bear children! It is a long and irrelevant story. In any case, I do not want more children. I love the ones I have and this is it.” said Luca, waiving his hand off.

Sabrina raised her face that had returned to stare at the ground while she was talking to scrutinize Luca, wondering about what he knew. Then, she bent her neck again and continued to stare at her knees.

“So you really think that I should marry her?”

“Do you love her?”

“Well, love is a vague concept to me. I am not sure about what the correct definition is. It is more like the air in the sky. I do not know where it starts and where it ends, where it comes from and where it goes. I loved and I was loved once and where did everything go? What did I mean when I said ‘I love you’ to my wife? What did my wife mean when she whispered ‘I love you’ to my ear at night? Do I enjoy being with Martina? Yes! Do I like to hold her in my arms? Yes! Do I think of her sometimes? Sometimes I do! Could I live without her? Yes. Do I love her? Probably not! I don’t know what you mean by love. What do you mean by love, Sabrina?”

“I do not know sir. I am not the one who should speak of love. I am just a humble servant who never had the chance to meet love. I was married at a very young age. My mother liked the son of a friend of hers so he became my fiancé. Once, he forced himself inside me while I was taking care of the laundry and my mother was in the other room. I did not have the courage to scream. I became pregnant. I had to marry him. I married that man who said that he loved me in front of my parents. I just did what was expected of me and after that, I kept working and working. He made me pregnant again and I had another child. I continued to work to support the three of them till I had to abandon them all because I could not make enough money to pay our debts. This is all I know about love."

"So you never loved anybody?"

"No, sir!"

A mischievous smile appeared on the face of Luca, who impertinently asked:

"Not even me?"

Sabrina's ears burned under her orderly tucked up hair but she did not answer.

Luca sighed profoundly, rose, walked to the desk, and said:

"Anyways, Sabrina, thank you for your advice, but I am afraid it is no longer needed."

From the desk, he fetched a letter unfolded over the hand–written envelope.

"Here, read this! See? People still write letters nowadays."

Sabrina looked inquisitively at her master and hesitantly took the letter:

"*My beloved Luca,*

I am sure that among others, you are the only one who will understand my decision because you alone knows my secret. As you know, I do not want to become a burden to anybody and most of all, to the one I love. I sacrificed once for someone I loved and I will do it again for you.

Yesterday, I told my Signora that I needed to go back to Ukraine to take care of my parents. It is not true of course, but it was the only story that would not hurt her feelings. I will go elsewhere instead where nobody will know, not even you, to start all over again. I am doing this because I love you and I know that you need your freedom. I know that they all want us both to marry, but for the wrong reason! It is all out of pity for me and has nothing to do with mutual love.

My dear Luca, I know that your heart is not with me. Your heart is with your Sabrina. I am a woman and I can sense things only a woman can. I can see how you breathe her. I can see how you feel her when you do not see her, how unconsciously you search for her. You have been so kind and wonderful to me, but your smile is not the same as the one you reserve for her. And I see how she looks at you. No matter how hard the poor woman tries to hide her feelings, I can see how she burns of passion for you. She looks at you with the devotion of a dog. She can anticipate all that you might think and desire, without need for words. She answers even before you ask. This, my friend, is love! It is exactly that love that you dismiss as an undefined word.

A few nights ago, I found a thick Asian hair on your pillow, just like Sabrina's long and beautiful black hair. Trust me, I am a jealous woman, but I am not jealous of Sabrina. She is just a servant like me, a woman who had to leave for whatever reason her family, her life, her familiar places to gratefully serve as a second class citizen in your country. She was a teacher, you know? She is more educated than I am and she is a servant just because she lives where she does not belong. She is a smart woman.

And as for me, I know when to make a dignified retreat. I want you to know that I loved you very much and I will probably continue to love you forever. You are a much better person than you give yourself credit for... but you need to follow your heart. You need to be happy. Maybe Sabrina could, one day, give you the children that I could never bear for you.

Good luck my loved one, be well!

With all my heart,

Martina"

Sabrina was flushed all over and her hands were trembling. She put the letter on the coffee table and ran to Luca's bedroom. She pulled out the blankets, scattered the pillows and searched with frenzy everywhere, even under the bed: not a single hair could she find. How could she have missed that one? She: the one who fussed so hard to keep things flawless.

When she turned around disheartened, Luca looked benevolently at her from the door's edge.

"I am so sorry. I have no idea how this could have happened! I always change the sheets every time a new woman comes. I am so sorry." she said, and she started sobbing.

"Do not worry, Sabrina. I never really intended to remarry. In particular, I never intended to marry Martina. I just needed to know how you would react to that idea."

Luca approached Sabrina and held her in his arms, where she let herself be for a few moments. Then she wiggled out of the embrace:

"I am sorry. I am confused! I need to go to my room! I hope you understand, Luca... Mister Luca! I mean Luca! I really need to go." and she left.

Luca sat on the bed. He took his shoes off and, at the same time, realized that the evening could not simply be over. He remembered the comfort of the prayers' routine in his childhood – a routine dictated by his despotic grandmother. Thus, he knelt at the side of the bed, hurriedly susurrating a Pater Noster, an Ave Maria and a Credo before jumping to bed in peace with the relief of having absolved simple and concrete duties. He fancied to kneel and revive the comfort of that obsolete routine. But he smiled instead:

"The power of habits. The addition to conformity." he thought.

Still, he could not figure what else could take him to a placating closure for the day. Barefoot, he walked to the kitchen and opened the refrigerator to do what any man would do in such a circumstance. But as he held the cold bottle of beer in his hand, he felt no interest in it and he returned it to the refrigerator. He walked to a cabinet and took out a crystal glass, thinking that something stronger would do. He went to the ice dispenser and released a few cubes. Holding the glass, he proceeded to the bar in the living room to pour some Cognac. But as he was about to dispense the liquor, he sensed that even this gesture was pointless, a deception to distract oneself, an act to dignify one's misery. He reckoned that he did not like to drink alone and that he was, as a matter of fact, completely alone – just as he was the night he found Christina with Jonathan. He was alone in the vast silence of life.

He returned to the kitchen, dropped the cubes in the sink and rinsed the crystal glass. Then, he deposited it on the table and placed his hands on its smooth edge, resting all his weight on his stretched arms.

"What am I going to do next?" he wondered.

And he meant it literally. It was not about what he would do for the rest of his life or for the next year or month, not even what he would do the next day. He could not figure out where to launch his immediate next step. He was paralyzed. Maybe... go to the restroom to release the extra fluids remnant of his party with the Old Boys? He felt no urge. He wished to go to Sabrina's room and lay close to her but she had just ran away from him and he had no right to disturb her. Maybe, go to the balcony and jump into the night? That was ludicrously dramatic, a pathetic hysteria, an unbecoming ending for a dignified existence. Perhaps, he should retire into the study to read once again Martina's letter. Why not call her? She still must have kept her phone with her? No! Martina was right. He did not love her... at least not in the way women think of love. He could tolerate her easily, he enjoyed being with her, and that was a lot to ask from a solitary man who still missed his wife.

But love? What is love? What do they all mean when they use this word? Perhaps, Martina was right. Despite his renitence to admit it, perhaps he did love someone – a humble soul who cared for him unconditionally... who waited and loved. Perhaps Martina was right that he cared about Sabrina more than he would admit. He reckoned that when evening came and it was time to go home, he anticipated with eagerness Sabrina's smile at the door. He recognized that he looked forward to the fragrances coming from the kitchen and the warmth that they aroused in his heart; lost memories of lives long ago when his grandmother was waiting for him, then his mother, then his wife; all those women whose only purpose in their existence was to serve him; all those simple joys that he had been taken for granted day after day. What was there left to live for, now that they were all gone? What was left for him? He thought of Sabrina's fussing around him to scout little imperfections that she could proudly fix, the little Tinker Bell who worships an aging Peter Pan. And he recounted the eagerness of her tidings about insignificant events of the day that were still important to her. And he thought of her tiny and nervous body that trembled in his embrace when he bothered to hug her for he was in a good mood. He thought of those who would scorn him for mingling with a servant – but why should he care? Nobody of consequence in his life was there to judge him. A pro of being alone is being free. And who was he to judge her status looking from the throne of privilege? What would have Sabrina become had she received all the opportunities that he had? Such a smart and thoughtful woman!

Again, he thought of going into Sabrina's room to find warmth in her embrace. But he could not resolve: he realized that he had taken advantage of the poor woman all along, of that impotent subordinate whom he had carelessly harassed... and he then felt embarrassment and regret.

"I should leave her alone, just like Martina, what am I doing? Why am I harassing an impotent woman? What's becoming of me?"

Where else could he go, then? The apartment was too small to run away from the embarrassment and the anguish. It was just a miniature reproduction of the boundaries of existence from which there is no escape. Finally, he succumbed to the comfort of routine and progressed toward the bedroom. There, he hooked the cell phone to the charger and took all of his clothes off. Finally, he lay naked in bed waiting for merciful sleep.

**

But in the middle of the night, Luca woke up to sense a warm weight pressing against his right side. It did not take much to reckon that the object was Sabrina's curled body, wrapped in the simple flannel nightgown and glued to his right flank. Gently, he wrapped his arm around her and moved her even closer. Sabrina murmured something undecipherable, probably in Filipino, and turned to the opposite side, pushing her back against Luca, her cold feet against his knees, and she continued to sleep. Luca in turn, wrapped his body around hers; with his left hand, he unbuttoned the familiar openings of her nightgown and thrusted his hand over her tiny breast to massage it gently till he also fell asleep – and in that sleep, they became one.

**

And on that same night, in the basilica, the impertinent candles with their flickering lights restored the smile on Saint Francesco's mouth.

Metamorphosis

Contributed by Anna Loza

Translated from Russian by Dmitry Akmal

That morning, the nurse did not come. Hope was laying on her bed and listening to the sounds emanating from the stairwell. The neighboring door creaked, and two sets of footsteps echoed from across the tiled floor; one pair of feet shuffled meekly, while the other had a meaningful stride. "It must be the neighbor across the hall", Hope thought to herself, before thoughtfully adding: "her son must have come to visit". The elevator began to rumble and Hope counted to herself: "One, two, three, four". As if on cue, the elevator stopped on the fourth floor, opening its doors with a metallic bang and slamming shut once more.

Hope looked out the window and saw, as she always did, a small patch of sky and the crown of the birch tree growing near her home. 'Birchy', she had lovingly named the tree – it was the only living thing that had never left her side after all these years. Everything else would come and go, each year less frequently than the last. Birds would perch on the windowsill and airplanes would streak across the sky, the low hum of their engines taking Hope to a far–away place she had never been and would never return to. Some years ago, birds had nested in the birch's crown, and Hope fearfully watched their home sway in the wind. Each time she would helplessly stare, and each time rejoice when the winged parents would return to the nest with worms in their beaks.

Often, she would return to memories of her youth – back when she could run, and climb mountains, and swim in the ocean. It was so long ago, yet these sensations seemed far more bright and vivid than her everyday reality – the sensation of wind against her face, the texture of soft, moist soil between her toes, the warmth of a newly–hatched chick resting in her palms. The memories were precise down to the smallest detail: the words spoken, the wrinkles on her mother's face, the dimples on her daughter's, and every feeling, every single tint. Hope painstakingly preserved her past, not permitting even the smallest memory to wither and die. Often, very often, she would unlock this treasured vault and experience each day anew. Whether sad or joyful, each fragment of the past held a deep importance and she would not let them go. "At least," she thought, "I'm re– living my own life, not someone else's". She had walked this road many times, from end to end, first regretting something, getting angry and repenting, but always coming to the conclusion that things happened exactly as they should have. She had finally accepted herself fully, from her harsh character to her sudden irritability, her each and every odd whim, and motionless body. She would not change a single thing. Except for one...the death of her daughter!

The disaster occurred unexpectedly, on one of the bright spring days from twelve years ago. It took them all by surprise, freezing the world like a malfunctioning stop–motion picture. The world outside petrified while her insides grew numb with unrelenting pain. Her house became deadly silent. It was not the silence itself that was awful, however – it was the absence of the sonorous chirping of a child. Hope's daughter had been hit by a car, and soon after the incident, paralysis had seized Hope's body. Her legs were first to go out from the grief, and the rest of her body shortly followed.

As the room sank into twilight, the shadows of the birch tree grew to encompass the opposite wall, the branches trembling and leaves shaking. Hope imagined herself moving with their frenzied dance, yet her body remained in place, yearning for food and water. Down below, the building's entrance slammed shut over and over as people returned from work, their chatter and laughter drowning out the sounds of the subsiding day. Hope tried to call out the window that had been left open on the previous day, but her voice was too weak, and her feeble call hardly filled the room.

A loaf of black bread sat on the table. Hope tried to take a deep breath, inhaling the pleasant and familiar smell. She succeeded, and conjured up images of eating the bread with a dollop of butter once the nurse returned tomorrow. Hope did not doubt that the nurse would return – Lana came every day, or had at least done so for the past two years. Once Hope's mother had passed, Lana regularly came to wash and feed the paralyzed woman. Hope had grown attached to her, although she understood that Lana, like many others, would only remain in her life for as long as payment was provided. The poor woman had accepted this, as she had learned to do for many things, with submission and humility. She did not complain when Lana began washing and feeding her less frequently and was grateful that Lana still came at all; the nurse was her last thread to the outside world.

This was not the life Hope led before her mother, who had cared for her paralyzed child for over ten years, passed away. Mother would sit with her for many weeks while her daughter mournfully stared at the ceiling; she read books for Hope and sang songs, doting on her child with such warmth and love that Hope occasionally forgot her tragic state. It was Mother who helped Hope accept her immobility and face her depression. Hope's grief was real, and her sadness melted away the surface layers of her soul, plunging deeper and deeper into its bowels. Hope's paralyzed body had become a cocoon for the incessant work of the spirit within.

The next day, Lana did not return either, and Hope suddenly realized that her nurse would never come again. Ever. The pain and nausea resurfaced, as Hope drowned her body and mind in a sea of self–pity. She had been abandoned, and she was frightened. Like an artifact forgotten in a storeroom gathering dust, or a stray dog left to the mercy of fate, Hope had been forsaken by everyone. She moaned softly and tears started slowly trickling down her lifeless cheeks. No matter how lonely we are, we live among others and can always call out for help, hoping until the end that someone will come. If left to die alone, everything for which you have lived becomes illusory and vain.

Hope closed her eyes and licked her dry lips. She patiently waited, attempting to control her strained nerves. "It's better to die at peace – to accept the things I can no longer change", she reasoned to herself, but it was in vain. Her soul forcefully protested against the barren path before her, fighting her motionless body. The clock on the opposite wall ticked, the minute hand crawling along the circumference of the timepiece. Each minute grew more painful and dragged on even more as the feelings of hunger were outweighed by a powerful, heated thirst. Evening settled, and Hope considered the strange possibility that it might be more pleasant to die in her sleep. She shuddered at such a likely outcome.

She lay pinned to the bed, as helpless as a dried butterfly specimen in an entomological collection. The woman tried to convince herself there was something, anything that she could do. "I can do this, this time I've got it" she urged herself on, pushing from the depths of her cocoon with incredible effort to try and spread her wings. A slight tremor ran through her body, but it vanished as quickly as it had emerged. Her arms would not move. Her body would not move. "I can, I can, I can" was the only thought ringing through her brain, blaring over the feelings of hunger and thirst.

Hope awoke suddenly, screaming in horror as she felt a pair of clammy hands upon her forehead. In the panic and disarray, she could not understand to whom these hands belonged. She lay there, as she had always done, with bated breath. As the terror subsided, she realized. These were not the hands of death. These were her hands. They belonged to her.

"Mush"

Contributed by Jamie Marincola

Why am I here? What is my purpose? If I were to never get out of bed again, would my life be any more meaningful than if I carried through the motions of my routine existence?

These are not questions pondered by a sled dog. A sled dog knows its purpose.

It's the crack of dawn in the Swedish Lapland. It's the first crack of dawn in nearly a month, but it's more than enough for the dogs. They howl and whine and growl and pull at their collars. Food is served. Some scarf it down; others pass on their breakfast mush in favor of mushing the sled. They've been through this routine regularly since they were puppies and know there's still two hours between food and pulling, but it's enough time to get pumped and energized for the day's trek.

Addi is the oldest dog on the trip; nearly ten years old; a pure Siberian husky. He waits patiently, indulging in his meal before taking on what's left of his neighbor's. In his youth, he had skipped his share of nourishment during the fervor of the morning, but now has the patience to get his fill. His legs are tired from yesterday, yet the ache he experiences isn't from exhaustion, but rather anticipation for the day's voyage.

He gets a visit from an enthusiastic visitor. She was his musher yesterday and may very well be again today. She also gives good pets. Addi takes the opportunity to stretch out for a hug. Mushers love hugs almost as much as Addi loves pets. The pets last a good minute, but only confirm that Addie loves pets more than mushers love hugs because this musher is on to the next dog before his hug is complete. There's always next time.

The sun meanders on the horizon as the hours pass. The anticipation is palpable. Jah Jah, a younger male whose aggression lead to his castration as a puppy, lets out a snarl and a leap hoping to get closer to his sled. Finally, the hour has come when the mushers surface from their cabin.

The forest erupts in disharmony.

Every dog expresses his or her eagerness through a unique combination of motion and sound. Once fitted with a harness, Jah Jah leaps to and fro, a sign that he is ready for action. Although each sled is facing the same direction uphill, coordinates mean nothing to Jah Jah until the journey begins. Addi is led more gracefully to his position, but not without delivering a significant tug to his musher.

All dogs are secured. They begin to pull in unison, but get angry when their straps hold them in place. Their musher mounts and uses her body to bolster the sled while she loosens the anchor. The sled budges, which only confirms to the dogs that their tugs are not in vain and that they should try harder until the musher succumbs to their efforts.

Finally, the sled in front disappears up the hill and their turn is near. The wood of the sled creaks as the reins quickly alternate between slack and taught. Jah Jah gives a quick snap at his partner who quickly alternates the direction of her pulling to maximize her distance from him. Even Addi loses his cool and shouts at his partner who returns the exclamation.

In an instant, their musher lifts her foot and the resistance that had been holding them back is gone. They are free. The energy that emanated from their jaws and unleashed towards their neighbors now singly focused on their sole purpose.

The tranquility of the forest is restored.

www.ingramcontent.com/pod-product-compliance
Lightning Source LLC
Chambersburg PA
CBHW031942130726
47905CB00002BA/400